Sweethand

Island Bites, Volume 1

N.G. Peltier

Published by N.G. Peltier, 2021.

SWEETHAND

First edition. March 30, 2021.

Copyright © 2021 N.G. Peltier.

ISBN: 978-1393353294

Written by N.G. Peltier.

For Corey. I did it!! ♥

COVER DESIGN: Leni Kauffman
Editing: A.K Edits

Chapter 1

FEBRUARY

Cherisse

"SHIT!"

Cherisse clapped her hand to her mouth as the loud expletive echoed up the quiet street, and she nearly lost her hold on the dessert boxes she was balancing. Of course, she would trip on a damn crack in the pavement, nearly falling on her ass, just as she got to the gate of the big house. Luckily the driver had already pulled off, so there wasn't anyone to witness her stumble.

She noticed a curtain fluttering in a nearby house, but no one in the posh area actually peered out. Thank the Lord for that. They'd probably have some sort of security come cart away the woman who dared disturb the peace of their neighborhood with her loud cussing.

Cherisse checked her heel. Not broken, just slightly scuffed. Dammit. She still called that a win. It was better than showing up at the Jones's house one hour late with a broken shoe in hand. She was already going to have to apologize profusely to her sister.

She'd texted Ava as soon as she was on the street to buzz her in, so the gate swung open easily. She paused mid-stride up the tiled walkway. *Holy fuck*. She'd known Eric's parents were rich, but *whoa*. She'd gaped at everything on the entire drive up to the Emerald View community, the houses getting bigger and fancier. The garages boasted more expensive vehicles, the closer the car got to the Jones's place. She shouldn't be shocked. Westmoorings boasted some of

Trinidad's wealthier citizens, but she blinked up at the massive cream two-story house with its red-tiled roof.

Shaking herself out of it, she made her way around the back as per her sister's instructions. Ava and Eric had been together for five years, but somehow, anytime his parents had one of their fancy get-togethers, Cherisse had either been hands-deep in flour and too busy to attend, or she'd been away from the island on pastry chef business. Finally, their schedules had synced. Besides, it wasn't like she could miss her sister's swanky engagement party.

She looked down at herself. A cute floral crop top and a matching skirt that made the entire thing look like one whole dress, and those damn death heels. Still snazzy, though, if a bit dinged now. Good. She'd worn her hair in loose waves today. The trip to the hairdresser for a wash, steam, and set on Friday had it shiny, bouncy, and smelling amazing. She looked good and was ready to mingle.

She pushed open the little gate that led to the big back yard, smile in place, and ran right into someone so hard she almost lost hold of the boxes again.

"Jesus f—" She bit off the almost-curse immediately, but when her eyes landed on the offender, she wanted to truly let the f-bomb fly.

"The Sugar Queen's late to her own sister's engagement party? Didn't think Her Royal Sweetness would know how to be tardy." The casual drawl heated her blood immediately.

No. Jesus, Lord, why? Why was she being tested this way?

Today had started off bad enough. Hungover from too much peopling at last night's charity event for the Arts, she'd woken up super-late, in a panic, because she'd overslept and gotten a late start on the cake and assorted desserts for the engagement party. She'd hustled her ass, having to improvise a bit. The cake turned into one layer instead of the planned two with the assorted cupcakes, which she'd snazzed up with fancy cupcake holders. She'd sent the cake stand ahead with her best friend and roommate, Remi. Everything would be assembled when she got there. Cherisse had texted Ava to let her know she was a tad late, but she hoped Remi would be a good distraction for a while.

She'd dealt with all that just fine. Mostly. She was thankful the party was set for evening rather than afternoon. She'd still arrived an hour late, which chafed at her always-punctual soul, but this? *No, no, no!*

"What the hell are you doing here?" she demanded.

His smile was the same as she remembered: annoying and even. His teeth had always been straight and perfect, which made her even more aware of her slightly crooked bottom ones, not that she'd ever tell him that. His grin flashed bright against his brown skin, and Cherisse was close to bashing him in the face with the dessert boxes. But she reeled in the urge. She wasn't about to ruin the damn cakes after she'd spent all that time making them.

"Did you crash this party?"

Keiran King cocked his brow—ugh, she remembered how much that arched brow annoyed her, too—and folded his arms. "I was invited, same as you."

No, that couldn't be right, but of course, it was. He'd been friends with Eric for years. She'd somehow forgotten that—or just ignored the fact like she ignored most things about Keiran.

His chuckle was low, and Cherisse bristled. "No one told you? I'm the best man. I have to say, Cherisse, you really know how to string people along. They're practically salivating in there, waiting for your..." He waved at the dessert boxes. "Whatever's in the box treats. Did you pull this fashionably late bit to make some grand entrance with your pastries?"

His words grated, but Cherisse's brain focused on only one thing.

I'm the best man.

"Did you just say you're the best man?" Blood rushed to her head. He had to be joking. He'd always known how to get a rise out of her since they'd been teens. Poke at Cherisse until she blew and lost her temper and said something her mother would deem unbecoming of a young lady, earning her a serious scolding. She was an adult now, and she would *not* let him rile her up. She went for flippant instead. "That sounds fake, but okay."

"You really don't believe me." His eyes crinkled as he laughed loudly. "Seriously, I'm not kidding. I'm the best man to your maid of honor. But, I don't know, your sis may have to rethink that if you can't even be on time for something small like this."

Walking right by was an option. Ignore all the words spewing from his lips. Anything but losing her cool. "I have a legit reason for being late, you asshole!"

Some heads turned her way, and her face grew warm. *Damn everything.* She'd completely forgotten where they were. Not exactly the impression she wanted to make on Eric's family. Cherisse got liberal with the swearing around her close-knit crew. Here, that wouldn't be acceptable.

Keiran's brown eyes twinkled at her outburst. He'd definitely won that round. Keiran King – 1 Cherisse Gooding – 0

"Whatever you say, Sugar Queen. Better get on. I'm sure everybody's waiting on your overly-hyped whatever." He bowed and moved to the side. She stormed by him, making sure to whack him in the side with the sharp corner of one of the boxes. His laughter echoed behind her.

She'd never hated the nickname she'd been dubbed with by her fellow foodies on the island. Sugar Queen. She liked it. The print and online magazines she'd been featured in used it all the time. Hell, she'd rolled with it all the way and plastered the damn nickname all over her bio on her website and social media accounts.

Except when Keiran said it in that smirky, condescending tone—then she hated it.

Thankfully, her best friend swooped in as soon as she saw her because Cherisse was about to have a meltdown.

"Hey, you made it, finally!" Remi Daniels hugged her as much as the dessert boxes allowed, then gave her the once-over. "Hey, we kinda match!"

They did indeed, hadn't even planned that. The cute floral romper Remi sported showed off miles of her toned deep brown legs. The deep orange color splashed with pink and white flowers complimented Remi's skin tone. Cherisse's floral pattern was all purples and pinks.

"Now, since you kept us all waiting on the goods, and I am your bestest friend in the whole world, I get first dibs on whatever's in there, right? You didn't tell me what you were bringing."

Remi bounced in her wedges, and normally, Cherisse would have slipped the box open a crack and allowed her to steal a cupcake, but there were other pressing matters. "I just ran into Keiran King. He said he's the best man? Please tell me I've somehow wandered into the Twilight Zone. That I'm still probably *so* tired from last night that I hallucinated him and that entire conversation just now?"

"Um..." Remi swept the bulk of her long curly black hair over one shoulder, fiddling with a lone curl. "I could lie to you and tell you that's the case, or we could go set out the cakes and make everyone happy. Thus making *you* happy as well, because I know how much you love seeing people enjoy your goodies. And we could forget you just found that out today."

Cherisse narrowed her eyes. "Wait, did you know about Keiran before today?"

"Ummm, well, you see..."

"Hello."

They both turned to the older woman who'd approached. Remi looked extremely relieved at the woman's appearance. Cherisse immediately pegged her as Eric's mother, her sister's future mother-in-law. The resemblance was clear. Mrs. Jones was a lighter shade of brown than her son, but they had the same hazel eyes that couldn't decide what color to be. Today, they leaned closer to brown. Her hair was styled into one of those pixie cuts, and she wore a flowy yellow dress that swirled around her knees. Her look was simple and chic, but Cherisse had no doubt that dress cost more than her rent, the gold bracelet she sported on her wrist possibly worth twice that amount.

"You must be Cherisse." Mrs. Jones smiled down at the boxes. "The cake we've all been so eagerly waiting on, I presume?"

Mrs. Jones's smile remained pleasant, but her words landed like a jab about Cherisse's lateness. "I'm *so* sorry to be late," Cherisse rushed out.

"Oh, no worries, it happens. Just be early for the wedding." Mrs. Jones patted her arm.

Cherisse laughed, but she wanted to crawl into a hole and bury herself. She'd started off with a shitty first impression. *She* wasn't marrying Eric, but Cherisse hated to keep people waiting. She knew perfection didn't exist, but it had been drilled into her enough that perception and image was everything. Being late for any reason made her itchy.

"These are worth the wait, I promise you, Mrs. Jones. They won't disappoint," Remi said cheerily.

Cherisse wanted to elbow Remi to shut up. She couldn't even promise that the cakes were her best work. She'd been hustling and worried they'd turned out subpar. What if her taste buds lied? Remi hadn't been there for a second opinion, and now she was second-guessing everything. Her reputation sure as fuck wasn't built on mediocre-tasting treats. Excellence had gotten her to the *Pastry*

Wars show last year, not the potentially inferior goodies she now clutched for dear life.

Oh, God, now her stomach decided to churn. Her fingers tightened around the boxes.

Remi flapped her hands in her direction. "Here, let's get these set up." She indicated the tables where the food was on display, with the cake and cupcake stands already laid out.

The urge to step back until she made it to the front gate and out to the street was real. She'd call the driver to come get her and take her back to her apartment with the offending *good enough* cakes.

"Cherry, what are you doing?" Remi's forehead creased. "Let go of the boxes."

"I can't let people eat these."

"Say what now?"

Cherisse smiled over at Mrs. Jones—who silently watched the not-quite tug of war she and Remi had going on over the boxes—then whispered to her bestie, "Everything was a rush. These are probably awful. I sampled before I left home, and I think they were okay? But...oh my God, listen to me. I think they were okay? I don't do okay, Remi. Okay isn't my thing."

"Nothing you make could ever be just okay. You know it, I know it. The damn feature in Island Bites magazine *and* on their blog sure as shit knows it. Didn't Merril Berry say your cakes were like magic in your mouth or something? I made sure those photos were drool-worthy, and you know they were."

The popular food blogger *had* raved about her desserts, and as a photographer for Island Bites, Remi had made certain the photos were on point, but... "Kieran basically insinuated they were overrated," she mumbled.

Remi made a face, mouth twisting to the side. "Keiran King is overrated. Why do you let that guy even get under your skin like this? You see him for a few seconds, and he's already making you doubt your food? C'mon, Cherry." She tugged at the boxes until Cherisse finally released them.

"You just want to get a taste before everyone else." Remi was right, though. Keiran was an irritation whose words meant nothing.

"Damn right, I do. Best friend perks and all that. Now, go find your sis and grovel for being late. I'll deal with this deliciousness."

Cherisse let Remi do her thing and pretended not to notice the questioning look Mrs. Jones shot her way. She hated the insecurities that popped up at the worst times, but after last year's fiasco... Nope, now wasn't the time to think about all that.

She found Ava chatting with their parents and Eric under the shade of several mango trees. Cherisse barely had time to throw a "hi" at them and receive any disapproving looks from her mother that said Cherisse's lateness was noted and not at all appreciated before Ava wrapped her up in a big hug.

"I thought you ditched us." Ava beamed. Cherisse's stomach settled a bit. She'd thought for sure Ava would be pissed.

"I'm really sorry. Forgive me?"

Ava played with the ends of Cherisse's hair. "Nothing to forgive. You're always on time, and I'm always late. I told Eric our wedding day might be the first and last thing I'm on time for, so he should appreciate that. He's already got a bet going."

Cherisse grinned. It was true. Ava and punctuality didn't go hand in hand, but she was good at charming her way out of being bawled at every time. One of the many ways they differed. Ava, younger by three years, taught at a primary school and had managed to snag a rich fiancé—who was sweet and totally in love with her sister, but yeah, still rich—which didn't hurt. Cherisse would turn twenty-nine before her sister's wedding and was single with no prospects in sight, a thing their mother kept harping on. Hopefully, with the wedding coming up in a few months, their mother would be too busy to hassle her about her man-less state for a while.

Her work took center stage these days. She aimed to position herself as one of the go-to pastry chefs on the islands. She hadn't grown Sweethand overnight; it had taken work, and there was still room to grow. If she sometimes got that twinge of loneliness, she curbed it immediately with a sugary treat or three. The time it took to craft her creations took her mind off everything just as much as the actual act of eating them did.

She tugged back on the ends of Ava's hair, where it brushed her shoulders. "Now, you gonna tell me why I didn't know about Keiran King being Eric's best man?"

Ava looked a little sheepish, whiskey-brown eyes not quite meeting Cherisse's. "I knew how you'd react. You two take this hissing at each other to the extreme. It's been years, you both need to get over this always poking at each other. Plus, Eric's one of his best friends."

"I don't poke," Cherisse huffed. "And since when is Eric even Keiran's best friend? I thought that was Scott?" She remembered Keiran and Scott being inseparable. She supposed Eric had sort of been in the mix too, but she'd never really noticed them hanging out so much.

"I said one of. You know Scott's his number one, but Eric and Scott are giant nerds, so of course, they all got closer." Ava hooked her arm with Cherisse's, her bronzy-brown skin glowing next to Cherisse's tawny complexion. Damn, she needed to hit the beach soon, get her glow on like Ava. "He's Eric's choice, and you're mine, so you're both going to have to deal with it." Ava chewed her lip, and Cherisse braced for whatever Ava was about to drop next. "Plus, we decided on a joint bachelorette/bachelor party, so the both of you will have to figure out how to get along," Ava rushed out, the words stringing so close together Cherisse couldn't be sure she'd heard right.

She blinked at Ava. "What?"

Ava grinned. "You know, I just realized, this is the first time in a long while you've both been on the island at the same time."

"This isn't funny. You can't."

"It's my wedding, and I can do what I want to," she sang.

Cherisse wanted to scream. Ava wasn't doing this out of malice and probably had a good reason for the joint party, but the combined event meant she had to work with Keiran to plan and pull it off. She envisioned this ending with her conking him over the head with a rolling pin or something. No good could come of this.

"Oh!" Ava's grin turned mischievous. Cherisse braced for more news she wasn't going to like. "Mummy's in matchmaker mode, just FYI. She's evaluating all the eligible bachelors here and definitely made one of her pros and cons lists in her head. Avoid her if you can."

Oh no, things *could* get worse. Her mother acted as if Cherisse being single was a personal offense to her. She and a handful of her aunts were always bringing it up in casual conversation. Cherisse wrinkled her nose. "She didn't put Keiran on that list, did she?"

Ava laughed. "Unlikely. You know she thinks he's bad news. He may be the only single man here not included on her list."

Bad news, indeed. Cherisse had been around enough music industry guys and had even dated one to believe that. There were also tons of rumors swirling around about Keiran. Cherisse wouldn't put any of those things past him. Being with Sean had brought her into his circle, and she'd seen and heard some shit and had foolishly thought her ex was different. She still frequented those circles sometimes because of clients, but she tended to stay clear of any advances from the men. Been there, done that, had the emotional scars to show for it. *Do not repeat* was her mantra where men in that industry were concerned.

"How do you know he's single?"

Ava's smile was enigmatic. "I know things." But it was obvious she'd know from Eric. Cherisse didn't give a damn about Keiran's love life but thank God for small mercies. Her mother would never dream to put Keiran on her radar.

Although she wasn't certain, which was worse: knowing she'd be seeing way too much of Keiran, or that her mother had now made it her mission to set her up with a bunch of men.

Fuck her life.

Chapter 2

Keiran

"THIS IS REALLY DELICIOUS. You should try it."

Keiran ignored his sister. She'd been pushing the cupcakes on him since Remi had announced they were available for devouring. Clearly, their twin connection was broken because Maxine should sense that Keiran wanted no part of the damn cupcakes. Guests scarfed the treats down like they were the last bit of dessert left in the world. He'd refused, for the simple reason that it annoyed Cherisse. He'd felt her eyes on him as he snubbed the cakes.

He continued to amuse himself by remembering how Cherisse had lost her cool earlier. The perfectly put-together Sugar Queen unraveling right before his eyes was satisfying. Petty of him, but hilarious, all the same. Keiran hadn't set out to tease to the point of that explosion, but her displeasure over him being the best man had annoyed him more than he'd let on.

She couldn't know that he'd also expressed shock over Eric choosing him, sure that Scott would be the better choice. Keiran didn't know the first thing about being a best man, having never been one before. Could he do a man of Eric's status justice when it came to something like this? Scott was used to rubbing elbows with the island's old-money types, Keiran not so much. Sure, Keiran produced music for some big-name local artistes, but their type of money certainly wasn't at the same level as Eric's family.

Not that Eric ever made his wealth an issue, but Cherisse's casual disapproval had irked.

"Nah, I'll pass," he finally replied, knowing his refusal to eat her dessert would aggravate Cherisse further.

Maxine rolled her eyes and shrugged. "Suit yourself."

He glanced over to where Cherisse chatted with Tyler Gray, who was decked out in a navy jacket thrown over what appeared to be a white t-shirt. He didn't know Tyler well, only that Tyler's father was a close acquaintance of Eric's family and that Eric claimed the man was boring as hell. Pretentious, too. Keiran frowned down at Tyler's bare ankles, exposed by the rolled-up hem of his pants. Was that the kind of guy Cherisse went for? One who didn't even bother with socks?

Cherisse had Tyler's attention as he nodded in agreement while her hands moved around. Her gestures made her crop top ride up ever so slightly to reveal a sliver of her torso. So, it wasn't really a whole dress, as he'd thought initially, but two pieces. Fashion was strange. What was the point of wearing a two-piece thing to look like a dress when you could just wear a whole dress? He'd have to ask Scott about that some time. His best friend had his pulse on all things fashion. Scott kept trying to get Keiran to "take risks" with his style, whatever that meant.

Scott knew how to pull together an outfit and always looked like he'd stepped off a runway. It was probably a skill all models learned. Keiran figured *he'd* just fall into the "trying too hard and failing" category if he ever decided to go for something new, so he stuck with his laid-back, casual digs.

"What's the point of having money if you dress like that?"

Maxine popped another sugary treat in her mouth. The damn things couldn't possibly be that good. "When you got that kind of money, you can walk around in a trash bag and call it fashion."

"Seems so. She's probably boring him to death about batter and cake pans," he mumbled, unsure why he would possibly care either way. "Match made in snoozefest heaven, I guess."

Maxine raised a brow. "You sound personally offended. Why's that?"

"I'm not."

Maxine didn't look convinced but didn't push the issue. "I think Mrs. Gooding is playing matchmaker. She's been casually striking up conversations with a bunch of dudes who she then casually introduces to Cherisse."

Sure enough, Mrs. Gooding was standing, not too far away from Cherisse, talking to a young man dressed in a short-sleeved shirt and jeans, and not so subtly gesturing at Cherisse, who, in between focusing on Tyler, kept tossing frowns her mother's way. Her smile looked strained even from over here. How interesting.

"You may be right," he admitted.

Maxine hooked her arm in his. "I need to hear this conversation."

Keiran let himself be dragged over. Curiosity got the better of him, and Cherisse's narrowed eyes as she spotted them coming over were sure to make for an entertaining time.

"Hey, girl. Long time, no see," Maxine said cheerfully.

Keiran noticed Cherisse's fingers tighten around her wine glass, but she returned Maxine's smile. "Hi, yes, it's been, what, about eight...nine years?"

"Yeah, about that. Good to be back home." Maxine had returned to the island late last year with his niece, Leah. "Sorry to interrupt your talk." Maxine looked the furthest thing from sorry, lips curved up in her trademark grin. "But I had to tell you, Cherisse, those cakes. Damn, girl, so good."

Cherisse shot Keiran a triumphant smile. "Thanks."

"I tried to get this one to taste, but he refused."

Oh, now Maxine was just stoking the fire.

Cherisse shrugged. "Well, he's obviously the inferior twin, and his loss, really."

"They are quite good," Tyler spoke up. "Hmm, I'll need to research the dessert offerings wherever we go on our date. I'll need to find something that matches up to a woman of your skill."

"Date?" Cherisse looked absolutely horrified at the idea but quickly covered up her less-than-stellar expression with a tentative smile.

Keiran suppressed a chuckle. Tyler and Cherisse, on a date? Now there was something he couldn't wrap his mind around but would pay good money to witness. Cherisse gave off that *I'm better than you* air; she was social, outgoing. He'd seen enough of her social media feeds and the pics from entertainment sites to know she frequented band launches, fetes, and other party-type events. Those sites treated her like some kind of local celeb. He supposed when you dated a popular soca star, it was to be expected; you ended up mingling with those in the local music scene and got to keep that semi-celeb status even if the relationship had imploded. And man, had it blown up in a big public way.

Tyler was known for turning up his nose at the local party scene, so the two of them going out together just wasn't something Keiran could picture. What would they even talk about?

"Your mother said you were on board?"

"No," Cherisse said, mouth set in a tight line. She tossed back the rest of her wine, earning a raised brow from Tyler and a cough that was clearly an aborted laugh from Maxine. "I mean, this is the first time we've spoken. It's a little premature to assume a date's a done deal, isn't it?"

Keiran hadn't expected to have this much fun at the engagement party, but he was enjoying himself immensely. "I think you should save yourself and take the out she's giving you, Tyler."

"And I think no one cares what the f—" Cherisse's words died away as Remi sauntered over and placed a hand on her friend's arm.

"Hey, sorry, I just need to borrow Cherry real quick," she said, dragging Cherisse away until they stood in front of some fancy white wrought iron benches. Remi appeared to be lecturing Cherisse. Cherisse's arms were folded, body language screaming defiance. She didn't seem to like whatever Remi was saying and kept shooting daggers his way. He couldn't resist; he gave a little finger wave that had her jerking her eyes back to Remi, who shook her head and looked to the sky as if asking for patience.

"Why the heck are you so willing to go on a date with her anyway?" Keiran asked.

"Her mother seemed to think we'd be compatible." Tyler rubbed his annoyingly square jaw.

"Dude, you being serious right now?" What sort of reason was that? He couldn't begin to gauge what Mrs. Gooding was basing this supposed compatibility on, but at the very least, Tyler should want to date Cherisse for more than that. They were both good-looking people, not that Tyler was Keiran's type. Cherisse, however...

He'd snuck looks at her in her shorty shorts lots of times when they'd been teens.

He remembered her scowling at him from behind her gate whenever he cycled by with Scott, who always threw a big wave and smile her way. Somehow, she'd become friends with Scott, who didn't even live in the area but visited Keiran for sleepovers and football games in the savannah so much it was like he was an honorary part of the community. He'd spent a lot of time at Keiran's when their school closed for holidays. Scott's step-dad had made his home life hell, so Keiran'd been happy to offer up a little haven for his friend. But then, Scott and Cherisse had gotten friendly. Keiran, however? Not at all. Their blood didn't take to each other.

But he'd still checked her out. His entire guys' crew gaped at Cherisse and Ava when they'd moved into the area. Even living two streets away at the time, word had reached him about the sisters.

Cherisse had all that wavy hair that, if asked, he'd say was brown, just brown, but that would be a damn lie. In the sun, her hair was a riot of browns, reds, and golds. The red was new. He remembered back when she wore her hair natural, how it had gone from kind of curly when still sort of wet and then poofed up into this fro that glinted golden in the sun when fully dry. Like a halo, except to him, Cherisse had been no angel. Did angels glare at people the way she had at him?

Her eyes were golden-brown, ringed with a darker brown that oddly enough reminded him of a tiger's eye stone he'd found once. Her lush mouth with its fuller bottom lip was reason enough too. If Tyler said he was eager to date Cherisse because he found her attractive, now that would make sense.

"Her mother thinking you're both a good match shouldn't be the only reason." Keiran risked another look over at Cherisse and Remi. They sat side by side on the bench, Cherisse's skirt rucked up to a little above her knees, and Keiran's traitorous eyes drank in her legs.

There was another reason, too. Her calves, fleshier now than back when they were teens, made Keiran wonder about her thighs. Were they fleshy too? Soft to the touch?

Whoa. Pump those brakes, buddy.

"She seems nice." Tyler's words brought Keiran back to the conversation at hand, dragged him away from wayward thoughts of possibly soft thighs.

"Nice?" he scoffed. "Cherisse Gooding isn't nice." Nice didn't mean a damn thing. The word was just too bland to describe Cherisse. She wasn't nice; she was a nuisance.

"Everyone says she's nice," Tyler insisted.

"Okay, buddy, whatever you say." Arguing with this guy was pointless. Cherisse had maintained a squeaky-clean reputation. Well, except for that major public meltdown she'd had last year, which in Keiran's opinion had been warranted.

And now it was like she was trying to over-compensate for that one less-than-perfect moment. Seemed exhausting to keep up a front like that all the time. But she was in the public eye more than he was. An intentional move on his part—all that attention made him squirmy—and yet, people still made shit up about him. He didn't have the time or desire to keep crafting statements to address any of them, so he ignored it all.

His music was his focus. Anything else was an annoyance that didn't warrant his attention.

Before he could protest further about Cherisse's supposed niceness, she came back, all traces of her anger gone, replaced by a smile so radiant it almost knocked Keiran back a couple of steps. Aimed in Tyler's direction, he got the full brunt of it. Tyler didn't look the least bit affected.

Cherisse waved her phone at Tyler. "Your number, please. So we can settle on date, time, et cetera."

This was really happening. Keiran struggled not to let his mouth drop open as Tyler complied, typing his number into Cherisse's phone. Her phone case had tiny cupcakes and donuts prints all over it. Of fucking course it did.

"This is ridiculous," he mumbled.

"You pronounced hilarious wrong," Maxine countered.

"See you soon." Cherisse flashed another of her blinding smiles at Tyler, waved at Maxine, and ignored him completely as she headed back to where Remi was still sitting on the bench. She'd barely gone two steps before a voice rang out.

"Hey, Cherry!"

She turned just as a body barreled past Keiran to wrap Cherisse in a big feet-off-the-ground swinging-her-around hug.

"Scott, oh my God!" Cherisse giggled. Keiran scowled as his best friend finally let Cherisse's feet touch the ground.

"You're wearing the hell out of that outfit, I gotta say."

Cherisse held the ends of her skirt out and struck a pose. "Well, I try to be as fashionable as you sometimes."

Ugh. Keiran couldn't believe this. Even Scott was fawning over Cherisse. Wasn't it common courtesy to greet your best friend first or something? Scott had almost bulldozed Keiran out of the way to get to Cherisse. He wasn't having any of that. He also needed to get away from Maxine's annoying snickering. She wasn't even trying to cover that shit up this time.

"Oh man, I missed home," she wheezed.

A hand landed on Keiran's shoulder, stopping him from stomping over there to reclaim his best friend. He flicked a glance at Eric. "They tend to have that effect on people." Eric sounded amused, too. "Nothing's changed, I see. You two are still like oil and water."

Keiran folded his arms. "Why'd you have to go fall for her sister anyhow? The island's small, but not *that* small, man."

"Love knows no rhyme or reason."

Keiran scowled at his grinning friend. "That makes no sense."

"Love makes no sense sometimes, but you roll with it when it's the right for you person."

"You'll be insufferable these next few months, won't you?" Keiran didn't know if he could deal with this extra moony-eyed version of Eric.

"Having second thoughts about this best man gig? I'm sure Scott'll fill in for ya."

"No." He wasn't about to give Cherisse the satisfaction of thinking she'd run him off. Plus, he *was* honored Eric had chosen him, even if it meant having to plan the joint party with Cherisse, which he'd protested when he'd found out. A lot of good that did—but he was going to run with it and be the best at it. He'd already started making plans for the epic gift he wanted to give the bride and groom. Now that he knew Cherisse was the maid of honor, he was determined to top whatever gift she had planned. It wasn't a competition, but Keiran would be damned if he was shown up.

"'Sup, guys?" Scott greeted as he strolled over.

Scott "don't call me Scotty, only I can refer to myself as such" Trim was all long, lean limbs, rich umber skin that was enviably smooth, ridiculously high cheekbones, and dark eyes framed by the longest damn lashes that he'd gotten hated on for back in secondary school. His tight black curls were trimmed low, the sides shaved down. Even with the pointy ears that Scott hated, he was ridiculously attractive. Keiran's teenage crush on Scott had blindsided him, but he shouldn't have been surprised. He'd gotten over it, but that didn't mean he couldn't silently appreciate the chiseled work of art that was Scott's face.

He'd never seen Scott take a bad photo, ever. No matter the situation—awful fluorescent light included—Scott made everyone around him look like a potato left out too long. It surprised no one that Scott had done modeling in his teen years. He only did it sometimes these days, occasionally sending people into a frenzy by showing off his well-sculpted chest in carnival costumes for band launches, preferring to focus more on his role as Creative Director of his own company. He dabbled in fashion and beauty editing, too, also doing the makeup artist gig on the side. Keiran didn't know how Scott juggled all these professional hats or when the hell he got to sleep.

Yet, somehow, Scott managed it all without looking frazzled. After a long session in the studio, without sleep, Keiran was liable to scare small children with how haggard he looked. Scott was always chiding them about proper skincare—perhaps he was onto something there. Keiran didn't live that ashy life, but it couldn't hurt to be more moisturized.

"Oh, so you see me over here now?" Keiran was still toting feelings about being ignored.

Scott gripped his shoulders, smile huge as usual. "Jealous much, K-2?"

Keiran rolled his eyes. Only Scott could get away with using that ridiculous nickname. "I'm just saying you sped by me like a full bus to greet Cherisse. Yeah, I'm going to feel some kind of way."

Scott patted his cheek. "No worries, you're still my fave, but Cherry's cool. I know you two have a thing. Why do you two get on each other's nerves like that? Unresolved sexual tension? Rivalry by osmosis? I mean, Remi and Maxi used to go at it like whoa, so I get wanting to have your sister's back, but you two gonna fight to the grave?"

"I'll take sexual tension for 500, Alex," Eric piped up, and Keiran wondered if it was too late to trade in his friends for more loyal models.

"There's no sexual tension." What were they even getting at? Cherisse couldn't stand him, and whatever ill-advised teenaged crush he'd had on her had long evaporated from his system.

Eric and Scott went on as if Keiran hadn't spoken.

"I'm telling you, there's something there," Scott insisted. "You two would be cute together, too."

"Right? If it's wrong to ship people, you know I don't wanna be right."

Keiran frowned. "You're saying a lot of words that don't mean anything to me, and there's no world in which Cherisse and I will ever happen. She's going on a date with Tyler anyhow." Why was he even mentioning that? Who Cherisse dated didn't mean a damn to him.

The idea of them as anything but two people who had mutual friends but preferred not to interact—if they could help it—was too absurd to imagine.

Scott and Eric exchanged shocked glances.

"Tyler?" Eric's nose wrinkled.

"And Cherisse?" Scott looked like the idea was the most farfetched thing he'd ever heard. Finally, a sensible response. The only reaction one *should* possibly have to that news. Sure, opposites attracted sometimes, but in this case, Keiran just couldn't see it.

Nice. Tyler had said she was nice. The concept of Cherisse being nice was so foreign to Keiran; he couldn't fathom how Tyler had arrived at such a conclusion. Okay, he knew how. Cherisse had carefully cultivated her persona, but how could Tyler not see the barely-contained fire underneath all that niceness? Or did it only come out around him?

And what was Cherisse's angle in all this? She'd done a complete about-face within minutes. His curiosity was working overtime. Was Cherisse going on this date to please her mother? Keiran knew how overbearing West Indian mothers could be. They were good at making you feel bad if you didn't at least try the thing they suggested, trotting out the '*after I carried you for nine months and had to go through X number of hours of labor, you can't even do this one thing for me?*' guilt trip.

Keiran ignored Eric and Scott as they also wondered aloud how this date would play out and whether Tyler would bore her to tears. Most likely. His gaze wandered the spacious back yard, seeking Cherisse out. He spotted her with Ava, their parents, and Remi. As if she felt his stare, she looked over. He could see her forehead creasing from here.

He smiled, and she looked away, but not before she casually tucked a stray lock of hair behind her ear with her middle finger.

Keiran laughed at the move. The months leading up to this wedding were going to be quite interesting.

Chapter 3

MARCH

Cherisse

THE CAMERA FLASH STARTLED her. She'd been staring at the dessert station way too long, obsessing over the setup. She glared over at Remi, who was still circling, taking photos from various angles.

"Just getting some shots of all this before the hordes descend and devour everything."

"Good plan." Next to her, Cherisse's PA, Reba, had her phone out doing the same. "We'll get some more good ones for Instagram and Twitter when we have some people around."

Right. It was why she'd hired Reba as her assistant. Reba stayed on top of stuff like that. Cherisse had forgotten all about photos, too busy fussing with the various stands that held the desserts for the post-awards cocktail party. Remi was there in her work capacity as a photographer for Island Bites.

With Reba and Remi dealing with the photos, Cherisse made one more circuit of the room. The formal portion of the People's Choice Soca Awards ceremony would be letting out soon enough, and hungry guests would be flooding this room in no time.

Last year, she'd attended the awards show as a nominee's date. Her then-boyfriend, Sean Daley aka Swagga D, had been nominated in a bunch of categories. Even though he'd imploded their relationship by being a lying ass cheater, she could still admit—grudgingly—that he was talented. He'd been nominated again this year, so Cherisse prepped herself for a run-in.

Reba had offered to stick around to dismantle everything, so Cherisse could spare herself from seeing Sean with possibly one of the women he'd cheated with, but no way would she pass up free eats, wine, and networking opportunities because her ex was a piece of shit.

Reba came over. "You good?"

"Yeah, everything looks great." Knowing Reba like she did, she wasn't referring to that, but Cherisse was tired of the concern. She could handle seeing her ex in public for the first time in almost a year without wanting to choke him out, right?

No matter what, you keep your cool. Don't let them see you sweat.

One of the many bits of advice her mother had given her over the years and something she struggled with. Why did she always have to be the one to keep her cool? Although ignoring that advice last year hadn't done her any favors. That video of her cussing Sean out backstage at the *Pastry Wars* studio hadn't been her best moment.

Reba peered at her over the top of her glasses, telegraphing that she knew what Cherisse was doing. Avoiding. Which she planned to do all tonight. It was best for everyone. Even though she'd push through, deal with it if she and Sean ended up in the same breathing space, she rather they didn't. The media would love that, hoping for another meltdown.

Sean's popularity had climbed steadily over the two years they'd been together, thrusting her in the media's eye too by sheer proximity. Her blow-up with him in public? Yeah, that had brought the thirsty gossipers out for blood.

The way random media still trotted it out when she did an interview, they clearly wouldn't let her live it down, which was fucking bullshit. Sean was the cheating ass, after all. She sure as fuck wasn't having a repeat performance because Sean would smile and charm his way into looking like a repentant angel. His fans had even spewed accusations of her using his fame to boost her business, which...fine, being with Sean had brought her better networking opportunities, but she hadn't gotten with him because of that. She hadn't set out to date a celebrity. They'd met at one of his events where she had been hired to cater the dessert. Even though they had hit it off immediately, Cherisse had been reluctant. The gossip about men in the music business was rampant, but she had decided to throw caution to the wind for once. Not that his die-hard fans cared. After obsessively checking comment after comment, she'd had to stop. Some fans had gotten seriously vile.

"Don't worry." Reba patted Cherisse's shoulder. "We got your back."

Tonight, Reba looked like a living, breathing Starburst, with her pastel pink hair in loose waves around her deep brown shoulders. Her tight off-the-shoulder dress was a deeper shade of pink than her hair, but it worked. Her eyeshadow was an explosion of orange and yellow. She looked sweet and fruity, but the determination reflected in her eyes said she would deal with anyone who tried to cross Cherisse. Her look alone would bring anyone to their knees.

She grinned at the thought of Reba destroying Sean with cleverly coded sarcasm. According to Reba, it was her one superpower, besides her baking skills. Reba wasn't just her PA; she was her Assistant Pastry Chef, too.

"It shouldn't come to anything serious. I'm staying clear of any annoyances in the form of Sean Daley," she assured Reba, and Remi, who had strolled over, camera slung around her neck.

Remi rocked a black jumpsuit and her signature wedges, and her miles of curly hair were trapped in a French braid tonight, with some strands coming loose around her face. She towered over Cherisse, who *was* wearing heels, making Cherisse feel small and very squishy, which was ridiculous and, she knew, just her nerves. She'd thought she looked pretty in her sleeveless royal blue dress with its beaded Peter Pan collar, opting for something cute and comfy because this was still work, even if they'd already set up and were free to enjoy the cocktails. She had to be in networking mode, break out her sweet-talking skills to secure more business for Sweethand.

"Sean is insignificant," Remi said, nose scrunched as if the very thought of the man disgusted her, which was accurate. Remi hadn't minced words when she, along with the entire island, had found out about Sean's infidelity. "I should warn you, however, that Keiran's here."

"What?" Could she not be free of him?

"Have you forgotten he's in the music biz too? He and his fellow producer got nominated for their Hopscotch Riddim."

Cherisse hadn't forgotten what Keiran did for a living, couldn't forget when her experience with men in the industry had left a bad taste in her mouth, but it had slipped her mind that he'd be present. Dammit.

"Who's Keiran?" Reba asked, dark brown eyes sparkling with curiosity. "And that riddim is wicked, though."

Great, another Keiran King fan. The riddim was a hit, and Cherisse found herself grooving along to that particular background instrumental accompaniment on the various soca tracks that radio stations had been blasting since last year, but she'd never admit it. Whenever she listened to the songs on the riddim, she conveniently wiped all knowledge of Keiran having a hand in the music from her mind.

"He's her nemesis," Remi said helpfully. "Since secondary school, actually. Although..." She tapped her cheek. "I think it's nemesis by proximity. I didn't get along with his twin. Hardcore rival back in the day."

"Not the only reason. Called me stuck-up plenty times just because I didn't hang with them like Ava did. Making it out like I was too good for them when my ass was failing at school. I didn't have time to fawn over a bunch of annoying fellas. He didn't even know one shit about me but made all these assumptions based on gossip from the street. I wish he'd fall into a black hole," Cherisse added, getting heated at just the thought of seeing Keiran right now. The damn island was small, but Jesus, she'd gone so long without seeing him around, and now, he was just everywhere.

"Wow." Reba raised a brow at her rant. "Why haven't I heard about him before?"

Cherisse didn't like the glint in Reba's eyes. "He's not worth my breath."

"Is he cute, though?" Reba asked Remi, completely ignoring Cherisse's rolled eyes.

Remi, the traitor, was enjoying this way too much. "Cute? Girl, no. Bunnies are cute. Keiran King is surface-of-the-sun hot. His siblings, too." She winked at Cherisse, who rolled her eyes again, refusing to confirm or deny that last statement.

"I don't see you denying this supposed hotness." Reba's eyes full-on sparkled with mischief.

"I don't have time to debate this."

Reba tapped her fingers against her pursed red lips. "Your silence on the matter is telling."

"What do you want me to say?" Cherisse asked, exasperated with the turn of the conversation. "Is he good-looking? Fine, yes. It doesn't make him any less annoying."

"Annoying can be overlooked."

"For what? There's no way in hell Keiran King would ever be a consideration for anything. Ever." The idea was ludicrous. "Besides, I have a date."

"With Tyler Gray. Some boring finance guy your mother thinks would make a suitable husband because he's loaded," Remi so helpfully replied. "Who also finds the idea of Carnival to be a stain on our dear islands?"

Reba gasped dramatically, looking ready to keel over at that little nugget of information. "He dissed Carnival, and you're still going out with him? You love Carnival! How the heck did this date even happen?"

How indeed? Cherisse loved a good party occasionally, and Carnival when she managed to secure a free costume, but that was mostly because networking for business was essential. She found most of her clients by referrals, but that didn't mean she didn't have to sell her brand herself. Getting contracts to cater fancy all-inclusive parties and Carnival fetes, high-end weddings, and corporate events didn't happen just by word of mouth. She needed to be visible and sell herself as a sought-after pastry chef to the stars. Of course, she took jobs from anyone, not just those in a higher income bracket, but it didn't hurt when she secured a wealthy client. Bills didn't pay themselves. So, she had to go where the local celebs went while not earning herself a reputation as a wild party girl but someone who happened to know the right people.

"He's very nice to look at." It was the truth. Tyler's monotone voice didn't take away from his good looks. It couldn't hurt to give him a chance, could it? Besides, he had a nice, safe, boring career, nothing close to the entertainment industry like a certain Mr. King.

She needed safe in her life right now.

After Sean, Cherisse had steered clear of men in the music industry, keeping any relationships she formed there strictly about her business. As much as she hated to even consider it, dating Tyler could help distance her from Sean and his shit. He didn't seem the type to create a scandal, and she didn't need another one of those. Ever.

The buzz of guests entering the cocktail reception prompted them to shift gears into professional mode.

"Hottie nemesis alert," Remi whispered, and Cherisse tensed. Surely they could be civil here, surrounded by all these people. She wasn't worried about him so much. *She* couldn't seem to control her damn mouth when Keiran was around.

Reba craned her neck to see, eyes following Remi's jutted chin movements. "Oh. My."

Cherisse refused to look. But even with her back turned, she knew Keiran had come up behind her. He just exuded this *'I'm here to ruin your day'* vibe. She refused to allow him to do just that, especially already being on edge at possibly seeing Sean.

"Keiran." Remi's voice lost all its warmth. She'd joked about him earlier, but right now, her tone could freeze the entire room and its guests. Cherisse could always count on her to go into protective bestie mode.

"Wow." Reba's was filled with awe and amusement.

Cherisse considered keeping her back to him forever. Almost said fuck it, but she had to be the effervescent Sugar Queen they all knew her to be. The pressure to keep up appearances was real and fucking exhausting. Always needing to be "on" because of those damn bills. Adulting was the ultimate scam. She wouldn't let Keiran make her act a fool. She pasted on her best smile and turned to face one of the two men she would trip down the stairs and feel no regrets.

Reba's "Wow" had been an understatement.

He was wearing a suit. She'd never seen Keiran in a suit. Ever. Had known she would see him in one for the wedding but hadn't even lingered on the thought. Why would she? She didn't care what he wore, only that his presence would annoy her. But now, he was in this suit, and Cherisse stared, blatantly drinking in the fit of his blue suit jacket on those broad shoulders, the cut of his pants on his trim waist. He had his jacket unbuttoned, and there were a few buttons undone on his white shirt as well, assaulting her eyes with a sliver of brown chest. Cherisse was attacked by a too-vivid image of her pressing her hand to his shirt, right above the waistband of his pants to test what lay beneath all that fabric. She'd been drinking him in, eyes taking it all in, from his shiny brown shoes right up to that bit of exposed skin, and when she finally got to his face, he was smirking, as if he knew just what wayward thoughts floated through her head.

Holy. Shit. This was the moment she hated Keiran King more than ever. Because he was too much in that suit. His goatee was perfectly trimmed. It framed those quirked lips perfectly. His smile was dangerous. She moved past it to the rest of his face. Those deep-brown eyes never left her face and brimmed with amusement. His hair was low, brushed down into black waves, the edges marked to precision.

She wanted to topple one of the dessert towers on him. Mess up that damn suit. Anything to ruin the picture of contained sexiness he gave off as he stood there.

"We match," he said, annoying smile growing wider.

Cherisse said nothing, refusing to acknowledge that they did indeed have on the same shade of blue. What were the fucking odds? And who gave him the right to walk around an event like this with that much chest exposed?

"Hey, lemme get a shot with your award?" Remi's question jolted Cherisse to her senses. She'd been hardcore staring at Keiran, having semi-lustful thoughts. She needed a drink or two, possibly more.

Remi got into work mode and posed Keiran and his co-producer, Dale Anderson, next to one of the dessert towers. Cherisse could always count on Remi to get in promo for Sweethand no matter what. Dale hammed it up for the camera, handing Keiran one of the two awards she hadn't even noticed Dale had been holding. Hell, she'd barely noticed Dale, which was unbelievable because his suit was this loud, shiny maroon number with a multi-colored pocket square that would probably singe her eyes if she got too close.

Dale plucked one of the small rose-shaped desserts from the tower and popped it in his mouth. "Lord Jesus, perfection as always." He grinned at Cherisse as he chewed. "Sugar Queen, you never disappoint."

"Thank you." Yes, focus on Dale. Ignore Keiran's very existence. In this moment, Keiran King and his offending suit did not fucking exist.

"How the hell did you get these to look like a rose and taste like heaven?" Dale gushed.

"A chef never reveals her secrets," she winked, and he chortled around the dessert in his mouth.

"Oh man, Keiran, you should get in on these." Dale waved the dessert in Keiran's face.

"I'm good. Shouldn't you be having dinner first?"

"Nah, man, I had to get to these before they all disappeared." To prove his point, Dale started going around the tower, adding each type of dessert to his small plate. "My mom loves your stuff. She gets those cookies you have selling in the grocery every month end. A little treat for herself. Can't go without them. You really have that sweet hand, for real."

Cherisse beamed. "You are so good for a girl's ego. Tell you what, I'm working on something new. I'll send you a sample package, maybe throw in some for your mom. Make sure she gets it."

"You're the best!"

Cherisse shot Keiran a triumphant smile.

"Buying customers with freebies, how creative of you," he drawled, unimpressed.

Cherisse wondered if she could bump into the dessert tower for real, make it look like an accident. Feign shock when the entire thing crushed him under its sugary weight, but there was no way she was wasting her hours of baking on him.

"Hi, I'm Reba. I've heard so much about you. All terrible things, but I love me a bad boy," Reba suddenly piped up, tossing in a wink. Cherisse had forgotten her presence, too busy being distracted by Keiran's suit.

Keiran's jaw tightened, and Cherisse found the tiny tic intriguing. Ah, so he could dish out the teasing but couldn't take it.

"Good to know my reputation precedes me." The muscle in Keiran's jaw jumped again, and Cherisse filed that away. How fascinating. The seemingly unflappable Keiran King wasn't so unaffected by gossip as he'd like people to think.

Oh, yeah, she was pocketing this little bit of information to use as ammo later.

Chapter 4
Keiran

SHE WORE THE SWEETEST dress, bright blue with a glittering beaded collar. The smile gracing her lips was anything but sweet. It promised vengeance, and Keiran felt an answering pull in his stomach.

He hadn't known she'd be here. He'd ducked out on the awards last year like a punk, but he'd definitely seen photo after photo of her and that fool Sean Daley. That guy had rubbed him wrong from their first meeting. Knowing Cherisse and Sean were no longer together, he'd figured she wouldn't be here. Keiran hadn't wanted to come. Dale was more the face of DK Productions, but Keiran had vowed to make more of an effort to be out there, support Dale at events like this. Even though the spotlight was *so* not his thing—which left him open to being gossip fodder for people in the industry—the guilt of leaving his partner to fly solo had finally gotten to be too much.

The Awards show had been long, and his tolerance had tipped into grumpiness the longer it ran on. He'd been so deep into daydreaming about the food at the reception and the instrumental combo he was playing around with in his head that Dale had to whack him on the shoulder to let him know they'd won their first category. Keiran had been shocked—not because he didn't believe their work was good, he knew it was. Their roster was full of artistes coming to them to produce their tracks and albums—but that meant he had to go up on stage.

"Do we have a speech?" he'd hissed at Dale. It hadn't occurred to him to prepare anything.

"I got a lil' something. We can wing the rest," Dale had whispered back as he'd dragged him up on the stage amid the loud applause and some whistles.

Keiran couldn't even remember what he'd said up there. He might have thanked his mom. He hoped he had; otherwise, he wouldn't hear the end of it, especially since she was stuck home getting over the flu and would be glued to the live stream of the show. The second time they'd won an award hadn't been any better. It had been a heart-pounding blur. Public speaking made him cold sweat. He preferred being in the studio, immersed in rhythm and bass, wrapped in the music.

Scott, Maxine, and Dale's boyfriend, Worrel, had come as their guests. They'd basically abandoned them for food when Dale dragged Keiran to the dessert stations where Cherisse and her team were.

Her earlier stare had near-incinerated him where he stood. Had she been aware that she'd been throwing him all that heat? Probably. She had to know by now how to get a rise out of him—they'd butted heads enough times over the years—and this time, it appeared she'd switched tactics. That stare had said she wanted to do dirty things to him, and Keiran's body had responded with *yes, please.*

"So much for being nice, huh?" He didn't bother hiding his annoyance at the whole bad boy comment. No doubt Reba would've gotten that impression from Cherisse. Clearly, she bought into all those rumors and gossip.

Cherisse didn't look concerned. "No idea what you're talking about." She glanced at Reba. "We should go mingle. Bye, Dale."

He'd been dismissed. It was becoming an annoying habit of hers.

"Well, damn. I knew you two weren't exactly friendly, but dude... That was..."

"Irritating." He cut Dale off. It didn't help that he was already on edge, having run into his father, who had several artistes nominated.

The press had loved that, urging them to get some photo ops together. The father-son music dynamo—their words, not his.

"If that's what we're calling it these days." Dale winked.

"Don't you start in on that, too. We should find the others." Before they could get on that, a woman in a tight white dress swooped down on them.

"Hey guys, congrats! I'm from ENT TT. Can I chat with you a bit?"

Dale shifted into super media darling mode while Keiran let his eyes wander, looking for some sign of his twin and Scott, as the woman asked Dale how they felt about their win and what she could expect from them after the Carnival season. Carnival was over, but it definitely didn't mean less work.

"We have some surprise collabs in the works, can't say too much on those yet. So you and the rest of the island can look out for that."

Her fingers flew as she typed on her tablet, then turned to Keiran. "It's good to see you out here. Was beginning to think Dale had you chained to the studio."

He smiled as charmingly as he could muster. "Well, those hits don't make themselves. Studio life sort of consumes all my time."

Her laugh was loud and tinkly. "Yes, yes, of course, and we do so love everything you guys have been putting out. All your riddims for Carnival had me wining low." She reached out and snagged one of the pastries off a nearby dessert station. "These are *so* addictive. I've been munching on them all night. Thank God Carnival's over so I can indulge." She patted her flat tummy. "I saw you and Ms. Gooding chatting earlier. I swear, the level of work that goes into her creations. I wonder how many hours she spends on them, and they literally disappear in seconds. You can see the work that goes into these, just like with your music."

"She probably has everyone fooled and just pops these frozen in an oven a few minutes before she leaves her house. I mean, come on, mixing music's gotta be way harder than mixing pastry batter," he joked.

The reporter popped the remains of the pastry in her mouth and smiled before asking them for a photo to go along with her blog post on tonight's winners.

When she floated away, Dale grabbed his arm. "You don't say shit like that to the media. They love those kinds of sound bites."

Keiran patted Dale's hand. "It was a joke, relax. It has zero to do with her post anyhow. She won't use that."

"Listen, I know you get weird about being in the spotlight, but be aware of what you're saying around the media. This is gonna bite you in the ass," Dale warned.

Keiran wasn't bothered. What use could his words even serve her article? He needed food and a drink. He made a pass at the food stations, head turning every time he caught a flash of bright blue and heard Cherisse's distinct laugh. It was infectious, loud, bordering on scandalous even. So incongruous with the rest of her persona. Made you wonder what had gotten that reaction out of her.

He caught sight of her at a table with one of their local carnival costume designers on her left, noticed Scott on her right, and sent his defector best friend the best glare he could muster, even if he couldn't see it. Scott, as if sensing he was in the line of fire, turned at the exact moment and had the audacity to wave at them before resuming his conversation.

"I think he's doing that on purpose," Keiran glowered.

Dale chuckled as they searched for a free table to perch themselves at while they ate. They found one occupied by Remi and Maxine, who seemed to mostly be staring intently at their devices rather than having conversation.

"Hey, you seen Worrel?" Dale asked, searching the crowd for his boyfriend.

"Last seen at the pasta station," Maxine replied. "That stuff is sinfully good." Dale announced he'd be back and went in search of his guy.

"So, does your friend only slander my good name to those in her inner circle, or...?"

Remi looked up from checking the shots on her camera, brow raised. "Is it slander if it's true?"

"You believe everything you hear?" he shot back.

This was the last place to get into it with Remi, but Keiran just couldn't seem to keep his mouth shut. Why did he care what Cherisse thought of him? Her opinion shouldn't matter, but it was rubbing him wrong more than expected. He had to be more tired than he'd thought to let even a hint drop that Cherisse's judgment was affecting him. He *had* been going hard in the studio for the entire Carnival season. He couldn't count how many late-night sessions they'd done.

The phone in front of Remi suddenly chimed. "Need to get this," she said, wandering away from the table. The reception had some music piping through the room. It wasn't loud, but that, combined with everyone's chatter, would make it difficult to hear whoever was on the other line.

"What are you doing?" Maxine asked, fiddling with her napkin.

"Nothing."

"You're being weird."

He forked some food in his mouth and chewed, not looking at the nail Maxine tapped impatiently on the table. He took his time swallowing before he said, "So?"

Maxine stole a piece of salmon from his plate and popped it in her mouth. "I can't wait to see you two try to work together. It's gonna be an epic mess. Don't disappoint me. I got a bet going. I need to make some extra money. Working with mummy in her office is driving me up a wall."

Maxine was way too excited about the potential disaster that would be him and Cherisse planning an event together. Eric's speech about wanting him and Ava's two main people to bond had sounded like BS to him, but what the bride and groom wanted, they got, apparently.

"So hurry up and fall into hate sex so I can get paid."

Keiran choked on his food. "A waste of time bet," he said after he caught his breath.

Him and Cherisse? Not happening. Fighting was their thing. The sizzling looks she'd thrown him earlier were obviously a ploy to keep him off-balance in a different way. He wasn't even angry at her for it; it was downright dirty-handed, and it made him grin to know he could have the perfectly put-together Sugar Queen on edge like that, to the point where she was trying different ways to get at him.

Maxine sipped her drink. "We'll see, brother. We'll see."

Chapter 5

Cherisse

HER POST-AWARDS SHOW cocktail party hangover was epic. Cherisse stayed in bed until after 9 a.m. Not late by most standards, but she was usually an early riser, greeting the sunrise so she could start her day. She wasn't a morning person, but years of training herself to be just that helped. Fake it 'til you make it. Whenever she had an event that required networking, the next day wouldn't start until later than she'd like.

Not that she could help it. Extrovert Cherisse kept going like the Energizer Bunny until she crashed, and then introvert Cherisse wanted nothing to do with anyone. Sometimes, she allowed herself the luxury of sleeping way in; others, she'd force herself to push through.

This Friday morning, she'd tried to strike a balance of sorts. She had a lot of upcoming things but nothing that was pressing for today, so she strolled downstairs, nearly tripping over her cat. The unrepentant furball insisted on curling around her feet since she'd disturbed his snooze spot by choosing that moment to come down the steps.

"Jello, Jesus, fuck!"

Jello yawned and went about his business of sleeping, stretching languidly across the bottom step. No love for her this morning. He'd probably already been fed by Remi, so he didn't need Cherisse for anything right now. She found Remi and Reba on the couch, heads close together, peering at something on Remi's laptop. Not an unusual occurrence since they were both better at bouncing back from these types of events than her. Remi was a true extrovert, who thrived on being around people, and Reba was just a morning person. Cherisse could be on when needed, but after that, get people away from her so she could recharge.

"Morning." She nearly cracked her jaw with the huge yawn that escaped. Remi and Reba both jumped. Remi pushed down the top of the laptop even though Cherisse couldn't see what they'd been looking at anyway. What was that about?

Remi shifted the laptop from her lap to Reba's, jumping to her feet to push a giant cup of warm goodness into Cherisse's hands. "I got your fave fancy Ritual's vanilla latte. Figured you'd need the boost."

"Have I told you lately that I love you?" She inhaled the yummy caffeine before taking a sip, and *yesss,* it was heaven on her tongue, but something was off here. Reba was being shifty, throwing weird looks while keeping a firm grip on the top of the laptop, and Remi kept urging her to drink more of the latte. "What's going on?"

She wondered if this was Sean-related. Last night, she'd managed to stay clear of him. Had briefly spied him and the woman he had glued to his side, but they hadn't collided. Good. She'd had enough moments of being around Keiran; she didn't need her ex thrown into the mix.

"I want to make sure you're properly caffeinated for this," Remi said. "Just don't kill the messenger." Her eyes cut to Reba, who hadn't relinquished her hold on the top of the laptop. "We'd rather show you before you found out from someone else."

Cherisse lowered the cup. "You're scaring me now. What. Is. It?"

Remi steered her over to the couch, where she sat next to Reba, who passed the laptop over to her. The ENTertainment site was up. Cherisse vaguely remembered the woman who'd made the rounds doing brief interviews with the winners. She'd cornered Cherisse to ask about last night's dessert display and what they could expect from Sweethand next. The woman, Carol, she thought her name was, had tried to bring up Sean, but Reba had swooped in and nixed that immediately.

She scrolled the article. Seemed normal enough. It spoke about the awards, and the night's big winners, then a sub-headline jumped out at her: **Is there a mini-feud brewing between the Sugar Queen and the Mixer King?**

What in the hell? The article that followed was no better than that clickbaity headline:

While last night's show was all about the music, no one could deny the presence of the delectable dessert towers at the cocktail function. Guests were seen practically razing the towers to get at the delicious desserts, courtesy of the Sugar Queen, aka Cherisse Gooding. Although, not everyone seemed enamored by the sugary goodness. Keiran King, one half of the dynamic music duo from DK Productions, said: "She probably has everyone fooled and just pops these frozen in an oven a few minutes before she leaves her house. I mean, come on, mixing music's gotta be way harder than mixing pastry batter..."

We at ENT think those are some fighting words. Sounds like a challenge to us. Which do YOU think is harder? Tell us in the comments.

And to Ms. Gooding, we say: Your move, Sugar Queen.

"Are you fucking kidding me?" If the article had been on paper, Cherisse would have crumpled that shit. No. She would have torn it to shreds, lit it on fire, then swept the ashes into the bin. She gently pushed the laptop to the side so she wouldn't be tempted to toss it. "That asshole!"

"Granted, he probably did say that," Remi said. "But Carol is known for this gossipy type shit. She's trying to escalate what was admittedly a foolish joke. A feud, really? That's a reach."

"I'm sick of him belittling what I do. I don't care if he was just joking," Cherisse fumed.

She'd worked hard to make Sweethand the success it was today. Last year's loss had been a big blow to her confidence, especially knowing she had no one to blame but herself. Yes, Sean, the *asshole*, had cheated, but she'd let it get to her. Making it to the finals of the *Pastry Wars* had been stressful enough. She had the entire weight of her island on her shoulders. Or so she'd felt. Then the news had broken the night before the finals, and she'd gotten zero sleep. Her phone had been buzzing constantly with family, friends, and random media trying to get at her. Her head hadn't been in the game. The morning of the competition, she'd totally crashed and burned. Everything had gone wrong. She'd broken down and had just quit the entire thing.

No doubt dating Sean had opened doors for her business, but she'd managed to keep most of those clients and gain more on her own merits by delivering an excellent service and always being on point. She couldn't afford an off day, not when dealing with food. People liked consistency. She couldn't do an awesome dessert today and a mediocre one tomorrow and expect to keep her Sugar Queen title. This shit was hard, but because it was food, people like Keiran thought it was a joke.

Well, fuck him. Food was important. Her work wasn't shit.

She pushed past Remi into the kitchen and started cataloging what ingredients she'd need.

"Cherry, what are you doing?" Remi sounded concerned.

"Uh-oh. Is she about to stress-bake?" Reba asked.

Cherisse ignored them as she started pulling ingredients and stacking them on the counter. "I promised Dale samples of the new thing I've been working on, and that's what I'm doing. If I make an extra-special batch of something for his ungrateful piece of shit friend, so what?"

"Uh, Cherry? Please don't send Keiran any poisoned goodies."

She spared Remi a glance and smiled. They'd followed her into the kitchen. "Don't worry. I wouldn't waste food that way."

"Cherry." Reba fell in beside her, eyes flicking over the ingredients as if Cherisse had stashed something deadly in there.

"Jesus. No poison, I promise!" She started humming as she got everything straight in her head before she began. *Sugar, flour, eggs...* Stuff for the mango white chocolate ganache filling, too.

Ava had texted to remind them about ladies' night tonight, so Cherisse definitely wanted these done and delivered so she could sit back and relax before then.

Tampering with food like that wasn't her style—that would be extreme—but she'd send Keiran a little message still. Poisoning the best man before the wedding would probably add unwanted stress anyhow.

KEIRAN

He'd fucked up.

The thought buzzed around his brain like a horde of flies as he tried his best to direct the artiste currently in the booth. They'd been cranking out some instrumentals while he tried to ignore the lambasting he'd received earlier.

None of his friends were shy about letting him know that he'd screwed up. Keiran had to pull his phone away from his ear as Eric shouted at him.

"What the hell did you do?" was the first thing he'd been greeted with when he'd finally returned Eric's *Call me now* text. Eric avoided phone calls like the plague, except at work. Couldn't escape that. That was Keiran's first clue that something was up. After the call connected, Eric had basically handed him his ass, and that was how he'd found out about the article.

Eric wasn't a loud guy, but when he was pissed off, watch out, he would let you have it. Afterwards, it always left you feeling like you'd gotten the scolding of your life from a parent who was highly disappointed in you. Even as an adult, that shit made Keiran feel bad. Because Eric was right: Keiran *had* fucked up.

He hadn't thought his offhand joke would be featured in that article in any way, but there it was. In all its splashy, gossip-inducing glory.

"Eric, really, I'll speak to the blogger about removing it," he'd tried to assure his friend.

"Too late, K." Eric's sigh had been long. "It was a shitty joke to begin with. You're going to have to apologize to Cherisse somehow. Do it before our thing later tonight. That's all I ask. Ava has her own lime with the ladies tonight, and I'm pretty sure you'd be wise to get in your sorry before then."

He'd forgotten all about the guys' get-together. Eric wanted to celebrate his engagement with his boys. The engagement party had been for his parents and family, but tonight they would grab drinks and rib Eric about his last few months of bachelor life. Keiran had been so deep in the beats as soon as he'd gotten up, basically holed up in the studio since this morning, that it had slipped his mind. Then this whole article debacle. Eric was right; the joke was terrible, to begin with, and shouldn't have made it past his lips.

Dale had joined him a few hours ago too. They'd been going hard, trying to put the finishing touches on this one track. Dale had been alerted to the article fiasco at the same time Keiran was, tossing him an *I told you so* glare before getting a call on his phone and disappearing upstairs, leaving Keiran to Eric's chiding.

He stared at his phone. He should call Cherisse, get the apology done with. They'd grudgingly exchanged numbers to arrange a meet-up to discuss this joint bachelor/bachelorette party business. Neither had used it. The wedding was in June, a little less than four months out, so they didn't have a lot of time. The short timeframe had gotten the rumor mill cranking, wondering if Ava was pregnant, but as Eric had told him, they'd been together so long, why draw out the engagement?

He was about to reach for his phone when Dale came clomping back down the stairs into the studio, hands full with three boxes. Boxes Keiran squinted at as he recognized the Sweethand logo, with the golden whisk and piping bag icons popping against the pink boxes.

"Sugar Queen came through!" Dale said, placing the boxes on the table. He picked one up. "Her PA dropped these off. My name's on this one. Oh. One for mummy, too, and...huh." He peered down at the last pink box. "This one's got your name on it."

Keiran signaled to the trumpet player to take five as he inspected the box. "You sure?" There was no way Cherisse had sent him anything good after that article mess, and Keiran knew she knew about it. So what game was she playing?

Dale held the box out to him while Keiran eyed it suspiciously. "Maybe you should vet it first."

Dale rolled his eyes, resting the box with Keiran's name on it off to the side. He peered into his own box. "Holy shit, these look good." He took a whiff of whatever was inside. "And damn, smells like heaven. Mango, I think. Mango macarons, hell yessss." He nudged his lid closed, then moved over to Keiran's box. "Let's see what she sent for—" Dale's snort made Keiran jump. It was so unexpected. Then Dale dissolved into loud cackles. "Dude!" He snort-laughed, pushing the box over for Keiran to have a look.

He'd gotten macarons too. Except, he was certain Dale's didn't have writing on each one that spelled out: **Go Fuck Yourself**

"What flavor did you get?" Dale wheezed out. "Apart from the saltiness that obviously went into making these. They're the same color as mine, so maybe mango too?"

"You don't think I'm actually eating these, do you? She probably put a laxative in them or some shit."

Dale whipped out his phone and took a photo of his set, then one of Keiran scowling at his *Go Fuck Yourself* ones.

"C'mon, man," he protested.

"What? This shit needs to be documented." Dale's fingers flew over his screen. "Hmm, what caption? Ah, yes, got it! I'm tagging you. Repost if you want."

Keiran shook his head but didn't bother to stop Dale. His own fault, really. He had this coming. The macarons did smell good, but he didn't trust them. He'd never really tasted Cherisse's hand, even back in the day, when Cherisse had started up her baking and convinced the neighborhood mini-mart to sell some of her treats. He'd see the cake slices at the counter when he went to pay for the items his mother always sent him for; had never tried them, even as curious as he'd been. He'd held fast to his pettiness. He sure as hell wasn't about to try these potentially suspect macarons.

"You really not trying one?" Dale asked. "I'm sure they're safe." He plucked one of his own out of the box and popped the whole thing in his mouth. "Oh shit, that's good. So, so good." Then he reached over for Keiran's.

"What are you doing?" Keiran snatched the box away.

"Look, I'm sure she didn't do anything to these. She already sent her message. She's too sweet to pull a laxative prank."

Keiran didn't believe that for a second. Cherisse might have them all fooled, but Keiran was convinced beneath the sugary smiles lurked someone who'd get off on silent revenge.

"I'm calling her." Dale had his phone to his ear before Keiran could tell him don't bother. "Cherisse, hi! Got your lovely package. Thanks so much! Uh, yeah." Dale glanced back at Keiran, eyes twinkling. "He got his as well. He's acting like it's poisoned or something. Yeah, *I* know you wouldn't do it, but I guess he didn't appreciate your message. Speaker? Okay, yeah, hold on."

Dale tapped his phone, then Cherisse's voice filled the studio. "You're an asshole,"—there was no doubt she was speaking to Keiran—"and my macaron message stands. But I swear, I didn't do anything to them. I wouldn't tamper with food like that."

"See, so it's okay for me to try one, right?" Dale piped up. He stared down at the box. "I'd take the smiley face, but I feel like it really drives the message home."

Cherisse laughed. "I thought so, too, and yes, it's safe for you to eat."

"Good." Dale picked up the one with "yourself" written on it and nibbled a piece off, making sure the "you" remained intact. Keiran rolled his eyes. Dale smirked, enjoying this too damn much. "Thanks again for the treats, Cherisse. Will have Keiran report back on the macarons."

"No need, I've said all I need to say. Bye." She hung up, and Dale pushed the box even closer to Keiran.

"Well? I'm not dead or rushing to the toilet yet, so either it's slow-acting, or they're fine."

"No." Keiran scowled at the damn things and shut the box lid, pushing them back over to Dale. "Let's get back to work."

He found his gaze sliding over to the distracting pink box as they worked. Perhaps he *could* take a nibble later after Dale was gone. Satisfy his curiosity. No one would know.

He jerked his stare away from the treats, realizing too late he'd had the chance to apologize to Cherisse and hadn't taken it. He could call her back and do just that, but now, he was annoyed. He had no right to be, but the darn macarons taunted him. Even with their **Go Fuck Yourself** message, he kept wondering if they tasted as good as they looked. Dale's chewing and moans of pleasure said they did, but Keiran refused to give in right now.

So he chose to be petty.

Chapter 6

Cherisse

BOOTLEGGERS WAS LOUD and packed; there was a rugby game going on. Cherisse wasn't big on sports, but she could appreciate a bunch of fit guys aggressively running around on the screens that were littered throughout the bar. The appetizers were good, and the drinks were strong and tasty. That was all that mattered. The conversation was entertaining too.

Ladies' night consisted of her, Ava, Remi, and Ava's close friend and fellow teacher, Julia. There was some prime Keiran-bashing going on, and Cherisse was grateful her girls had her back. Not that she'd expected anything less, but it felt great to know they'd take Keiran to task on her behalf.

She'd baked her anger into those macarons, hoping to be in a better mood for tonight's festivities, but it still lingered. The article played over and over in her mind. She'd memorized the entire thing already, having obsessively read and reread the offending words.

"Did you see this?" Remi pulled up an Instagram photo from Dale's feed, showing a scowling Keiran next to Cherisse's macaron message. "That caption, though."

The caption under Dale's photo made her laugh so loudly she almost snorted her martini through her nose.

When the sugar queen gets salty #dontmesswiththequeen #henotready #thatsmileyfacetho

"Accurate," Ava said, giggling. "Best revenge. Simple yet effective. I told Eric to tell him to apologize to you, did he?" Ava swirled her Long Island with her straw. Cherisse could imagine her sister's face when she'd laid down that proclamation. You messed with one Gooding sister, you were going to face the wrath of the other.

"No." She wasn't holding her breath for that apology.

This wedding made certain they couldn't escape each other, so it would be best for everyone if he genuinely said sorry for the shitty joke. Cherisse told herself she didn't even care, but the anger swirling in her chest said otherwise. But she could handle Keiran. She didn't have to like him to survive this wedding. It would make things a lot easier, but once he fell in line with her plan, they'd pull off the best joint wedding shower ever.

Ava frowned, and Cherisse patted her sister's bare shoulder. "It's your night, let's not sully it with thoughts of Keiran. I'll deal with it."

"Fine!" The vengeful look in her sister's eyes cleared, and she leaned over, smile mischievous. "So, tell us about this date."

Julia perked up. "Oh? Date? Do spill."

"She's got a date with one of Eric's family friends," Ava piped up before Cherisse could say a word.

Cherisse rehashed how her mother had basically thrust this guy on her, but eventually, she'd given in because really? It was easiest to just roll with what her mother wanted. Fighting it would just make her more persistent. Cherisse should've known Ava's wedding wasn't going to deter her mother from her mission: seeing all her children hitched and happy. Cherisse wasn't resting romantic hopes on this date. This was a shiny thing she'd dangle in front of her mother to distract. Act like she was willing to dip her toes back into the dating scene, keep her mother satisfied. Yeah, she was an adult who lived on her own, but when her mother got going, it was best to just let her believe she was making an effort.

Especially since Ava had shown her mother how to install and use WhatsApp. There were only so many photos of random sons of her friends that Cherisse could handle receiving. She figured if she gave in just a bit, her mother would stop.

"What y'all doing?" Julia asked.

"Dinner at Amaretto's."

A chorus of oohs went round the table. Amaretto's was one of the fancier restaurants. She'd never been because it was way out of her price range. Tyler had acted like he frequented the place regularly, and maybe he did. Cherisse didn't have a clue what to wear, worried nothing in her closet would live up to such a place.

Her mother had been impressed when—after badgering her about where they were going—Cherisse had revealed the location. Her mother's screech over the phone meant she approved and was possibly already planning a fantasy wedding for Cherisse in her head. She'd gone on about being so lucky as to have two daughters who secured rich men, completely ignoring Cherisse's reminder that she and Tyler hadn't even gone on the date yet.

Times like these, she was glad she didn't live at home anymore. Best decision of her life. She'd used needing her own kitchen to craft her creations as an excuse to strike out on her own. Her mother was overly possessive of her cooking space. As a teen getting interested in experimenting with baking, Cherisse had had to create a schedule that she'd run by her mother before getting the okay to start on her baking. Serious overkill. But what could a teen who lived under her parents' roof do but comply? Taking on Remi as her roomie to make her mother less antsy about the entire thing had worked better than any other excuse would have. Not that Cherisse hadn't wanted to live with Remi, she had, but her mother's soft spot for Remi worked in her favor. Cherisse wasn't above using it to keep her mother from constantly calling or randomly showing up at her place.

Hell, her mother still tried to do that, dropping by unannounced, which Cherisse had tried to curtail, especially because her mother would always find something in her apartment to critique.

Why these curtains still up?

The floor near the living area looks so bare. A rug would look nice here, not that I'm telling you what to do at your own place.

When last you cobwebbed?

But she rolled with it, just like she'd do with this date. She wasn't particularly enthusiastic about it—Tyler hadn't wowed her with his conversational skills—but perhaps he was better on a one-on-one basis, without a matchmaking mama watching them nearby.

Ava's sudden shout of glee drew Cherisse's gaze up. She spotted Keiran first, standing next to a grinning Eric. Scott waved from his left, and Maxine and a couple other guys Cherisse didn't know stood behind. What were they even doing here?

"Hey, you!" Eric planted a kiss on Ava, and Cherisse scowled.

"Are you guys crashing ladies' night?" Remi asked.

"Uh, no." Eric's grin got wider. "Would you believe we're having a groomspeople night, and we just happened to end up here?"

"Are you telling me Ava didn't tell you where we'd be?" That seemed far-fetched. She glared harder at Keiran, who looked on with a mildly sheepish smile.

Eric made some cross-his-heart-and-hope-to-die sign. "No, honest. A happy coincidence."

"Well, you all best get your asses at another table. This is ridiculous," Cherisse grumbled.

"Aw, c'mon Cherry, don't run us." Scott broke out his usual charming megawatt smile. She almost relented, but the smirk on Keiran's lips had her seething. She'd thought she hadn't cared whether he apologized at all, but now, she wanted him to grovel.

"Your boy here can't sit with us," she huffed, arms folded to punctuate her point.

Maxine snickered, and Keiran rolled his eyes, but he suddenly dropped to one knee, right there in the middle of the bar, and took Cherisse's hand. Too stunned to pull away, she gaped down at him. "Please forgive me, Sugar Queen. I was a fool, and I didn't mean it."

Cherisse yanked her hand out of his grasp. "You weren't invited to touch me, and get your ass up!" All eyes were on them, with Keiran making a spectacle of himself. She didn't need wacky proposal rumors spreading around, linking her to Keiran in any sort of intimate manner. "Apology *not* accepted. I'll accept nothing less than sponsored drinks for all of us and a public apology."

"What? Come on, that's a bit extreme. This isn't public enough?" He got to his feet.

"Stingy and a pathetic apology?" She pointed her olive-laden toothpick at him. "You're not winning any points here. You said that shit to a blogger known for bacchanal. Are you new?"

Keiran glanced at his guys and Maxine, who shrugged and didn't look the least bit inclined to offer assistance. Good. He wasn't getting any backup there. It was what he deserved anyhow. Eric was smart. He knew better than to go against his wife-to-be on this. Scott's grin said he found this way too funny to help a brother out.

"Drinks, that apology, and maybe I'll *think* about forgiveness," she pressed.

Keiran looked ready to argue, lips slightly curled in a show of annoyance, but he eventually sighed. "Fine. Whatever. Your public apology'll come tomorrow."

"And I don't mean some half-assed status update that don't mean shit. A video. Let me see you're really sincere."

"Seriously?" He frowned.

"Seriously." She munched on the olive, waiting, gaze challenging. Did he really think he could shit on her livelihood and get off so easily?

He shook his head, gaze stormy. "It'll be done. What drinks does everyone want?"

The ladies tossed out their orders, and Cherisse grinned triumphantly. Score one for her. Keiran turned to head to the bar, and she fell in beside him. He looked down at her. "I don't need a chaperone."

"I got a link at the bar. I can get us the drinks faster."

His skeptical look said he didn't believe that. "What? You think you got more bar game than me?"

"You're rapidly losing points here, and yeah. You think cuz you got all this going on"—she drew a circle around his body with her finger—"you can get through faster?" Oh, she would show him.

"Glad you noticed what I got going on."

God, she wanted to smack that grin right off his face. Damn, her loose lips. She would have never made such a rookie mistake if she hadn't had a few drinks. "You're not all that." Weak as a comeback, but she couldn't let his ribbing stand.

"I haven't had any complaints."

"Well, neither have I!" she shot back, heat rushing up to her face as she grew more pissed off. "We'll see who gets the bartender's attention first."

Challenge flared in his eyes. "Game on."

This was a game Keiran was going to lose, he just didn't know it yet. In spite of her increasing urge to cuss up a blue streak at Keiran, she smiled. Poor man.

She waved him forward, glaring at the way his white t-shirt clung to his back as he passed her by. Damn, the workout he must do to get muscles like that.

Nope. What the fuck was she doing checking out his back muscles?

She shook away her wayward thoughts. *Get a grip, girl.* The bar was crowded. Keiran didn't bother to push through the people packed around, trying to get the bartender's attention. He stood back, obviously hoping to use his height to his advantage, and possibly his annoyingly charming smile. He had that grin set to stun as he signaled to the Chinese woman with the long black hair who was sliding a beer over to one of the patrons.

"Hi." Keiran ramped up the bright smile.

Cherisse kept her grin in check. Barely. This was going to be hilarious. The woman's slight frown transformed into a full-blown grin, lighting up her round face. "Hey, darling! Am I glad you decided to grace me with your sexy self tonight."

Keiran tossed Cherisse a victorious smile before turning back to the woman. "Glad to be of service. Can I get...?"

The bartender's brow went up. "Not you." She waved Keiran away, his mouth dropping open at the obvious dismissal. Cherisse suppressed the urge to cackle at his stunned face.

"Hey, CK." She smiled back.

They'd gotten friendly when CK had been roped in to work the bar at a fancy event last-minute. Cherisse had been there too, having supplied the desserts. They'd struck up a conversation after CK had tried flirting with her but soon realized nothing would come of it, which they'd had a good laugh about. Then they kept running into each other whenever Cherisse came here, and a sort of friendship had formed, one where CK did some harmless flirting, which guaranteed Cherisse got her order quickly. A trade of sorts, which they both found amusing and just rolled with.

Cherisse rattled off the drink orders and fixed Keiran with a smug stare as CK went off to fix them right up.

"What the hell just happened?"

Cherisse patted the front of Keiran's shirt, ignoring the way his solid chest felt beneath her palm. She snatched her hand away before she could dwell on that. "Sorry, buddy. You're not her type."

He mumbled something she couldn't catch over the excited shouts of the sports fans. She was enjoying this way too much. They stood waiting on the drinks, not saying a thing until CK returned. Keiran muttered thanks as he slid his card over. When CK returned his card and the drinks, she propped her elbows on the bar, leaning over.

"Tell me something, though. How you always getting finer every time I see you?" CK asked, winking dramatically.

Cherisse grinned, shrugged. "Well, when you have a messy, public showdown with your cheating ex, you gotta make sure you keep it all on point going forward, right?"

CK nodded. "Giiirl, yes." Her gaze slid to Keiran. "This the new man?"

"No. *Hell* no." Her and Keiran? What a joke?

She snorted at his affronted look. He could twist up his face all he wanted. Cherisse wasn't going to pretend that was a thing. That *they* were a thing.

CK eyed Keiran up and down. "Shame," she said, looking back at Cherisse, mischief dancing in her brown eyes. "Y'all look kinda good together." CK was pushing things now. Time to exit.

Cherisse grabbed what drinks she could, threw a "later" at CK, then carefully made her way back to the table. She didn't need to wait on Keiran; he'd served his purpose.

When she got back, the table was deserted. What the fuck? She looked around for her sister and Remi. Maxine was absent too. Cherisse set the drinks down. She spied Julia dancing with Scott and tried to signal to them, but they were both too busy boogying to notice her waving.

Keiran finally showed up with the rest of the drinks. "Huh, we've been ditched."

Eric was suspiciously missing as well. Cherisse could bet she knew where her sister was. Seriously, those two couldn't even be separated for one night?

"I'd bet anything Ava and Eric found a dark corner somewhere. Those two, I swear, disgustingly in love."

"You really think so?" Keiran asked, sipping his beer.

"This place has sentimental value for them. First date, first make-out session in the car park, first bathroom sex moment."

Keiran choked on his beer. He wiped his mouth. "What?"

"Oh, yeah, my sis loves to overshare this shit."

"Wow, I didn't think Eric had it in him to do public sex." He gulped at his beer as if it was too hard to wrap his mind around that.

The sudden jolt of their table signaled Ava's return. Ava giggled as she tried to steady herself against the tabletop. Cherisse eyed the massive hickey on Eric's neck.

"Whoops." Ava held on to the table as she slid into her seat. She'd nearly knocked over the drinks, clearly tipsy. They had been hitting the drinks hard since they'd arrived at the bar. "Had to go to the bathroom."

"And I, uh, helped her do that." Eric didn't even try for a good excuse. It seemed ladies' night had been truly invaded.

"Did you see my sister in there?" Keiran asked.

Eric and Ava exchanged secretive looks, then both said, "Nope," at the exact same time and busted out laughing like that was the funniest thing. Cherisse hoped the guys had a designated driver because either Eric was high on whatever fooling around he'd done with Ava, or he was just plain drunk.

Their crew had hired a taxi because Julia had to leave early, and the rest of them planned to get as tanked as they wanted. They were celebrating, after all.

"We saw nothing," Ava sang out.

"We know nothing," Eric added.

Cherisse glanced at Keiran, who shrugged. Guess he didn't know what that was about, either.

"Hey, let's dance!" Ava cheerfully proclaimed, dragging Eric over to Julia and Scott.

Cherisse took a big swig of her drink just as Remi returned and announced, "I really had to pee. Sorry to abandon you to this." She waved at Keiran. "It was one of those neverending ones."

"Thanks for that info," Keiran said dryly.

Remi pointed a finger at him. "No one cares what you think." She grabbed up the drink Cherisse pointed to, eyes extra-bright. Oh yeah, Remi was also on her way to Tipsyville.

So was she, because she didn't bother to filter herself or her desire to rub Keiran's loss in his face. The mini bar challenge wasn't anything much in the grand scheme of things, but any little leg up she could get over Keiran, she would take it. "Keiran failed at getting CK's attention. He thought he could beat me."

Keiran's brow creased, and that frown was a lovely balm to the tiny bit of lingering annoyance over his presence and his general existence.

He shook his head. "That entire challenge was rigged from the start."

Remi laughed, and Cherisse emptied her glass, sliding it over to Keiran. "Be a darling and refresh my drink, won't you?"

She jumped up and linked arms with Remi, pulling her toward the dance floor while she left Keiran sulking.

KEIRAN

The separate crews' night had turned into one giant co-thing. Cherisse's protests from earlier had died away, possibly swallowed up by the drinks Keiran still supplied. They'd all jumped on the "make his sorry ass pay" wagon, milking it until the end, maybe even until the bar was ready to close and toss them out. Even Maxine. Traitor. Somewhat luckily for him, there was now a two-for-one special going on in honor of whatever rugby team was winning.

Some hot wings joined the myriad of glasses that littered their table, and the women descended on them.

"Oh my God, these are *so* good," Cherisse crooned. Eyes growing increasingly brighter as the night went on, she'd gotten more cheerful, at his expense. The shots flowed liberally.

This exuberant Cherisse was deadly, carefree, swaying from side to side, mouthing along with the hip-hop song currently blasting through the bar. Long hair swished around her shoulders, cheeks flushed from the dancing and the drinks, as she chowed down on her chicken right there on the dance floor, not caring one bit. The rugby game had finally ended, transforming the bar into full-on dance session mode.

"Best. Wings. Ever." Maxine bumped his shoulder as he reached for a wing in the quickly depleting pile. She was having fun too. He was glad for that. His sister deserved a good time.

She swatted his hand. "Nope. I've been charged with making sure you get none of these. Cherisse's rules."

"Since when do you do anything she says?" They weren't downright hostile to each other anymore, but they weren't friends either.

Maxine pointed a half-eaten wing his way. "Since you were an ass and deserve to be punished and wingless."

"Et tu, Maxi?" Standing guard over the wings seemed a bit excessive. Maxi swiped up the basket, wiggling her fingers in a little wave as she left him.

Keiran was pondering how desperate he was to get his own damn wings and hide in a corner to eat them without being judged when Eric rolled up. "Dude!" Eric shouted in his ear as he draped his arm over Keiran's shoulder. "I'm *so* lucky. So damn lucky she said yes!"

Happiness dripped off his friend. A tiny twinge of jealousy beat against his wingless stomach. He needed to rectify at least one of those feelings. The chicken was the easiest to remedy. The happiness

Eric so obviously felt was something Keiran realized he'd lacked in relationships. Had he ever truly had that? With his music, sure. He could say without a doubt that made him happy. His past relationships had mostly been great, except his last one that had been damaged beyond repair. Thinking on it now, he could say he'd cared for his exes while he'd been with them, but this level of joy? He didn't know.

"Happy for you, man." He meant that.

"You'll have that too. I know it!" Eric pointed with his chin. "Ask her to dance."

He expected Cherisse to toss her wing bones at him if he even breathed too close to her. Asking her to dance seemed life-threatening. The drinks had been accepted, that didn't mean she wanted him all up in her space to dance. Why the hell would she after what he'd thoughtlessly said to that blogger?

"Nah. I don't have a death wish."

Eric pouted. "Just let my OTP sail, man."

"I have no idea what that means, but it's not happening."

Still, he observed Cherisse as she danced with Scott, body limber, movements growing more relaxed with each drink she downed. There'd been a time when he'd been outright jealous of Scott's easy way with Cherisse. He knew nothing but friendship would come of it. Scott was gay and hung up on someone else. Someone who wasn't Keiran. Both things had irked him at the time, even as he'd scolded himself for caring. It hadn't helped any of the confusion he'd been dealing with. Teenage Cherisse had been aloof with him, didn't even give him the time of day, but Scott? Got the biggest of smiles, the tightest of hugs. After things didn't go as expected with Scott—he still cringed at that day he'd almost imploded their friendship—his teen self had been bitter at the attention his best friend showered on Cherisse. Irrationally so, which didn't help the tenuous relationship he and Cherisse had.

Then he'd foolishly somehow slowly fallen into crushing on Cherisse. The worst idea. That also hadn't helped his panic over discovering he wasn't straight.

He watched as Scott and Cherisse pretended to twirl each other now, her head thrown back as her body shook with genuine laughter. Ava came over and pulled Eric back on the dance floor, leaving him alone to watch. Keiran had danced a bit with Julia earlier, but it felt a bit as if everyone was punishing him for messing up. The bridesmaids, for sure. His own damn fault, but it was getting to him.

He found himself drifting closer as Scott and Cherisse kept at it. Their movements grew bigger and wider—no doubt they were having fun—until Scott whirled over to him, and Keiran suddenly found his arms filled with an equally surprised Cherisse as Scott shouted, "Bathroom! Take over for me!"

She blinked up at him but was either too shocked or tipsy to move out of his embrace. "Uh." She peered around him, watching Scott hustle away.

Keiran, too aware of Cherisse in his space, was at a loss for what his next action should be. Release her and go back to being a pariah? *She* hadn't moved away yet, but he should. Except the feel of the soft skin of Cherisse's arm under his made it hard to do anything but hold on, and for once, she wasn't looking at him as if he was something unpleasant that had gotten stuck to the bottom of her shoe.

"Do you want to dance?" It slipped out before he could stop himself, before he thought better of it.

She stepped away from him, looking horrified at the idea. "I'm not *that* drunk. But now I need another drink." She shot him another incredulous stare, shook her head as if he'd asked the most ridiculous question, then walked away.

Well, he'd tried. A lot of good that did. Damn Eric and his nonsense talk about OTPs or whatever.

Chapter 7

Cherisse

A HAND, FLUNG IN HER face, jolted Cherisse awake, mouth parched, and feeling grimy. Had she even brushed her teeth last night before tumbling into bed? Cherisse carefully removed the hand that she realized belonged to Remi. Remi shifted to her side, so her back was to Cherisse, the blanket pulled up until it almost covered her head, her messy bun the only thing visible.

Something tickled her shoulder, and she nearly screamed as she reached to brush it off and encountered her hair unbound. Dammit, she hadn't even wrapped her hair last night.

The throb in her temples made her wince. She'd forgotten to drink water before bed—her dry mouth was indication enough—and vaguely remembered shucking her clothes and crawling into the bed. She moved the cover down, and yup, she was in just her underwear. God, she was a mess, and so was her hair probably, since she hadn't slept with her silk head tie. She squinted around the unfamiliar room. Where the fuck?

Clearly, her brain was still alcohol-soaked. She recalled dancing with Scott and Eric, even a random guy or two from the bar. The latter half of the night was sort of fuzzy, and there *had* been one guy she'd been laughing up a storm with as he twirled her around, but that had been the extent of it. Dancing with a bunch of people, except Keiran. She remembered the small look of hurt when she'd shot down his offer. But she must have imagined it. Keiran didn't even like her. She'd just made him buy drinks for them all last night, so he couldn't have been serious.

Cherisse nudged Remi. She mumbled something unintelligible and didn't move. Cherisse felt like shit. She pressed her hand to her aching head, trying to will the pain away. She looked around—taking in the bedroom—when it clicked. Her parents' house. The guest room. There'd been a reason for them crashing here instead of going home, but damned if her hurting head would let her remember why. Ugh, fuck this morning seriously, with its bright ass sunlight seeping in through the not-heavy-enough curtains.

The bedroom door flung open, and Ava hustled in. "Wake up!"

Cherisse flinched as something cold landed on her chest. The fuck? She grabbed at the bottle of water before it rolled down her stomach. "Wha—"

Remi snuffled next to her but didn't get up. In fact, she burrowed even further under the covers.

"Get up, Cherry. I'm serious!" Ava looked frazzled, her hair all over the place. Judging from the pillow marks on her cheek, she'd just gotten up too. She was still in her sleep shorts and top that boasted a Winnie the Pooh print.

"Where's the fire?" Cherisse eased up into a sitting position, clutching the water bottle. Her head kept up the throbbing. Thankfully, there was no urge to throw up. As actual hangovers went, this one wouldn't have her immobile.

"I forgot! Forgot my own dress appointment! April called, and I had to act like I knew it was today all along, but I. Did. Not. Remember. We're late. We need to leave in the next hour, and God...I'm never drinking again." She pressed a hand to her stomach, mouth twisted into a grimace. "Just get your asses up."

Things slowly fell into place. April was Ava's wedding planner, and this would be Ava's first time trying on dresses. Ava was definitely hungover too. Her eyes were heavy-lidded, barely fully open as if shielding against the morning brightness.

"Shit, I need to shower. Seriously, wake Remi up. I think I have time to do something about this horror show." She circled her face with a finger and then stormed out.

By the time they assembled downstairs, they were the sorriest bunch. Ava's eyes were hidden behind giant sunglasses, and she was downing water like her life depended on it. Cherisse and Remi had completely forgotten a change of clothes, and there wasn't time to swing by their apartment. Cherisse was wearing some wildly patterned leggings Ava had tossed at her. Unable to shimmy into any of Ava's shorts or jeans due to being bigger in the hips and thigh area, it would have to do. She refused to roll up to the fancy bridal store in sweatpants, so she'd ignored those in the pile. She'd borrowed a t-shirt too. One that said *MATURE-ISH* on the front. One that, as she squinted at it long enough, looked like her t-shirt that had mysteriously gone missing forever ago.

Remi, with her tall ass self, didn't try to borrow anything, not even a t-shirt. She'd shrugged and, after showering, put back on the same dress she'd worn last night. The dress was horribly wrinkled, having been slept in, but Remi didn't seem to care. She slipped on her wedges from last night and slumped on the couch, blinking at them sleepily, not giving a shit, her almost waist-length hair tumbling across one shoulder.

Then the guys and Maxine showed up because they were getting fitted for their suits today as well. Eric looked fresh as ever, and Cherisse immediately hated him. She was suffering, and he was smiling like he hadn't had a damn thing to drink last night. She pretended Keiran wasn't there, even though she got a little satisfaction that he wasn't looking as chipper as Eric. Scott didn't look too bad either, but then again, when did he ever?

"Jesus, you look like a zombie horde," Julia remarked when she showed up. She'd left early last night and had obviously gotten the most hours of sleep, looking the freshest of them all in ripped skinny jeans, a cute camisole, and sandals, sunglasses perched atop her head. Her hair was pulled back into a perfect bun, baby hairs slicked down so that not a strand of hair was out of place. Brow hiked up, Julia looked Remi up and down. "Is that the same dress from last night?"

Remi shrugged. "It covers my ass, mostly." Mostly was right. A slight breeze would have the dress swirling up to show Remi's entire backside. Cherisse had borrowed underwear too. Ava always kept an unopened pack of the most randomly patterned undies in her drawer. Cherisse was currently sporting ones with turtles. She had no idea what Remi had on under there. As if she knew exactly what Cherisse was thinking, Remi flipped up the back of her dress to reveal Snoopy boy shorts.

"Cute, right?" Remi asked, popping her booty. "I'm keeping these."

Ava wrinkled her nose. "Why would I even want them back? You wear 'em, they're yours. Can we just go, please?" She waved her phone around impatiently. "We have an appointment, and mummy is two steps away from trying to force-feed us some nasty ass hangover remedy."

That got everyone moving. Their mother was known for always having some bush concoction at the ready for all situations.

Eric had procured a nine-seater van, so they were rolling together, which was annoying as hell because she ended up next to Keiran, who merely grinned and held up his phone.

"Public apology incoming."

"Now?"

"Yeah, you can witness it firsthand. I really am sorry. I hope you know that."

She stared ahead as Eric maneuvered the van onto the Solomon Hochoy highway. It was at least an hour's ride to Princes Town. Keiran's apology sounded sincere enough, but Cherisse felt the anger brewing all over again.

"Do you even realize the assholes that came out their holes to spew shit on that post? I know I should've run far from the comments, but fucking bros talking about my place being in the kitchen or under them, there's no in-between, made me see red."

Keiran's eyes widened. "You read the comments? First rule of the internet, don't read the comments."

"Yeah, well, I'm too curious for my own good, clearly. Doesn't change the fact your joke prompted that."

Keiran stared down at his phone. "Shit. I'm... I fucked up."

"We *females*." She shot him a pointed look. "This one fucker kept using "females" in his comments. What a gem he was. Know what? I'm not repeating what he actually said, you can read it yourself if you want. I'm tired of having my job looked down on. Oh, you bake? For fun? What's your real job? Like the food industry isn't a thing? I don't get it too much, but once in a blue moon, so your joke? Not funny."

He looked appropriately embarrassed now. Good. Why should she feel bad about pointing out the shittiness of it? He squared his shoulders and opened his camera app, shooting her an apologetic smile.

"Okay, I'll make this right." He held his phone up to his face. "Happy Saturday, peeps. Most of you might have heard about the article by now. I'm not linking to it to boost any more hits to it, so don't ask. Well, I made a really not cool joke, and I'm truly sorry. Women have guys belittling everything they do every damn day, and I added to that. Which was frankly fucked up. My mom would have my ass if she knew I did that." He winced. "I guess she'll ask me about it after this, Lord, help me. So, I wanna say, flat out to Cherisse, I'm sorry. And I'm grateful for you calling me out on it." He glanced over at her, then back at the screen, corner of his lip quirking up as he fought a grin. "In a unique way, but message received."

She bit her lip to hold in her snort. The macaron message was still hilarious, and she had no regrets about sending it.

"So, I'm gonna do better. I don't expect her to forgive me, it's her right not to, but I just want her to know I'm truly sorry. Last thing..." His eyes hardened. "To the assholes commenting utter shit under that article, grow up, get a fucking life. Oh! And go check out her Sweethand website for sweet treats. I'll leave the link in my post. That's it. Laters." He threw up deuces before stopping the video, played it back, then looked to her for approval. She nodded, and he posted to his accounts.

"Are we good?" he asked, and Cherisse pursed her lips. Did he think it was that easy?

Cherisse folded her arms and leaned back in her seat. "It's a start."

Keiran shrugged. "Damn, you're a tough one, but thanks for not poisoning those macarons, I guess."

She cocked her head. "So, you did eat them?"

"I admit nothing," he said, looking out the window.

They made it to the bridal store, late as expected. Eric and Ava parted ways so the groom's party could see about their suit fittings.

The store attendant peered at them over the top of her glasses. They looked a hot mess, but Ava wasn't about to be judged while in this fancy ass store. She adopted a haughty stare as she tossed out her future mother-in-law's name. It was amusing how quickly the woman's disposition changed, suddenly turning charming, attentive.

"How 'bout dem dollar signs, huh?" Remi whispered out the side of her mouth. Not a single lie detected. Mrs. Jones's name clearly held weight here.

Cherisse grabbed a seat as her sister described the sort of styles she was looking for, so one of the store girls could pull up the options on her tablet. Cherisse switched between watching Ava as she tried some dresses on and her phone, going through updates from Reba.

As maid of honor, she felt a little guilty not giving this her full attention, but work was never done, and multi-tasking was a thing.

Apart from doing the dessert stations at Ava's wedding, she'd booked a job for another wedding a few weeks before. Plus, Reba had sent her the stock numbers for the Sweethand goodies she sold in select bakeries and groceries. She'd need to restock soon. Lots of cookie and cupcake baking ahead, but Cherisse loved it. Surrounding herself in the sugary baking smells made her happy. Had since she'd hovered around her mother's kitchen, watching the delicious-smelling batter become tasty treats.

A loud gasp and a nudge from Remi tore her gaze away from her phone, which nearly slid out of her hand.

"Well?" Ava turned to them, smile hopeful, but Cherisse, used to Ava's facial expressions, knew right away—Ava had found the one. She was in love with this dress, no doubt. Cherisse could see why.

The entire top portion of the dress was this intricate lace pattern. The halter style showed off Ava's toned arms. The skirt was a gorgeous ivory color and swished around Ava's legs as she twirled. As her sister kept twirling, Cherisse got a look at the back, which dipped low, revealing a lot of skin.

It was a good thing the wedding wasn't happening in a church because they'd definitely want Ava to toss a shawl or jacket or something over the top, which would have been a shame because that bodice needed to be seen. Cherisse wasn't sure how her sister and Eric had pulled off not getting married in church. Her parents went to the Roman Catholic church in their area every Sunday and dragged Ava and Eric with them more often than not. They'd given up on getting Cherisse to go regularly. So Cherisse had expected her parents would push for a traditional church wedding. She'd have to ask Ava how she'd managed that magic.

"I have never been queerer in my entire life," Remi muttered, and Cherisse bit her lip to keep her snort in.

"Stop lusting after my sister," she mock-glared, elbowing Remi in the ribs.

"I'm not," Remi insisted. "Just appreciating the gift that is woman." She winked and continued to smile up at Ava from her seat.

"Eric'll die." Julia beamed at Ava, eyes a little shiny like she'd burst into tears any moment.

"Or cry," Cherisse added. "You look gorg, sis. He's not ready."

Ava placed her hands on her hips, smile wide. "Good. If he doesn't cry or at least gimme an open-mouthed gasp, I'm leaving him at the altar."

That had everyone getting a good laugh in and Ava doing some more preening in front of the full-length mirror. Even some of the other customers complimented her. She truly looked stunning, even with her sunglasses pushed up atop her head and her eyes still a little squinty, courtesy of the hangover.

"He won't know what hit him," Cherisse assured her sister.

After donning her own clothes again, Ava whipped out a fancy-looking card that just screamed money and paid for the dress in full. At their raised brows, her sister smirked. "I'm not marrying him for his money, but it sure doesn't hurt." She winked at them, indicating it was time for the next order of business.

Bridesmaid dresses. They were getting theirs made, which was fine by Cherisse, especially since her sister insisted the dresses have pockets. Not exactly an easy thing to find ready-made. Cherisse cherished the few dresses she'd found that actually had pockets because apparently, designers didn't think people who wore dresses needed them, which was ridiculous. Plus, they'd all voted on styles that were slightly different yet still complimented each other, and that wasn't an easy thing to find in stores here.

"Just don't make us wear anything hideous," Julia declared as they shuffled next door. This place was an extension of the bridal store, and just as fancy with its buttery-looking couches lining the wall. The seamstress's assistant offered up a variety of beverages.

"What's the color scheme again?" It took Cherisse a moment to realize Julia was asking her, as Ava was busy chatting with the seamstress.

Cherisse should know this. She was the maid of honor. She should have this info stashed away, right? Ready to trot out at times like this, except she was drawing a blank.

"Uhh, it's...um, this sort of peach, I think."

"How do you not know this?"

"I got a lot going on, okay? I have to plan that joint party with Keiran. That's enough of a headache on its own. Then, I'm doing the dessert stations..."

Julia folded her arms. "Uh-huh."

"It's coral, with different complementary yet lighter shades." They both turned to Remi, who shrugged as she sipped from her glass of something bubbly. "What? I listen when it suits me. Plus, that's gonna pop with my skin tone. I'mma look like a brown dougla goddess in that flowy coral stuff."

Cherisse had steered clear of the offered bubbly, choosing to play it safe with water. "Seriously, Remi? Champagne? Aren't you hungover enough?"

"Listen, this is expensive bubbles. I'm playing never see come see right now, I'll admit that. We don't get this luxury often." She sipped her drink. "And, you know what they say? The cure for a hangover is more alco."

Cherisse rolled her eyes, wetting her throat with her cool, refreshing water. She felt Julia's judgy look, which was fair. She *should* have known about the color scheme. She was already failing at this maid of honor gig. She'd never been one before. Bridesmaid, sure. That was low pressure. You just had to show up to things when told to. This was different. It being her sister ramped up the pressure even more. She needed to take a more active role. First thing on that list: actually set up a planning meeting with Keiran. She wasn't looking forward to it. Had to be done, though. Sooner rather than later.

As if he'd sensed she'd been thinking bad thoughts about him, Keiran appeared in the shop. "Hey, sorry to bother you, ladies, but I need to borrow the maid of honor a sec."

KEIRAN

Cherisse's wrinkled nose shouldn't be cute, but it was. Something about that coupled with the colorful pattern of her leggings and the t-shirt with *MATURE-ISH* printed across her chest made her seem less like the perfectly put-together Sugar Queen and more approachable. Except that last part wasn't exactly true. She wasn't amused by his appearance—he'd seen that look enough times to know—but this was too important, and as the best man, he had no choice but to face her wrath.

"What do you want?"

"Just..." He gestured for her to follow him; he needed her away from the rest of the bridal party.

She rolled her eyes but walked with him towards the door.

"This could've been avoided if you'd replied to my message or answered your phone," he pointed out. More discreet that way too, but fact was, she could avoid her phone. She couldn't avoid him in her face like this.

"Phone's in my bag, and we were a bit busy fawning over Ava. Just get on with it. I'm too hungover for your shit."

"Ah, a chink in your impenetrable armor."

She closed her eyes, taking a deep breath before reopening them and exhaling loudly. "Get on with it."

Oh, how he wanted to continue teasing, but charm would be better suited here. Cherisse was likely to strangle him with one of the colorful shawls that hung near the door. "You'd be saving Eric's life here. We're trying to explain the color scheme, but all we've got is it's sort of peachy? Eric's not the best with color names, and he obviously didn't want to ask Ava."

Cherisse cocked her head. "You serious?"

"Yes."

Her laughter was unexpected, as was her muttering, "Oh universe, you are so funny." But the haughty look that replaced her laughter wasn't. And there was the Cherisse he knew. "Coral, obviously. Things the best man should know."

Of course, she knew. Cherisse probably had a binder filled with important details or a dedicated folder on her phone. She wouldn't be scrambling like he'd done in the store. The clerk had been unimpressed, not bothering to conceal his disgust that neither the groom nor the best man had the answer to such a simple question. Another thing on the growing list of things for Cherisse to hold against him. He'd basically shown his soft, exposed belly to a predator, and no matter what anyone thought about Cherisse being nice, that was so not the case. Her sweetness masked a devious interior.

"Keiran, are you over here spying?"

They both turned as Ava strolled over, Julia and Remi not far behind.

"Nope, definitely not."

"Well, since you're here, I may as well mention this. I mean, it could be fun? Will be fun." Ava grinned. "I need everyone's help making flower crowns. Entire bridal party gets ones with real flowers, and the rest of the guests can get the fake ones. Everyone's gonna look so cute in them!"

At least he knew it was a garden wedding theme. The flower crowns would be a nice touch.

"So I want to start on making the fake ones soon as a sort of trial run? I know we're three months away, but I'd rather see if we suck at this before it's too late. The real ones'll be done closer to the wedding day."

"Wait, you want *us* to make them?" Cherisse looked horrified.

"Well, yeah." Ava flung an arm around Cherisse's shoulder. "Think of it as a wedding party bonding moment. All hands on deck."

"Sounds fun," Keiran chimed in. Cherisse scowled. He'd seen those crowns on Pinterest before. How hard could they be?

Ava squeezed Cherisse's shoulder, waving bye to Keiran as she steered her sister over to the woman patiently waiting to measure them. "It *will* be fun. I promise."

Chapter 8

Cherisse

THE PROMISED FUN WAS a damn lie.

Her first attempt at a flower crown looked a hot mess and nothing like the creation in the video she'd been trying to follow. It was closer to one of those Pinterest fails.

"Well, this isn't so bad."

Cherisse's fist closed around one of the silk flowers, crushing it in her palm, jaw tight as she looked over at the perfect flower crown Keiran was holding. Of course, *his* was an exact replica of the one in the video. The universe was definitely having a laugh at her. What were the odds he'd be good at this?

"I hate you." She couldn't stop it from slipping out. She'd been fighting with her one crown for what felt like forever. Apart from the one in his hand, Keiran had three others already made and placed off to the side.

Keiran laughed, eyes scrunching up in the corners. "I can show you if you want. Yours isn't that bad. You just need more flowers to fill up this side."

She ignored him, going back to doing battle with her crown. She'd get it done without his help, thank you very much. Hopefully, when the others arrived, at least one of them would have as much trouble as she did, so she wasn't the only one with pathetic-looking crowns.

She reached for her phone and texted Remi, again: **where are you? If I have to be with him another minute you'll find a crime scene when you get here >.>**

Remi: five mins away. Promise ;)

That wink said it was more like ten or twenty minutes. She'd been at Eric's for an hour already, and only Keiran had shown up so far. Everyone else was late. Typical. Eric's place was a short walk away from his parents. Cherisse wondered how Ava felt about that, having in-laws that close. The house had apparently belonged to Eric's late aunt, who'd left it for him. It wasn't as ostentatious as his parents' but pretty damn close, boasting a couple of guest rooms and a massive kitchen that Cherisse envied. The pool in the back yard looked inviting right about now, too. Eric and Ava had enticed them over for crown-making with mention of a potential pool party after. Except they'd both been gone forever, doing Lord knows what—she hoped it involved getting stocks for later—leaving her here with Keiran and the damn crowns.

"Why are you so bad at this?" Keiran asked, gesturing at her pitiful-looking flower. "You're supposedly good at creating these delectable treats everyone raves about, and yet..."

"Food and flower crowns are totally different," she shot back. Her creativeness only extended towards food. Any other sort of craft was beyond her. Her hands felt clumsy as she tried to get her crown to look like the ones in the video, and her patience had since evacuated the house.

Being stuck beside Keiran as he effortlessly churned out crown after crown didn't help. But she refused to give up. Their point system that existed only in her head had them even right now, but with her Pinterest fail, the scales were tipping in his favor. Not happening. She stared down at the video on her phone and reached for her crown again.

"So, what do you think? I pull this look off or nah?"

Cherisse looked up from her phone to find Keiran wearing one of his crowns on his head. Her first instinct was to say how ridiculous he looked. Except that would be a lie. He looked charming, and she hated it. Coupled with that lopsided smile, the crown made up of orange, pink, and white flowers made him look like some mischievous wood nymph. One who promised loads of not-so-rated-PG fun.

She shrugged and looked down at her phone again. "It looks fine."

"Aw, come on. Fine? I worked my fingers to the bone, getting this just right. Fine, she says." He shook his head. "Would it kill you to admit it looks better than fine?" He picked up one of the other finished crowns and held it out to her. "Try this on. Please," he added after she pursed her lips at his request.

She rolled her eyes and pulled her hair out of its high bun, letting it fall around her shoulders in a wavy mess, before sticking the crown on her head. "Well?" She probably looked silly, wearing this crown with her rolling pin pendant, a blue tank top that said *They see me rollin', I'm bakin'* on the front, and leggings. Except, Keiran wasn't looking at her like she looked silly.

His dark eyes were suddenly serious. "You look...great," he said before looking away to grab his phone from the floor. When he looked back, amusement and smirking had replaced the brief intensity. "Selfie?"

"I'll take my own, thanks." She snapped a couple for Instagram and Snapchat, while across from her, he did the same.

"We should get one with both of us. Best man and maid of honor. I already snapped a bit of my making-them process."

"What?" She hadn't even noticed he was doing that. "I'm not in your story, am I?" He better had not been snapping her when she cussed up a storm while fighting with her one crown. That would be just what she needed. She had a rep to maintain that didn't include her clients hearing her dropping f-bombs every other word, and wouldn't that be another point for Keiran in their not-so-silent war?

"I didn't. I'd ask first." He grinned. "So, I'm asking now. Selfie with me? Let everyone see you've maybe forgiven me for my, uh...foot-in-mouth incident."

Right. That. Except she hadn't, had she? She didn't think she was being unreasonable here, but who knew? Where Keiran was concerned, her emotions flip-flopped all over the place. People were still talking about his foolish joke in that article. Fine. It *was* just a selfie. Even with a public apology posted on his social media, this wasn't just going to die down. Trinis loved a good gossip, and if posing with Keiran would squash it, she'd do it.

"Okay, a quick one, then I gotta get back to my monstrosity." She indicated the misshapen crown on the floor then scooted over, so they were close enough to both fit in the photo. Her bare shoulder brushed his. She registered his warm skin against hers, all too aware of his bare arm in that sleeveless basketball jersey. His face was close as he angled the phone for the shot.

"Big smiles," he prompted before taking the photo. He looked at his phone before showing her. "Does it have the Sugar Queen's approval?"

"Yeah." It would do. His flower crown had slipped down to a jaunty angle, and she was sort of smiling, but Keiran had his full-on stunner grin going, and it brightened the entire mood of the photo. She realized abruptly that this was their first selfie. Hell, the first photo they'd ever willingly taken together.

"Huh." Keiran looked down at the photo again. "I think this is our first one together in ever."

Was he a mind reader now? "Was just thinking the same thing," she admitted.

There *were* photos from their teen days where they were both present, but they'd always had people between them. They never stood together for group shots. Cherisse had been irritated enough that Keiran hung out with people she actually liked, which meant she was forced to see him sometimes. So when they'd all gone out as a group, it was easier to ignore him.

"Feels like I should frame this momentous occasion. History in the making." Keiran chuckled, which then made Cherisse look down at his mouth. His scruff framed his lips, made them look enticing. Biteable. Which, in turn, made her realize how close they were still sitting and how very still Keiran had gone. *Whoaaaa K.* She needed to get back to flower crown-making and abort this line of thinking.

"Hey, the gang's all here," Remi called out from the front door. Cherisse scooted back over to her spot just as Remi came in, followed by Reba, Maxine, Scott, Julia, Eric, and Ava. The last two carried several bags. "I bribed Reba with baked treats so she'd help. So, at some point, you'll need to make some." Remi plopped down next to Cherisse.

"She can make her own, though," Cherisse pointed out, thankful for their timing. Uncomfortable with the direction her thoughts had been taking, the interruption was welcomed. The only thing she should be thinking about Keiran's mouth was how punchable it was. Lips looking so soft and plump. Perfect for punching. Yup. So punchable.

Remi shrugged. "That's for you two to sort."

"I mean, I'm good, but not Sugar Queen good. Yet. I can admit that." Reba slid down next to Cherisse, brow raised at her mess of a crown. Her gaze cut to Keiran's perfect pile then back to Cherisse's. Cherisse glared. Reba bit her lip, not saying a thing.

As the others got settled in around them, claiming their spots on the floor, Keiran directed his attention to the bags, their little moment seeming to have had zero effect on him at all. She needed to get on that track ASAP. "What we got?"

"Meat. Food things. Driiiinks. Once we get the crowns done, party tiiiime," Eric sang out, following Ava to the kitchen, leaving Keiran to show the others the DIY flower crown video.

"This shit looks complicated." Scott poked at the silk flowers strewn about. "But I'll look really cute in these, no lie. Hmm, I'm already thinking up some makeup looks that'll go great with these, too." Scott was doing the makeup for the bridal party, and having seen his work, Cherisse knew he'd come up with something stunning.

"It's easy enough," Keiran said, all casual-like, shooting Cherisse a wink.

Oh, he was going to regret that.

KEIRAN

The pile of flower crowns had grown significantly as the day wore on. Keiran was actually enjoying the repetitive motion of weaving the flowers so the crown took shape. Who knew he'd be so good at this? Outside of his musical talents, he didn't particularly have hobbies. When would he find the time? For him, music was work but also the thing he loved, so he wasn't bothered that he dedicated the majority of his time to it.

But this, he was into. It was sort of soothing.

Another thing he was enjoying was Cherisse cussing up a storm as she struggled with her crowns. Refusing to accept his help and glaring at anyone else who gave suggestions, she'd stormed to the kitchen to help Ava out.

Eric had already excused himself to get started on seasoning the meat, letting it marinate a bit for grilling later.

"I think my ears are still scandalized from all those four-letter words," Scott joked, poking at Cherisse's pile. The crowns had gotten marginally better than her initial set, but not by much. "How is she so bad at this?"

"Your pile isn't exactly going to win any awards there, buddy," Remi piped up, ready to defend her friend.

"Maybe, but Remi, come on, this is atrocious." Scott picked up one of Cherisse's attempts and stuck it on his head. A few flowers dangled off the frame, ready to give up and just fall off.

Keiran agreed but wisely kept his mouth shut. He wouldn't win any points with Remi if he bad-mouthed Cherisse's crown. Maxine chose the same route, working studiously on her set as she glanced up every few minutes as Remi and Scott talked. Scott could get away with that. Everyone adored him. Keiran was on thin ice already.

Finished with his batch, he got to his feet, stretching out the kinks in his body. He'd been sitting in the same position for too long.

"I'll go see if they need any help with the food." A ploy to score some eats. His stomach was protesting.

He'd almost walked right in through the open door when he heard his name.

"Why are you making Keiran and I do this? It would be so much easier if you had separate parties so I could do my thing without seeing his face."

Well, okay, Cherisse, tell us how you really feel, he thought.

Ava sighed. "It's what we want. We want everyone to celebrate together."

"That's what the wedding is for," Cherisse huffed. Keiran bit his lip to keep his chuckle at bay. He could imagine the frown that creased her forehead and that wrinkled nose.

"Come on, he's not that terrible. Not like I forced you to work with Sean or some shit."

"You may as well have."

Ouch. That one struck a nerve. Her ex was a piece of shit, cheating asshole. Keiran had run into the guy before; it was hard not to when he was one of his father's artistes. He'd never had to work with the man professionally, thank God.

"Keiran messed up with that joke, yes, but he's nothing like Sean."

"You're really defending him right now? Knocking someone up and acting like she doesn't exist sounds pretty shitty to me. These music guys think the world revolves around them."

What the fuck? That goddamn rumor was still getting traction? And Cherisse bought into that bullshit? Keiran told himself to turn around, go back to the living room.

Do not engage with this nonsense.

But he was tired of being dragged over shit that was so far from the truth. He stalked into the kitchen. Ava's eyes grew wide.

"You don't know a damn thing about anything."

Cherisse cocked a brow, unperturbed that she'd just been discussing him like that. "Why don't you clear the air, then? Silence is pretty damning."

"Because it's no one's damn business what happens in my private life!"

"So, it's not true?" Cherisse persisted.

Ava placed a hand on Cherisse's shoulder, but she ignored it, continuing to face off with him. Keiran had never addressed the rumors because it was easier to let everyone think whatever they wanted of him than address some foolish talk. He didn't have time for media speculation. Opening that door to even comment on the gossip that reared up every so often was not something he was willing to do, but hearing Cherisse talk like this was pissing him off.

"You believe everything you hear? I hear some people say you used Sean to boost your business, but that doesn't make it true, does it?"

"What you've heard, or what *you* think?"

"I don't think that, Cherisse. Sure, I think this whole sweet act is just that, an *act*, but I also think you're quick to judge me based on nothing. I'm nothing like Sean."

"Funny how you still haven't denied the most important thing I mentioned." She shrugged. "I mean, you wouldn't be the first man to shirk your parental responsibilities."

"Okay, you two, let's just simmer down," Ava tried, but they both ignored her. The sliding door that led to the outside patio slid open, and Eric stepped inside, eyes bouncing between them.

She was prepared to think the worst of him just because he hadn't refuted any of it. Why did that feel like a jab right through his chest? He'd already known Cherisse didn't think much of him, but damn, this was a lot. He was tired. He'd been gritting his teeth and holding back every time someone trotted out this rumor, but her last words obliterated the tiny bit of patience he'd been clinging to when he'd decided to walk in here.

"You wanna know the truth?"

"Keiran, you don't have to say anything," Eric said.

Oh, he knew that, but he wanted to wipe that self-righteous look off her face. Wanted to clear his name for once.

"My ex and I hit a rough patch. Then, she fucked around with someone else and got pregnant. So, I ended it, and of course, people thought I'd dumped my pregnant girlfriend when she started to show. We'd been drifting apart for a while, but I figured we could work it out but clearly not. I didn't want people to vilify her, so I took the brunt of shit and just ignored it all. Not that I need to make a public statement about it. It hurt me, but fuck, I didn't hate her, and if that makes me a fool, then whatever. Mistakes were made, and I just wanted to move on with my fucking life, okay? Happy now? There's your truth."

Cherisse didn't say a word, but she looked appropriately chagrined, eyes darting everywhere except to his face, so he dropped one last parting shot. "Cat got your tongue? Convenient." Then he turned to Eric, said, "Let's go check on the meat," and walked out to the patio.

Chapter 9

Keiran

HE WAS LATE FOR THE first party planning meeting with Cherisse, which, considering how they'd left things after the flower crown session, wouldn't mend anything between them. Even more so because of who he'd been with. Cherisse wouldn't care that he'd want no part of working with Sean Daley. She wouldn't care that he hadn't been pleased to be summoned to his father's office for this meeting at King Kong Entertainment.

It was almost as if he'd jinxed himself when he'd thought about never having had to work with Sean before. He'd initially told his father "no" flat out when he'd mentioned they were bringing Sean in on this track with Sheila. There was no fucking way he was doing it. His father had claimed Sean's vocals on the track were just what the song needed to add that extra punch. It didn't hurt that Sean had enough fans who would be eager to listen to anything he was on, which could, in turn, help boost Sheila. He'd wanted to stick to his gut reaction and refuse but had already signed on to work with Sheila and couldn't back out just because of Sean. Sheila was going places, and unfortunately, his father had been right about Sean's popularity bringing his fans out to boost the track.

Not that he could mention any of this to Cherisse.

The pounding rain outside didn't help getting to her apartment any quicker, and he was umbrella-less too—the rain had come out of nowhere—so he was stuck in the car, watching his phone blow up with **Where are you??** texts from Cherisse.

84

He'd thought of telling her he was outside now, but whatever, he was actually amused by her texts, so he'd let her stew. After a while, it was clear the damn rain wasn't stopping, so he decided to make a run for it, the rain battering him as he prayed he wouldn't skate on the wet ground and bust his ass. He arrived unscathed but soaked, water running down his face as he rang the bell. The door swung open, and Remi stood in the doorway, umbrella in hand. She swept him with an up-down look, taking in his drenched clothes. "Your guest is here!" she called over her shoulder. "Good luck," she told him cheerfully, brushing past, giant umbrella whooshing open as she made her way to her car.

Left on his own to face Cherisse's wrath, he took a deep breath and entered the apartment, shutting the door behind him. Dammit, he was creating a puddle in the doorway. He'd get more shit for that.

Stuck in that one spot, he waited for Cherisse to appear. The first thing he noticed was the singing. Perfect pitch and tone, belting out a song he didn't recognize. It was the type of voice that made you stop and listen. Calming, yet burrowing deep in your chest, grabbing hold. He froze as Cherisse exited a door just off the kitchen, head bent over her phone, probably about to send him another scathing text, while effortlessly hitting notes that had goosebumps popping up along his arms.

"Holy shit," he breathed, stunned.

The song died on her lips as she shrieked, hand pressing to her chest, phone nearly flying as it fumbled in her hand. "Holy fuck! When did you get here?"

"Literally just this second. Guess you didn't hear Remi announce me?"

"I sure as shit didn't! Jesus, fuck." She took several deep breaths to calm herself, hand gripping her phone as if she intended to throw it at him.

"Sorry."

She took one last deep breath, folded her arms across the front of her blue romper, and said, "You're late. And wet."

Her hair secured in two plaits, face bare of makeup, she was even more casual than she'd been at the flower crown-making session. In spite of the fission of anger that reared up at the memory of what she'd said, Keiran stared, cataloging her bare feet, with toes painted a bright pink. It was throwing him off as much as her voice had.

He realized he was staring, so he let his eyes flit about the apartment.

The front door led right into her living area, where there was already a whiteboard set up with scribbled bullet points and a notepad and pen tossed on the couch. The apartment was cozy. The living room led to a spacious kitchen area with a portion sectioned off for dining. A staircase led up to what Keiran assumed would be the bedrooms. Bright cushions added some color to her chocolaty brown couch, and Keiran noted framed photos hanging on the walls, some gorgeous scenery shots, and people silhouetted against a firework-lit sky. He wondered if these were Remi's pieces or stuff they bought from other photographers.

"Forgot an umbrella. Can I dry my clothes?" He tugged at the t-shirt sticking to his chest.

Her eyes followed the movement. "Why didn't you tell me? I could've met you outside with an umbrella."

He shrugged. "I don't know, Cherisse, maybe I figured you wouldn't care to do something like that."

She tugged on a braid, eyes not meeting his. "Listen. About what I said, I'm really..."

"Can we get to that after? I'm cold."

"Okay, just follow me. I'll get you a towel, and I don't know what you'll wear in the meantime, but I have a dryer for your clothes."

"I don't want to drip on your floor more."

"You can't strip right here. It's okay, I have a mop."

"It's less of a hassle if I just keep the puddle to one spot."

"It's *fine*."

He followed her upstairs, conscious of the water dripping behind him, but if Cherisse didn't care, why should he?

She pointed at one of the closed doors. "Bathroom. Towels are on the shelf in there. I'll see what you can wear when your stuff is drying."

"I can mop up for you," he offered, even though he really wanted out of these soppy clothes, but he'd made the mess, so it was ingrained in him to offer.

She sucked in her bottom lip before releasing it with a pop, fiddled with her braid again. Was she nervous? It wasn't an emotion he'd ever seen from her. Cherisse oozed confidence or haughty superiority when she was dealing specifically with him. "Don't be nice to me. It's weird, and I don't deserve it."

"Well, you catch more flies with honey than vinegar."

"I was a bitch."

"Yup."

"So, yell at me or something."

"Nope."

"But why?"

"Too tired." Which was the truth. Arguing with his father at that meeting while Sean looked on smugly had been exhausting.

Cherisse shook her head. "I'll get you something to wear."

He'd slipped into the bathroom, tossed off his wet clothes, secured the towel around his waist, and was peering at the ceramic cat on the toilet tank by the time Cherisse knocked on the door. She stumbled back when he opened the door.

"Fuck me. Jesus." Her eyes drank in his bare chest and dipped down to his hand, clutching the towel.

"As much as I'm enjoying the look on your face right now, are those for me?" He indicated the bundle of clothes cupped in her hands.

She jerked her gaze up. "Yes, here." She shoved the clothes into his hands. "Sean's stuff. Guess I forgot to give these back. Feel free to keep them, burn them. I don't care. Let me put your wet stuff in the dryer."

Seriously, Keiran couldn't be free of Sean today, but clothes were clothes. He couldn't afford to be picky when remaining in only a towel while waiting on his clothes to dry wasn't an option.

Cherisse's eyes made another sweep of his bare chest before she literally shook herself and muttered, "I'm downstairs," before briskly walking away.

Keiran grinned as he got changed and joined Cherisse in the living room. That look in her eyes didn't lie. Coupled with the surprise had been flat-out appreciation. Cherisse had definitely liked what she'd seen. Something darted in front of him, and Keiran paused. A white cat with orange and black spots stood at the bottom of the stairs staring at him, tail up and curled.

"You have a cat, and you can sing? Just full of surprises today." He stared down at the feline, who didn't look pleased to see him. But you just never knew with cats. Maybe that was just its resting cat face, and it wasn't actually plotting to claw his eyes out.

"Yup. Jello. Don't worry, he won't attack or anything."

"Jell-O? As in Jell-hyphen-O?" Keiran skirted around the cat as he entered the living room and sat on the couch opposite Cherisse. "You for real named your cat Jell-O?"

"No hyphen, but yes, I named him after the wobbly treat because who doesn't like Jell-O?"

Keiran snorted. "That's interesting."

The cat strolled over to Cherisse, bumping his body against her legs before sauntering over to stare up at Keiran quizzically. It was pretty cute. He sported a little pink collar with donuts printed all over and a Pusheen pendant dangling from it. He hoped Jello was just curious about him and not about to go into attack mode. The cat *was* staring at him intensely.

"Dissing my cat's name won't win you any points."

"I wasn't," he assured her. "Just thrown off by you having one, and like I said, your singing. Where the hell you been hiding that? You have an amazing voice."

She looked down at Jello, but not before he caught the flush creeping into her cheeks. "Eh, it's alright."

Alright? Was she being serious? Her singing had been more than alright. "Cherisse, for real. Your voice would go so good on this one track we're working on."

Her head snapped up, eyes narrowed, skepticism clear as day.

"I'm not playing," he insisted. As he thought on it, he could hear how her voice would fit in as background vocals, add something special to the track. It wasn't quite where he and Dale wanted it to be, and damn if he didn't think he'd found the missing link.

She laughed. "Yeah, right. I'm not a professional singer. Is this your way of getting back at me for being awful to you?"

"Trust me, I wouldn't lie about this."

"Trust isn't something I give freely, but I do apologize when I'm wrong. I'm sorry about how I acted. It was so uncalled for. I know you don't think so, but I'm not usually like that. You just make me..." She clamped her mouth shut. "I'm just sorry, okay?"

"Well, I *was* an asshole with that joke, so I guess we're even. Listen, just come into the studio. We can record a bit. No pressure. See how it goes. I think you'd be a good fit. What do you want me to do to convince you?"

She eyed him thoughtfully. Perhaps he should've dialed back on the desperation there, but he was already arranging the piece in his head around Cherisse's vocals. If he added some piano right there at that note, they'd have it. He just knew it.

"I'm not saying I would do this, but I have a challenge for you. You don't really get what goes into what I do, do you? That joke pissed me off so damn much, and since I'm short my assistant for this thing, I dare you. Be my assistant for the day, and I'll do the vocals. Tit for tat. Then we're even."

"Your assistant? For what?"

"Easter brunch with my mother's old school buddies. This weekend. I'm doing a full dessert bar."

"A brunch? That's all?" Didn't sound so terrible to him. How difficult could it be to prepare for something like that? Frankly, it sounded like he was getting the better end of the deal. A small part of him did think doing this with Cherisse could be intriguing. Seeing her in her element. "How bad could it be? Older ladies love me."

Cherisse scoffed. "Uh-huh. So, that's a yes? You be my tagalong, and I'll do your thing. Desperate times and all."

Keiran stuck out his hand. "Alright, we'll call this a truce of sorts, then. Sold. Shake to seal."

Cherisse rolled her eyes before shaking on it, then frowned down at Jello, who was attempting to climb Keiran's leg. "Jello, no!"

"It's cool. Animals love me." Keiran grinned down at the cat. He was more used to dogs, but animals, in general, did seem to be cool with him.

"Whatever. We should get crackin' on the planning." She leaned down to retrieve her cat, but Jello sped up Keiran's leg, claws digging in as the cat made it all the way up to his shoulder.

"Seriously?" Cherisse glared at him and then at Jello, who merely perched on his shoulder like it was something the cat did every day. Huh, well, wasn't that something? Her cat liked him, and that pissed her off.

"Okay, before you end me with your murder eyes, this isn't my fault." He petted Jello, and the cat butted at his neck.

"Goddamn traitor," Cherisse huffed.

Keiran chuckled. Oh, this was going to be fun.

CHERISSE

"So, I had some ideas."

Keiran sat across from her, arms resting on his knees as he leaned forward to check out the bullet points on the board. Jello made himself comfy next to Keiran, and Cherisse pretended she wasn't offended by her cat ditching her to cuddle up to him—but oh, it chafed. So did the smugness radiating off of him. She could read it easily in the quirk of those damn lips. He figured his end of their little deal would be easy. She couldn't wait for him to be schooled and surprised at the work that went into preparing for something like this.

They'd supposedly squashed things between them for now, but Cherisse could still appreciate the tiny, vicious part of her that was looking forward to seeing him struggle to keep up with her. He *so* wasn't prepared.

And she hadn't been prepared for Keiran when he'd emerged from the bathroom, *Jesus.*

She'd nearly swallowed her tongue. Keiran had stood in that doorway in just a towel, one he'd clutched for dear life like it would slip down his hips any moment. Cherisse had never wanted gravity to have its way with something as much as that towel.

She'd drank in all that gleaming brown skin like she'd been a woman parched. Her brain had snapshotted broad shoulders, toned arms, abs. Glorious, glistening abs with a treasure trail that disappeared beneath the towel. She'd forced her eyes away from lingering on the bulge behind it, but *fuck*. She'd imagined his ass had been perfect, biteable handfuls—not that she'd been able to see with his back to the inside of the bathroom, but she'd seen said ass in pants and jeans before, so she assumed.

Lord, she needed to get it together. She'd had moments of seeing an attractive man and full-on lusting, but this was Keiran, for God's sake. This visceral reaction was unexpected and unwanted. She did not want this.

"So, your ideas?" Keiran prompted. Jello was basically draped in his lap now, kneading at his thigh. *Same, boy, same,* she thought before she could stop herself. Nope. No way. She wasn't having lustful thoughts about Keiran. *No.*

She waved at the board.

"Movie-themed. Romance movies. OTP?" he read, wrinkling his nose. "Shipping? I see you speak Eric. I never know what any of this stuff means when he gets going. I really should Google this."

Cherisse folded her legs under her. "Lemme save you the trouble. OTP means one true pairing. Like your favorite combo of characters in a fandom? The ones who get together or who you want to get together. Then there are NOTPs and BROTPs. So, I was brainstorming some things I know Ava and Eric like...did I lose you?"

He was staring at her as if she was speaking gibberish, which to him, she probably was. He obviously wasn't big on fandom lingo. The crease between his eyes kept getting more pronounced, and his lips were pursed.

"Yeah. How exactly does any of this translate into a theme for the party?"

"Well, I was thinking we have movie-centered games, based on their fave movie fandoms, and we can make all the food around their favorite movies? I know they're both obsessed with rom coms and romance novels."

"Yeah," Keiran chuckled. "Eric basically got hooked when he found his mom's romance books one day. He'd hide in the bathroom at school to read 'em at lunch so the other guys wouldn't give him crap for it. Meeting in a bookstore when you both reach for the same book. Who even does that?"

"It was the cutest meet-cute." Cherisse agreed. Her sister was a voracious reader, and finding a guy who was into romance as much as she was, was pretty awesome.

"Okay, I get where you're going with this idea, and I'm liking it, but how 'bout this? We set it up like this giant slumber party. Dress code is sleepwear. We have drinks, food, and games that are movie-themed. I already checked some things online, and the invitations can be shaped like those sleep masks. We can maybe even give out actual sleep masks as souvenirs, with the date and their names on it. Not sure what the budget allows, but there can be a giant sheet set up as the screen with movies projected on it if you want to go old-school. Karaoke can be involved. Imagine drunken singing. That would be hilarious. I can arrange the music part of things if we agree on this."

"That's..." It was an amazing idea. She was genuinely floored. She'd expected Keiran to just stroll in with either zero ideas or some ridiculous plan that she'd have to veto, but this was brilliant. "Sounds like you put a lot of thought into it." Like he'd actually taken the entire thing seriously. She was a tad peeved she hadn't thought about the slumber party angle.

Keiran stroked Jello's fur, back and forth, the movement of those hands hypnotizing. Jello seemed to be enjoying his touch. Damn traitor. "Not really," Keiran drawled. "It just came to me on the ride over."

And there went her moment of awe. She should've known. "Do you ever take anything seriously? I have an entire Pinterest board dedicated to this, and you, what? Just pull an idea out of your ass?" Albeit a good one, but damn him.

"So much for that truce. Look, I don't have a fancy board or whatever, but I've thought it through. Just because I spent less time doing so doesn't make my idea inferior. Everyone works differently."

"Stop making sense. I don't like it."

"Well?" Keiran prodded. "We can pull portions from each idea, so everyone wins. I'm not here to just monopolize the entire thing."

Which had been her plan. She blew out a breath and allowed herself to stop getting worked up over things that were trivial. "It's a really good idea. I...wow...blanket forts. There could be blanket forts. Can you imagine the entire thing set up as a blanket fort slumber party?" She flapped her hands at the whiteboard. "Write! Put all the ideas down!"

He didn't move, but his lips quirked up in a small smile.

"What?" Why was he grinning at her like that?

"You excited is a thing to behold. I like it."

She frowned, and he chuckled, getting to his feet to grab up the whiteboard marker. Jello mewed as if he didn't like that at all.

"I didn't see this going like this," she muttered. He was setting her off-balance again.

"Oh, I know. You expected to just walk all over me, and I'd agree with whatever." The squeaking of the marker stopped, and Cherisse's frown deepened as he sank back onto the couch. She didn't think he'd heard her. "I don't mind bossy women one bit." His lips curved into an infuriating smile. "But regardless of whatever, we need to be a team on this. I'll defer to you where desserts are concerned, obviously, but don't think you can just do your own thing and not consult me. Eric's my friend. I get a say on this."

"Fine," she gritted out after too many minutes had lapsed with both of them just eyeballing each other. Him still smirking, her grinding her teeth together so she wouldn't snap or go into a curse-filled rant.

"Ready to flesh out the details now?" Keiran asked.

She could be the bigger person. His idea had been a good one, and he was right. They could incorporate thoughts from both and make the party something special. They could do this. Work together without fighting. Attend that brunch together. Get through a studio session. Cherisse still couldn't believe those were things she'd agreed to.

"Sure," she muttered, but an annoying voice in her head kept nagging at her, demanding to know: What the hell was she doing?

Chapter 10

Keiran

KEIRAN SQUINTED UP at the streetlight as he waited for Cherisse to open the door. Still dark out and a little chilly too, he tugged the sleeves of his Henley down to cover his forearms, wondering if Cherisse was even awake. Had her 3:30 a.m. call time been a joke to play with him? Because he wasn't amused. Did she really need to be up this early to prep for this brunch?

He released a jaw-cracking yawn just as the door swung open to reveal Cherisse, who didn't look any happier to be awake at this ungodly hour, her usually loose waves up in a lopsided bun. She didn't say a word, just waved him in, and stumbled towards the kitchen. There were already ingredients all over the counter. She ignored all of them and reached for a huge coffee mug, the thing so big the cat could probably do some laps in it, held up a finger and said, "Don't talk to me until I've had my coffee. For your own safety."

Keiran raised a brow as she took a long sip and sighed. Okay, so she wasn't a morning person. How unexpected. He was beginning to realize there was a lot he didn't know about Cherisse. "Might work faster by IV," he quipped.

She shot him a death glare. "I said, don't speak to me yet. I will murder you and toss your body into the bushes." She resumed drinking her coffee, her blissful sigh so incongruous with her threat he couldn't help but laugh, which earned him another narrow-eyed gaze over the mug's rim. She finally nodded. "Okay, you're safe now."

"Are you sure?"

Her smile was less deadly when she nodded. "It was a near-death experience for you just then, but yup. All good now." She swept the counter with her hand. "Welcome to where all the magic happens. Since you're a newbie assistant, I printed out the menu in order of what we'll be tackling first. Waffle bar is last. All cakes will be done first because it'll take longer. Well...after the eggs. I'm doing marshmallow Easter eggs, and I already made them and let them set overnight because of timing, so all you'll have to do is cover in chocolate."

"Waffle bar?" He didn't have a clue what that was, but he supposed he'd learn soon enough. "And you *made* marshmallows yourself?"

"Well, yeah. I wanted the egg shape, so homemade was the way to go. Anyway, let's melt the chocolate so we can get these out of the way."

Keiran had never heard of anyone actually making marshmallows from scratch. He knew about buying them from the store, so he stared at Cherisse as she instructed him on melting the chocolate, then how to cover the eggs. The tiny, from-scratch, egg-shaped marshmallows. He couldn't get over that as he did as she instructed and dipped an egg into the chocolate. How did you even make marshmallows?

"Keiran, focus!" Cherisse snapped. "Your egg is dripping."

Sure enough, he'd forgotten to let the excess chocolate drip into the bowl before moving it to the parchment-lined baking sheet.

"Shit, sorry, I'll clean up."

"Nope, just keep going. I'll get it."

Cherisse was a drill sergeant in her kitchen. As soon as they completed one thing from the list, she checked it off and had already ensured the next item was prepped and ready to go. Keiran's eyes went round at the photo of the cake they were about to attempt, a multi-colored four-layer mini cake, with some sort of cream in the middle of each layer, and on top, a bunny nose and ears.

"How many of these are we making?"

Cherisse's grin was a little evil. "Enough for about one hundred people or so."

Keiran groaned. His energy was already lagging. Working in the studio until late meant he'd gotten two hours' sleep before making it over here. Which Cherisse wouldn't care to hear. It was his own damn fault for underestimating this entire process. Despite her grumpy moment before her coffee, Cherisse had gotten increasingly animated as she'd explained everything and instructed him on what they were doing. Her love for baking was clear, and he truly hadn't anticipated the work that went into this.

"Not quite the popping frozen items in an oven for a few minutes you anticipated, huh?" she said, casually throwing his ill-advised words to that blogger back at him.

"Yeah, I—"

She waved away his words. "It's squashed. I just couldn't resist. Now, batter time."

By the time the different colored layers of cake were in the oven, Keiran was somehow covered in flour while Cherisse looked fresh as ever. They were both wearing aprons, but Keiran was so clearly out of his depth here that it hadn't mattered.

"Uh, you have a little flour there." She reached out to wipe at his cheek, and Keiran froze. Cherisse snatched her hand back. "Sorry, I shouldn't have done that without your permission."

"It's fine." A lie, because that tiny touch had felt like fire trailing across his skin. He was too tired to shield himself against Cherisse this early in the morning. His defenses were down.

They'd called a truce, but Cherisse willingly touching him like that was an anomaly. Perhaps her defenses were down too. He didn't know what had prompted that move, but the awkwardness was growing, so he pointedly asked, "Frosting's next?"

That propelled Cherisse into motion. "Yes! Right, frosting, yup."

They maneuvered around each other for the next few hours, the moment's discomfort forgotten as sunlight gradually shone into the kitchen. At one point, a sleepy Remi shuffled in long enough to swipe a chocolate-covered egg, ignoring Cherisse's protests. Jello appeared in the doorway too but didn't enter, as if the cat knew better than to even try his luck here.

"Hey! You didn't want to help. You get no treats."

Remi ignored Cherisse and kept chewing on her marshmallow. "Too late to stop me now. Besides, you two seem to be doing just fine. Reba may want to watch her back," she joked.

Keiran scoffed. "Her job is safe, don't worry."

Remi suddenly raised her phone and snapped a photo of Keiran and Cherisse. "I think I'll caption this one: Sugar Queen puts Mixer King to work. Sweet victory." She chuckled as Keiran pretended to be offended, but he couldn't care less. Besides, Remi's post could help with squashing the feuding rumors.

"I hope you got my good side," he said as he added some vanilla to the buttercream frosting under Cherisse's watchful eye.

She was close enough to him that he clearly heard her mutter, "Every damn side is your good side, fucking annoying."

He snorted but pretended he hadn't heard a thing.

HE HADN'T KNOWN WHAT to expect, having never attended any sort of brunch, no matter how many times Eric and Scott expounded on the joy of brunching. He took in the sprawling back yard as he followed Cherisse over to the dessert and waffle bar area. He'd soon discovered the waffle bar was a setup with mini waffles with various toppings and syrups to choose from. Cherisse hadn't been kidding about the variety of toppings. There was homemade whipped cream, various types of nuts, fruit, sprinkles, chocolate chips, M&Ms, and more.

The food and drinks area was set up under a covered portion of the yard. Guests could swing by the buffet-style spread, grab their drinks and eats, and make their way out to the lawn where round tables had been set up with extravagant centerpieces that were garlands with bright flowers and a selection of fruit woven in. It was legit fancy, and Keiran couldn't stop himself from gaping at everything, covertly poking at the fruit to see if they were real or plastic.

"Holy shit." His finger squished into the very real grapefruit, and he hastily drew it away, peering around to see if anyone had noticed that. The caterers were busy bustling around. The host was nowhere in sight, either.

His shower had revived him somewhat, but he'd been schooled. He could admit that. This had been an experience. Especially after the cakes had emerged from her giant oven, and they'd put together the layers for the finished cake, complete with the marshmallow bunny ears.

As they set up, an older woman who could've been in her forties or fifties sauntered out, with a glittery top hat on, a silver bow and giant bunny ears stuck to the front. Her toned golden-brown arms glowed against her sleeveless white pants suit.

Keiran's eyes widened at the hat, and the woman laughed.

"Cherisse, why's this boy looking at me like he don't know about the hats and other assorted headwear?"

"Uh..." Cherisse flushed, clasping her hands behind her back and rocking slightly on her heels. "I may have forgotten to mention it?"

The woman clucked her tongue and smiled at Keiran. "At my Easter parties, all are required to pick the gear of their choice and wear it throughout the day. Makes for some fun photos. We've got hats, bunny ears headbands. Think I even saw some nest and eggs contraption this year, I don't know. I swear Mira looks for the weirdest of the weird." She winked at them, sticking out her hand. "I'm Laney Johnson-Reyes, and you are?"

"Nice to meet you, Ms. Johnson-Reyes. I'm Keiran, Cherisse's assistant for the day."

"Huh, interesting." Laney's gaze moved between them, speculative. "How nice of you to help out, but I thought Cherisse already had an assistant? And by the way, it's Mrs. Johnson-Reyes. My wife's around here somewhere."

She was still smiling, but her gaze was challenging. Keiran had no doubt she'd dropped the bit about her wife as some sort of test. He could imagine the reactions she'd gotten before. She didn't have to worry about any of that from him, but of course, she couldn't know that.

"Can't wait to meet her, and I'm in no way replacing Reba. She couldn't make it, so I'm the poor sub Cherisse had to make do with."

Laney threw Cherisse a dazzling smile. "Oh, I like him. Well, let me find Mira. She's probably off cuddling the dog somewhere to build up strength before the hordes descend. She's not the social butterfly I am."

Keiran watched Laney retreat, then returned his gaze to Cherisse, who'd gone back to fiddling with a dessert box, gently extracting the mini cakes within and situating them on the dessert stand. "Laney seems nice."

"She is. It's the others that are a bit much." Cherisse brushed a wayward curl from her face.

Keiran shrugged. He hadn't been kidding about charming older ladies. It was a well-honed skill from interacting with his mother's friends on numerous occasions. He figured he'd do alright here.

"I'll be fine," he said confidently. Cherisse's grin said she thought otherwise.

By the time the guests arrived, he'd been eye-fucked by a trio of ladies, who seemed in their fifties. Their gazes had taken him in from head to toe, and in spite of the discomfort of being mentally undressed by the three women, Keiran graced them with a smile. As he stared down at the food spread, he was certain he felt their eyes on his ass. But he ignored that, piling his plate high with waffles and other yummy things. He'd given in and tasted one of everything back at her apartment. Cherisse had looked on smugly as he'd fought back groans of delight at the taste.

Why had he been petty about her desserts for so long? They were amazing!

Cherisse came over to the bar to fill her plate as well. "Hey, lemme ask you something. When you came to my apartment for the meeting, did you have tuna on you, by chance?"

"Uh, what?"

"Jello was all over you, so, just wondered."

Keiran didn't hold back his snort. "Really? You're really annoyed that your cat liked me so much, huh? Why would I be rollin' with random tuna in the first place? I didn't even know you had a cat."

Cherisse went down the line, placing toppings onto her waffles. "I don't know what you're into."

"Oh, my God." This was too much and so much fodder for teasing. She was legit not pleased about her cat being all over him. "I told you, animals just love me."

"Right, like the damn cat whisperer or something. Whatever." She picked up her plate, lips spreading into a wicked smile. "Older ladies whisperer too, as I recall. I gotta go see Laney about a thing."

"Wait, what're you—?"

She waved over her shoulder, and Keiran was suddenly on alert. That smile didn't bode well for him at all. Truce or not, Cherisse was up to something.

It wasn't long before his "Older ladies love me" comment was biting him in the ass, and he was eating his words, along with some chocolate syrup-drenched waffles, which made it a little easier to swallow. Although, he hadn't expected an audience for that.

He looked around for Cherisse, but he'd been abandoned, left at the mercy of the three women who'd undressed him with their eyes earlier. They'd ushered him to their table that was now littered with glasses of mimosa, half-eaten foods, and fruit from the centerpieces. He'd been trying to excuse himself for the last twenty minutes. His charm had backfired—had, in fact, worked too well, it seemed, judging from the lazy hand that suddenly found itself on his arm.

"A healthy appetite *and* toned arms. Everything a woman could ask for." The woman currently petting the bare skin where his short sleeve ended wore a wide-brimmed hat with little bunnies and Peeps on the brim. Blonde hair brushed her pale, freckled shoulders as she leaned forward. "That syrup looks *so* good. Chocolate's my fave."

Oh, Jesus. Just what Keiran needed, a white woman with a taste for chocolate. He scanned the other tables, the food stations, and the rest of the back yard. Where the hell was Cherisse? Or their host, for that matter?

"Becky, leave the boy alone," the woman on his right admonished. She shook her head, bunny ears headband bouncing in her fro as she peered at Becky from behind her cat-eye glasses. "Quit trying to be all jungle fever up in here. I told you that shit's not cute."

"What?" Blue eyes wide, Becky removed her hand from Keiran's arm. "I was only talking about the syrup, Celeste. That's all."

"Sure, Becky." Celeste sipped her sangria, eyes brimming with censure. "If you think you've got anything he's interested in. Girl, please. You see he came here with Nyla's daughter, Cherisse? He may like 'em a little light-skinned, but not your brand of pale, sweetie."

Becky glared at her friend. "You don't even know what you're talking about!"

Celeste raised a brow. "You're not as slick as you think."

While the two bickered, the other friend, a tall, slim woman with short, tight curls and deep brown skin, watched on with glee. This seemed to be a routine of sorts. Keiran wondered if he could slip away as the two women went back and forth. He didn't want to be collateral damage if stuff started getting thrown around.

"So, how's it going?"

He latched onto the voice like his last lifeline. At this point, he didn't care if he was being rude. He didn't know these women—would probably never seen them again, if he was lucky. He sprang to his feet, hooked his arm with Cherisse's, tossed back an "Excuse me," and towed her away. By the time they'd left the table behind, she was gasping for breath, she was laughing so hard.

"You ditched me!"

Hand pressed to her mouth, a loud snort escaped. "You said you'd be fine. My God, your face. Priceless. Just..." She snickered loudly. "Fucking priceless. I wished I'd captured it. This was a great idea. You distracted them so much they didn't even badger me about my love life or give me life advice or anything. They basically forgot I was here. Thank you. I should bring you to things like this more often."

"There will never be another opportunity like this," he vowed.

"Never say never. I mean, if you're looking for a sugar mama at any time, Becky'll be happy to oblige." Cherisse winked.

"I'm good, thanks." He narrowed his eyes. "Were you really that pissed about Jello? That's the height of pettiness. Leaving me at their mercy." He tried to muster a scowl, but it was pointless. Cherisse's laugh was too contagious, and the bright yellow bunnies angling forward and back from the springs that were attached to her headband made it even more difficult to maintain a frown. She'd chosen the headwear to match her sunny yellow dress.

God, she's adorable. It was like a punch to the gut. Her smile, her everything.

"This has nothing to do with Jello." She didn't bother to keep a straight face. She pressed her lips together, but it was useless. "What?" Her laughter died off as she swiped her hand beneath her eyes. She'd been laughing to the point of tears. "You're looking at me funny. Do I have something on my face?"

Yeah, your smile. It takes my goddamn breath away, was what he wanted to say. But of course, he didn't. They were being cordial, even teasing each other in non-vicious ways, but a truce could only withstand so much.

"No, but you do have something funny on your head." He went with the safer option. When in doubt, joke it out.

She looked pointedly at his head. "Ahem."

She had him there. Laney had chosen one of the more ridiculous hats out of the box, claiming that as it was his first time at one of her events, it was the host's choice. He currently rocked a giant top hat with glittery eggs, a bird's nest, yellow baby chicks sporting bow ties and glasses, and tiny bunnies on the brim.

He shrugged. "Whatever, I make this look good." He'd posted a silly selfie to Instagram. Might as well get something out of the ridiculous thing.

"Becky definitely seems to think so," Cherisse quipped, giggles starting up again.

"You did that on purpose."

"You can't prove it either way. I thought you were the older ladies whisperer? I'm sure whispering in her ear would've been quite...effective."

Oh, she was truly devious, just as he'd always known, and Keiran wasn't even annoyed about it.

Before he could formulate a reply, Laney's voice rang out. "Attention, all. I hope you've filled your bellies and loosened those inhibitions because now," she paused dramatically, "we have the games."

"Games?" He was realizing that simple didn't apply here. Was this another thing Cherisse had failed to mention?

"Uh, those didn't exist last year."

They both looked across to where Laney was waving them over, then glanced at each other, hesitating to leave the safe zone that was this orange tree they'd found themselves under.

Keiran took the plunge and offered his arm. "M'lady, shall we?"

Cherisse hesitated for a beat before sighing, then taking his arm. Keiran ignored the feel of her skin against his and marched them towards the games zone.

CHERISSE

The game turned out to be a scavenger hunt. Each team of three—Cherisse, Keiran, and Becky had been teamed up, much to Keiran's dismay and Cherisse's delight—was given plastic eggs with clues inside. Once the whistle sounded, they had to open their eggs and dash off, using the clues to find the golden eggs. The team with the most won the whole thing.

This bunch took the game seriously, grown people dashing off, bumping into their competition as they took off to solve their clues and find the eggs. Their scrambling to get the most eggs was successful. They won the prize, which was hotly contested by several super-competitive people who felt their team had an advantage of some kind because Laney had blatantly been rooting out loud for them. Cries of cheating went ignored as Laney silenced the dissenters with a sweep of her hand.

"Brunch is brutal," Keiran whispered in Cherisse's ear as one extremely vocal guest stormed off.

"Bye, Carl," Laney sang out after the retreating man. "Who keeps inviting that guy anyway? Never liked him."

Keiran snorted. "Holy shit, Laney's awesome."

Cherisse chuckled. "She is one of a kind. Also, super-rich, so no one dares cross her. They're always glad to get invited. I guarantee you Carl'll be back next year. My mom's gonna be pissed she missed this."

"How'd they even meet? They seem so different."

It was true. Laney and her mother were complete opposites, personality-wise. Laney with her don't-care attitude—which Cherisse suspected she'd had to adopt to deal with those who side-eyed her out-and-loud queerness—and her mother, who was so wrapped up in appearances. Cherisse had gotten a lot of that from her mother—it had been driven into her head enough times to take root—but her mom took it to the extreme sometimes. Her mother, Laney, and Remi's mom had somehow gravitated towards each other in school and had remained friends ever since. There was an epic tale of Laney verbally destroying another girl who decided to bully Cherisse and Remi's moms, and thus, the friendship was born. At this point, Cherisse wasn't sure what was fact and what had gotten embellished over the years, but it sounded like something Laney would do.

Keiran's eyes widened at her retelling of the tale, and his gaze swung back to Laney, who was now cradling a giant hamper. "Wow, she's great."

"Yup," Cherisse agreed.

Laney ushered them over, eyes gleaming as she presented the winning hamper. Cherisse suspected Laney was already tipsy. She'd been guzzling mimosas like juice. But if you couldn't get drunk at your own brunch, what was the point?

"Whoa, this is..." Keiran gaped at the hamper. The thing was enormous and, as Cherisse tried to peer through the clear wrapping, seemed to be bursting with goodies, gift vouchers, and what looked like an expensive bottle of wine.

"Congrats!" Laney corralled them in for a winner's photo. "I'd hoped you two would win. None of these other heifers deserve it." She cackled, and Mira shook her head, releasing a small laugh as Laney planted a loud smack on her cheek. "I'd have gone for the lips, but I don't want to scandalize the heteros." Laney's smile grew mischievous. "On second thought..." She shoved the hamper into Keiran's hands and dipped Mira into a scorching kiss, leaving her wife flustered, cheeks pink as they came up for air. "If anyone's got a problem with me kissing my wife in my own damn house, they can get the fuck out."

Not a single soul made any movements. It truly was some sort of miracle that Laney and her mother became friends in the first place and managed to remain so.

"Excellent!" Laney clapped her hands. "Now, if you'll excuse us." She linked her hand with Mira's. "That kiss was hotter than anticipated, so now Mira and I need to take care of some business." She waggled her brows.

"Laney, oh my God, you can't just say things like that," Mira protested, face getting redder. Laney dipped her head to whisper into her ear. Cherisse had no idea what she'd said, but judging from the way Mira blinked at Laney before dragging her in the direction of the house, it was safe to assume it was something naughty.

"Well," Keiran said, hefting the hamper. "This has been the best first brunch ever."

Cherisse agreed. By the time they decided to leave, half the guests were well into their day drinking. Laney made them both promise to return next year. Cherisse wasn't sure how that would work out. Keiran was only here because of their 'you show me yours, I'll show you mine' deal, but he seemed enthusiastic about the idea.

She'd actually had fun. With Keiran. Sometimes at his expense, but who would've thought that possible? He'd shown up on time this morning. Had taken all her instructions without complaining. He'd rolled with the eccentricities of Laney and her bunch, hadn't even batted an eyelash when Laney launched into a drunken rendition of Notorious BIG's "Hypnotize" while Mira tried to talk her wife down from climbing onto one of the tables to reenact Julia Stiles' moves from *10 Things I Hate About You.*

"I don't think I've laughed this much in a good while," Keiran admitted as he drove away from the house. "That was wild."

"You've been Laney'd," Cherisse said. "It's always an experience." She looked through the hamper as Keiran headed back towards the highway. Drowsiness was kicking in. She'd had a few mimosas as well. Laney had topped off her drink several times, going light on the orange juice. She focused on the hamper, curbing a yawn that threatened to escape. "Oh, they're spa vouchers. I'd like to have those if you don't mind. My birthday's coming up. These chocolates are expensive too. We can share up the goodies. Holy fuck!" She clasped one of the gift certificates. "This is dinner for two at Prime. That place is fancy as fuck. I couldn't even afford to stand outside there. Wow, Laney's the best."

Keiran laughed. "I'm sure you and Tyler will have fun."

She peered at him. She hadn't mentioned her first date with Tyler at all, simply because she'd been bored out of her mind. Tyler was chatty and name-dropped a lot as if stuff like that should impress her. It didn't, so she certainly wasn't wasting her Prime dinner on him. She wasn't certain yet if she'd give him another chance in a different setting.

Keiran glanced over at her briefly before returning his gaze to the road. "How'd that date go, by the way?"

"Fine."

"Just fine?"

She sighed. "Fine, it was terrible, happy now?"

"Not at all." He drummed his fingers on the steering wheel, lips pursed like he wanted to ask something but was unsure of her reaction. Keiran never seemed to care whether his questions were well received or not. Was he actually taking their truce seriously? "Why did you agree to the date? Was it because you found him attractive?"

Unsure where he was going with this, Cherisse considered brushing him off with a sarcastic reply. It was so ingrained in her to be like that with him, toss some snark that would satisfy her desire to be petty, but not today. It could be the mimosas running the show because she gave him an honest reply.

"When you're a woman of a certain age, your family feels it's their duty to point out your singleness and help you out. It's just easier to seemingly go along with my mom's not-so-subtle suggestions of eligible men. And if these guys want to get me free meals, who am I to argue? I'm not about to do a tug of war with the bill because it offends their sensibilities for a woman to pay. I'm just gonna eat my food and decide whether I want a repeat or not."

"Is that what Tyler did?"

"Hell no, I didn't even offer. That place is way out of my budget."

Keiran laughed, and Cherisse couldn't help responding with a smile of her own.

"So, you gonna see him again?"

Cherisse shifted the hamper on her lap, digging further into its depths. "I don't know." They hadn't exactly clicked, but after a year off the dating scene, was she being overly critical? Tyler hadn't truly said or done anything offensive. Yes, the name-dropping had almost made her roll her eyes, but was she giving him a fair chance? She was by no means obligated to. Perhaps he'd been nervous, and therefore rambling on about nonsense. Dating required too much damn thinking.

They drove in silence until Keiran's phone beeped, and he checked it at the next light, his jaw clenching.

"Everything okay?"

"Fine. Just studio stuff."

His tone said otherwise, but Cherisse didn't push. There were surely limits to their brief ceasefire. Neither of them was inclined to share things they didn't want to. They weren't friends. He'd done as she'd asked, and now she had to reciprocate in the studio.

When they got to her apartment, he helped with the hamper, holding it until she got her keys out and opened the door.

"We can share these up now if you want," she offered.

"Maybe later. Just send me a list of everything in there, and we can figure it out. I'm serious about the Prime dinner, though. Yours to use as you please. The spa vouchers, too. The rest, we'll sort. I trust you to list everything." He winked, his mood after seeing that message having shifted back to his usual self, and a loud laugh escaped her mouth, which had Keiran snickering too as he placed the hamper on the floor of her living room.

"That laugh, I swear. I love it."

She stared after him as he waved goodbye, closing the door behind him. People didn't usually say they loved her laugh. In fact, she'd grown up extremely self-conscious about it because her mother had drilled into her that it was too loud and scandalous, unbecoming of a young lady. That ladies must be seen, not heard. Over the years, Cherisse had started giving no fucks where that was concerned. She'd given up on trying to do some subdued version of it. Her genuine laugh was loud, boisterous even. But it was part of who she was.

"Was that you and Keiran laughing just now?" Remi asked as she came down the stairs. "Had to see if the apocalypse had begun because what the hell?"

Cherisse shrugged. "We had fun."

Remi gawked at her, face twisted in disbelief, then she noticed the hamper. "Oooh, what'd we win?"

"We?"

"Like you're not gonna share with me." She crouched down to inspect the goodies.

"Some of that belongs to Keiran."

"Uh-huh." Remi kept searching through, releasing a gasp as she held up the Prime gift certificate. "Oh, wow." She glanced up at Cherisse. "You wouldn't go with Keiran, would you? When your bestie's right here?"

"He did help me out today." She had zero intention of going to Prime with Keiran, but she loved teasing Remi too much. "Plus, we got spa passes, which I figure we'll use for our birthdays."

Remi got to her feet, eyes narrowed. "You're already doing that studio thing for him. He can't have Prime."

Remi was the only one she'd told about the challenge she'd thrown out to Keiran and his wanting to use her voice on a track. Her response had been surprise—then she'd begged to tag along to the session. Cherisse shut that down immediately. She didn't need extra witnesses to her screwing it up because she would. She had no doubt about that. Solos in front of other people? Not her jam. And even worse, it being Keiran. The one person who would gladly use her failure against her.

"Besides, Prime is a date spot," Remi added. "Going with Keiran would be kind of weird. But a bestie date would be fair and appropriate."

It would be weird. How would something like that even go? They'd had fun today. A fluke. Possibly never to be repeated. But an actual meal at a place like Prime? It was best not to tip the balance of their dynamic too much. Who knew what shift in the universe they might create?

Prime with Keiran wasn't happening. "Maybe I should offer to take Tyler," she mused.

"I think the hell not!" Remi protested. "I thought you weren't going for a second date?"

"I might give him another chance. Just to be sure."

"Well, do that some other place."

Cherisse extracted the voucher from her bestie's hand and grinned. "We'll see."

Chapter 11
APRIL
Cherisse

"WEAR THE FUCK-ME HEELS."

Said heels slipped from Cherisse's hand and fell to her bedroom floor as she shot Reba a glare. Grin still in place, Reba shrugged. "What? Those shoes are hot, and Tyler's cute."

She stared down at the shoes, a treat-yourself splurge that she had basically done with her eyes closed, not looking too closely at the price tag. Post-breakup shoes. They were these hot neon pink stilettos that made her feel super-sexy, and she'd only worn them once.

In between working with Keiran on the party, baking up a storm to replenish her goodies in the groceries and bakeries, and brainstorming the dessert station ideas for Ava's wedding and the other wedding that came before her sister's, she'd decided to give Tyler another chance. She really had nothing to lose, told herself she was doing this to keep her mother off her back and show that she was giving her dates a fair chance. Two dates was fair enough time to decide this wasn't going to work, right?

"I have no intention of fucking Tyler." She nudged the shoes with her foot. Tyler was good-looking, but there was zero chemistry on her end. She'd gotten more of a jolt when she'd touched Keiran's face to remove that smudge of flour, which was an entirely weird thing to recall in this moment.

Reba twirled a pink lock of her hair around her finger. "They give the illusion of being DTF. You don't actually have to, obviously." She drummed her bright yellow nails against Cherisse's bed. "He might end up showing a different side of himself. I mean, you and Keiran have been getting along lately, right? You had fun at the brunch. The world is full of strange and wonderful happenings."

"Yeah, we have, and we did."

The planning process with Keiran was an odd mix of small arguments but mostly them actually getting shit done without any major blow-ups. They'd split the tasks evenly and provided each other with updates. The party was scheduled for a few weeks before the wedding, so they were steadily getting things done. Cherisse breathed a sigh of relief with each item she crossed off her lists. They'd made it through the baking session, with Keiran actually admitting he'd been genuinely surprised at what the preparation entailed.

The one point of tension between them was the pending studio session. A date hadn't been set, and Keiran wasn't prodding her about it, but that would change soon. Surely, he had a deadline where that was concerned. But right now, the focus was the party planning.

"He even complimented my checklists." That had been a surreal moment.

"*Giiiirl,* those checklists of yours are scary." Reba pretended to clutch some imaginary pearls. "I'm okay with lists for work-related purposes, but your system gives me hives! Digital's the way to go. Get with the times. That notebook makes my head hurt. I love you, but that damn thing is just...no."

"Checklists are a godsend," Cherisse said. They both busted out laughing. She'd said that many times over the course of their working relationship. She couldn't help it. Checklists helped a lot. Hers were damn near indecipherable, though, basically scribbles with lots of bullet points, arrows all over the place, even some terrible drawings to illustrate a particular point. It gave most people a headache, sent them running screaming in the opposite direction, but she preferred paper to digital in this instance. There was something appealing about finally crossing off a finished task with her pen. "He said they made a weird kinda sense. He was actually able to read them."

Reba gasped. "For real? Okay, just marry that dude already. You won't find anyone else capable of that."

Cherisse shook her head. Marry Keiran? The apocalypse would happen before that did. "I'll pass on that, thanks. Anyways, back to the shoes." She kicked at them again and thought, why the hell not? She had the perfect dress to go with them too.

"Oh, by the way." Reba waved her phone around. "If you feel to meet up after, I'll be chillin' downstairs with Aleem. Him and his friends are having a sushi night at Hyatt. Nice coincidence, right? If you need a pep talk or just a weirdo in the background giving you an exuberant thumbs up, I'll be there. These fancy events always have rabbit food that can barely sustain anyone, so feel free to crash sushi night."

Reba wasn't wrong about the food. Cherisse had attended events like this before, and sure enough, she'd always been starving after. The food was usually gorgeously plated, but the portions would never appease her appetite. "You're hanging with Aleem? You know he's totally in love with you."

Reba didn't seem too concerned about it. "He knew what was up with our arrangement and that relationships aren't really my thing these days. The sex was good while it lasted, but then he starting getting all mushy and ruined everything. I told him being friends is fine, and he acted like I tried to murder his dog or something. As if my offer of friendship was the worst thing ever. So, I'm basically there for the free sushi because I told his ass not to fall for me." She shrugged. "He's paying."

"I can't keep up with your drama." Cherisse had heard about Reba's escapades countless times. Casual sex sounded like a nightmare waiting to happen. For her, at least. Her emotions always got in the way. Reason enough for her taking time for herself after Sean. She hadn't wanted to dive into anything too soon.

Although she'd missed being intimate with someone. And while she got herself off just fine, thank you very much, she did crave being close to a warm body again.

"I'm prepped to also be your wingwoman if needed." Reba gave an enthusiastic thumbs up.

"Just don't make it weird."

"When do I ever make anything weird?"

Cherisse gave Reba a pointed look, and she rolled her eyes. "What do I do with my hair?"

Reba didn't look up from her phone. "Wear it up. Show a lil' neck. People are always about legs and cleavage, but the neck is for real a sexy part of the body." She placed her phone on the bed and came over to scan Cherisse's open closet. "What you wearing?"

Cherisse pulled out the one she was considering, and Reba clapped her hands, mouth stretching in a happy grin. "Yes, good. I approve. Looks easy to remove, in case you change your mind about Tyler."

"Reba, seriously." But she found herself wondering if Tyler had a distracting set of abs like Keiran. Then she chided herself for even going there, shut that down before her brain conjured up Keiran in that towel, again. No good would come of those wayward thoughts.

Focus on the date. Maybe Tyler would surprise her.

CHERISSE'S MOUTH DROPPED open as they strolled up the stairs. The Building An Appetite Project displays were outside the

Regency Ballroom and were so much more than she'd expected. It turned out to be an ambitious undertaking between culinary, art, and architecture students, an experiment to mesh all three subjects and display the results. It was also an event sponsored by the architectural design firm where Devon King worked.

Devon, a broader, older, more serious-looking version of Keiran, shook Tyler's hand as they perused the desserts. Tyler was related to one of the executives at Devon's firm. "Thanks for supporting," he said to Tyler before turning to her. "Hi, Cherisse."

"Hi, Devon." Cherisse gaped down at the desserts inspired by geometrical shapes. "Holy shit. This is amazing." She loved coming up with unique creations for her desserts, but these were just mind-blowing, and she was in awe.

"Yes. We've been working on this since last year. Conceptualizing et cetera. Didn't think we'd pull it off. Hopefully, now my boss will stop looking at me like I've lost my mind."

"Wait, this was your idea?" Cherisse checked out a dessert that looked like a chocolate geometric abstract art piece, the grooves of the cube-like shape filled with some sort of red jelly. It looked like a design you'd find displayed on someone's desk, rather than something edible. She was beyond impressed, and obviously not the only one. Guests were oohing and ahhing over everything on display.

"Well, no, not really. We have an intern who also studies the culinary arts. The idea was hers. I just ran with it and helped get it in the door to the company's higher-ups. Other firms will definitely try to snap her up after this, but they better back off." The steely glint in his eyes made Cherisse raise a brow. So, Devon did have feelings under that cool façade.

The intern in question was one of the students smiling at guests from behind the display tables, eagerly explaining the inspiration for and technicalities of their creations.

"Oh! I know you!" the short woman exclaimed when Devon introduced them. Kim Cole was bubbly with long box braids and a dimpled smile. "I was rooting for you on *Pastry Wars!* Someday I'll make it on there."

Kim's excitement was catching, and Cherisse found herself grinning back at the younger woman, in spite of her awful memories of the show. "I've no doubt you'll get on there and win. These are so amazing!"

"Aww, you're sweet." Kim said. "Anyway, boss man, you better go make the rounds, talk up the company. I'll be over here holding it down." Kim's hand swept over some smaller versions of the bigger-sized chocolate cubes. "There are minis for sampling, so take as many as you like!"

Cherisse didn't have to be told twice. The designs looked too pretty to eat, but damn if she wasn't going to anyway. She was curious about the taste. Tyler didn't look as excited.

"Not a fan of sweets," he admitted when she asked what he was having, which wasn't a strike against him because the way Cherisse saw it, she could take his share.

They took in the other desserts on display, while Cherisse sampled and snapped pics to tease Reba and Remi. She basically blew up their group chat with the tantalizing photos.

Reba: Ohhh myyyy gawwwsh. I want this in my face.

Remi: You are a cruel woman. How dare...

Cherisse: these are so good. If only you could taste them LOL

Reba: smuggle some downstairs in a napkin.

Remi: If I show up with my camera no one'll know I'm not really scheduled to take pics at this event.

"You're eating all of that? That's a lot of sugar."

Cherisse stiffened. And there was that strike. She hated people commenting on her food choices. She got enough of that from her mother and other family members. Who the hell did Tyler think he was?

"It's why I'm so sweet," she quipped, instead of handing Tyler his ass. He had the sugary treats to thank for making her so mellow. There was certainly *not* going to be a third date after this.

She was grateful for the moment Tyler ran into some "very important people he just had to catch up with" because she was quite fine on her own, roaming, admiring the backdrop of the expanse of glass that ran along the side of the cocktail area. The lights from the Waterfront down below illuminated the sea that surrounded the Hyatt.

With a plate of sweets in one hand and a glass of wine in the other, Cherisse ducked outside onto the balcony area, enjoying the feel of the cool night air against her skin. She plopped down onto the cushions of the wicker couch and balanced the plate of desserts on her knee carefully. Her tight white dress may not have been the best choice for tonight, considering she'd been surrounded by sticky treats, but she hadn't had any accidents yet. Plus, she looked damned good in it. It was worth the risk.

"Thought that was you." The voice floating out of nowhere almost made her knock over her plate and drop her glass. Keiran emerged from a semi-lit corner. Guess the balcony wasn't as deserted as she'd thought.

"The fuck are you doing here?"

He stood a little off to her side, not quite hovering over her, a small smile playing on his lips. "Here to support Devon. The entire fam's here."

Keiran hadn't mentioned he would be attending, but then again, why would he? She hadn't mentioned she was going either. "Why are you lurking out here?"

"Not lurking. Avoiding my parents being in the same place after so long. Divorce is fun." His tone dripped with sarcasm. "My dad brought his girlfriend, who's younger than us, so you can probably imagine how well that's going."

"Well, damn. How's your mom doing?" Cherisse remembered Sheryl King as a vibrant, funny woman who, whenever they'd run into her, would always go on and on about cavities and proper dental care. To be expected, when she was a dentist with her own practice.

Keiran shrugged. "Last I saw, she was on her third glass of wine. Could be more by this point. It would've been best if he'd just refused the invitation. I'm not even sure Devon knew he was bringing this woman."

If she remembered correctly, the divorce had gone down five years ago, after Sheryl had apparently caught wind of her husband's infidelity. Gossip had been rampant. It couldn't have been easy for any of them to deal with.

"I can't even avoid the asshole if I wanted to." His laugh was brittle. "What I get for going into basically the same business as my dad, I guess."

Cherisse had completely forgotten. Mr. King ran King Kong Entertainment, where he managed talent that included musicians. They were bound to run into each other. Even Sean was signed with the label. It seemed assholes of a feather flocked together.

"I'm sorry." She didn't even know why she was saying that. It wouldn't help put his family back together. She just didn't know what else to say. Keiran looked dejected. She'd never seen sadness like that in his eyes.

"So, Tyler, huh? That's still happening? Quite an entrance you two made. You're not exactly blending in that dress. Which is my terrible way of saying you look really good in it. Sorry," he tacked on after an awkward beat of silence. "I'm in a shitty mood."

The media had fussed over her arrival with Tyler. Not something Cherisse had enjoyed, but Keiran was right. She *didn't* blend in this dress, and certainly not at Tyler's side. "Not happening for much longer," she admitted.

He leaned against the railing, legs crossed, silence growing thick between them once more when Cherisse had expected some sarcastic remark from him.

She shifted, switching her crossed ankles from one side to the other, refusing to be the first to break this intense quiet.

"You think I'm like him, don't you? My father. That's why you were so quick to believe the rumors."

She clutched at her glass. "Keiran, I..." And what could she say to *that*? He wasn't wrong. Her bad experiences with Sean had colored her experiences with men in the music industry, and Keiran's cockiness hadn't helped her think he was any different. Which may have been wrong of her, but cautious was the only way she knew how to be. He hadn't exactly helped his case by that foolish joke, but clearly, he was torn up about his dad. "Do you want a hug?"

Ill-timed. So out of left field. *What the fuck was she doing?* The question clearly surprised them both. Keiran blinked down at her, brow furrowed. It was possibly time to lay off the wine now.

"I've been told I give good hugs." The words kept pouring out. Why was she persisting with this? Yes, she was a hugger, loved giving them and receiving them, but this seemed like a bad idea, and yet, he looked like he could use one. It had to be hard facing his father at all in any setting, let alone one where he'd brought along a date, a much younger date. Cherisse could only imagine what his mother was feeling in this moment. The passage of time didn't always mend all wounds.

"I mean, if you're sharing them, I wouldn't say no to one." He was back to looking slightly amused. Now was a good time to backtrack, say she was joking. Get back inside and find Tyler. Hell, ditch Tyler entirely and go meet Reba downstairs. Tyler didn't deserve another moment of her time. She'd given him a fair chance, and boy, had he not earned it.

But she found herself resting the dessert plate next to her and tossing back the dregs of her wine, stashing the empty glass on the floor before she stood. Her heart was hammering away in her chest. Why? This was just Keiran, just a hug. She hugged her friends all the time, was great at it. Except, they weren't friends. They were two people who'd butted heads for years and were now forced to work together for the sake of people they cared about. Two people who had a shaky understanding that they'd ease up on antagonizing each other, for now. There was no friendship in that.

Why was she even making a big deal of this?

Hug and retreat. Not that hard.

So why the hell was her heart still trying to pound itself right out of her chest?

Chapter 12
Keiran

TONIGHT HAD SWIFTLY moved into surreal territory. The audacity of his father flaunting his date in his mother's face. Keiran would have never imagined he'd pull such a move. He didn't care one shit who he dated, but the over-the-top PDA was so unexpected. Even his date had looked slightly uncomfortable over the extra-long kiss his father had planted on her.

He didn't know who this man was anymore. Who had such blatant disregard for the woman he'd once professed to love so deeply?

You would think a man who'd been blasted in public after the news broke about his having fathered a child while still married to his wife would be sensitive to keeping a low profile, but the flack hadn't lasted long. His father hadn't truly had to pay any price. He had issued some half-ass statement, looked appropriately contrite, and then continued on with his life.

While his mother still got pitying looks and had to deal with randomly encountering his father's outside woman and child in the grocery. Keiran hadn't been present, but his mother had calmly mentioned it and gone about her day. Except he'd definitely heard her sniffling silently in the bathroom. They'd never talked about it because that's what his mother preferred, but Keiran could never and *would* never forgive his father.

No wonder Cherisse was leery of guys in this industry.

But in this moment of emotions battering his insides, he could admit it hurt. The idea that Cherisse thought he was like his father, another no-good, piece of shit guy. He'd brushed off her coming at him about that rumor, but it had fucking hurt.

Like you've given her a reason lately to think otherwise.

He shushed that voice and focused on her in that damn dress. It clung to every curve. When he'd seen her coming up those steps with Tyler, everything had fallen away. His father's annoying presence, his brother's uncomfortable stance as he pretended the awkward tension around his parents wasn't growing thicker by the second.

Hadn't lasted long. The moment Tyler casually slung an arm around her waist to pose for a photo op, Keiran had tossed back his drink and guided his mother over to check out the desserts.

And now, here they were. He'd word-vomited all over her, and she'd felt enough pity to offer a hug, of all things. Talk about bizarre.

Her body language indicated she regretted her casual offer. Keiran wasn't about to push. If she wasn't comfortable hugging him after all, so be it. It was probably for the best. There was something about those startlingly pink heels that was sending his thoughts into overdrive.

Thoughts that conjured up silky sheets, bare skin, and just those bright shoes, heels digging into his back as she wrapped her legs around him.

He shoved his hands into his pockets and rocked back on his heels, nonchalant. As if his mind hadn't gone *there*. As if his stomach wasn't twisting at the thought of exiting this tiny bubble of quiet he'd stepped into, to get away from family drama. Watching his father not give a damn about any of them.

"Hey, no worries. I'll get me some of those cool-looking treats and not think about pushing my father down the stairs."

"Shut up," she said, and then he was wrapped up in her softness. Her bun tickled his jaw, and Keiran allowed himself to relax, drink in the feel of her. Allowed himself to slowly return the embrace as his arms came around her.

He'd never in a million years pictured he'd be here. Ever. Having Cherisse willingly hug him, and it was a good hug. She really was good at this. She threw her entire self into it, and *God,* she smelled amazing. Like vanilla. Like something good enough to devour whole and go back for seconds.

She mumbled something against his neck, her breath washing over his skin, and Keiran nearly shivered. He didn't want to let go but figured he better not push his luck. He was about to pull back and ask her what she'd said when someone cleared their throat.

The way they both pulled away had to make them look guilty as hell—not that they were doing anything wrong. Just super-weird because they did *not* do this—but he hadn't actually expected anyone to walk in on this hug.

Tyler was the first one he saw, face blank, not one indication of what he was thinking as he let the balcony door slip shut behind him. Then Maxine, whose mouth was hanging open. His mother was busy sipping from her wine, seemingly unconcerned by anything they'd walked in on.

Cherisse put space between them immediately, and Keiran figured he better tackle the giant elephant in the room. "Sorry for taking up your date's time. I was being a whiny baby about something, and Cherisse was nice enough to offer a hug."

Tyler's face remained impassive, but his mother squinted at Cherisse. "Cherisse Gooding, is that you?"

"Hi, Ms. King. Nice to see you." Cherisse gave a little wave, then looked startled when his mother clasped her hands in hers.

"Haven't seen you in so long. Look how lovely you are!"

"Thanks, Ms. King. It has been a while."

"Well, we must change that. Come over for Sunday lunch sometime soon, okay? I'm having a barbecue soon." His mother held Cherisse at arm's length and smiled. "That dress." Then she looked to Tyler. "And who's this? Your boyfriend?"

"*No.*" Cherisse seemed unbothered by her forceful reply and didn't seem to care about Tyler's frown. Looked like this date wasn't heading for a happy ending. How sad for Tyler. The man now appeared utterly confused.

"Okay, mummy, we need to get some food in you. Let's see what they have downstairs because I don't think those dessert samples did much to soak up that wine." Maxine didn't wait for confirmation, just linked their arms and dragged their mother towards the door.

"Food sounds good," Keiran agreed. Anything was better than the discomfort that was settling in the longer they all stood here.

After a short conversation with Tyler, who looked displeased, Cherisse left him scowling after them and followed downstairs, where they all met up with Reba. She jumped up, waving them over to where she was having sushi with friends at the bar. It wasn't long before they all ended up outside, claiming a table that faced the waterfront.

Keiran kept an eye on his mother. Maxine was steadily supplying her with water, but his mom was still very much tipsy. Somehow, she had Reba's friends eating out of her hand, cackling, gesturing wildly as she recounted some hiking trip gone wrong. The two guys with Reba were enthralled by his mother's story. One of them was hanging a little too closely on her every word. Keiran narrowed his eyes at him.

"Your mom's still got it."

Cherisse's voice in his ear startled him. When had she moved to sit next to him?

"I'm keeping an eye on that dude. He best not get any ideas." He glared at the guy to drive the point home. Pointless move because the dude was too busy staring into his mother's eyes to notice anything around him.

"He's cute."

Keiran swung his gaze to Cherisse, who was trying, and failing, to hide her grin behind her glass of juice. She'd switched from the wine a while ago.

"Not happening."

"Your mother's an attractive woman. Come on, don't cramp her style."

"There is no way in hell that dude is..." He narrowed his eyes at her. She was biting her lip, barely keeping her laugh in. "You're joking, aren't you?"

"Yup." She looked so pleased with herself.

He liked this, them hanging out. It was tipping the weird balance they had into unchartered territory. Them maybe being friends, outside of their truce, something they'd never been the entire time they'd known each other. It was odd, yet he liked it. Didn't want to look too closely at why that was. *Like you don't already know.* He brushed that pesky voice away. His teenage self was living a long-buried dream right now. He'd never actually hated Cherisse, not really. She'd frustrated him, sure, but at some point, their back and forth had gotten fun. He'd just kept that to himself.

As the night wore on, his mother sobered up enough to be less chatty, but clearly not enough to realize this Adam dude was full-on flirting. The last straw was Adam asking his mother for her number.

"Hey, whoa." Adam threw up his arms when Keiran got to his feet the minute the question left Adam's mouth. "She's a dentist. I need a dentist. Teeth care is important."

Adam *had* asked for the number of his mother's practice, but Keiran wasn't buying that shit. His mother's laugh was loud enough to have some patrons, dining inside, look out to where they were all still seated.

"I'm flattered you think this young man's giving me the time of day," his mother said, patting his cheek.

Adam looked too pleased with himself. This swirl of annoyance was leftovers from dealing with his father, who had thankfully left with his girlfriend as soon as they'd all come downstairs. He'd been on edge the entire time. His sole moment of reprieve had been that hug from Cherisse, which he shouldn't think too hard about.

He needed some air before he caused a scene and punched a guy out.

He didn't go far, just a little way from their table, leaning against one of the columns as he stared out at the dark water.

"A dollar for your thoughts."

He swung his head to the side and watched as Maxine leaned against the column opposite his. "A whole dollar? Lucky me. What happened to a penny?" he teased.

Maxine shrugged. "I figure a dollar may be more of an attractive incentive for you to share your thoughts."

"A dollar can't buy shit, but I mean, money is money."

"You okay?"

He see-sawed his hand from side to side, and she nodded. Didn't ask him to elaborate. She obviously got it. Had to be feeling some of the same weariness, anger, and frustration at the entire situation. They both stared out at the waterfront for a while, deep in their own thoughts, until Maxine interrupted the silence.

"Are you thinking about how weird that hug was that we walked in on? Because I sure was."

Of course, she wouldn't let that slide. Maxine wasn't Devon, who didn't care to be involved in his siblings' business. Not that Cherisse was Keiran's business in any way that didn't involve wedding stuff.

"Nope." This time, he strived for casual, uncaring. That hug? No biggie. Didn't affect him in any way. "I'm taking in the scenery, calming myself so I don't rail that Adam guy."

"Don't deflect. What's going on with you two? You were *hugging*."

"Nothing is going on. We decided to be civil, that's all. And I got all up in my feelings, and she felt sorry for me. Just like I said."

"Cherisse doesn't even like you. Would probably not pee on you if you were on fire, but you're at the hugging stage now?" Maxine's stare burned the side of his face. He loved having a twin, but times like these, Maxine's perceptiveness was unwanted.

"Look, I needed a favor from her, so we paused our arguing, called a truce. That's it. Really. Don't ask me what favor. I'm not telling."

Maxine sighed loudly and resumed leaning against the wall, arms folded, lips pursed. She was legit pouting, but Keiran wasn't revealing a thing. Cherisse was already nervous about it, and he'd promised he wouldn't tell anyone about the studio session except Dale.

It was easy enough to get Cherisse in and out of the studio without anyone knowing. His mother, sister, and brother would be at work, and Leah was still at school until the July/August break. They had enough time to get it done.

The knocking of glasses and scraping of utensils against plates jogged something in his brain, a rhythm formulating. Keiran tapped out the beats on his thigh. It was always how it began, some random sound that lit up his brain and shouted *yes, you've got something here!* There was a new potential beat in that chaos of sound. He'd extract it. He always did.

"You're doing that zoning out thing again." Maxine turned to head back to the table. "I'm going back inside to rescue that boy from mummy, cuz she'd eat him alive."

Keiran flapped his hands at Maxine. "Shh," he hissed. That beat, right there. Cherisse's voice, layered over it, would be something magical.

"Okay, I'm out."

He didn't acknowledge Maxine's exit, only smiled to himself as he tried to coax out the fledgling beat, excitement coursing through his veins at seeing what Cherisse could truly do with that voice.

Chapter 13

Cherisse

THE BOOTH FELT SUFFOCATING. It wasn't claustrophobia making her feel like the words were caught in her throat. It was Keiran watching intently from the other side of the glass. In here, he was different, less carefree. He'd donned this super-serious studio mode mask that left her skin prickly like she'd break out in hives at any moment.

She was fucking this up, had no clue what she was doing. Just as she'd anticipated. Even as Keiran tried to guide her through it, she felt like she was croaking through the entire verse.

Music wasn't hard for her to catch; learning a new song came quickly to her. Hell, anything sung to a tune was faster to learn. The song was clear in her head. She knew her part. But she kept freezing up.

"Alright, let's take a break," Keiran suggested, not a bit of frustration in his voice. Either he was good at faking this, or he was genuinely not about to shout her ass down for wasting his time. This was the second break they'd taken since Cherisse had come down to the studio.

It was a random day in the week when everyone else was off at work, and his niece was off at school, so no one was around to witness this utter shitfest. Not even Scooby, who wasn't allowed down here, apparently. The dog's mournful face was the last thing she saw before Keiran closed the door and headed down the steps to the studio.

"Sorry, I'm not good at this." She exited the booth and threw herself down onto the couch, face on fire, as Keiran swiveled his chair to face her.

She'd been in choir in primary school and had some vocal talent, but this? This was vastly different to singing along with a bunch of other people, guided by a choir mistress. In choir, she'd had no solos except for her audition to get into the choir, and that had been a heart-pounding experience.

Here, with Keiran, it was just his eyes on her, and it made her itchy, made her skin feel too tight. She was close to dashing up the stairs and out the door, but she'd promised. Keiran had even come to pick her up, brushing away her comment about taking public transport to his house. No judgment about a woman her age, not driving. She was uncertain whether he'd been trying for chivalry or making sure she didn't duck out on their deal. Maybe both.

Bet he's regretting this now.

"Am I making you feel uncomfortable?" His question drew her out of her thoughts. His legs spread wide as he rocked back in his chair, arms resting on his stomach as he held her gaze. Her disloyal gaze that dipped right into the V his thighs created, for hopefully the briefest of moments. So brief that Keiran hadn't noticed. Staring at Keiran's crotch certainly wouldn't make any of this less stressful. But it was just right there, practically begging for her eyes to trace the outline in those barely decent sweatpants.

Focus.

"No, it's not that. It's me." Boy, was it ever. She'd never done this before, obviously, but Keiran had tried to prep her beforehand. He hadn't just tossed her in the booth, but she wasn't getting into that relaxed headspace. "I'm not a professional singer. I mean, sure, I've been in a choir, but it's absolutely not the same."

Keiran cocked his head. "The secrets keep getting revealed."

"Choir wasn't a secret. Just a part of my life I left behind. A fun thing to do while in school." She'd loved it while she'd done it but had zero desire to take it further. She'd had no dreams of trying out for the national choir, no matter how much she'd been prodded. The most singing she did these days was in the shower, around the apartment, in Remi's car, or at karaoke when she was tipsy enough to not care.

"What can I do to make this less painful for you?"

"Not look at me?" She was only half-joking.

"Here's what. Let's try again, okay? You know the verse, no doubt about that. It's your nerves tripping you up, but it's your first time. You show me yours, I show you mine, right? I'm asking you to bare your soul basically, so I'm getting on the piano to try something, okay?"

Piano? She'd, of course, noticed the sleek black instrument near the booth but hadn't for one second thought Keiran knew how to play it. She'd figured the electric keyboard setup was more his style, and maybe the piano was for show, which was a ridiculous assumption to make. Why wouldn't he actually be able to play any of the instruments in here?

"You can play that?"

He sauntered over to the piano and sat, brow raised. "It's not in here for style. I'm a terrible singer, so I put my musical talents elsewhere, and don't even ask me to prove how bad I am. I don't sing in public. Trust me, I'm saving your ears." He ran his fingers over the dark wood, his touch a slow caress. "My father would scoff at this Kawai. He's all about the Yamaha, but this upright will give just the sound I need. Always works for me. The lower tensile strength of the strings gives a more dynamic range. And don't get him started on the electric piano over there." He pointed at the keyboard setup. "He gives me grief for that too, but it works for certain tracks. Can't please the man. Not that I still try to."

"Um..."

He grinned. "Of course, none of that piano talk means anything to you, but just trust me."

Trust him. When it came to this, maybe she could. She was in his domain now and had no choice but to follow his lead. As his fingers danced lightly over the keys, Cherisse focused on his face, wanting to see the emotions there as he played what she soon recognized as Twinkle Twinkle Little Star.

"Just warming up," he said, grin wide. "Any requests?"

"Can you play soca on this?"

"Of course." Confidence oozed off of him as the familiar sounds of a popular soca song echoed around the room. "Most people are usually surprised at what songs you can play on a classical instrument. Maxi can play just about anything on a viola. That's *viola,* not violin."

"What's the difference?"

Keiran sighed like he'd gotten the question many times before. Cherisse hadn't known his sister played any instruments, and she sure as hell didn't know how a viola and violin differed, choir and the recorder being her only forays into music.

"Quick lesson," he said as he continued playing song after song on the piano. "Violas are larger. Heavier, too, and have a deeper, mellower sound. Gorgeous instrument, but the piano is more my style."

Of course, it was. She could imagine Keiran charming the pants off someone as he coolly and casually stroked the keys like he was doing now. But her pants were staying firmly on, thank you very much.

"Tell me. How many times have you used this piano to get laid?"

His fingers faltered on the keys, but he didn't stop. "You really think the worst of me, don't you?" Cherisse gave him a pointed look, and he chuckled. "Fine, one time, and I didn't plan some elaborate seduction. She asked to see the studio, then asked me to play her something. The rest is history. Literally, because she's the one everyone thinks I knocked up and left. But you know how that went."

Fuck. Cherisse opened her mouth to apologize again, but he shook his head and launched into something she didn't recognize, but it tugged at her, causing goosebumps to pop up on her skin. It sounded like a tune that would perfectly back a groovy type soca song, like the one she couldn't quite nail. The type of song you'd hear in a smoky bar that wrapped around you like a warm hug.

"That's beautiful," she whispered.

He didn't reply, but his mouth quirked up in his trademark smirk she was getting used to. She'd never dreamed Keiran could wrench a sound like this from his fingertips. She wasn't quite sure where to look. Her eyes darted from his fingers stroking the keys, coaxing that mellow sound out, to his face, full of concentration, but something lighter, too. As if he not only took great joy in breathing life into the instrument but sharing that with others. With her. Damn, talk about baring your soul.

The song trailed off, and Cherisse had no words left. This Keiran she'd never seen. Knowing what he did and hearing the finished product on the radio was completely different from this moment. This raw, in-your-face moment of him replicating and creating sounds like these while his fingers danced across the keys like a lover's touch.

Cherisse had never paid much attention to Keiran's hands, but at the moment, she wondered what music he could wrench from her if he touched her like that.

Whoa, okay. She needed to reel this in.

"Something like that would work," he said, and she blinked at him as if coming out of a trance. Perhaps she was.

"Yeah, okay, let's try. That was...wow. Thanks for sharing that with me."

"Knives and forks on glass."

"What?" She furrowed her brow, confused.

"Nothing." He got to his feet. "Ignore my weird ramblings about my process."

He gestured for her to put the headphones back on.

"Let's try this." Keiran watched her intently, voice coming through her headphones, calm. "Close your eyes. I need you to really feel the song. I'll layer the piano over you after. Don't focus on me. Focus on the lyrics and what type of way they make you feel."

She chewed her lip. Okay. He wasn't asking her to do anything too weird, and after what he'd shared with her, she could at least try again. It was what she did when she was home alone, cleaning, belting out a tune. Her eyes wouldn't be closed then, but she allowed herself to just feel, throw her whole being into the song, not caring how silly she looked. She did it in front of Remi because she felt comfortable with her; anyone else was a different story. But she could try.

"Alright." Keiran grinned, the curve of his mouth an enticing distraction she didn't need. "Wow me. No pressure or anything."

She took a deep breath, closed her eyes, focused on the music filtering through her ears, and sang.

KEIRAN

"Well?"

"That's me." Her eyes were wide, mouth hanging open. "I sound...good. I do sound good, right? By your professional standards, I mean."

Keiran chuckled. "You do. I knew you'd get it."

When her voice faded away, she asked him to play it again. And even though he did, hearing her voice again was like a kick to the gut, especially with the piano draped over it like warm caramel. She wrapped up the words with raw emotion, just what he'd asked for, but his heart was thumping. He was trying for a neutral face but had no idea how successful he was because *damn*. He wondered what she'd been thinking of as she sang. Her voice was battering his every sense right now, and he needed to not be getting swamped with all these feels.

"You're good at making me sound good," Cherisse said.

"Nah, that's all you. I just bring out what's already there, act as a guide. Package it up a lil' nicely, but that's all you." She leaned against the wall, arms folded. "Take the damn compliment while you can get it."

"Fine. Thank you."

She kept up her casual stance, watching him. Her earlier nervousness was gone. Here was the Cherisse he was familiar with. That brain of hers was calculating how to ask him something. Whether to ask at all, but he knew she would.

"You love music," she said. "So why didn't you work with your dad? Before the divorce, I mean."

A question he got a lot, especially in the rare interviews he did. His father had built a music empire which he'd made no secret about wanting to leave in Keiran's hands, but he hadn't wanted that.

"I do work with him in some capacity. I produce stuff for some of his clients, but working at KKE just wasn't for me. I just wanted to do my own thing. Make my own path. It's funny, but not really, that my dad keeps insisting about me being his legacy when it's no secret Maxi wants that. She went to school for Music Management, and he just ignored all that, kept insisting he wanted his son at his side. Devon couldn't give a shit about music, so that was a dead end. My dad has this old-school 'my son is my legacy' thinking."

"That's bullshit," Cherisse said.

"Totally. He uses the fact that Maxi did the degree, then stayed up there, got married, had a kid, and didn't come back here to justify why he didn't insist she come work for him. Talk about an asshole. I'd be miserable there."

He had his own style of doing things, worked well with Dale because they wanted the same things, had the same vision, but under his father, he'd have a hard time. Maxi always said she could change all that if she'd just get a foot into KKE, but Keiran didn't have the patience.

His father was already driving him to contemplating murder with this Sean Daley thing. Keiran felt a pang of guilt at that, working with that piece of shit even though the man had talent oozing out of his pores. He couldn't get rid of Sean soon enough.

His phone beeped, and like a summons from the devil himself, a message from Sean—who he'd saved as That Mofo—popped up: **need to reschedule next session. Can't do this week, will be off island.**

This fucking guy. Sean had confirmed his availability, and now this. Prolonging this process was not ideal. He was likely to strangle Sean before this was over.

"Everything okay?"

He shoved his phone into the pocket of his sweats and nodded. "Yup. You hungry? A successful session calls for some food. My treat."

She gave him one last piercing look then patted her stomach, sustenance clearly more important than her curiosity about that message. Good. Sean Daley wasn't a topic he wanted to raise. He was, in fact, doing her a favor by not ruining her day. "Food sounds like heaven right now."

"Right. So, let's head up, so I can get started on cooking."

"You're cooking?"

"I'll have you know, Ms. Gooding, my hands are good for things other than making music."

She raised her brow at his choice of words, but neither of them touched the obvious innuendo there. Instead, he focused on her skepticism over his cooking skills. Granted, he didn't have a vast repertoire of fancy dishes he could make, but he was thrilled to introduce her to his fish broth masterpiece. He'd had some kingfish thawing out this morning. It was time to bubble a pot.

It was the oddest thing having Cherisse hovering, watching him as he prepped the dish. He refused to let her help. Not because he was fussy about people in his space when he was cooking. Far from it, he liked company in the kitchen, but he figured he'd put her through enough this morning. She'd earned her rest. He felt the prickle of her gaze on the back of his neck as he added the seasoned fish pieces to the pot.

"You use the heads and all?" she asked.

"Of course, best part." He turned away from the stove in time to see her nod in agreement. "My dad loved to eat the eyes," he admitted. "I was grossed out by it enough as a kid that I'll eat the meat but never the eyes."

"I eat the eyes." Cherisse tossed him a challenging wink, and Keiran gave a full-body shudder.

Scooby trotted into the kitchen, jumping up on Cherisse, begging for some affection, and acting like the most neglected dog in the world.

"Scooby, down!" Keiran chided. Scooby knew how to manipulate those who weren't privy to his tricks.

"It's fine," Cherisse said, patting Scooby's head. That sealed it—she'd won over Scooby forever. He was easy. Head pats and belly rubs were all it took. She was winning Keiran over, too. Even being a cat owner, she obviously liked dogs as well. Points in her favor.

"He knows he isn't supposed to jump on guests." Keiran leaned against the counter, watching as Scooby basked in the attention. Was it pathetic to be jealous of your dog? Cherisse was down on her haunches now, letting Scooby wriggle himself into a frenzy over her touches. Keiran couldn't help but wonder if he'd react the same. Foolish thought. As if he'd ever get touched by Cherisse like that.

When the fish broth was ready, Keiran was suddenly overtaken by a barrage of nerves. Used to cooking for his friends, he was confident his fish broth was on point. Watching Cherisse take her first sip, the flipping feeling in his stomach was back—different this time, but still battering his insides.

"Oh, this is good." Cherisse seemed genuinely surprised as she dug into her bowl for another spoonful. "You should have another early morning baking class with me. With this soup and my treats, you'll be marriage material in no time," she joked.

"I think I manage with what I've got, but thanks," he replied drily.

"I'm telling you, baking will level you up."

"You're just trying to find another way to boss me around for fun, aren't you?"

Cherisse shrugged, but her mischievous smile said he wasn't too far off with his assumption. "But you're so good at taking instructions." She rooted around in her bowl, breaking the skin of the fish and scooping out the eye. "Consider it." She waved the spoon with the fish eye close to his face.

"Hey, now, that's playing dirty." He slid his chair back.

"But it's so much fun to play dirty."

Keiran's breath whooshed out his mouth. His brain went right to the gutter. She hadn't meant it that way, surely, but his body tightened all the same. Playing dirty with Cherisse sounded downright fun. He cleared his throat. "Right."

Cherisse's hand hovered there, the fish eye smack in the middle of the spoon, swimming in broth. The feeling in the room shifted, wound tighter as if any sudden movement on both their parts would shatter the tension that was swiftly building. Keiran swallowed. Cherisse's eyes dipped to his throat, then back up to his face, so quickly, he was sure he'd imagined it. Their staring match went on for what felt like minutes but had to be a couple of seconds, at best.

Scooby's nails clicked against the floor as he padded over to them, and the spell was broken. Cherisse pulled back her hand and popped the fish eye and broth in her mouth, cheeks hollowing like she was sucking a sweet—instead, she was cleaning the meat that clung to the eye. She spat the eye out and grinned at Keiran.

"Delish."

Now she was the one teasing him, in more ways than one. The double entendre had been unintended. Didn't stop his brain from trying to go *there*. Her massacre of the fish eye didn't put a damper on that. If anything, it weirdly made him wonder how she'd use her tongue otherwise.

Bad brain. Stop this.

"I'll eat yours if you want?"

Keiran choked on his broth. She definitely hadn't meant that the way it sounded. Had she? He peered at her as she stared back at him, the question magnified by the way her head was cocked, waiting for his reply.

"Uh, sure, yeah, it's yours. All yours." *Be cool. Be the guy who was in the studio earlier, not this awkward loser.*

Except, studio Keiran didn't quite know how to deal with perceived double meanings that sounded way dirtier than they'd been intended.

He should've just let her leave, not prolonged their time together. This felt too intimate all of a sudden. Cooking for friends was one way they bonded. They'd each bring a dish. He'd whip up his own thing. Drinks, food, and lively conversation was their MO. With Cherisse, it felt too cozy, too...everything. His brain was rapidly supplying all sorts of nonsensical ideas.

He didn't need any of this. He sure knew how to add unnecessary complications to his own life.

Jesus, take the wheel.

Chapter 14
Cherisse

HER KITCHEN SMELLED like heaven, a delicious mix of the cakes in the oven, and the sugary concoctions in the shot glasses before her.

Perfect. The red velvet shooters were ready for sampling. Jello had clearly thought so, too—she'd had to shoo him away from the shooters several times. He hadn't liked that one bit, but he strolled out of the kitchen, tail swishing as if he didn't care that he'd been denied a taste. He generally stayed clear of the kitchen when she was in the baking zone, but after, he'd come sniffing around to try his luck. Not that he ever got lucky.

She licked away a smidge of cream cheese frosting that somehow managed to get on the side of her hand, then grabbed up the two shot glasses and one of the extra treats she'd whipped up for herself, a strawberry Jell-O mousse parfait.

She allowed herself a small smile as the sounds of Frank Sinatra's "I Did It My Way" piped through her apartment.

"I see we're going way old-school here," she noted.

Keiran looked up from where his laptop and speakers were set up. Jello had planted himself right next to Keiran, looking mighty cozy, so disloyal. "Well, it *is* a classic. I say it makes the list."

Cherisse plunked the shot glasses and the cup down on the table. Keiran eyed them with interest. It was still weird that he no longer acted as if her treats were poisoned. He'd never actually admitted to eating her macarons, but Cherisse suspected he had. Jello's yellow stare was fixed on the glass, too.

"I need some feedback. I'm making a variation of these for the wedding, so I wanted to do a smaller setup for the slumber shower, and since you're already here, you get to sample."

They'd decided to meet up at her apartment to discuss music for the wedding shower. Cherisse had already chosen today for her baking test runs, so Keiran coming over was easier. He'd been going through a playlist while she sorted herself in the kitchen.

She slid one of the shooters closer to his hand before digging into hers. She'd gone really simple with these: layers of red velvet cake, with cream cheese frosting in between, and homemade whipped cream, topping everything off. She debated whether to have some chocolate shavings on top and decided she'd try with her next batch.

"Looks good," Keiran said.

"High praise from the King himself."

The last couple of weeks, they'd been texting and meeting sporadically, schedules permitting, to discuss all things shower-related. She'd noticed little things about Keiran that had slid right by her oblivious teen self. He enjoyed pushing her buttons. That wasn't anything new; she'd known that. She recalled a particularly heated argument they'd had over sucker bags. The frozen treat had been a staple on a hot day. Their neighbor sold both fruity and milky options. The treat was simple enough for anyone to make themselves since it involved pouring the juice or milk into plastic sandwich bags and placing them in the freezer until they froze, but the neighborhood still supported by buying. Cherisse couldn't even remember what prompted the fight, but a shouting match had erupted over which kind was better. By the end of it, she'd been red in the face, ranting, while he'd stood there, smirking at her for having lost her cool.

What was new was the realization that it was truly not done out of malice. Every time he said something ridiculous, she'd scowl, then he'd smirk, and his eyes—those deep brown depths that made her think of chocolate ganache—held amusement and affection. The kind you'd maybe give to a friend.

Did that mean they *were* friends now? Had they outgrown their petty squabbling? She sensed they were slowly making their way there. Maybe.

"Tastes even better," she said, spooning a mix of the cakey goodness in her mouth. He watched her intently. She focused on the shooter. The cake was moist and flavorful, not too teeth-jarringly sweet. The frosting was an excellent counterbalance, and her from-scratch whipped cream was on point. "Oh yeah, this is good."

He cracked an amused smile. "Why do *you* sound so surprised? You made this."

"Just good to know I'm not losing my touch." She buffed her fingers against her shoulder then blew on them.

He had the glass in his hand, just twisting it around and around, observing her as she ate, before finally digging his spoon in. "Red velvet?" he asked.

"Yeah."

"My fave." He stuck the cake in his mouth and chewed. She watched his face closely, trying to gauge his reaction. Even if he hated it, it didn't mean she would scrap the entire idea. She'd just get another opinion. But she was curious to see his reaction.

As she watched him, "I Did It My Way" gave way to another Sinatra song, "The Way You Look Tonight." She made a mental checkmark next to that one. It should definitely be on the list. Her sister loved this song. She did, too. They'd grown up with their father blasting Sinatra songs every Sunday afternoon.

"Jesus, this is..." Keiran's tongue darted out to lick away a trace of whipped cream from his spoon. "Heaven on a spoon," he finished.

Cherisse felt her face split into a wide grin. He scraped the bottom of the shot glass, doing another of those slow spoon licks that had Cherisse following every move his tongue made. His eyes caught hers, and Cherisse's neck felt warm. Busted.

His smile was slow, sultry, as he dropped the spoon in the glass. "This definitely makes the dessert menu."

Her head bobbed up and down. "Yup." He needed to quit looking at her like that as if she were the next thing he wanted to sample.

He pointed at the parfait cup. "What's that one?"

She swiped up the cup. "Off-limits. It's a strawberry Jell-O parfait. Not for sampling." She dipped her spoon in the mousse on the top and popped it into her mouth. Delicious. She had a few more in the fridge and could share, but did she want to? Not really. She was selfishly possessive of her Jell-O treats.

Keiran shook his head, shoulders shaking with silent laughter. "You weren't kidding about liking Jell-O, were you? What's the fascination with it?"

Cherisse shrugged. "I always just liked the wobbliness of it when I was younger. I dunno, it's a fun thing to eat."

"You do know what gelatin's made from, right?"

She narrowed her eyes at him. Of course, she did. Her curiosity about her favorite dessert had sent her on a Google spree. She'd gotten the shock of her life, but then she'd shrugged it off. Who cared what it came from? Jell-O was life.

She polished off the Jell-O at the bottom of the cup. "Don't care. Still gonna eat it." She licked her spoon clean, and his eyes tracked every swipe of her tongue. He wasn't even being subtle about it. *Payback, motherfucker.*

He abruptly got to his feet and stretched out his hand. "In keeping with our you-show-me-yours, I-show-you-mine theme, I sampled your thing; now, we test run mine."

She frowned at his hand. "What does that mean?"

He bent over his laptop, played around with the mouse until "The Way You Look Tonight" was back on repeat, then motioned again for her to take his hand. "Only way to know if the song works is to test it."

He was asking her to dance. Just like at Bootleggers, except this time, it was just them. She stared up at him as if he'd lost it. Their truce didn't include *dancing*.

"I don't think—"

"It's just a dance," he interrupted. "No big deal, right?"

Oh, this motherfucker. There he went again, pushing her buttons. She was onto him now. That widening grin said as much. If she protested too much, it would seem like dancing with him *was* a big deal when it wasn't. It really wasn't. She could do this, no problem.

She rose to her feet, placed her hand in his, and squeaked in surprise when he spun her right into his embrace. The closeness was shocking. She felt every bit of his hard body against her, the same body he'd bared to her hungry gaze in that fucking towel. Cherisse nearly tripped over her feet at that memory as they swayed around her living room. Dammit. Her heart was pounding so loudly, at least to her ears. She wondered if he could hear it. The pulse in her neck hammered away. Fuck, this was new. She didn't like it one bit.

That why you're clutching his arm like that?

Was she really? She relaxed her grip. He couldn't know that this, their closeness, was affecting her in any way.

"You okay?" he asked.

"Fine. Great. Marvelous." Pathetic. That's what she was. Where was the cool-as-a-cucumber Sugar Queen who could give back anything Keiran could toss at her?

"Heart's beating a bit fast there."

"You can feel that?" she asked, absolutely mortified.

He laughed and spun her away, not missing a beat with the music. This time when their bodies met again, their faces were so close, she felt his breath on her cheek when he said, "I can feel everything."

Just what the hell did he mean by *that*?

And his words made her all too aware of the lower half of his body. Those thighs clad in those cursed sweatpants.

As they swayed, it was getting harder to catch her breath. The song clearly worked. They should stop this. Keiran's proximity was too much. If she said she was feeling uncomfortable now, he'd stop, except discomfort wasn't her current emotion. Keiran's gaze never left her face as they kept swaying. His touch at her waist felt like it would burn its way through her clothes to her skin beneath.

"Cherisse." Her name was a whisper, one she could barely hear over the roaring in her ears. That damn heartbeat, triple-timing it. But oh, she heard it. Heard the way her name sounded like a prayer on his lips. Noticed the way his eyes dropped to her mouth. It was a question, too. *May I?*

"Yeah?" Her casualness belied the banging of her heart against her chest. Was it normal for a heart to race like this? How was she still alive?

"I...this will sound...Jesus, I don't even know, but can I...?" He swallowed hard, Adam's apple bobbing. He drew in a deep breath, eyes still fixed to her mouth, his tongue darting out to wet his lip, which in turn drew her gaze. Lips slightly parted, his breath unsteady, the mood shifted, tension crackling between their bodies.

"Do it." The words slipped past her lips before she could instruct her brain to reel them in, hold them back, but she held his stare. Waiting. Consent had been given, and in the same breath, a challenge had been issued. She didn't move. She was waiting too now. Wanting...

She felt the brush of his lips against hers right down to her toes.

Keiran was kissing her, and she'd let him. Knew she could've ended it before his lips ever touched hers, but the wanting got the better of her. She was even more shocked when *she* turned the simple brush of his lips against hers into something deeper, hotter. Her hands gripped the back of his neck as her tongue tangled with his. He tasted sweet, like the dessert he'd so hungrily licked from his spoon. Now she had that same tongue in her mouth, feasted on it, pressing into his body as much as she could.

She felt him hard against her. Sweatpants truly were a gift from God. She should pull back, stop this. She was kissing Keiran King! There was nothing to prepare her for that. But her touch-starved body was leading the show, enjoying the way his hands rested right above her ass, slowly kneading at her lower back, driving her wild. He couldn't know it was one of her zones—she loved having her ass fondled—but damn if he hadn't found it without even really trying.

She envisioned him grasping her ass firmly in his hands, rubbing, teasing, learning the feel of her, and before she'd even made the conscious decision, she was moving them backwards towards her couch. He was helping. They were both in sync on where their bodies wanted to go as they kept on kissing, exploring each other's wet heat. This was definitely hazardous, this blind shuffle to the couch. She hoped Jello was observant enough to get out of the way, but she didn't want this kiss to end. Her body wanted one thing: to get him down there so she could straddle him, keep kissing, keep nibbling, do something about the building ache between her legs. The bulge she felt against her could help with that just fine. A slow grind against that hardness was next on her agenda.

They were almost there when a loud, incessant chiming made him pull away, frowning. "What—"

Shit! Her cakes!

She untangled from his hold, reality rushing back in. She'd been kissing Keiran, while another Sinatra song swelled around them, while her oven had been signaling the cakes were ready. She had no idea how long the chiming had been going on for. All she knew was panic was setting in.

She'd kissed Keiran. Jesus, what was she thinking?

"Cherry," he started. Using her nickname jolted her into action. She didn't wait to hear the rest and fled to the kitchen instead to remove the cakes from the oven and clear her head because she'd fucked up. Her heart was a drumline, threatening to leap right out of her chest—this time, not in anticipation.

She had her head cupped in her oven-mitt-covered hands, the cakes cooling on the counter next to her when Keiran came up behind her.

"Cherisse." Perhaps he'd realized the effect the use of her nickname had on her. He sounded wary, unsure. As he should be. She had no idea what she would do if he came any closer.

"You should go," she said without turning around, lifting her head to stare at the wall beneath her cabinets. "Send me your playlist suggestions. We'll go from there." Calm, so calm. Something she didn't feel at all right now, but she'd fake it until it felt true. She might need to take care of some other business when he left because she'd gotten riled up from that kiss alone.

"So, that's it?" His tone was incredulous. What was he expecting exactly? That they'd carry on, make out some more, like that was normal for them? Because it wasn't.

"Just please go. I can't right now, okay?"

"Alright," he said. She listened as his steps retreated, glanced over her shoulder to ensure he'd really gone. The slamming of her front door was proof enough of that.

She touched her lips, fingers tapping along the seam. The swirl in her belly swiftly gave way to dread.

Fucking hell, what did they just do?

Chapter 15

Keiran

EVERYTHING HURT. HE'D been going at it the last hour or so, and finally, his body said enough. The gym was mostly empty on a Sunday, so he could wallow in the pain as he basically flopped onto his back, body coated in sweat, muscles screaming. Not that it mattered. Surely, he wouldn't be the first person to just lie on his back like this in the gym, like his spine was now fused to the floor, and he'd never get back up again.

He just needed to lay here a bit. Not think about sugary kisses. Definitely not dwell on hands that held his head in place to deliver more of the same sweet kisses he was totally not thinking about. She'd taken charge of that kiss, had steered it into something more intense, and Keiran hadn't minded at all. It was so hot following her lead.

Dammit! Clearly, his intense workout hadn't tired him out enough because sure enough, his brain went there, tossing in the feel of her body against his as an added fun bonus.

They hadn't spoken in a week since the world's most ill-timed kiss, but they'd have to eventually. It was already April. There were shower details to finalize. They had to pull this off. Eric and Ava deserved the best. Then, the wedding after that. Avoiding each other forever wasn't feasible. Keiran didn't even want to—that was all Cherisse. He wanted to explore where that kiss had been about to go. If they'd made it to the couch, he suspected they'd catch the damn thing on fire with the heat that had been rolling off them both.

"Yo. What you doing, man?"

Keiran opened his eyes and stared up at his best friend. Scott was frowning down at him as he wiped away his workout sweat with a towel, two bottles of water cradled against his side.

"Taking a nap. Contemplating life. You know, the usual."

Scott dropped down next to Keiran, placing one of the bottles near him. "What's going on with you? You were wailing on that punching bag like it insulted your mother or something."

Keiran blew out a breath, cheeks puffing up as he exhaled. He hadn't told Scott about the kiss yet. He'd told Maxine. Well, more like she'd pried it out of him. His twin had a knack for that.

"Nothing, I'm good. Just blowing off some steam."

"Uh-huh," Scott said, voice heavy with disbelief.

Scott and Maxine were way too in tune with his moods; it was annoying and yet sort of comforting, knowing that they knew him so well. They were two of the most important people in his circle, and he knew he could trust them to offer up advice, tell him like it is, hold nothing back.

He should just blurt it out, get it over with. Scott was his boy, his best friend. They held each other's secrets safe. It shouldn't be so hard to answer him honestly. Scott already figured there was something there with him and Cherisse, at least on Keiran's end anyway. Cherisse had been into the kiss. Her reaction didn't lie—she'd kissed him back, enthusiastically—but her actions after were loud and clear. Regret.

Scott watched him intently, sipping his water, waiting, trying to wear him down into spilling.

"I kissed Cherisse. Not sure how to process it yet? It's been a long week," he said, creakily getting to his feet. Damn, he'd really gone too hard. He needed to get home and rest before people descended onto his back yard. His mother was throwing Maxi a welcome home BBQ. A bit late after the fact, but any excuse to feed and entertain people.

Keiran had been roped into DJing, which would be a simple laptop and playlist affair. He wasn't inclined to do anything else.

Scott spewed cold water all over Keiran. "Holy shit. When? What'd she do? Why the hell didn't you tell me this before?"

His own fault, really. He could have timed that better. After wiping at the water trickling down his neck, Keiran spilled the whole story, snickering as Scott's face went through a range of emotions. A smirk at the dancing, waggled brows at Cherisse's challenging words and the kissing, then pursed lips when Keiran got to the not-so-great end.

"Ah, well. She was right there with you with the kissing, escalating things too. That's got to count for something." Scott sounded way more confident than Keiran felt.

"She thinks it's a mistake."

"Did she say that?" Not out loud, but Keiran just knew. Plus, she was avoiding him. "There could still be hope," Scott insisted. "Or, I don't know, maybe she just hates your guts even more now."

Hope. Something Keiran didn't want to allow to grow. They headed for the showers while Scott continued to theorize on Cherisse needing some time to process.

BY THE TIME HE GOT home, it was almost noon. His mother had been blowing up his phone because guests were set to arrive at 1 p.m. as if they ever would. Most of his family worked on Trini time, which meant the guests wouldn't show up until two at the earliest.

He needed to figure out how to come at this Cherisse situation. Should he approach her? Be the one to reach out first, so they could stop avoiding this and just talk about it? He shoved all that away. Right now, his main focus was a power nap, if his mother would let him be.

His niece greeted him at the door, Scooby trailing behind, tail wagging. "Uncle Keiran!"

"Hey, sweetie."

Leah grabbed his hand, dragging him inside. "The pretty lady brought cupcakes!" she announced, thick plaits swinging as she jumped up and down excitedly. Keiran stiffened. Pretty lady with cupcakes could be anyone; it didn't have to mean Cherisse. Yes, he recalled his mother's casual mention of this very BBQ, but had she extended an official invitation and not mentioned it?

Leah led them towards the kitchen just as Maxine swept out with a tray of food. "Finally! Go set up the music before I have to hear another grumble about it."

He gently slipped his hand out of Leah's. "Is she here?"

Maxine didn't ask who he meant. "Yes, with her mom."

"A heads-up text would've been nice."

Maxine shrugged. "I was busy. Just get your laptop and set up. Don't go in there."

He ignored Maxine, who rolled her eyes and gestured for Leah to follow her outside. Taking several deep, calming breaths, he pushed into the kitchen, not quite believing Cherisse was really here, but of course, she was. After ignoring him all week—except to discuss party planning—she was leaning against the counter, laughing with his mother. In that split second before she turned and caught sight of him, Keiran drank in her laugh, genuine and loud. He adored it.

Her laughter died away, causing his mother's gaze to shift to him. "I'm setting up the music. I promise."

"Good. Let me see if Devon got enough ice. I swear, just because I didn't give him a precise headcount, he's trippin' over how many bags to get."

As soon as his mother breezed out of the kitchen, Keiran demanded, "What are you doing here?"

"Your mother invited us."

"I didn't think you'd come, considering."

Her cheeks reddened. Her hand kept plucking at the skirt of her maxi dress. It was sleeveless and yellow, with little blue flowers. Cute. She was always cute. And sexy. And bossy. Especially when grabbing the back of his head to kiss him harder. He needed to redirect his thoughts right now.

"Look, you know your mother. I couldn't refuse her invitation. My mother would also think it weird if I did."

"You've been avoiding me, and then you just what? Expected to show up like nothing happened?" No point in wasting time on small talk. He was addressing this now.

"Yes. With good reason. I know I said what I said."

Do it. The challenge had been clear.

"Ask, and ye shall receive," he said calmly as if the very notion of her being here didn't have him on edge. Any one of his family members could walk in. It wasn't the best place to have this talk, but she'd stepped into his domain. He wasn't letting this chance slip by. He leaned against the counter, letting his gym bag slip to the floor so he could fold his arms and wait.

"Why didn't you tell me you'd be here?" he asked the same time as she blurted, "It was a mistake."

And there it was, just like clockwork. "Your mouth's saying one thing, but, Cherry, the way you're staring at *my* mouth is singing a different tune."

Her eyes snapped up to his. She opened her mouth, clamped it shut, chewed her lip as she glared at him, then finally said, "Don't call me that. We're definitely not at nickname tier yet. Look, I got caught up in the moment. That's it. What's your excuse for wanting to kiss *me?*"

He shrugged. "I've always wondered what it would be like. Kissing you." He let his voice go low. "Gotta say, my imagination didn't prepare me for any of it. Don't think I'll look at red velvet cake the same again."

Her eyes shifted to the dessert box, resting next to her on the counter. He hadn't even noticed it. Cherisse was all he saw the minute he'd entered the kitchen.

"I didn't think this through," she muttered.

"Neither did I," he admitted. He'd seen a moment, felt the tension swirling between them. He was certain he hadn't imagined it, so he'd taken a leap. The kiss would change their dynamic, had already done that. So much for that truce. He hadn't given a second thought to what came after the kiss.

Cherisse huffed out a breath. "Let's just forget it happened, okay?"

Like he could. Like it was so simple. There was no forgetting. Not for him. "Why did you let me kiss you?"

Her mouth worked open and closed, but she didn't say anything. It would be amusing, except Keiran was in pain and wanted to just hide out in his room. Or the studio, where he could listen to the rough cut of her track again and remember every minute detail of that kiss. He moved to close the space between them because why not? Why not make it worse by getting close enough to drink in her scent?

The kitchen door swung open, and Cherisse's mother swept in, effectively destroying their moment, a huge smile on her face until she landed on Keiran. Her smile vanished completely as she said, "Keiran." As if the letters of his name left a bad taste in her mouth.

"Mrs. Gooding. Nice to see you." It wasn't, but Keiran had been raised to always be polite to elders, even if they didn't follow that same rule.

Mrs. Gooding had certainly made no secret about her feelings towards him. She obviously believed the rumors too, but Keiran knew she was also protective of her daughters and had incredibly high standards for them. In her mind, he'd been lumped into Sean Daley's category and didn't deserve a lick of her time or Cherisse's. But she was civil when his mother was around.

Not so much now.

He stepped back from Cherisse, and her mother dismissed him with a flick of her honey brown locks as she turned to her daughter. "There's someone I want you to meet."

Cherisse's mouth pursed. "Who?"

"Don't do that with your face, it's unbecoming. Let's not dismiss him until you meet him. He's good-looking, polite, and a pediatrician, which means he's good with kids. Sheryl assures me he's a nice young man. Respectable."

Mrs. Gooding punctuated that last word by looking right at Keiran. He continued to say nothing but sent her a winning smile because he wasn't going to satisfy her by letting on that he was in any way affected by her insinuation that he wasn't respectable.

And did she say, pediatrician? Keiran had a cousin who fit that description, but shit, it couldn't be. Jerome *was* all those things but also gay, which wasn't a known fact in his family. In fact, he was the only one Jerome had outright told, as far as he knew. To everyone else, it was hushed speculation or downright cluelessness.

Cherisse spared Keiran a brief glance before grabbing up the dessert box. "I need to take these cupcakes outside." She breezed by her mother, who shot Keiran another look like he was to blame for Cherisse's reluctance.

In this instance, a tiny part of him hoped he was.

Chapter 16

Cherisse

KEIRAN'S EYES WERE on her, burning into her skin.

Calm. Cool. Collected.

Her mantra since she'd sat down across from Jerome, who had awkwardly turned out to be Keiran's cousin. She should have aborted the whole thing then, but her masochistic streak wouldn't let her, apparently, and she couldn't help comparing Keiran and Jerome, even though the only thing they had in common was their smooth brown skin. Jerome was clean-shaven, and right now, Keiran had more stubble going on, which wasn't ideal for her wayward thoughts.

Soft. It looked so soft.

Fuck.

Cherisse kept up her nods and smiles, occasionally joining in when she was asked something, but barely. Too caught up in her thoughts. This wasn't her. She was good at this, great at making small talk, came with the job when you had to put yourself and your business out there. But she was too aware of Keiran stationed behind his laptop as he cranked out song after song. And the damn kiss that hung between them.

Then dessert.

It was her fault, really. She hadn't even thought about the cupcakes when she'd decided to make them. Red velvet. Fucking hell.

Don't think I'll look at red velvet cake the same again.

Keiran's eyes had gone wide when his mother opened the dessert box, then that smirk. God, how she hated it, and yet, it sent a flash of heat through her body, had her remembering those lips moving against hers. He sure as hell wasn't helping by swiping his finger through the frosting, sucking said finger into his mouth, then saying, smile still firmly in place, "My fave."

"Hey, cuz." Jerome's drawl ripped her away from the memory of that damn finger disappearing into that sinful mouth.

When had he left his DJ post? And did he have an endless supply of those short-sleeved t-shirts that always seemed to fit him just right? This one was blue and snug, just at the curve of his biceps. Keiran sank into the chair opposite her. Cherisse could feel her mother's displeasure from here. Everyone had so obviously been told to leave them alone. Not a single person had come over to join them after they'd sat. It was weird, being put on display like this, but Jerome had taken it in stride, so she'd rolled with it too. Keiran clearly didn't give a shit.

"'Sup, J?"

"Nothing much, just enjoying the company of this lovely lady here."

"Hmm," Keiran hummed, leaning back in his chair, hands resting on his stomach. They exchanged a loaded look that Cherisse had no means of deciphering, then Keiran said, "Lucky man."

"From what I hear, you've been lucky too." Jerome grinned. "How's the party planning going?"

"Great." He fixed her with that infuriatingly amused stare. "Our mouths are getting quite the workout..."

Cherisse choked on her potato salad, face surely turning red as she coughed. She reached for her glass of lime juice and took a huge swig.

"...from all the talking about our plans," Keiran finished casually.

"Whoa, you okay?"

Cherisse waved off Jerome's concern, shooting Keiran a glare over her glass. She was going to murder him. He shrugged, broad shoulders making his t-shirt way more appealing than it needed to be.

Her patience shattered, and she jumped up, chair nearly toppling over behind her. "I need to, uh...bathroom! Excuse me." Not exactly the smoothest exit. Damn Keiran and his...everything. How dare he? She just couldn't be around him anymore.

In the bathroom, fingers gripping the sink, she stared at her reflection in the mirror. She'd have some explaining to do. But what could she even say?

"Get it together, girl," she told her mirror image. Now wasn't the time to have a meltdown because of that kiss. She could be cool. Go on like it didn't mean a damn thing. Because it *didn't*. She'd gotten caught up in the music and the dancing. That was it.

Her phone vibrated in her dress pocket, and she took it out, grateful to see Remi's smiling face staring back at her.

"How's it going?"

Cherisse looked around the bathroom where she was currently hiding out and considered lying, glossing over her current situation. She hadn't told Remi about the kiss yet, but she could really use her friend's soothing right now.

"Well, I'm hiding out in the King bathroom because Keiran and I kissed last week, and now, it's a tad awkward. The way he was licking that damn cupcake icing is obscene, and mummy basically tossed his cousin at me, which is beyond fucking awkward, and I dunno if I want to throttle Keiran, or...or..." She hadn't meant to say that last part. Dammit.

"What!" Remi shrieked so loudly Cherisse winced, pulling the phone from her ear. "Keiran kissed you?"

"Well, the vibe was there, and I may have thrown down a challenge, and he took it up, and kissing happened?"

"Wait. Hold up. What you mean, you threw down a challenge?"

"My exact words were 'Do it'? I, yeah, I don't even know. In my defense, there was music and a lot of sugar in my system at the time, so I, maybe, no, definitely got caught up in the moment? But it meant nothing." She barely sounded convincing to her own ears—she could imagine Remi's *I'm not buying this* face.

She was still unsure about what had prompted her to drop that not-so-subtle dare. She could've pretended the tension wasn't there. Could have pulled back. Something. Anything but uttering those two words that propelled everything into motion. She wondered what would have happened if that damn timer hadn't gone off.

"Cherisse."

"I know."

"You and Keiran kissed."

"I *know*."

"So, do you plan to kiss him again?"

"No!" Her lapse in judgment wasn't something she planned to repeat. Ever. There would be no more kissing Keiran. No matter what he'd revealed to her in that studio, it didn't mean she wanted to get caught up in his charms. Been there, did that with Sean. The door rattling almost made Cherisse drop her phone. Shit, how long had she been in here? "Talk more later, Rems, gotta go."

She pocketed her phone and opened the door. Keiran was on the other side because her life was basically a joke now. "Good to know you didn't fall in." His chin jerked at the toilet, and Cherisse felt her face get hot.

"Fuck off." Cherisse stepped out, closing the door behind her. Most men were put off by her potty mouth. Not Keiran, apparently, because it only stretched his grin wider.

"Bye-bye, truce."

She was an adult and refused to get pissed off enough to lose her cool. Not today, Mr. King. "We're going to keep going. Get this party planned. Not kill each other, and *definitely* no more kissing. Now, if you'll excuse me, your cousin's waiting."

"You're not interested in Jerome, so why bother?"

The nerve of this man. "He's good-looking, funny, and a pediatrician." She waved three fingers in his face. "Sounds interesting to me."

"I'm at least two of those things."

Cherisse rolled her eyes. "You're not even in the running. Not even a consideration. So, bye." She walked around him, heading back outside, draping her Sugar Queen cool around her.

"Everything okay?" Jerome asked.

It would be. She needed Keiran back where he belonged, as the guy she tolerated for this wedding, nothing more. The shower planning had forced them together, but there wasn't anything that said they had to be friends. Being friendly had made working together easier, which was already throwing things out of order. Adding kissing to the mix had tipped the scales so far over, shit was spilling out everywhere. She had to fix that. She didn't need this added complication in her life.

She mustered up a classic Sugar Queen smile. "Yes, all good."

Chapter 17

Keiran

WEDDINGS WERE USUALLY fun. Free food, drinks, and enough going on that he didn't have to be a scintillating conversationalist. With Dale next to him charming everyone they met, Keiran didn't have to worry about making small talk. Except, Dale had abandoned him to go socialize.

They'd both been invited as a thank you for working on the bride's album, and it wasn't like Keiran didn't know anyone here. He just preferred to get lost in the crowd. A lot of heavy hitters in the music industry were in attendance. Sierra Gale was one of the big-name Trini soca artistes, and she was marrying another major player in the industry, Ricky Simons, a music exec, so the reception was overflowing with the who's who of the local music scene. Keiran had even spied a few regional and foreign artists mingling. But Dale was the god of small talk. Keiran always hung back.

The sit-down dinner portion of the evening was long over, and the vibe had switched over to party mode. Most people were either getting down on the dance floor or schmoozing. Keiran spied Sierra making her way over to him, the long train of her wedding dress trailing behind her. Moments before, she'd been grinding on her new hubby. He had no idea how she'd managed that in her dress.

"Keiran!" She planted a quick kiss on his cheek, mouth spread wide in a toothy grin. "Did I thank you guys for coming? I can't even remember."

"Well, it's been a busy day, so no worries," he assured her. The invite had been thanks enough. A good way to get his mind off of

Cherisse and the kiss, but that had backfired. Being at this wedding dredged up all sorts of feelings. He'd spied an elaborate cupcake tower when they'd entered the venue, and his thoughts had gone right to Cherisse.

"Boy, you tellin' me! I'm glad the stress part is over, and I can have some fun!"

"You look like you're having a time."

She really did. She was radiant in that dress, cheeks flushed from either her blush or happiness or both. Sierra made a stunning bride, hair in loose curls around her face, brown eyes shining every time she glanced over at her husband.

"Oh, I am, and I have so many people to thank for that. Especially a certain life-saver." Her eyes searched the crowd. "She's around somewhere. I called in a cake emergency, and she delivered." She looked back at him. "I think you two even know each other?"

Keiran stiffened. *No.* No damn way. The universe wouldn't be this cruel. But of course, it was. A group of people parted at just that moment, giving Keiran a clear line of sight to the cake table.

She was wearing an orange dress that molded to her curves, hair pulled back in a ponytail, the curled ends bouncing as she nodded along to the music echoing through the venue.

"Oh, there she is!" Sierra went on, waving in Cherisse's direction as if his entire world wasn't being upended by Cherisse in that dress. "My cake person had to cancel last minute. Chickenpox, of all things! I remembered Cherisse because Sean was coming, and...wait. Shit."

That snapped Keiran out of allowing his gaze to trace the outline of Cherisse's hips in that dress. "Sean. As in, Sean Daley. As in..."

"Her ex. Oh damn. I didn't think about that." Sierra was hastily looking around. "I didn't even consider them bumping into each other. I was in crisis mode, and his name jolted me to remember her, and she was so sweet to do this rush job for me that I told her she could bring a plus-one too, in case she felt uncomfortable being here alone. But she came alone."

"I'm sure it's fine."

Keiran wasn't sure of that at all. He had no doubt shit would go down if Sean and Cherisse ran into each other, especially if Sean mentioned that he was working with Keiran. They were keeping that under wraps from everyone, including the press for now, so Keiran felt a smidge less guilty for not telling Cherisse. Getting the album going was a slow process because Sean worked on his own time, but Keiran had been working towards getting at least a teaser sample of the track out there to create some buzz.

"I'm gonna say hi, real quick," he told Sierra, pasting on a smile that he hoped looked genuine enough as he made his way over to her. "Hi." He pulled out his most charming smile, which wasn't reciprocated. Cherisse kept blinking at him as if that would make him disappear. Her open body language from before vanished.

Cherisse tugged on her ponytail, wrapping the ends around her index finger as she frowned at him. "Are you here to make trouble?"

"Why would I do that? Sierra invited Dale and me. We worked on her album. Why do you always think I'm crashing something just because we end up in the same place?"

"I didn't say you crashed." Cherisse fiddled with the cupcake stand, moving the remaining cupcakes around, so they closed up the spaces left by cakes that had already been taken by guests. She kept at it even after all the spaces were filled. Anything to not look at him, it seemed.

He snatched up the cupcake she was pushing around, and finally, her head jerked up. She yanked the cupcake from his hand and plunked it back on the cupcake tower. This was getting ridiculous.

"Where's Jerome? Not as interesting as you'd thought?" He sounded like a jealous fool, which he had zero reason to be, especially knowing Jerome had no real interest in Cherisse, and just because they kissed, he had no claims on her. Cherisse's gaze sharpened like a predator scenting a weakness in her prey's armor. Shit. *Distract, distract, distract.* "You can't keep ignoring this. We've talked around it all week."

"Sierra's request was last-minute, so I didn't extend my plus-one to anyone. Also, we have more important things to discuss than *that.*"

He couldn't agree more. Like the way she'd gripped his head to deepen that kiss, that said she wasn't shy about going after what she wanted. And she had wanted to turn up the heat level. He didn't doubt that for a second. They could definitely discuss that. His eyes dropped to her glossy lips, remembering the feel of them against his.

"Stop." Her voice sounded strangled, pleading. He was playing with fire here, but he took his time sliding his eyes back up to meet hers. "Stop looking at me like...like you..." She swallowed, fiddled with the cloth that covered the cake table.

"Like what, Cherisse?" he whispered.

Her chest rose and fell. "Like you're thinking about it. Like you want to kiss me. Now. Again."

He leaned in. "I am, and I do. Seems you want to, as well."

She shook her head, jaw tight, eyes suddenly ablaze. Like she was telling him he wasn't going to get to her with his blunt confessions. Like she wasn't having any of his shit. This Cherisse—the one who wasn't all smiles and calm, modulated friendly tones, the one who looked like she was thinking about kicking his ass—really got him going. He relished sparring with her.

"Please, you couldn't handle me kissing you again. You think I'm all shook up by that kiss? Well, lemme tell you something, Mr. King, you'd be weak if I really put my back into a kiss."

"Then, do it." He tossed her words right back at her, and what he'd realized about Cherisse was she had a competitive side, and maybe he'd be damned for always pushing those buttons to get her to that point, but he had zero regrets.

Her nostrils flared, and Keiran couldn't help the laugh that escaped. "You are a piece of work," she said. Definitely not a compliment.

"Hey, I'm not the one out here making outlandish claims," he shrugged and secretly enjoyed the moment Cherisse snapped, grabbed his arm, and dragged him away from the chatter and music.

He wasn't prepared for being pressed to a wall in the dimly-lit corridor that led to the bathrooms. Not an ideal place for making out, but if Cherisse didn't care, why should he? Her lip gloss tasted like strawberries, and her tongue tasted like wine.

She tugged at his bottom lip and pressed her body against his. Shit, she'd definitely be able to tell he was hard. These slacks weren't hiding a thing, but Cherisse didn't seem put off by his erection. In fact, sweet God, her hips mimicked the thrust of her tongue against his, and Keiran's hand dipped to her ass. Cherisse arched into his touch, her moans and his steady pants the perfect soundtrack to this moment.

She pulled away too soon, the drag of her teeth on his bottom lip wrenching all the curses he knew from his mouth. She pressed a hand to his chest and said, "Point made." She gestured to his mouth. "Might want to wipe that off. It isn't quite your shade."

God damn. He wiped at his mouth. It was hard to follow her after that, but he refused to remain slumped against this wall, heart racing. The tiny smirk she threw over her shoulder was enough to send him up in flames. But he managed—on slightly wobbly legs—to walk back into the main hall, eyes glued to her swaying hips until he drew up next to her, stopping her forward motion with a gentle hand on her wrist. He needed a drink, preferably water, so he could douse his entire body.

She turned, not dislodging his hand yet, allowing him to keep touching her. To keep drinking her in. She'd pull away soon enough. The guests were occupied on the dance floor, but Cherisse was too aware of public perception to let this go on for too long.

"What's the matter? Cat got your tongue?" she teased.

He found words from somewhere. "If you're calling yourself a cat, then yeah. I'll say so."

One beat, then two. Back to silent stares and racing pulses, he supposed. Or was the beating pulse just him? He couldn't quite tell if Cherisse was as off-balance as he was.

"Well, isn't this cozy?" The deep, mocking, familiar voice was like a splash of cold water on Keiran's face. They both turned to face Sean Daley. Well, fuck.

Chapter 18

Cherisse

CHERISSE KNEW SOMEDAY the sliver of impulsiveness that lurked deep down inside of her would come back to bite her in the ass. She usually liked order, some measure of organization in her life, but her damn rebellious streak was always waiting, ready to drive her to do things she knew she shouldn't.

Case in point: Sean Daley. She'd been warned about him the moment they'd started dating. Cherisse had brushed off the concerns. She'd heard them all. Sean was a good-looking light-skinned black man in the music business, so of course, he'd been pegged as a playboy with women on the side.

Cherisse had rolled her eyes, ignoring her mother's rants about, "Dem redmen and dem feel they too nice and yuh cyah trust dem."

Cherisse had seen women try to be all up under him while they'd been dating, but she'd never thought for one moment he was a cheater just because of his looks. That was ridiculous stereotyping, so she'd ignored the warnings.

Joke was on her, though. Sean *had* been playing her.

He looked the same. Same curls, same bright grin, same square, clean-shaven jaw, perfect for punching. She braced herself before meeting his gaze, unsure of what her reaction would be, wondered if there would be a hint of regret there, in spite of all he'd done to her. They'd been good together, or at least so she'd thought. There was nostalgia rearing up and trying to smother her. She just felt indifferent to his smiling ass and hoped like hell he couldn't tell she'd just been kissing the shit out of the man next to her.

Which she blamed entirely on that streak of rebellion. She calmly removed her wrist from Keiran's hand. No jerking or pulling away guiltily to signal to Sean that this wasn't something she wanted to draw attention to.

"Sean." *Good. Yes. Maintain that calm, even tone, layered with a subtle unspoken, "oh, it's you."*

Sean thrived off of attention—it fueled him. He fed off a hyped crowd when he got on the stage. The more excited the crowd, the more energy he exuded. He was a great performer, engaging. Still an asshole, though.

"Looking nice and rosy," Sean said, smile reaching leering levels.

Cherisse didn't need to be friends with her exes, especially one who'd shown himself to be a lying, cheating dirtbag. Regardless, she wasn't about to make a scene either.

"When you're loving life, it shows, I guess." She smiled back.

"More like loving up on some cake," Sean chuckled, and Cherisse felt Keiran shift next to her.

The thrill of having rocked Keiran's world with that kiss evaporated. Her smile faltered. She'd loved how she looked in this dress when she'd put it on. Yeah, it showed off every bit of thigh and ass, but it had made her feel powerful, sexy. Dangerous curves ahead and all that. Now, Sean's words just made her feel too aware of the bit of weight that had settled on her hips after their breakup that hadn't quite left. It shouldn't matter what he said, but it flashed her back to her insecurities about having the public eye trained on her when they'd dated, and she'd been critiqued for everything.

"What the hell is wrong with you?" Keiran growled.

Sean's head swung his way, looking him up and down. "Just kidding around with an old friend, don't see how that's your business."

"Friend?" Keiran scoffed. "You're not friends. Pretty sure your joke would still be shitty even *if* you'd been friends."

"It's fine." Her voice sounded small.

God, she hated that. So much for Sean not affecting her. And it wasn't fine. She should tell his ass off, but she was too aware of the other guests. Too aware of the last time she'd melted down over his ass. Too aware of her mother's voice warning about appearances and causing a scene. Granted, she'd had a right to get pissed off, but the gossip after? She could have done without. So, she'd been hyperaware ever since then about not getting caught up in bacchanal. She should just walk away.

"It's not fine! This asshole doesn't get talk to you like that." Keiran's voice drew looks. Awesome. More gossip fodder.

"So, you her bodyguard now?" Sean moved into Keiran's space, their chests almost touching. "You've been holding out on us, Keiran. That why you've been acting like a little bitch all this time? Didn't you just make some shitty joke about her not too long ago?"

Cherisse frowned. What did Sean mean about Keiran acting like a bitch? It made no sense. Keiran's jaw clenched, and his hand landed on Sean's chest and shoved him back. "Not someone who got time to deal with your punk ass."

Shit. She'd never seen Keiran like this. Lips twisted, stance broadcasting he was ready to rumble if needed. This wouldn't end well.

"Listen, it's *fine*. Just leave it—" she tried, but neither of them was paying her any attention now.

"You put your fucking hands on me, man?" Sean said loudly. "Daddy dearest isn't going to like that." Heads turned their way, murmurs growing louder. Wouldn't be long before someone started recording all this on their phone. None of them needed this to escalate into them becoming some social media meme.

"Apologize, and we're good," Keiran snarled.

"Nah, is a joke. Relax, hoss." Sean brushed Keiran off and turned to Cherisse. "Might wanna tell your guard dog to stand down...what the fuck!"

Keiran had a fistful of Sean's shirt, which prompted Sean to shove Keiran back into the cake table. Shit! The cupcakes toppled off of the tower, rolling across the table, some falling right off the edge to the floor, as Keiran's back slammed into it. Hard.

"Stop!" Cherisse cried. They were too busy grappling to listen. She looked around at the stunned faces, and *fuuuuck,* there were already phones being held up to capture everything.

"Jesus Christ, just stop, dammit!" It was a bad move the minute she stepped closer, tried to pry Keiran away. Should have known the minute Sean started spewing something about "pussy" and "sweet" that it would take a turn for the worse, but her flaming cheeks weren't enough to dissuade her from trying. Keiran's back was to her, and his arm reared back to either shove Sean or punch him. Shit. She stepped back quickly, letting his arm go, completely forgetting the table was at her back until she crashed into it.

Fuck. Her hip took the brunt of it. She vaguely thought that was going to leave a mark as she went down hard, knees scraping against the floor as her palms met the ground.

She actually considered just staying down there. Her hip throbbed, and her knees felt raw and less a few layers of skin. Shiny brown shoes hastily appeared in front of her.

"Jesus, Cherisse." Dale stooped down, eyes filled with worry. He looked over her head a split second—Cherisse could still hear the scuffle behind her—then looked back to her and asked, "You alright?"

"Just please." She didn't know if he could hear her. She didn't even want to lift her head right now to see the faces looking back at her. She was too embarrassed. "Take me home."

"Of course." He helped her to her feet.

She didn't look back at Keiran or Sean, ignored the guests around her. She just wanted to get home and sleep forever.

"YOU SURE YOU'RE GOOD by yourself?" Dale asked for the millionth time.

Her hip twinged a bit, the scraped knee throbbed, too, but she'd live. The minor physical bruises were less on her mind than her embarrassment. She'd stayed away from her phone the entire drive, certain she'd find something online already. She'd rather not know right now. Shower and sleep were her main plans.

"You should go before that becomes more than a drizzle." The sky looked ready to open up, the constant patter slowly turning into heavier drops. "I'm good, really." Remi was out and not sure to be back tonight. The small bag she'd had draped over her shoulder was the one she used for overnighting, so Cherisse wasn't entirely sure if this date Remi was going on involved after-hours activities. She hadn't asked, and Remi hadn't volunteered any information. She expected a text either way, at some point.

Dale looked uncertain. "I'm going to kill him, I swear," he mumbled but gestured for her to go inside, which she happily obliged, watching from the window as he ran back to his car.

She wanted to bury herself beneath her covers and not come out again for a while. Just have Remi push some food into her room, and she'd be good to go. Except, rent didn't pay itself, and her job couldn't be done while she hid away in her room.

She decided to shower and tend to her boo-boos. She'd been right about her hip—there was a small bluish mark forming there when she checked in the shower. Her knee wasn't in bad shape, just some scrapes she cleaned with Dettol, gritting her teeth at the burn.

A cupcake-decorated bandage slapped over the knee, and she was all good.

At some point, she'd dozed off in front the TV but the constant plings from her phone jerked her awake. The pounding of the rain on the roof had been a soothing rhythm to help get her to sleep, but her message notifications certainly weren't that. Cherisse squinted down at her phone. The time showed 11 p.m. Just an hour after she'd left the wedding. The text she'd figured would be from Remi wasn't.

Keiran: Cherisse I'm so sorry. I just wanna know you're ok. I didn't know you fell until...after

He'd sent a bunch more before that. She scrolled back up, checking the time of the first one. Not too long after Dale had whisked her away. She considered ignoring him, but her fingers flew over the screen.

Cherisse: I'm fine.

She'd said that a lot tonight. Three bouncing dots appeared immediately. He'd clearly been waiting on her response.

Keiran: I...ok uh...I'm outside. You didn't answer before and I got worried so I came by. And I know you probably don't wanna see me now but...

Cherisse: WHAT! YOU'RE OUTSIDE?

She hadn't expected that, especially not with the way the weather was raging out there. Again, this night. Could she get back her balance at all?

Keiran: Please. And it's cold out here

She considered refusing. Leaving his ass out in the cold rain would serve him right, but she was already moving to the door, replying to his text while she did that, aware of her ratty shorts and equally worn sleep top. The thin straps were so stretched out. Whatever, she didn't need to impress Keiran.

Ugh. She was going to regret this, but she could hand him his ass to his face, and that would be satisfying, at least.

Chapter 19

Keiran

SHE LOOKED PISSED OFF and ready to run him from her front door, but Keiran was too busy being thankful she was alright. He'd known she wasn't seriously hurt—only after he'd been forcibly separated from Sean, he'd realized she was gone. He'd been filled in on how she'd tried to part them and the fall, and that didn't diminish his concern. He'd also obviously embarrassed her, so he had a lot to apologize for.

He shivered as the rain howled at his back. He'd run towards her apartment, caught without an umbrella again, so he was soaked.

She glared at him, eyes settling on his bruised cheek. Sean had gotten in a shot after Keiran's punch. His hand was still twinging from connecting with Sean's jaw.

"This is emotional blackmail."

"What?"

"You show up here in a goddamn storm, looking like a drowned puppy, so of course, I feel sorry for you and let you in. Too guilty to turn you away in this weather."

Shit. She was right. He hadn't considered any of that. Obviously, he wasn't thinking anything through tonight. He was cold and shivering, and it would be hell to see to drive in this, but maybe he could just wait it out in his car.

"I'll go. I didn't mean to guilt you into anything. I'm sorry," he repeated.

"Just get your ass inside, Jesus, fuck."

For the second time, he stood inside her apartment, dripping water in front of her door.

"Just fucking stay there."

He didn't move. She obviously wasn't letting him drip water through her place like last time. Not that he blamed her. He was lucky she'd even let him in.

"I'm truly sorry," he said again as she returned with a big fluffy towel that she tossed at him.

"Yeah, you said."

"I really am. It should've never escalated to that extreme, but Sean shouldn't have spoken to you like that."

"I'm a big girl. I can take it."

Cherisse had looked stricken by that asshole's words. Sean's jab about Keiran's careless words added fuel to the fire and set him off. Because Sean wasn't wrong. Sure, he'd made the public apology she'd asked for. Didn't make what he'd said any less shitty.

She sat down on the couch, cross-legged, and gestured to the floor. He wasn't getting any dry clothes either, so he'd have to ride out this storm soaked.

"How's the face?"

"Little sore," he admitted. He stretched out the fingers on his right hand. "Hand's a little twingey, but not too painful."

"You should put some ice on it, but my ass isn't getting up to do it." Her steely gaze pinned him in place. "You should've just walked away. I haven't even checked social media at all, but I can imagine what everyone's saying. I'm not trying to blow up my career because of you two. Sean likes the attention. I doubt this is the kind of thing you want sticking to you when it comes to your work."

It wasn't. Shit. Sierra would be within her rights to blacklist him. She'd probably never want to work with DK Productions again. He hoped this wouldn't lose them business. He hadn't even thought of that in the heat of things.

"I messed up." He scrubbed a hand over his face, blocking out Cherisse's face for a moment. When he brought her in his sights again, she was looking at the TV.

She sighed deeply. "I didn't ask you to come to my rescue, and definitely not like that."

"I know. I wasn't thinking about anything but shutting his ass up."

"Yeah, I won't lie to you, his words hurt. Not because I'm ashamed of any additional pounds on my ass, but he just knows how to pick at my insecurities and get under my skin. I'm so angry at you right now, but myself, too." She ducked her head, finger picking at the hem of her top. "I thought he couldn't make me feel so small ever again, but I was wrong, clearly."

"Fuck him. He didn't deserve you."

She gave him a sidelong glance, eyes flashing. "And what? You think you do?"

"I never said that." He truly hadn't fought Sean with any ulterior motive. He'd just wanted the guy to shut the fuck up and not hurt Cherisse. Okay, maybe he'd also not wanted him to let on about them working together. Which, if he told her about now, wouldn't go over well.

"Did you fight him thinking, what? I'd fall into your arms with gratitude?"

"Jesus, Cherisse. I wouldn't do that."

She shrugged. "Well, Keiran, I didn't expect you to fight a guy in the middle of a wedding, but here we are." The sudden boom of thunder made them both jump. "Even the weather can't get its shit together tonight," she mumbled. She jabbed a finger his way. "You shouldn't have punched him, but I know you were sticking up for me, so thanks, I guess."

She was letting him stay. He was grateful for that. This weather would be a bitch to drive safely in. He wasn't keen to try. She was allowing him to hang around a bit, and that was fine by him. He'd ruined enough things tonight. He wasn't about to do the same with this.

KEIRAN AWOKE, TO CHERISSE snuggling into him, chest rising and falling as she slept. For a moment, he thought he was still dreaming, but it came back to him. The *Cat Mom* t-shirt he wore was a good indication.

She'd finally taken pity on him and offered him the biggest-sized sleep shirt she had, that still fit snugly across his chest. Pants were a no, so he'd wrapped the big towel around his still-wet boxer briefs. He'd tossed his shirt and slacks into the dryer while Cherisse had kept her head facing the TV. Until she sighed and allowed him onto the couch, all the way on the other end from her.

At some point, they'd both drifted off and had gotten wrapped up in each other like this. The rain hadn't let up, the pounding on the roof practically drowning out the TV. Could explain why they'd both knocked out. Rainy nights were perfect for sleeping. The steady thrum of it against the roof always made snoozing easier.

He should go before Cherisse woke up and realized he was still here. But, the damn rain and wind howling like a banshee. Still not a great idea to drive through it.

He maneuvered so he could retrieve his phone out of his pocket without waking her. It was a couple of minutes to 1 a.m. As unlikely as that seemed, he hoped the weather would take a miraculous turn for the better. No telling when Remi would come strolling in. He didn't think Remi would appreciate him being here, especially if she'd caught wind of his foolishness tonight.

He checked his phone. Several missed calls and texts from his father. He was definitely ignoring those for now. In fact, he was ignoring all social media too. That was best left for morning after he'd had some sleep. He hoped like hell his family and friends hadn't seen any of his brawl with Sean. He didn't want to have to explain any of it.

He looked back at Cherisse, stared at the faint dusting of freckles decorating the bridge of her nose. There was even a smattering of them on her shoulders. The urge to trace them, follow the dots into some sort of discernable pattern, was great. He kept his hands to himself. That way led to trouble.

"Shit." The softly muttered curse jerked his gaze away from her arms. Eyes open, she blinked up at him. "Fucking hell, I fell asleep on you. Were you watching me sleep this whole time?" She scooted back a bit, rubbing her eyes.

"Not the entire time," he admitted sheepishly.

"Because that's not weird at all," she said around a jaw-cracking yawn as she stretched her arms over her head, her top molding around her breasts. For the first time, Keiran noted she wasn't wearing a bra. The worn material of her top did nothing to hide a damn thing. He tore his eyes away from her nipples, poking against the top.

"I wasn't being a creeper, promise. I should go," he added even as he'd all but told himself moments ago that wasn't a good idea. He was also way too aware of her soft thighs in those shorts.

"Wait it out. I refuse to be labeled a completely heartless bitch to send you out in some freak storm weather like this." She got off the couch to peer out the window. "Looks real bad out there."

Keiran was proud of himself. His eyes didn't linger on her ass. He merely snuck a quick look. But when Cherisse returned to the couch, he maybe had some of that lingering heat in his eyes because the concern melted away as she cocked her head at him.

"You're doing it again."

"What?"

"Let's not pretend like you don't know." Her tongue swiped out and wet her bottom lip, and well, that was just unfair. Had she done that on purpose, or was it just an unconscious nervous move?

He did know what he was doing. She wasn't wrong. He wanted to kiss her. She wore the soft and sleepy look well, but it was the concern he'd seen in her eyes that made him want to risk it all for another kiss. She'd actually cared about him going out in this rainy mess, even after all the shit he'd done tonight. But he needed to dial it down a bit. He didn't want Cherisse feeling uncomfortable around him like he'd pounce on her at any moment.

"Sorry," he muttered, all too aware of his tight boxer briefs beneath the towel. He should've tossed those into the dryer too, but it would've been too strange sitting on Cherisse's couch bare-assed, even with the towel. "I probably wouldn't survive another one of your 'putting my back into it' kisses, anyway."

"You sure won't." The little smile quirking up the corner of her mouth made him hard, promised so many naughty things.

Her hand drifted up slowly, hovered near his face as if giving him time to move away. Why would he ever? Her hand brushed his cheek, and Keiran didn't move, barely released a breath in case any sudden movements would jolt her to her senses. Make her realize what she was doing. He wasn't sure what was happening right now.

"What are you doing?" he whispered, not wanting to shatter whatever this was but compelled to ask.

"I don't know," she admitted. Her thumb moved on from his cheek to the corner of his mouth.

"Something you'll regret tomorrow?" His brain wouldn't stop trying to find ways to ruin this for him.

"I don't know," Cherisse repeated. "I'm still angry with you, but curious too, I guess. To see if lightning strikes three times."

He had no idea what had brought this on. He didn't care. Any misgivings he had vanished as soon as her soft lips brushed his. The hand that had been caressing his face slipped down to his neck. Keiran let her take the lead. He was on board for the ride. She could take him wherever she wanted. At this point, he was going with whatever.

That didn't last long, though. The minute her tongue swept in and deepened the kiss, he was sending her backward on the couch. Her leg wrapped around him, strong thighs tugging his body forward, so he was up close and personal now. Kiss turning frantic, tongue seeking the wetness of his mouth, hips tilted up until there was no way Cherisse couldn't feel his response to her.

He was pressed up between her legs, and fuck if he couldn't stop himself from thrusting forward, the same way their tongues were going at it in each other's mouth right now. He slid his hand in her hair, gently tilting her head back so he could get at her throat to pepper her skin with light kisses.

"Motherfucking fuck." The curses spewed from her lips. Her thigh rode higher on his hips, threatening to dislodge his towel. He let his hand slip down to grab a handful of her ass, and he found bare skin.

Oh, sweet Christ.

Her shorts had ridden up until a good portion of her behind was hanging out of it. Bless this soft cotton and her thong, truly. Easy access. He kneaded her soft flesh as his mouth roamed back up to hers. He wanted to go further, push her top down so he could tongue her nipple until she screamed, but all in due time. If she allowed it. He was still braced for her to call mistake on this and shut everything down. But he was milking this for everything he could, as long as she was allowing it.

"Why'd it have to be you?" she groaned into his mouth. "God, the first guy to make me feel like this. Been so long, and it's you? God help me."

"Sorry to disappoint," he said dryly.

He wasn't annoyed by her words. He was on fire, and so hard. He had Cherisse's hands on him. He. Did. Not. Care. He understood what she was saying. It had been some time since he'd been with anyone like this too. It was blowing his mind that he had Cherisse under him like this at all. That her hand was reaching between their straining bodies to grasp him under the towel.

"Wet," she said. "Not just me, your briefs. You should take them off." God, he was going to die before he really had a chance to savor her. She molded him through the wet material, and his short-circuiting brain wondered if this was her revenge. Murdering him by touch. "Just don't stop," she panted. "Don't stop touching and doing what you're doing," she instructed.

"So bossy." He grinned down at her.

She narrowed her eyes. "What'd I just say?"

He pulled back. The leg around his waist fell away. "Hold that thought." He made quick work of the towel but left his wet briefs on, enjoying the way Cherisse watched him, teeth pressed into her bottom lip, eyes heavy-lidded with lust as they made a slow perusal of his body. It made him wonder if he should have just gone for it anyway.

He returned the favor, drinking her in as she lay there. Her hair spilled out around her head. One flimsy strap of her top had fallen down her shoulder, which led his gaze right to the breasts that pressed softly against her top. His hands had helped her already ridden-up shorts along so much that they were bunched up, pressing the material snugly between her legs and, fuck him, it wasn't hiding shit. He bit his lips, imagining his mouth right there, drinking, lapping, sucking...

"Fuck, you're gorgeous."

"Yeah?" Her hand moved along her thigh to rest right between her legs. Her middle finger caressed herself through the shorts, and that settled it. This was how he would die.

He hadn't expected her to be so brazen. She was proving what he'd known all this time. Cherisse wasn't as sweet as everyone thought.

"Where's Jello?"

The hand between her legs stilled. "Really?"

"What? It's a legit question. It's weird if he just shows up to watch." Keiran loved pets but not *that* much.

Cherisse bit her lip but didn't quite hold back her smile. "That really the thing you care about right now? The most important question you have? Because I don't have a clue where Jello got to."

"No, not the most important question," he agreed, eyes jumping from her hand to the way her teeth dug into her lips, amused smile gone, replaced with need. "What do you want? At this moment, what do you want, Cherisse? God, you could ask for anything right now, and I just...tell me." Dangerous words, but oh so accurate. The power was in her hands. He was enthralled by the motions of that finger, and Cherisse was enjoying this. Her eyes reflected her smugness.

"Anything?" she asked. Eyelids lowered until a gleam of golden brown remained. "Take me upstairs, Keiran. That's what I want right now."

Chapter 20

Cherisse

THE WORDS TUMBLED OUT as the throbbing grew between her legs. She was really going for this? Yes, yeah, she was. Horniness had definitely clouded her judgment. This was Keiran, after all, and she'd just asked him to take her upstairs, where they'd take this teasing further. She shushed the part of her that was trying to tell her what a bad idea this was. That it wasn't worth the regrets that would descend later, the mess they'd have to wade through. That she was still angry with him over the fight.

But, Keiran was looking at her with a whole load of want in his eyes, and Cherisse hadn't had anyone look at her like that in a while. She was relishing every bit of heat in those dark eyes. The way his gaze fixed on her hand moving between her legs made her feel more powerful than she'd ever felt lately. Especially after Sean and his shit. The fucking asshole.

"Are you sure?" he croaked. His palm kept rubbing against his thigh. Was he aware he was doing that? She allowed herself a wicked smile. Either he was trying to stop from touching himself, or he was imagining taking over for her hand. She was good with either. The idea of them getting off together like that had her body growing hotter. That was new. She'd never thought she'd be turned on by that, masturbating in front of someone, but oh, she could visualize it clearly now.

"That it's a good idea? No," she admitted. "That I want to? Yes. So, do you want to fuck? Yes, or no?"

He swallowed. She grinned. "Yes," he said. "Condoms? Please say you have condoms. I know I said I'd do anything, but driving in that wetness isn't my idea of fun."

"I do." Remi insisted they keep restocking, whether they were getting any use out of them or not. *Be prepared* was both their mottos. "Besides, there's more fun wetness to drive into right here, so..."

Keiran snorted. "That was awful."

"But oh, so true." She winked, ready to see this through. She wasn't prepared for Keiran swooping her up in his arms. She blinked at him as she hung on, the hand she'd been using to pleasure herself digging into his shoulder as he held her, waiting.

"Tell me where I'm going?"

The short trek upstairs to her bedroom was ample time for sense to prevail, but when Keiran deposited her on the bed and began stripping out of her sleep shirt and those ain't-hiding-shit wet briefs, any lingering hesitations went right outside into the pounding rain. *Holy Jesus.*

"Fucking hell, dude, what the fuck?"

She'd seen him shirtless before, but now there was no towel to block her view. Her eyes flitted from the muscles bunching in his arms to the pecs she was more than eager to take a bite out of, to his nipples, dark against all that smooth brown skin. Her tongue was eager to trace those abs, and *Jesus, take the wheel,* her gaze slipped lower to his hard length. He was primed and ready. His hand gripping himself as he watched her ogling him made her press her legs together to ease the throbbing.

The thirst was real. She was ready to get down there and take all of him in her mouth.

"I swear, that filthy mouth of yours does things to me." He sounded like he was smirking. Damned if she knew with her eyes fixed on his hand as he kept up his lazy strokes, up and down, with a twist at the head.

"Oh, I'll show you filthy," she promised. "Get over here." She let her eyes trail back up to his face. Yup, he was smirking, head tilted to the side as he continued palming himself. He didn't move.

Oh, so he wanted to play right now? He would regret that. She grabbed the hem of her top and pulled it off, then got rid of her shorts until she was just in her thong. Ah, now she had his attention because it wasn't long before she had a face full of bobbing dick. She looked up as he stood over her.

"Ready or not," she taunted.

They were too worked up to go slow, kisses wild, hands grasping, cupping, and kneading every bit of flesh they could reach. Cherisse arched into the touch between her legs. Her thong had gone the way of the floor at some point, so there was not a thing to stop Keiran's fingers from exploring, dipping inside. She rode them shamelessly. She had a brief moment of self-consciousness when he replaced them with his tongue, licking at the juncture of her thigh and pelvis. The lights were on. There was no darkness or candlelight to hide flaws in its golden glow. She shook away the doubts, refused to let Sean's words mar this for her. All such thoughts fled as Keiran worshiped at her flesh like he was having the finest feast.

She urged him on with the motion of her hips. With one last slow lick, Keiran raised his head, his tongue flicking out to taste her wetness from his lips. Fuck, that was hot. She pulled him in for a messy kiss, tasting herself, pressing into him as his hardness nudged her wetness. She needed him inside her now.

"Get that fucking condom on," she ordered.

By the time he fumbled the condom on, Cherisse was so wet from his fingers and tongue she was ready to blow, but she was going to savor this, every slow slide, every groan that wrenched from him.

"Jesus, fuck...just...God...lemme just..." He flipped her around to her hands and knees, and *oh,* he couldn't know how much she enjoyed this position, but he'd clue in soon. She threw a sultry look over her shoulder, eyes locked onto his hips as he drove forward, reveling in the feel of his hands as he gripped her hips. She wiggled back onto him, and Keiran groaned.

"Fuck, Cherisse." His hand caressed her behind. She arched into him further. "You got a fucking dimple on each cheek. Who the fuck even has those?"

She chuckled for all of a minute until he sped up his thrusts, and her laugh dissolved into a loud moan. Keiran was all heat and grinding hips at her back, punctuated by his deep groans. "Yes, harder, fucking *yesss,*" she spurred him on, body arching further as one big hand came round to cup her breast. Lightning sizzled to center between her legs. She was so close to coming, so close. She bit her lip, trying to stop herself from crying out when Keiran's hips did this particular swirl move. Jesus, he was good at this.

"Don't hold back." His lips grazed her ear as their bodies, slick with sweat, moved together.

The loud boom of thunder happened at the exact movement she cried out, face pressed to her sheets, which did nothing to mask her loud moan as she came. Cherisse wondered if the spots of light behind her eyes were lightning, but then, that didn't make sense, did it? Lightning came first, not after thunder. Although she'd heard one time that wasn't entirely true—that they happened at the same time, but light traveling faster than sound and all that. Well, then, it seemed her brain was severely dick-addled at the moment. Did that orgasm just fry her brain?

But they weren't done. Keiran was still going. "Need. A. Minute?" His breath tickled her ear, and he punctuated each word with an annoyingly slow thrust. Oh God, that was too much.

She shivered. "No, just...water, maybe? Fuck." She eased away from him, turning over, so she was on her back. Keiran grinned down at her, mouth curved into a self-satisfied smile.

"Okay, let's get you hydrated. We're not done yet."

Cherisse shamelessly ogled his taut ass as he disappeared from the room. He returned quickly, sans condom, a cup of water in hand. She wondered if he'd actually run, worried the time apart would have her nerves settling in. At this point, she was too wrung out for her brain to even conjure panic.

His gaze was locked on her as he approached the bed. Her body flushed with heat, and Cherisse was ready for more. She couldn't be certain she'd come again, but it would be fun to try.

Almost at the bed, Keiran tripped on who the fuck knew what—discarded clothes, maybe—but Cherisse squealed as cold water sloshed from the cup onto her bare skin. "Fucking hell!"

"Oh shit, sorry."

"If you weren't eyeballing the girls," she huffed, wiping at the water on her stomach.

"Well, damn. You laid out like the best buffet I've ever been to, what you want me to do? The girls just there, looking like my next favorite meal." Keiran shrugged, unrepentant, eyes locked on her breasts. Cherisse snorted. He handed her the cup. "I can fix this." He ducked his head, warm tongue licking at the water on her skin. Oh, fuck. The cup nearly fell out of her hand. "Drink your water, Cherisse," he instructed.

How she managed it while his tongue flicked at her nipple, she didn't know, but she drank it all. Heat pooled between her legs again, and what she did know was she needed him inside her again. She placed the cup on her side table with shaky hands. Easing him back with a hand on his shoulder, she scooched down until he hovered over her. He reached for another condom and rolled it on, slowly, eyes never leaving her face. Their playful banter was gone. Only the heat arcing between them, intense stares, and heavy breaths remained.

She wondered what he saw reflected on her face. She felt too raw. Nerves too exposed. But she needed that look again, the one where he looked at her like she was everything. She shouldn't do this. It was selfish of her to feast on his adoration like this, but she needed it. God, she needed it, especially with Sean's cruel words still there, echoing.

Without a word, he brought her leg up, anchored it on his hip as he eased back into her body, eyes blazing with heat and lust and awe. "You're so fucking beautiful," he whispered, hips back to their slow torture again.

Cherisse held on, meeting him thrust for thrust, basking in it all as she let his words fill up her tiny cracks.

Chapter 21

Keiran

KEIRAN TENDED TO THINK of himself as a fairly patient man. Came with the job when, more often than not, he had to try several different iterations of a beat before they got what they needed. But he loved his job. This session, however, was set to destroy that whole idea. He didn't need this shit, not after last night with Cherisse.

Keiran had slipped out of Cherisse's apartment as soon as he'd gotten up, leaving her sprawled on her bed. He'd sent her a quick text about leaving since lingering to find something to write on would take some time. It had been a struggle not to stick around. He'd hesitated, but he didn't want to invite trouble by running into Remi, and the rain had stopped, so he'd had no excuse to stay. Luckily, he hadn't seen Remi on his way out. He *had* run into Jello. The cat had eyed him balefully as if judging him for sneaking away. He'd rather deal with a stare-down from Jello than Remi, so he'd left, squinting against the bright sun.

He'd gotten home a few hours ago, not getting much sleep, his mind racing. So, waking up to Sean Daley, Sean's publicist, Mara, and Sheila at his front door not too long after had been like a nightmare. Not Sheila so much, but definitely Sean, whose scowl suggested he was ready for round two of their brawl.

Mara had ignored his loud, "What the fuck?" and announced that since he'd been ignoring his father's phone calls and messages, she'd been sent to issue orders.

"It's imperative we finish the single for the first teaser promo. So, we'll be utilizing your incident," she wrinkled her nose before pressing on, "and painting the fight as a publicity stunt. Sheila's track speaks to being fought over by two guys, so it's perfect."

Keiran had gaped at her. "You've gotta be joking."

"I take my job seriously, and I bet you do as well. Your lack of judgment in this situation could very well affect both you and Sean. Damage control is needed. This has already created a buzz, so now we'll take control of the narrative and spin it our way. No one is allowed to leak a word of this to anyone yet, so I suggest you say nothing until we're ready to launch."

Of course, his father would find a way to use Keiran's poor choices to his advantage. But as reluctant as he'd been to let Sean into his space right now, Keiran realized he had no choice. He was already receiving backlash from his family and friends for once again acting before thinking. The media was possibly also having a field day with this—he hadn't looked online—adding fuel to all the rumors about him he'd refused to address. He'd also tried calling Sierra to grovel, but she was off on her honeymoon and obviously in no mood to entertain him. He'd made a mental note to send the largest bouquet of her favorite flowers for when she returned.

It was his own fault that he and Dale were now stuck in the studio with Sean and his watchful publicist when he should have been lost in sleep, daydreaming about the taste of Cherisse.

"How's that sound to you?" Dale asked.

"Fine. Hey! What the hell?" Keiran jerked away from the fingers flicking his forehead. Dale sat back in his chair, arms folded. "What was that for, man?"

"You been spacing." Dale nodded at Sean and Sheila in the booth. "We don't do fine. Fine ain't gonna cut it, and you know that. That line needs some work."

Keiran rubbed his forehead. "Well, if you damn well knew that, why'd you ask?"

"Because Sheila deserves our best. Regardless."

"He's right," Mara piped up. "Sean isn't going to want to have his vocals associated with a mediocre track."

She'd been filming on her phone as they recorded, with the footage to be used as part of their social media promo. Keiran wasn't comfortable with any of that—his studio was his sanctum—but he'd sucked up his protest because behind-the-scenes moments would help build their Instagram engagement too. Not that Mara was posting the full thing. It was another avenue to capture footage for the teaser. Keiran usually left their social media accounts up to Dale, who he trusted. Mara, not so much. She was an anomaly in their space, one under his father's employ. Her loyalty was to King Kong Entertainment and his father. Not Keiran.

Keiran's jaw clenched. Dale *was* right on all counts. He chose to ignore Mara's statement. She was in Sean's corner, so chances of getting any sympathy there were zero.

Keiran didn't want to jeopardize Sheila's rise to stardom, and they needed Sean for that, apparently. He needed to fix this, give it his all like he did every time he got down here. Apart from Sean and Mara invading his space, it was also a little hard to focus when his mind helpfully supplied flashes of how Cherisse sounded and looked when she came. Of her head thrown back, skin flushed. Hips, soft thighs, and sex-sleepy eyes were the real distraction, not that he *could* or would admit that.

Keiran bit his lip, pushing the memories into a corner in his mind. He'd revisit those later. "Yeah, Dale, I get you. I'll fix it." All too aware of Mara, he lowered his voice. "I messed up big time. Eric's also disappointed in me. Again. I'm surprised he hasn't revoked my best man status."

"How's that going? You and Cherisse getting along with this party planning?"

If he could call steamy, spontaneous sex getting along, then they were doing just fine. So much for tucking those memories away. A discussion needed to happen at some point. He had no idea if he should broach it first. What would he even say? He hadn't stuck around long enough to see the regret in her eyes, but he'd been waiting for a reply to his text. That they wouldn't do this again.

Instead, he got silence. It was only the day after. He imagined her working up to it, but he was itching to text her again. That way lay trouble. He had to reel himself in before he spilled his guts at her feet. It would be easy, too. One heavy-lidded look from Cherisse and he was putty in her hands. It was better for both of them that he kept those feelings to himself, for now at least.

"Yeah, we're good." Eager to move on from any discussion of Cherisse, especially with Mara and Sean around, he refocused on their task. "Let's run that again."

Sheila gave a thumbs up. She was easy to work with, pleasant, had talent oozing out of her pores. Her voice was phenomenal. She readjusted the headphones over her braids, ready to jump back in.

Sean scowled his way. "Yeah, let's hope it doesn't sound like shit this time."

Dale patted Keiran's leg before he could release a scathing comment. Keiran took several deep breaths. *Lord, please grant me the patience to not strangle this man.* He allowed Sheila's vocals on the upbeat track to wash over him. The song, titled "Have Your Cake And Eat It Too," was a cheeky rendition of a woman having fun with two guys who end up fighting over her, but in the end, the woman doesn't choose either of them.

Keiran imagined Cherisse would get a kick out of the title. There he went again, dragging her into his thoughts without even trying. To be expected, since he hadn't gotten to savor his morning after as much as he'd hoped. Sean had effectively soured that with his presence.

Dale eventually called a break because his co-producer was attuned with his moods and knew when he needed a breather. "Let's take five, and we'll get back to it," Dale suggested. Sean didn't look pleased, but he toned down the animosity a smidge. Great, because Keiran wasn't going to stand for any more of the man's shit in his studio.

"This is the worst idea," Keiran muttered, swiveling in his chair, his back to the recording booth, eyes on Mara, whose head was down focused on her phone, but Keiran couldn't be certain she wasn't listening.

"Agreed." Dale arranged his body on the couch, legs dangling over one of the arms. "I could really go for one of Cherisse's goodies right now. I wonder if she'd deliver to us again."

Keiran walked over to the couch and sat next to Dale. "Not with this asshole here," he mumbled, eyes on Sean as he chatted with Sheila in the booth.

He didn't want to think about Cherisse walking in and seeing Sean after last night's events. Knowing they were going to use their fight and spin it like something they'd planned all along didn't sit well with Keiran at all. Mara had said they were all supposed to remain mum about it, but it wouldn't be so bad if he told Cherisse right before the teaser promo dropped, would it? That way, Cherisse wouldn't be completely blindsided, and Mara wouldn't murder him in his sleep for leaking information way ahead of time.

Yes, he would tell her right before they went live. Hopefully, it would be soon, so he could stop feeling like he was lying.

Chapter 22
MAY
Cherisse

"FUCK."

"Yeah."

"*Fuuuuck.*"

"Cherisse, if you keep saying 'fuck' like that, I'll..."

"Come?" she whispered in his ear. "That's the point. We don't have much time." She pressed her hips into his, trying to get this show on the road. No idea how long they'd been in this supply closet. "Please." She nibbled at his earlobe, and Keiran grunted. What a sound. It made her wetter, and she tried to draw him in more with the leg she'd wrapped around him, one hand pressed back on a giant bale of toilet paper, of all things. She refused to think about that too much.

Hurry, hurry, hurry was the chant in her head as he rolled into her, frantic now. So close, so fucking close. *Fuck.* She bit her lips as she came, her moan extra-loud to her ears. Keiran pressed his face into her neck, body going still, the slow lick of his tongue at her clavicle so unexpected and sexy. She shuddered.

"That was..."

"I know." Leg hoisted up around his waist, he was still inside her, bodies pressed so close, and even through the layers of clothing, she could feel the wild thumping of his heart. Wearing a dress today had either been worth it or the worst idea. She hadn't decided yet. She'd just had the hottest quickie of her life, thanks to Keiran, and nothing was making sense right now.

How was she supposed to wrap her head around that?

"We should get back before we're missed," she suggested. Or before they got busted in this supply closet.

Keiran slid away from her, looking around for some means to dispose of the condom, probably. The place got points for the well-stocked bathrooms. Condoms, mints, pads, tampons, cozy seats. All that had played a major part in selling her on this venue for the wedding shower. Eric's mom being a member of this country club didn't hurt, either.

She hadn't expected she'd be making use of the condoms, especially not during their walkthrough. The guy giving them the tour had excused himself to take a call. They'd decided to take a little roam of the place while their tour guide had been preoccupied.

They'd been tense with each other when Keiran had picked her up. Their conversations had mostly been by phone the last couple weeks of April, sorting out details. They were in shower month now, with wedding month not so far off. Avoiding each other wasn't possible.

They weren't talking about it, which was fine by her. The sex was a one-time thing, no matter how much she kept remembering how Keiran sounded in the throes of passion—that throaty groan, fuck, that had been hot—or how their eyes kept sliding off each other as they'd strolled the venue. One and done. That was it.

Except she'd somehow found herself dragging him into this tiny space, their mouths fusing together, his hands finding their way under her dress, grasping a bare ass cheek before tracing the edge of her thong.

"We can't do that again," she added when Keiran didn't say a thing.

He'd zipped himself back into his jeans and wrapped the condom in some toilet paper. Good thing she'd chosen this supply room to lose her mind in. He was holding the wrapped condom in his hand, grin extra-wide.

"Sure."

"I mean it."

Keiran shrugged. "Whatever you want, Cherisse. I'm just going with the flow here."

"Why?" Prolonging this was ridiculous. Getting away from this too-small room where she'd just let Keiran fuck her should be her priority. They'd started slow then quickly grown frenzied as if they couldn't get enough of each other. The way he'd rotated his hips...had torn all sorts of sounds from her lips, especially that last one.

Please, Lord, don't let anyone have heard me.

His expression was way too serious. She didn't like this. If they were going to do this—which they weren't going to again, dammit, this had been a fluke—it needed to stay in casual, easy territory. Which made no sense because she didn't even do casual sex.

"You don't want me to answer that." He moved towards the door. "I gotta get rid of this. I'll meet you back in the main room."

She didn't turn around until the door shut behind him. *What the hell was she doing?* Adding unnecessary complications to her life, apparently. But her needs were being met—was it so bad to want more of that? She inhaled deeply, re-wrapping her Sugar Queen persona back around her.

Her phone beeped as she made her way back to the main room. Reba. Good, she'd use her as a buffer. She wouldn't be tempted to drag Keiran off anywhere with Reba around. She'd asked Reba to swing by as she was assisting them now that they were in the final phase of planning. They would wrangle the rest of the wedding party for the setup closer to the event date.

Cherisse made it back to the room just as Reba strolled up. She grinned as the tour guide caught sight of Reba, pastel pink hair in two ponytails on either side of her head, face beat, highlighter throwing off that perfect glow. Today, she rocked double gold nose rings and a slouchy top that slid right off her shoulder, drawing the eye to her clavicle, black leggings, and pink/purple ombré canvas sneakers.

"So, what'd I miss?" Reba asked cheerfully, oblivious to the tour guide staring at her.

Cherisse felt Keiran's hot gaze on the side of her face, but she kept her expression neutral. "Not much. We're just about to get the official walkthrough going."

"Sweet! Hey, Keiran. Hope you and boss lady been getting along," she teased. "Also, just so you know, Sean's a dick, and I, for one, am Team King."

Cherisse sighed, and Keiran's smile was a tad sheepish, but he rolled with it. She'd given in to her curiosity and had watched the video. The comments were mostly speculation on whether they'd been fighting over her, but Cherisse hadn't delved too deeply into them. That was a time suck, and she'd possibly get pissed off again. But not enough to *not* have sex with Keiran, in a goddamn closet, of all things. She didn't recognize herself. Cherisse Gooding didn't have hot—God, *so* fucking hot—sex in public spaces. The risk of being caught was too great, as well as a threat to her carefully crafted persona.

"Hey, Reba," Keiran said. "We're getting along just fine, aren't we?" He winked at Cherisse, and she looked away, cheeks flaming. Damn him.

The tour went smoothly, for the most part. The only hiccup was when Reba asked what door that was—the supply room door—and tour guy enthusiastically went on about it. It was literally just a place to stash stuff; why was this guy so excited about it? Cherisse chalked it up to his default setting, but it didn't help that he was lingering here. Reba had ended up walking next to him, which left Cherisse and Keiran trailing behind, side by side.

"He's really selling this closet. Not that he needs to, to me." Keiran's voice was so close to her ear, it startled her. "Ten outta ten, would bang in it again."

Cherisse snorted. She couldn't help it. She'd meant to scowl at him, elbow him for bringing that up. Tour guy and Reba looked over at them.

"It's a really nice closet," Cherisse said, head bobbing, struggling to keep a straight face.

Reba's eyes swung back and forth between her and Keiran. Cherisse could see the wheels turning. She hoped they weren't giving off any *we just had sex in this closet* vibes because she'd told no one about that rainy night. Not even Remi. Not yet. She would, but she was trying to wrap her head around what she was doing. And since she'd gone and done it again, her just-a-one-time-thing excuse was slowly unraveling.

The rest of the visit went by as expected. The guy, Aron, he reminded them, kept on his overly enthusiastic spiel all the while trying to impress Reba, who wasn't having any of it but was obviously amused. Cherisse kept her work armor on, refusing to get drawn into Keiran's jokes and quips. That was as distracting as his chest in that t-shirt. Knowing what his chest looked like under the damn thing made it even worse.

She needed to get her mind off this, so when Remi texted about going to the gym, she jumped on that. Remi had been trying to get Cherisse to come be her gym buddy for a while now. Cherisse could admit she'd slacked off, been inconsistent, so it could be just the thing she needed. She grimaced at the thought of Remi's trainer. The guy was a beast and didn't like excuses. Cherisse was full of them.

Maybe she'd just stick to an aerobics class or something. She actually liked those.

"Need a ride back?" Keiran asked after the meeting wrapped up.

"No, thanks, I'm good." There was no way she'd get into the car with him again today. Her self-control needed adjusting. Hopefully, the gym would help her work off these lustful feelings.

"I'm going to the gym. I'll grab a ride home with Reba."

"You're going where?" Reba sputtered. She pressed the back of her hand against Cherisse's forehead. "You good? You're willingly going there?" She narrowed her eyes. "Who are you, and what have you done with Cherisse?"

Cherisse nudged Reba's hand away. "Yes, yes, the world's ending, better prep the bunkers with snacks," she joked. She was pretty vocal of her hatred of the gym. Reba and Remi employed good-natured ribbing at her expense all the time. But it was true. Usually, she'd have to be dragged kicking and screaming. Awkwardly sweating her ass off in front of other people was not her thing. She could get her sweat on at home.

"I'm tagging along. I need photographic evidence of this," Reba said gleefully.

Cherisse rolled her eyes. "You know damn well you're only going to gape and take selfies."

Reba cocked a hip and grinned. "Well, boss lady, cute gymwear isn't gonna photograph itself."

Reba was gym-averse as well, preferring her swimming and yoga to anything else. Remi was the gym beast among them. Cherisse got tired just watching Remi's workout routine.

"What gym you go to?" Keiran asked. He was doing that intense stare thing again, knowing smile plastered on his lips. *Act natural*, she willed herself, even as she felt heat prickling up her neck.

"Jungle Gym." She hoped to God he wasn't about to invite himself because there was no way she'd be up for that. She didn't need to drop heavy weights on her foot because she was distracted watching Keiran craft those lickable abs. She wasn't strong enough for that.

His smile grew wider. Oh no. "I go there too, sometimes. But not regularly, and not today. Music never sleeps. I'll probably get in a quick workout at home or something."

"Mmmhmm." Reba eyed him up and down. "Whatever gets this package together, I'm here for it."

Cherisse linked her arm with Reba's, not the least bit excited about getting to the gym, but she needed to get out of Keiran's space. Thinking about the private workout they'd just done was a big no. "Bye, we'll talk. Text. Whatever. Bye." She dragged Reba away to her car.

HER FRIENDS KNEW SOMETHING was weighing on her. Reba had been giving her sidelong glances since they'd left the country club and swung by Reba's place for Cherisse to borrow something to wear. Now, she felt both their eyes on her as she and Reba did the aerobics class, and Remi went through her reps with her personal trainer. She sensed a tag team coming. She had no clue what she'd say where Keiran was concerned.

She and Reba sprawled on the floor after the aerobics class and watched Remi do her thing.

"Jesus, my eyes are tired just watching this," Reba huffed, taking a swig of her water.

"Same."

They were both breathing hard, trying to catch their breath from their workout while Remi went through some rope workout, abs tensing, muscles in her toned arms bunching. They watched in awe until Remi finished and high-fived her trainer before walking over to plop down next to them.

"How in the world, Remi? That shit looked like a case of noodle arms." Cherisse slid Remi a bottle water.

"The burn's good." Remi grinned and nudged Cherisse. "You should try sometime. Gavin's not so bad."

"Nah, I'm good. I don't like people yelling at me."

"He hardly even yelled today."

"Uh-huh." Cherisse wasn't about some dude screaming in her face for any reason.

"So, I'm thinking pizza night," Reba piped up. "We haven't done that in a while. Pizza-movie-catch-up night. My parents won't be home, so we can even watch something R-rated." She waggled her brows. "What say you?"

Ah, so that's how they were going to do it. Their exchange of sneaky glances wasn't lost on her. Feed her, then pounce with the questions. She couldn't even be annoyed about it because she did love pizza.

"Sounds good to me," she said.

"Good!" Reba got to her feet, hands on her hips. "Then you'll tell us what's been up with you these past weeks."

"You aren't even being subtle about this food bribery." Cherisse stuck out her hand for Reba to help her up.

Remi got to her feet, too, bouncing on her toes. Cherisse wondered if she could siphon some of her bestie's energy. "We know the way to loosen your lips."

Cherisse groaned. "We're gonna need a lot of pizza."

REBA LIVED FIFTEEN minutes away from Jungle Gym, but they'd decided to shower at the gym so they could get right on with making the pizza. Reba and Remi still weren't asking any questions yet, so they chattered on about other things. The upcoming wedding. Cherisse's sweating over the dessert stations setup for that and her other Maid of Honor duties. The gift she'd decided on for Ava. She and Reba even ran through a list of emails that needed addressing.

Once the pizza was done, they grabbed their slices and drinks and cued up Magic Mike XXL. Remi and Reba settled in on either side of her on the big comfy couch. They silently lusted after Channing Tatum as he went through his dance routine on that wooden table until Remi stretched her long legs onto the table, plate balanced on her stomach.

"Well." She raised a brow at Cherisse.

"You not even gonna let me finish my pizza?" Cherisse asked, second slice already in her hand, ready to munch.

"You can eat and talk," Reba pointed out, ever helpful, as she reached for her ginger-flavored beer that no one liked except her.

Cherisse sighed. She'd been trying to formulate her story. Once she dropped the truth, she'd be bombarded by questions she just wasn't sure how to answer. She and Keiran kept falling into whatever this was, and she didn't know how to justify the why of it.

She took a deep breath and just said it. "Keiran and I had sex." She paused. "Twice."

Reba spewed her drink all over the coffee table. "What the hell!" she choked out, coughing wildly as she wiped at her mouth. She disappeared into the kitchen and returned with the paper towel roll. "In case you decide to drop some more surprises," Reba said as she wiped up the spewed drink.

"How did this happen? When did this happen?" Remi asked.

"I'm not sure how it happened."

"Don't even try telling me you tripped and fell on this dick because I swear to God!"

"Okay, relax." She cut Remi off. "I just meant it wasn't planned, obviously. Just sort of happened. It was the night of Sierra's wedding, after the fight."

Remi pursed her lips. "Of course, it was that night. I leave you alone for one night and this. But wait." She narrowed her eyes. "You said twice."

"Um, well, today may have been another lapse-in-judgment day."

Reba choked on her pizza this time. "Dammit! Eff this! I'm not eating or drinking a damn thing 'til you're done with this. You tryna kill me for sure."

Cherisse laughed. "Sorry."

Remi slowly chewed her pizza, listening. "So, what are you doing exactly?"

She shrugged. "The Lord alone knows. This wasn't supposed to happen once, let alone twice or in a supply closet."

Reba's brow popped up. "Damn, girl. At the venue walkthrough? I knew something was up."

Cherisse picked at the pineapple on her pizza, popping the pieces in her mouth as she avoided looking at her friends.

"You don't do casual hookups, so..."

"I know. It's not happening again."

"Right." Remi didn't sound convinced.

Cherisse wasn't entirely convinced, either. They'd be seeing each other at the party, and there was still the wedding to go, not to mention all the little Maid of Honor/Best Man shit Ava and Eric were sure to need them both for, in between all that. She could be adamant about not having sex with him anymore, but dammit, she hadn't planned the quickie in the closet either. Self-control. She needed to get some of that from somewhere.

"I just don't want him thinking this could be more than a one-time thing." Remi shot her a look. "Fine, a two-time thing.

Whatever. Rolling into FWBs with Keiran isn't something I want, or anything serious either."

"This'll get messy as hell." Remi sipped her drink, pointing the bottle at Cherisse. "You get to choose how you handle this, but maybe try to minimize the fallout. And what about these guys your mom keeps throwing at you? Are you gonna keep that up now that you're getting some regular D?"

"It's not regular D. I just told you." She exhaled exasperatedly.

"But it could be," Reba pointed out, needlessly, because *she wasn't having sex with Keiran again.*

Cherisse had sensed some things bubbling beneath the surface between her and Keiran. Things she'd pretended not to notice. Things she couldn't ignore after the kiss, but she'd chosen to. Now, here they were. Why was she even pretending like she didn't know how this could go sideways?

She didn't want to keep talking about this. "So, who else is making a mess of their lives?" she asked cheerfully.

Remi's gaze returned to the movie. "Well, that date I had the other night was going okay until I called her by another name while my hand was up her skirt. And with all the rain, I couldn't leave right away, so it was an uncomfortable night."

"Oh, shit." Remi hadn't mentioned the date, and Cherisse had been too occupied silently freaking out over having had sex with Keiran to ask Remi about it when she'd gotten home. God, she was a terrible friend.

"Whose name?" Reba asked.

Remi didn't look away from the TV. "Let's just say, Cherisse isn't the only one having King-sized problems."

Cherisse stared. "Oh."

"Shit. We're gonna need some stronger drinks and more pizza." Reba got to her feet. "Mummy's got some tequila stashed somewhere."

"Yup."

"I..." Cherisse had a ton of questions, but Remi shook her head, obviously not wanting to elaborate further. Which was fine. Remi was right on the mark about one thing, though. Cherisse did have a King-sized problem and no idea how to deal with it.

Chapter 23
Keiran

THE VENUE LOOKED JUST like he'd imagined, with the cozy corners, as they'd dubbed them, mini blanket fort sections set up with comfy pillows and cushions where people could go off and watch the movies being projected. There were snack sections, a selfie station equipped with props, and games to be played. They'd also set up a prize for the most creative sleepwear. Keiran was pleasantly surprised that they'd pulled this off.

The guests wore various types of sleepwear, ranging from cutesy sleep sets to ridiculous onesies. People had really gone all out with the dress code.

Eric and Ava had swept him and Cherisse up in a suffocating hug when they'd arrived, the bride and groom wearing matching wide-eyed looks of awe as they'd surveyed the décor.

"Oh my God, this is awesome!" Eric had gestured wildly at the cozy corners. "Blanket forts, yes!" He'd waggled his brows dramatically. "If the fort's a-rockin', don't come knockin.'"

Keiran had rolled his eyes. "Dude, it's not that kinda party."

"But it could be," Ava had said, leering at her fiancé.

Keiran felt a sense of pride that they loved it. He and Cherisse hadn't murdered each other; they'd survived working together. Of course, now they'd plunged headlong into this weird limbo because of the sex. The sex they were now pretending didn't happen. At least Cherisse was, or maybe she was just a good actor. It was all Keiran could think about.

He stood near the snack table, eyes scanning the area until they landed on pajama pants sprinkled with cupcakes. He'd have spotted Cherisse easily, even without the brightly-patterned bottoms. He was too attuned to her not to. "I Sugarcoat Everything" was splashed across the front of her top with a mini cupcake at the end like a full stop. Tousled hair down around her shoulders, wide grin on her face, she'd explained she was going for that just-woken-up bedhead look, and she'd nailed it. God, had she ever. Her lips were glossed with this deep red that had him picturing how that mouth would look stretched around his cock. She looked adorable and sexy at the same time, and it was doing a number on him.

It didn't help that he was so acutely aware of what they'd done in that damn closet. The closed space was like a siren's call to him now.

Cherisse held the game sheets they'd prepared, going over the rules with Reba, who'd been happy to help run the games. Dressed in silky grey pajamas, one button done up, the rest unbuttoned and showing off her toned midriff and the top of her black boxers, Reba drew a lot of eyes. He could admit she rocked that TLC style well, but his eyes slid back to Cherisse's ass in the soft cottony fabric. The urge to make use of that closet again was real. He was remembering those ass cheek dimples when Scott rolled up, decked out in a silky belted robe over some equally shiny PJs.

"Yo, this setup is awesome! Thanks for creating the nap zones for after the itis kicks my ass with all this food." Scott grabbed up a popcorn container from the table.

"Cozy corners," Keiran corrected. Scott laughed at him but kept on eating his popcorn. "What? The sign says so and everything."

"You're really into this."

Keiran shrugged. "We spent a lot time on it, hell, yeah, I'm into it. Lots of sweat went into pulling this off."

Scott munched on his popcorn, a knowing look in his eyes. "Yeah, I know 'bout the sweaty activities you two been up to."

He'd told Scott everything. Maxi knew about the kiss. Eric didn't know any of it. Not because Keiran didn't trust him, but he figured Eric had enough going on. And okay, he could admit he wasn't completely certain Eric wouldn't spill the beans to his wife-to-be. Keiran had no idea if Cherisse had told anyone since they weren't discussing it. Was he even allowed to ask her that? This was all new to him, so he was treading lightly, erring on the cautious side.

Scott clapped him on the back, grinning. "Living that dream."

"Yeah? What dream is that exactly? Us secretly sleeping together while she publicly goes out with Jerome?"

He sounded bitter, but he hadn't been prepared to hear from his mother that the two had gone to Fleur's Tea Shop on some cozy date. His mother had mentioned it casually, in passing, and Keiran hadn't been sure how to react. It was ridiculous to be jealous of Jerome when his cousin wasn't interested in Cherisse romantically. But she didn't know that, and he couldn't tell her because he wouldn't out Jerome like that. But maybe if he told his cousin what was going on between him and Cherisse, perhaps Jerome would find someone else for his ruse.

The problem was he didn't know what Cherisse's intentions were. Had she agreed to the date because of pressure from her mother? Did she genuinely like Jerome? His cousin was a great guy, so it wasn't that unbelievable, but where did that leave him and Cherisse?

They'd had amazing sex, which he'd never expected in his wildest dreams, but it didn't give him the right to expect anything from Cherisse. His jealousy was his problem, but damn if hearing about these dates didn't chafe. He could admit he wanted that, too. Seemed unlikely he'd get it.

Scott rooted around in his container. "Sorry, man. I know you really like her."

Like? What a joke. His heart hammered in his chest from just watching her smiling with her sister, who'd joined the conversation with Reba. He was screwed. He should've shut everything down before it had gotten this far. Adding sex just revved up all the twisty annoying feelings that had been simmering since they'd come back into each other's orbit. Now, he knew how she tasted beneath his tongue, felt in his hands, and sounded when she came. He shrugged like Scott's words weren't a dagger to the chest.

"It is what it is. I'll live."

Scott leveled him with a look heavy on the skepticism but kept on eating the rest of his popcorn, not saying a word. Keiran told himself to go check on the status of the games, anything but standing here feeling sorry for himself while Scott patted his shoulder.

"It'll work out, somehow," Scott assured him. "By the way, your FWB's heading this way, so good luck with that."

"Scott, what the f—" Too late. Scott had already sailed off, stopping briefly to wave at Cherisse before he power-walked away like whatever was happening on the other end of the room was so important.

"Hi." Her smile was a little frayed around the edges, but Keiran chose to pin that on tiredness—they'd been here late last night and early this morning setting up—rather than *I know what you look like naked* awkwardness. It was possibly a mix of both. "Everything okay over here?"

"Yeah, why wouldn't it be?" She tossed him a questioning look. His tone had been a bit curt. His brain supplied nothing else. Well, nothing except wanting to ask her about Jerome and why she hadn't mentioned the date. It *did* register how good she smelled, though. Vanilla. She always smelled good, sweet. Today, she smelled all vanilla-y, like... "Cookies," he blurted out.

"Cookies?" Her brow furrowed because, obviously, that made no sense.

"No, I meant you,"—Jesus, he was going to sound like a fool—"smell like cookies." He scrubbed his hand over his face. Her snort made him drag his hand away. She was smiling at him, at least, a real, full-on, genuine, make-his-heart-beat-faster smile.

"I get that a lot. Sorry to disappoint, but it's just my perfume. I didn't make any cookies for this thing. I did the, uh..." She cleared her throat. "The red velvet shooters that you liked so much, and other desserts, obviously." Her hand swept the table behind him.

Like he was ever going to forget what those red velvet shooters were. He associated their first kiss with them. He wasn't losing that memory anytime soon.

"I've had people say I smell like bread, cookies, cake." She ticked them off on her fingers.

"Not bad smells to be associated with. What was the weirdest?"

"Hmm." She tapped her cheek, rolling her bottom lip inward before releasing it with a pop. "Honey roasted peanuts."

He dragged his eyes away from her mouth, chuckling. "They do smell good, so that's a fair comparison. You smell good everywhere."

Well, now, he'd done it. Ratcheted up the already present tension by referencing the one thing they were actively avoiding talking about.

"I should get back," she said hastily. "Time to start the games."

"Shit, sorry. I didn't mean to make this any weirder than it already is."

She shook her head. "It's fine. Don't stress."

"Except it's not." Why wasn't he shutting up? This wasn't the place or time. But dammit, he had Cherisse here now. When would he get the chance to discuss any of this? The wedding? He didn't think so. "Look, I'm gonna be real with you. I can't stop thinking about you and me. And...we had sex. There's no way I can pretend it didn't happen. I can't. I know that's what you want, and I get it." He blew out a breath.

Cherisse opened her mouth then snapped it shut like she wasn't sure what to say. He'd put her on the spot, but he was tired. Tired of walking around on eggshells. He was distracted in the studio too. That was never a good thing. He couldn't blame Cherisse for that. It all just added to his frustrations, which were bubbling over at the worst time.

Cherisse looked around. She rubbed her arm, eyes flitting about before her gaze came back to rest on him. "I can't stop thinking about it, either. That what you wanted to hear?"

"Yes. Then why'd you go out with Jerome?"

Cherisse reared back in surprise. "That's...none of your business."

"Maybe. Doesn't hurt any less."

"What are you doing? Don't say shit like that. We're not doing this." She shook her head. "I...I need to go. The games need to get started." She turned to leave him with his heart in the dust.

"Just vomiting my feelings everywhere as one does." *Stop this.* Cherisse wasn't obligated to like him back, and he damn well knew that. Sex didn't mean she felt anything other than lust for him.

She turned back, a ball of anger in his face now. "Now isn't the place for this. You wanna hash this out? Fine. Later. Don't make this about you."

He was pissed. Hurt. Acting a fool. Yet seeing Cherisse like this made him want to kiss her. The damn closet was basically calling to him now. A fired-up Cherisse was a goddamn beautiful thing. As if she knew what he was thinking, her eyes dropped to his mouth for several heartbeats. She tore her gaze back up to meet his stare.

"God, you're pissing me off so much right now."

He leaned in. "Maybe, but you still wanna fuck me. When you're ready to talk, come find me. My tongue's ready to do whatever you want."

He walked away. Her sound of outrage was satisfying.

Chapter 24
Cherisse

THESE PING-PONGING emotions were annoying. As was Keiran. The damn man. How dare he try to make her feel guilty for hanging out with Jerome? Which was really what going to Fleur's Tea Shop had been about. She didn't even like tea, but the shop was so cute and served other beverages, and Jerome was a cool guy to hang out with.

She liked Jerome. He was easy to talk to, and they'd bonded over both of their mothers' ridiculous attempts at matchmaking, so it had been the perfect distraction from this Keiran mess, not that she'd told Jerome any of that. He was still Keiran's family.

Was she a terrible person for leaving him to believe she was in any way interested in Jerome romantically?

"What'd that pencil do to you?" Remi whispered in her ear.

Cherisse looked down at her grip on her pencil. She'd crumpled one corner of the games sheet, too, without even realizing. She was supposed to be chipper and ready to host the games with Reba, not thinking about Keiran or that parting comment. Or that his words had heat pooling everywhere, even as she was fuming. She hated this.

She tried to smoothen the crinkled edges, eased her death grip on the pencil. "Nothing," she said.

"Something happen before I got here?" Remi asked.

"Keiran King happened, that's what," she muttered before plastering on her best smile. "Nothing I can't handle." She found his smug face among the guests, remembered that discreet middle finger she'd tossed him at Ava's engagement party. Unsure she could pull off the move as smoothly, this time, she didn't try it. She just returned his grin and then got into host mode.

The games ran smoothly. Reba was a great co-host, ad-libbing jokes, hyping everyone up, even managing to capture all the fun moments on her phone. Ava and Eric were clearly having fun, which was all Cherisse had hoped for during the course of planning this. That and surviving Keiran. She was crashing and burning at the latter because right now, even as pissed as she was at him, her eyes kept finding his.

She needed air. The games were over, and people were either heading off to the cozy corners or engaging in conversation with the bride and groom-to-be. The perfect opportunity to slip away, especially with fatigue lingering in her bones. It would hit her hard.

She'd expected the crash to descend a bit later on after she got home. Planning events, in general, was exhausting, but working with Keiran had her emotions all over the place. As she stepped outside, she hoped no one would need her for anything. She should have taken advantage of one of the cozy corners, but that meant still interacting with others while they had movie time. Why hadn't she thought of having a single cozy corner made for herself?

The slumber shower was being held in the main event area of the Marigold Club, a spacious hall that they'd transformed into the cozy corners, food areas, game spots, and the props and self-photo area. The outside of the club boasted lush grounds peppered with fruit trees and different types of flowers, adding spots of color amidst all the green. There was a pool and tennis court somewhere in the back, but Cherisse stuck to a corner of the main hall porch area, arms pressed against the handrail that wrapped right around the hall.

She retrieved her phone from her pocket. Reba usually took care of the bulk of Sweethand emails, but sometimes, she'd get some stuff sent to her personal email, so she ensured to at least peek at her inbox daily. After deleting a bunch of spam and flagging a legit email about catering for a birthday party, she perused her social accounts. She'd already been tagged in a bunch of photos. There was even one with her and Keiran chatting with Ava and Eric. It had been taken just when the couple had arrived.

Her fingers had a mind of their own because they pulled up Keiran's Instagram. She skimmed his feed, noting a photo of them that he'd reposted from Scott. They'd been captured working side-by-side, getting the place ready during the setup this morning. They both wore shorts and tees, flip-flops on their feet. The sexual tension swirling between them wasn't obvious in the photo, but she remembered how hard it was for her not to think about the sex. The hot, satisfying, "this is gonna be a problem, but my body is a greedy bitch" sex.

They should talk. Lines were blurring, and she needed a firm grip on some self-control right now because no matter how sure she'd sounded to Keiran when she'd said they weren't doing it again, her body would do the opposite. She'd gotten a taste, and damn if she didn't want a repeat. There was a lot of that hard body she hadn't explored yet. The last time hadn't quenched her thirst. If her plan had been one and done, scratch an itch, sprinkle a little water on this drought period of hers, it had backfired spectacularly because it just fueled the want that was churning inside her.

"So, this is where you're hiding." As if she'd conjured him with her filthy thoughts, Keiran settled beside her.

Her body tightened, responding to his proximity, while he remained casually propped against the railing.

"I'm not hiding." She forced herself to relax. He was doing it again, trying to get a rise out of her.

"Well, I'm here. Care to finish our chat from earlier?"

She didn't want to do this. She wanted to go home. She wanted to feel his strong hands cupping her ass again, massaging her flesh, stroking her thighs. Her fingers dug into the railing. She drank in the way his black sleeveless tank fit to his chest and showed off his arms but refused to let her eyes drop below his waist. No. She'd caught enough glimpses of his ass and thighs in those plaid boxers. His sleepwear wasn't flashy in any way, but she'd had to mentally slap herself several times throughout the party to stop from gaping.

"You couldn't think of anything a lil' less boring?" she quipped, gesturing at his get-up. She wasn't in the mood to continue their earlier conversation right now.

"My usual sleepwear isn't quite this...decent."

"Oh." She'd walked right into that. Dammit. She wouldn't ask. She would not... "Are you saying you go bare-assed on the sheets, or?"

His lips slowly quirked up. "Boxer briefs."

Oh, sweet Lord. That was somehow even worse. If he'd shown up here in tiny boxer briefs, that supply closet would have gotten more use, guests be damned. She'd bite into a shoulder to keep her ass quiet if she had to. Because Keiran, in tiny briefs, would break her. Her mind worked overtime, picturing that. His dick would definitely be pressed up all indecently at the front, fabric molding that ass in the back, and his muscled thighs would be on full display.

He straightened from his casual lean, fingers drumming the flat top of the railing. "So, I threw on these longer boxers over them so I wouldn't give anyone an eyeful. My public service for the day."

"How commendable of you," she said wryly even as her throat dried out at the knowledge that he had those briefs on under his boxers. Now would be an excellent time for her to leave. Find her ride and get gone. But that pull between them that she just couldn't seem to escape was taking the reins now, and she found herself closing the distance, hooking a finger in the waistband of his boxers and tugging him closer.

He didn't fight, allowed her to reel him in. A small part of her was confident that Keiran wouldn't refuse her. She'd seen that heavy serving of want in his eyes enough times now to be sure of that. His reaction to her not-date with Jerome was proof too.

Maybe. Doesn't hurt any less.

Those words should be enough to send her in the opposite direction. She was being selfish. She *knew* that. Using him to get off when he probably wanted more. She'd seen a spark of something other than lust in his gaze, too. But he hadn't refused her yet, so was it so wrong if they both got something out of this? Even *if* Keiran wasn't getting exactly what he wanted, he obviously wanted this.

And she was so damn weak.

"No one has to know." She could have her cake and eat it too—as messed up as that was—because what was the point of having cake right there if you didn't eat it? If Keiran was willing to be on board with it.

"Is that what you want?" His gaze was intense, searching as if he was trying to root out what her real angle was here.

"I can't deny this sex we keep having is...distracting. I know I keep saying one and done, but we both see how that's been working out. Tell me to go to hell if you want to. I'd deserve it for even suggesting this." She kept toying with his waistband until his hand came down on her wrist, stilling her movements.

"We're both adults here. If we say what we're doing upfront, no one'll get hurt, right?"

She looked up at him. "Right."

"What are the rules?"

"Rules? We have sex when we want, then go about our lives. Lather, rinse, repeat. We don't need to make a production of this."

He frowned, releasing her wrist, hand moving up to tuck a strand of hair behind her ear. "So, basically, a booty call, and you still go on dates?"

"Yes."

His hand moved from her hair to trace the shell of her ear. Cherisse shivered at the featherlight touch. "I suppose anyone's a more feasible option than me. Can't even say I blame you right now. I haven't exactly been at my best." His touch burned all the way down her jaw. "Just tell me when you're done with me. When you've gotten whatever it is you need out of this."

"Keiran." God. His words made her feel like shit.

He cupped her jaw. "Don't feel bad about what you want. You're being upfront with me. So, you set the end date, yeah?"

"Fine."

He bowed his head, mouth hovering inches away from hers, waiting. She nodded, and he captured her lips in a soft kiss as if to seal the deal. She was already on edge, body wound tight, ready for release. She couldn't do this softness. She pulled him into a corner of the porch.

As their tongues tangled, she palmed him through the boxers. His erection tented the front of it. There was no way he could go back inside without giving the guests an eyeful. She sucked on his bottom lip, hand still stroking, tugging. "You got your car keys?"

His head thunked back against the side of the hall. "Yeah. Handy pocket in this thing," he panted out, hips moving in time with her hand.

"Gave anyone a ride here?"

"No."

She gave one last slow stroke that had him groaning. "Good. Take me home."

Chapter 25

Keiran

THEY'D BARELY MADE it inside her apartment before Cherisse was on him, biting at his lip as she pushed at the bottom of his tank top to scrape her nails over his stomach.

"Get this shit off," she demanded, eyes flashing with lust and a hint of lingering annoyance.

"You're so beautiful when you're angry."

"Is that why you keep pissing me off?"

He laughed. "No. Just a pleasant side effect."

He wanted to go slow, bask in her body, but she wasn't allowing it as she pushed him back until he bounced onto her couch. Seconds later, she was straddling him, and his hands went to her hips.

"Cherisse."

"That isn't what this is," she breathed against his lips. "Fast. Hard. Make me fucking scream. That's what I want."

Well, shit. He would be a fool to say no to that. For the second time, he swept her up in his arms, and she squealed.

"A little warning next time," she huffed as he took her upstairs.

"You said faster. And this is faster than walking."

He'd barely set her down on the bed before her top was thrown off to the side and her pajama bottoms kicked off. Keiran nearly tripped while removing his boxers because, sweet Jesus, Cherisse wasn't in the mood to wait. Her finger was already rubbing at the center of her thong. "Come take these off. Now."

So goddamn bossy. He loved it, and he loved the little sounds he wrenched from her, loved the crescendo of it as she got louder with every touch and stroke. In the end, he did make her scream, but it was the way she snuggled up next to him, head on the pillow she'd dragged into his lap as she sighed, that was nearly his undoing.

At the risk of losing a limb, he took a chance and stroked her hair away from her face. Eyes still closed, cheeks flushed, and breath a bit ragged, she was the most beautiful woman he'd ever seen.

"I can feel you looking at me, weirdo."

"Do you think people will notice we're gone?"

"Probably." She yawned. "Don't care."

"Do you want me to leave?" It was a reasonable question. Snuggling wasn't exactly part of their casual sex deal. Or was it? They hadn't exactly hashed out a list of Dos and Don'ts.

"What I want you to do is shush while I snooze. If you want to leave, that's up to you."

"Wow, sex really mellows you out, huh?"

Her finger unerringly found the one place between his ribs where he was ticklish and poked at it.

"Hey!"

"Shut. Up."

His phone rang from somewhere on the floor, and Cherisse groaned. "Maybe you *should* leave," she grumbled.

"That's Eric. I should get that."

Cherisse got up from his lap, pillow and all, and flopped back down onto the bed as he got up to search for his phone.

"How many squats you gotta do to get an ass like that?" Cherisse asked, and he looked over his shoulder to see her eyes dipped low.

He chuckled as he retrieved his phone. "Too damn many."

"Hey, where are you?" Eric asked.

"Um." Keiran met Cherisse's gaze as she waited for his reply. She turned onto her side, hand on her cheek to prop herself up. "Cherisse wasn't feeling well, so I offered to take her home."

"I hope she's okay."

"What's happening? Is Cherry alright?" Ava piped up in the background. Dammit. The last thing they needed was them worrying enough to come over here.

"Yeah, she's okay. Really. Just probably tired. I sent her straight to bed."

Cherisse's grin turned naughty, fingers trailing down her side, drawing Keiran's eyes to the curve of her hips then down between her legs.

"Shit."

"What?" Ava sounded mildly panicked, having taken the phone from Eric.

"Nothing. She's fine. I'm coming back to the party in a bit," he choked out as he followed the motion of Cherisse's finger. Up and down, then, oh God, in and out. "Okay, bye. I'll see you in a little."

He ended the call, tossing the phone back onto his discarded clothes. Before he could move back onto the bed, Cherisse crawled over to him, reaching up to trace his lips with the same damn fingers. "Remember how I said to shut up?"

He nodded as she put his mouth to better use.

Chapter 26

Cherisse

SHE SHOULD'VE KNOWN the fatigue from the wedding shower was the first sign, but she'd ignored it, worked up a different, more delicious kind of tired with Keiran back at her apartment. He'd left her sated, her entire body languid.

Now, two days later, after somehow bullshitting her way through a client meeting without collapsing, Cherisse felt like shit, probably looked it too. Keiran's lie to Eric and Ava had become a reality. She was sick. Achy and tired, she had to actively work to concentrate on where the taxi was going so she wouldn't fall asleep and miss her stop.

She staggered into the apartment, and Remi looked up from her laptop, caught sight of her, and jumped to her feet.

"Jesus, you look horrible!"

Cherisse tossed her handbag on the couch, body thumping down next to it. "I might be coming down with something. I don't have time to be sick," she wailed, arm covering her eyes as she thumped her head back on the couch. Her throat felt like she'd swallowed glass.

"Did Keiran infect you or something?" Remi's voice came from above.

"Shit, I probably spread my germs to him. I should text him."

"Symptoms check," Remi demanded, her pseudo-mom voice switched on.

"Achy, sore throat, head's pounding. Just...tired." Her bed and meds were much needed. "Ugh, our birthday's soon. I can't be sick."

"Don't worry about that. I'm making you tea. Then you can have some of the fun drowsy stuff, and bed."

She peered up at Remi. "Okay."

Remi's eyebrow winged up. "Oh lord, you're sicker than I thought. You're actually going to drink tea without kicking up a fuss?"

"Your honey-lime concoction thing worked last time when you forced me to take it, so let's not get carried away. No other tea-like beverage shall touch these lips unless they're in dessert form and made by someone that I trust cuz you know *I* don't willingly put tea in anything I make."

Remi patted her head. "Alright, Miss Tea Basher, I'll take care of you."

Remi did just that—made her the tea to soothe her fiery throat, got her some drowsy meds, and helped her up to bed. Cherisse waved Remi off when she offered to bring her work up. Remi was busy sorting photos to upload to the Island Bites site, as well as some test shots for her first gallery showing that she had coming up in the next few months.

"Don't be a weirdo. I'll text if I need anything." Cherisse waved her phone.

She wanted to shoot Keiran a quick text too. It was the right thing to do, in case she had unknowingly shared her germs. She didn't need Remi hovering around for that. She'd already made her feelings about the casual sex with Keiran known—silently, with a heavy dose of side-eye. Plus, the meds were doing their thing. Her limbs felt heavy, and she needed to send that text before the phone fell on her face or something.

"Go." She shooed Remi, who still hovered in the doorway.

"Fine. Sleep." Remi left the door slightly ajar, and Cherisse rolled her eyes. Sometimes, Remi was a worse worrier than Cherisse's mother.

Cherisse tapped out a quick text to Keiran:

Cherisse: think I'm coming down with the flu. So heads up flumaggedon maybe heading your way.

Keiran: oh damn how you feelin'?

Cherisse: I've been banished to bed and drugged up. Remi's orders. Anyway meds kicking in so before this phone meets my face...

She didn't wait for his reply. The phone had already almost slid out her hand, so she pitched it next to her and let the drowsiness pull her under.

SHE WOKE UP GROGGY, eyes burning. She had no idea how long she'd slept. She squinted at her curtains, which told her nothing. Then she remembered her phone.

Cherisse patted the bed beside her until her hand landed on it. Keiran had messaged back. She'd slept right through that.

Keiran: hey, you like soup right? I can bring you some?

That had been three hours ago. She checked the time, already after 6 p.m. Why was he trying to bring her soup? This wasn't part of their hooking up. It hadn't explicitly been said, but Cherisse was sure she'd made it clear this was just sex, hadn't she? That didn't involve soup.

Did it involve post-sex cuddling?

"Shush, you," she hissed at that annoying inner voice. She was definitely worse off than expected if she was openly talking back to herself.

Cherisse: yes and not necessary. Not part of the deal. Thanks tho.

Keiran: oh you're up. Well uh I'm not saying I'm downstairs but...

What? He couldn't be serious. She opened a new chat window for Remi.

Cherisse: is Keiran here?

Remi: uh...

Cherisse: dammit Remi!

Remi: he brought food. Otherwise I wouldn't have let him in. I think it's soup. Which is kinda sweet, I guess. How u feeling?

Cherisse: like shit.

She thought about going downstairs and decided she wasn't ready to move yet. Fucking flu. She burrowed deeper under her covers. Her fan was on full blast, adding to her chills, but reaching across that short distance to turn it down or off completely felt like a chore. She was hungry, too. Her tummy rumbled. At least she hadn't lost her appetite yet. That soup sounded like a good idea. She should tell Remi to bring it up, and...

She woke up again, thinking she'd slept another few hours, only to see twenty minutes had passed. The damn meds always dragged her under deeply, throwing off her sense of time.

"Hey."

Cherisse's eyes jumped to her bedroom door. Keiran. Oh, God, why? He hesitated as if he wasn't sure how she'd react. If she had any energy at all, she'd throw a pillow at his head.

"No," she said, tossing her cover over her head. "Why're you still here?" Her voice came out muffled from under her blanket cocoon.

"I have soup. Remi said I could come up." His voice sounded closer.

"I'm gonna kill her." Seriously, what was Remi even trying to pull with this?

"Not entirely sure this isn't some set-up for me to face your wrath. She told me I should be able to find your room on my own, considering."

Cherisse huffed, pulling the cover down just enough so she could glare at him over it. She was hyperaware of her hair falling out of the bun she'd wrestled it into at some point.

"Hi," he grinned, gesturing with the tray. "It's really good, promise."

She pushed herself up into a sitting position, letting her cover fall away. "Did you make that?"

"Yes." He placed the tray on her lap. "Can I sit?"

He'd made her soup. It was sweet. *Nope. Stop that right now.* She glared harder. "No."

Seemingly unbothered by her curt reply, he stood there, rocking back on his heels. Why wasn't he leaving? Was he actually going to watch her eat the damn soup?

"You served your purpose, you can go now." She was being rude, but she hated being sick.

"You're cute when you're irritable."

She ignored him and took a sip of the soup. Damn, that was delicious. "It's good."

"Course it is. I know what I'm about where soup's concerned."

She slurped up more soup. Her throat still ached, but the soup was easier to eat than anything too solid right now. More broth than anything else, with a bit of noodles, she could manage without too much pain. A round of honey and lime was in order after this or more of Remi's tea. "You this eager to get yourself sick?"

He shrugged. Even feeling like death, she could appreciate his shoulders in that white t-shirt. She dipped her spoon in the soup again, brought it to her mouth so she wouldn't actually say that. She felt grimy. God, she needed a shower, and he was here, being all nice and looking sexy. She hated it.

"I just wanted to check up on you, that's it. Is it so wrong to want that?"

"Stop being nice and caring and shit."

He cocked his head. "You saying I can't be nice to you cuz we're having sex?"

She let the spoon clang against the now-empty bowl. "I'm trying to prevent the catching of feelings and shit."

"Don't worry, I won't fall in love with you."

She narrowed her eyes at him. Wasn't sure she believed him, then thought she was being full of herself to think he'd fall in love with her. She blamed the germs that had invaded her body and the grogginess from the meds. He'd admitted to liking her, sure, and being hurt about Jerome. But that didn't automatically mean he felt anything deeper, at least not to that extreme.

She pushed the tray to the side. Keiran swooped down to grab it up, body hovering over her, face too close. "You're breathing in my flu germs," she pointed out.

He took his sweet time pulling back. "I'll be fine. If I do get sick, you'll be the first to receive a whiny "I'm dying" text. Need anything else?"

She needed him gone. He'd done enough already. She appreciated the soup, but she didn't need the guy she was hooking up with buzzing around while she looked a hot mess. "I need a shower," she mumbled, "and no, you can't help with that."

"Wouldn't dream of offering." That smirk said otherwise.

She slid back down onto her back. After Keiran left, she'd get her shower sorted out. "I just need to be better before my birthday," she mumbled.

They'd been planning it for weeks. The gift vouchers she'd won were going to be put to use. Spa day with Remi for their actual birthday on the Friday which would lead into clubbing later in the evening. They'd also planned to overnight at the Hyatt so no one would have to drive back after whatever tipsy shenanigans bar hopping brought. Then Saturday night was the surprise party Cherisse wasn't supposed to know about, but Remi had given her the heads up, thankfully. Cherisse wasn't keen on surprises, but her mother never listened.

She had two weeks to get rid of this cold so she could enjoy her twenty-ninth birthday. She really should get up for that shower, but her foggy brain and tired, achy limbs were making that difficult.

"Sweet dreams, Sugar Queen," she heard before she drifted off again.

KEIRAN

Remi ignored him when he came downstairs with the tray and empty soup bowl. She was still staring at her laptop. When he'd shown up earlier, he'd been certain she wasn't going to let him in. She'd stood at the door, eyes raking him up and down, brow raised at the Tupperware container of soup.

"Brought food. Smart." Then she'd stepped aside for him to enter.

He'd expected some kind of *'what are your intentions with my friend?'* type interrogation, but she'd merely told him Cherisse was likely already in dreamland courtesy of some cold meds. He'd been surprised she'd let him hang out until Cherisse woke up, and he could take the soup up to her.

"Do I just leave this in the sink?" He lifted the tray.

She didn't look away from her laptop. "Sure."

He considered leaving the bowl in the sink, but his mother's voice in his ear scolding about washing up after himself was loud enough for him to rinse out the bowl and spoon and stash them in the appropriate slots on the draining board. He left the tray on the counter. His mother's Tupperware bowl had already been washed and dried off, so he grabbed that up. Figured this was his cue to leave.

He walked back out to the living room, expecting to just sail out the door.

"Tell me something, Keiran. How you think this will end, hmm?"

So damn close. Body angled to face him, her fingers drummed against the desk, other arm draped over the back of the chair.

"She'll get tired of me eventually and move on." He shrugged, even as the idea made his chest ache. He knew what he'd gotten himself into here. Knew he was full of shit when he'd agreed to this whole thing. He didn't just want this to be sex, and it would blow up in his face soon enough.

"And you're good with this?"

"Doesn't matter if that's what she wants."

"You like her—" He opened his mouth to protest. Remi held up a hand. "Don't even try to lie right now. You're both being ridiculous as hell here. I don't know what she's doing. Hell, I don't think she knows. Guess your pipe-laying skills are that good."

"She likes what I do well enough." He wasn't trying to be cocky. Cherisse had been vocal enough when coming for him to deduce that. But he sure as hell wasn't going into details with Remi.

"Someone's gonna get hurt," Remi announced.

"I won't hurt her."

"Yeah, I didn't mean her."

Of course. Because he was the sap in this situation. The one most likely to let his emotions tie him up when Cherisse was just here for a good fuck. He couldn't blame her. She'd been upfront. He was the one lying. About more than one thing.

He spun the empty bowl in his hand. "Anyway, thanks for letting me in. I need to go. Promised Maxi I'd babysit. She'll suffocate me in my sleep if I bail, and she doesn't get to go out."

"I wouldn't lose any sleep over that. She's the cuter twin anyways."

He clutched his chest. "Damn, tell me how you really feel."

"Bye, Keiran."

"Laters, Remeena." He chuckled all the way to the door as she tossed some seriously inventive curses at his back.

Chapter 27
Cherisse

IT TOOK THE REST OF the week and into the next one to fully ditch the cold, which set her back workwise, even with Reba handling details with that other wedding she had before Ava's. That bride had apparently been a hair-trigger away from going full-on Bridezilla with Reba because Cherisse hadn't shown up to the meeting. Reba's explanations that Cherisse was sick didn't help. The bride had shouted in Reba's face about being sent an assistant instead of Cherisse, which had then turned into Cherisse getting on the phone—still feeling like crap—to soothe the woman and fit in a reschedule of the meeting because no matter how Cherisse tried to tell her Reba was capable of running the meeting, the client didn't care.

Cherisse had been willing to dissolve that working relationship immediately. She didn't want to deal with someone who was condescending to Reba like that, but Reba had talked her down.

Coupled with that, Cherisse had apparently gotten a couple of offers for TV shows. One pitched a co-hosting segment with a popular local chef, Patrick Simmons, who had a weekly segment, and another was for some type of regional cooking contest. They'd both piqued her interest, especially the contest since the prize money was enough for her to put towards funding that project she'd been thinking about for a while—her own bakery. She didn't plan to work out of her apartment indefinitely, but spaces were so expensive to rent. A loan was an option, but Cherisse preferred to exhaust all other avenues first. A small part of her also needed to redeem herself after *Pastry Wars*. But, putting herself out there again was scary too, so she'd told Reba she would think on it a bit.

While she'd been trying to play catch up, she also caught herself glancing down at her phone. Keiran hadn't returned to check on her since the soup, but he'd been sending her ridiculous memes every day since then. He claimed they were to cheer her up, and she had found herself laughing at them while trying not to hack up a lung. Luckily, the damn cough mostly cleared up because her mother had come over to force-feed her some foul flu-be-gone concoction, which had turned into an interrogation about Jerome.

As they sat on the couch, her mother trying to pick her mouth about "the date," her phone chimed, and just like all the days before, it was another meme. This time, it was one of those 'What people think I do vs. what I really do' ones for pastry chefs. She snorted because it was so accurate.

"Is that him?" her mother asked, scooting over to peer at her phone. "See how he has you smiling? A true sign of something good. If a man can't make you laugh, then it's no good. Your father is ridiculous most times, but I can't help myself. I love that man."

"Mummy, come on!" Cherisse protested, putting her phone face down so her mother couldn't see the screen. As cute as that reveal about her father being able to still charm her mother was, she had no intention of letting on that her reaction had been to Keiran's message and not anything Jerome had sent.

That wouldn't go over too well, and she was in no mood for a lecture.

"Fine." Her mother scooted back, giving her some space. "But you always tell me stay out of your business, but see? I chose well. You like him."

"Let's not get carried away, okay? Just because I laugh at one thing doesn't mean it's time for a wedding."

Her mother sniffed. "Whatever. You never want to listen to me. But, just remember to tell my grandchildren I had a hand in their parents' love story."

Cherisse rolled her eyes. Nyla Gooding always knew how to lay it on thick, especially after the Sean fiasco. She'd definitely have a fit if she knew what Cherisse had been up to with Keiran. She'd been clear on her opinions, especially after seeing the fight video. *Keiran King was trouble.*

Cherisse agreed—not quite in the same way her mother meant, at least not anymore—because she couldn't wait for her mother to leave so she could reply to his silly meme. Trouble. So much trouble.

"You should invite Jerome to the wedding," her mother continued.

Cherisse rubbed her forehead. *That* was not happening. She could envision how terrible an idea that was. Bring the cousin of the man she was currently having sex with to the wedding? As a date? Absolutely not. Not that she planned to still be having sex with Keiran by then. He'd given her the power to end their arrangement whenever she wanted. So why hadn't she done that yet?

"The guest list is all set. I'm not going to upset Ava and Eric's carefully laid plans." Ava hadn't shown any Bridezilla tendencies, but Cherisse had seen her sister and Eric poring over the guest list and seating chart intensely. No way in hell was she messing with that. "Anyways, I got shit...uh, stuff to catch up on, so."

Her mother didn't call her on that slip of profanity. A miracle. But she did release an exasperated sigh before she tapped the jar of dark liquid and rose to her feet. "Take this for the lingering cough. It'll be gone in no time. Just don't let it touch your tongue because the taste is awful."

Arguing was pointless. It was easier to just let her mother have her way. Nod and smile until she left. As soon as she was gone, Cherisse checked her phone. Another meme from Keiran and a couple of new messages in the bridesmaids' chat group. She replied to Keiran first.

Cherisse: don't you have work to do?

Keiran: it's called multitasking

Cherisse: looks like playing de fool to me.

Keiran: much needed stress reliever more like it. How you feeling?

Cherisse: better. Thanks for the soup. And I guess the memes too

Keiran: just trying to be a good friend.

Cherisse paused. Friend? She wasn't certain she'd call them that. Fuck buddies? FWBs? She didn't know. It was something people did all the time, but she didn't like blurring the lines, didn't know how not to. She and Sean hadn't exactly been friends prior to them becoming a couple. They'd met randomly at an event, sparks flew. They'd hung out, and things had gotten serious pretty quickly. Sex had come after they'd been together a few months. This thing with Keiran was new territory for her.

Before she could respond, her phone chimed with another message from Ava, which turned out to be a notification that she'd been added to another group chat with the other bridesmaids.

Ava: hi my lovelies! Please meet me at the address below at 4pm and wear something nice!

Julia: ...

Cherisse: what's happening?

Ava: no questions, just be there!

Cherisse: this is sketchy as hell

Ava: omg it's nothing bad I swear

Remi: k

Cherisse: you're not even gonna ask what's going on?

Remi: nope

Ava: and that's why I love you. Ok mwah! See you all at the address k byeee!

Cherisse clicked the link Ava sent. The address turned out to be the same country club where they'd held the wedding shower. Why would Ava want them to meet her there, and what was with the secrecy? It obviously involved something wedding-related, but Cherisse couldn't begin to know what. She returned to Keiran's chat.

Keiran: so Eric dropped a weird meet me at this location text and a link to that country club. Weird.

Cherisse: Same here with Ava. What are they up to?

Keiran: No clue but he said to dress nice. What you wearing??

Cherisse: goodbye

Keiran: so mean

Cherisse: you like me this way

She pressed *send* on that before she thought better of it. Fuck. Would he take that as flirting? She hadn't meant to. It just seemed to come easily with Keiran, which, *no*. This flirting banter with him was a terrible idea and possibly sent mixed messages.

She switched back to the chat with Remi and Julia, where the conversation was still ongoing minus Ava, who'd dropped her summons and vanished.

Julia: it's the country club. That means we should dress fancy

Remi: I got that one dress that shows a lot of leg

Julia: anything you wear shows a lot of leg Madame Gazelle

This was safer territory. God, she was making this worse for herself.

It was so easy to let the banter fly when it wasn't face-to-face, but it wasn't helping to keep things casual. She realized she'd looked forward to his annoying meme messages, which weren't so annoying at all. Funny. Cute, even. Which was bad. So very bad. And he'd been so sweet bringing her the soup when she'd been sick, even if in the moment, she'd acted put-off about it.

End this.

She tossed her phone on the couch. She had too many things to get done before meeting Ava at the country club for whatever mysterious reason. Cackling at memes was nowhere on that list. Thinking about how sweet Keiran had been and how maybe he wasn't as terrible as she'd thought was going into a danger zone.

She ignored her phone while she finally typed up the list of names of persons who'd given Ava gifts at the wedding shower. Ava needed those for her thank you cards. But the constant pling of her phone kept beckoning, and finally, she sighed and picked it up, swiping to check the chats, but mostly Keiran's reply to her ill-advised message.

Keiran: you know I do

Her heart, pounding in her chest, startled her. God. Why had she checked that? Should she reply? He'd know she read it, but what could she even say that wouldn't make things more awkward when they met up at the club later? The country club. Where they'd had sex in a supply closet.

Congratulations, you definitely played yourself.

By the time Remi came home, showered, and got ready to head to the country club, Cherisse had worked herself into a tizzy. She'd popped on her sunglasses inside in preparation for stepping into the afternoon sunlight. After a week of confinement, the sun was sure to feel too bright. She'd also hoped to hide her growing anxiousness from Remi long enough that the drive would soothe her.

It was ridiculous to get worked up over seeing Keiran today. So, she liked his memes, looked forward to his messages. That didn't mean anything. What was her problem? Seriously.

"What're you thinking about so hard over there?" Remi asked as they rolled to a stop at a traffic light.

"Keiran." Remi was her best friend. Keeping stuff from her was always a waste of time.

"Ah."

"He's not fitting into the box I tried to put him into. I don't like this."

"Hmm. Human beings are unpredictable like that sometimes. But not you, you're super-predictable."

"What?" Cherisse asked, offended. "I am *not.*"

The light changed, and Remi drove forward. "You know you don't do casual but yet acted like you could. After I reminded you that you don't. Sex is important to you in that it's all wrapped up in your emotional connection to someone, and yet, you thought, oh, hey, it's Keiran, so this'll be easy."

Cherisse stared straight ahead, arms folded across her seat belt. "So, this is your long-winded I-told-you-so?"

"Yup."

"What do I do now?"

"I don't know. You jumped on his dick, you figure that shit out."

Cherisse continued to sulk the rest of the way to the club while Remi sang along jovially with the radio. But she was right. This was a mess of her own making, and she was the one who had to decide how to fix it.

Chapter 28

Keiran

MAXINE AND SCOTT WERE full of theories about why Eric and Ava had called them to the country club, ranging from Ava being pregnant to more outlandish things like a plan to elope. Keiran was too busy thinking about Cherisse and the supply closet to add anything useful.

"There's no way in hell they're eloping after all these preparations," Maxine mused as they walked in.

"Eric's parents are rich. They won't even feel that loss of money," Scott chimed in.

The attendant led them to the dining room, to a table where Ava and Eric were already waiting, big smiles on their faces. Remi, Julia, and Cherisse were already at the table too. Everyone was standing as if they, too, had just arrived.

Keiran's gaze clashed with Cherisse as he came to stand next to her.

"Well, you're looking better."

She fiddled with the belt on her jumpsuit. "I feel better. Thanks again for the soup. You're sweet. I mean, *it* was sweet. The gesture. Jesus fucking Christ." She looked away as Ava urged them all to sit. He was close enough to have heard her muttered curses, but what intrigued him the most was her fumbling. Was Cherisse nervous? Interesting.

"Thanks for meeting us here, everyone."

Keiran focused on Ava. He could ponder on Cherisse's babbling later.

"Are you pregnant?" Maxine blurted out, and everyone stared at her. Ava chuckled. "What? We're all thinking it."

"Not pregnant," Ava announced.

"You're eloping, aren't you? Or about to spring a surprise wedding right now, right here?" Scott nodded as if it were fact. "I knew it! I brought some makeup kits, *just* in case."

"Seriously?" Eric looked more amused than anything else.

"So, am I right?"

"Sorry, bud, but no."

Cherisse shifted next to him. "Are you calling off the wedding? Because I swear to God if you made us craft those damn crowns for nothing... Wait." Her eyes narrowed. "Are you gonna force us to make more of those? Is that what this is? Soften the blow by taking us somewhere fancy, so we can't make a scene? Because no."

Keiran covered his laugh by reaching for his water. Cherisse looked prepared to murder everyone if that was indeed the case.

"You're all ridiculous and wrong." Ava beamed at Eric, who grinned back.

"Well, tell us, dammit!" Julia had been silently observing and had now clearly lost all patience.

"Okay, Jesus. Eric and I wanted to thank you all for being so great. Taking every task we asked of you in stride. Well..." She turned to Cherisse and Keiran. "Most tasks. You pulled off an amazing party and didn't kill each other. Yay."

If only Ava knew what it took to get there. He and Cherisse exchanged a look, and Keiran couldn't be sure, but hers looked mildly panicked. What was going on?

"So, to thank you all, we've gotten you a one-year membership to the club!"

"Hell, yes!" Remi shouted.

"Isn't it customary to give the wedding party gifts closer to the wedding?" Cherisse asked. "I mean, we're not that far off, but it's still a few weeks."

"True," Eric piped up. "But we figured you get to make use of the facilities before that. As in today. We've already planned a little pre-wedding pamper session for you all. And Remi and Cherisse, you can use it for your birthday week as well."

"We already got the spa vouchers from Laney's brunch, but we'll see. May as well make a spa tour of it."

"This is the best gift ever," Scott said.

"Thank my rich fiancé for that." Ava clapped her hands together. "We should eat then get to the fancy spa stuff."

"Hey! I thought you were marrying me for my body?"

Ava blew Eric a kiss. "That too, darling. Make no mistake about that." Her slow perusal of Eric from head to toe could've singed them all. Eric flushed and coughed, causing the entire table to erupt into raucous laughter, earning them a few looks from the other guests around them.

They probably wouldn't be too pleased about their group regularly descending on their club, but Keiran was looking forward to using the facilities for some regular self-care. It wasn't a thing he did often or enough. After dealing with Sean, he was certainly going to need it. He'd been carrying around way too much tension.

"God, you're both so disgustingly cute." Maxine made fake gagging sounds, and Ava and Eric just shrugged before closing the gap between them for a quick kiss. Scott wolf-whistled, and the rest of the party piled on the teasing.

Yup, this club was not prepared for them at all. Well, the rest of them, at least. Eric's family had been members for years, which was probably how they'd gotten them memberships without going through some rigorous vetting process.

As the others decided on the menu, Keiran leaned over to Cherisse and whispered, "Do you think our closet's been lonely without us?"

Cherisse didn't look at him. "I'll stab you with this fork if you don't shush." But there was no real heat behind her threat.

"Once it's nowhere important."

She cocked her head. "I'll leave your mouth alone. It's of most use to me."

"God damn, woman." His cock twitched. He shouldn't be turned on by that, but it would seem that Cherisse could say anything, and he'd be on board.

"Are you scared, Keiran?" she taunted.

"Terrified, actually." And not for the reasons she believed. *Because you're everything that I want and can't have.* He reached for his water so he wouldn't say that because God knows he would fuck up their already shaky situation.

"Good. Gotta keep you on your toes."

"Already there."

They dispensed with their sneaky conversation as the server came to take their order, and Keiran met Remi's sharp gaze over the server's notepad. Her words came back to him.

"Someone's gonna get hurt," Remi announced.

"I won't hurt her."

"Yeah, I didn't mean her."

The sensible thing to do was end it before Cherisse did, but a small part of him hoped she wouldn't. A foolish notion, but here he was, unable to. Remi's words continued to echo in his head as Ava's group went off to get their pampering done.

He could barely enjoy the chocolates that were offered for guests of the spa or the full-body massage.

"You're very tense," the masseuse noted as she worked at his shoulders.

No kidding. He had too much going on. Sean. Cherisse. The wedding. His overwhelmed brain refused to allow him to enjoy this. The others were happily sighing while getting their massages. Keiran needed a breather. The music being piped into the room was supposed to be soothing, but it was grating on his every nerve. He got up, surprising the poor masseuse as he flung on one of the fluffy robes. He gave the woman a tight smile and announced to his sister and friends, "Bathroom calls."

Except this section of the club was unfamiliar to him, the wedding shower having been held on the other side, so he found himself wandering around.

"It can't be that hard to find the bathrooms, come on," he muttered as he turned down a corridor and ran into none other than the woman occupying a good portion of his thoughts.

"We've gotta stop running into each other like this," Cherisse said, dressed similarly in one of the spa robes, face covered in some sort of mud mask. "Looking for the bathrooms too?"

"Yeah."

"I think the directions I got said left, but clearly not."

"Better off than me. I didn't get any directions. Just sort of winged it."

"Well, we're quite the pair." Cherisse plucked at her robe, and there it was again. The sense that she was nervous. But why?

"What's going on with you?" he asked.

Her brow furrowed. "Looking for the bathroom, same as you."

"Not what I meant. You're acting weird."

She stuck her hand into the robe's pockets. "We're in a weird situation, aren't we?"

Yes, they were, and her discomfort could be from trying to act like nothing was going on between them, but something else was up here. What he'd learned about Cherisse over the time they'd known each other was that she was good at keeping her cool and, as amusing as it was to see the moments where he ruffled her feathers, this was different. Cherisse might lose her temper with him, but she'd never fumble or fiddle like this.

"I told you, you can end it at any time."

"Why's that pressure on me?" she demanded, eyes blazing.

Pressure? Hold on. He looked at her face—really looked. She was barely meeting his gaze, and her teeth kept worrying at her bottom lip. Oh. Cherisse wouldn't be talking about pressure if...

"Cherisse, I know why it's hard for me to end this. It's why I gave you the power. But why is it hard for you?"

Her eyes widened as if he'd caught her in a private moment. "I-it's not."

"*You* mentioned pressure. You feel something, don't you?"

"The only thing I feel is a tummyache coming on from all those complimentary chocolates I ate," she said, but the smile plastered on her lips wasn't reflected in her eyes. "I'm gonna go."

Had he read her wrong? But what did he expect from Cherisse? She'd made it quite clear what she'd thought of guys in his business. But hadn't that been before they'd gotten to know each other outside of their initial dislike? Besides, even if she did feel something for him, it wasn't fair for him to demand she reveal it, here and now.

He forced a smile to his lips. "Yeah, wouldn't want them to worry." He turned away to head back to Maxine and the guys, but the unexpected touch to his arm halted his steps. He looked back, surprised to see Cherisse still standing there.

"I don't even know what I'm doing," she mumbled before looking up at him. "I do feel something," she rushed out. "But I don't know if I'm going to do anything with that."

"Because of Jerome?" he asked carefully, not wanting to give away how much her hastily spoken words affected him. Calm was the word of the day, even though he felt so far from it.

"Jerome's got nothing to do with it. I made you think he did, but no. He's nice to talk to, but..." She reached up to scrub at her face then remembered the mask. "Shit, I gotta wash this off. I don't—"

"Trust me?" It made sense, considering her history with Sean. *Tell her, tell her, just fucking tell her.* It was on the tip of his tongue to blurt it out, about working with Sean, about what they were going to do with the video. But her confession was so tentative, and she was standing there looking like she wished she could take the words back. What would *his* confession do to that?

As selfish as it was, he didn't want to destroy the already fragile moment.

"I thought I could easily trust you with my body, and I did, but when I trust someone with that, it's never *just* that. I don't know why I thought I could do that."

"Cherisse, I..." He didn't want to say the words out loud in case he jinxed it, and God, why was he being such a coward about Sean?

But she stepped back, shook herself hard, and said, "I have to go," then turned to walk briskly away.

Well, then. What the hell was he supposed to do with that?

Chapter 29
Cherisse

SHE HAD NO CLUE HOW she made it to her birthday without combusting.

The spa pampering afternoon at the Marigold Club had been much needed, but she'd ruined it for herself. Everyone else had been relaxed after, but how was she supposed to do that after that encounter with Keiran?

She'd basically admitted to having feelings for him and then run off.

Talk about terrible timing for a confession of that magnitude. On top of all of that, he'd sent a **Can we talk?** text, which she was still ignoring. Regardless of knowing the topic of discussion, her anxiety was dialed all the way up. She had no idea how to approach this talk they needed to have.

Why hadn't she just kept walking, not turned back to utter those words? That damn impulsiveness again, just waiting to cause problems. He'd sensed something was off with her. She'd done a poor job of keeping her nerves under wraps, but he wouldn't have known that if she'd kept her mouth shut.

"This is orgasmic."

"What?" Yanked out of her anxious thoughts, she turned to her mother, who sat across the table from her devouring her waffles. Her parents had insisted on treating her to a birthday breakfast at Lola's, which was delightfully empty at the moment, so they had the place all to themselves.

Lola's breakfast was amazing, but Cherisse did not need to hear the word 'orgasmic' coming out of her mother's mouth.

"Mummy, please." She grimaced but shoved another bite of her waffles in her mouth. Heaven. She'd opted for chicken on her waffles because why not?

Her father chuckled. "Honey, don't embarrass the child on her birthday."

"What?" Her mother didn't look the least repentant. "Isn't that how the young people talk these days?"

"I'm hardly one of those young people you're referring to," Cherisse pointed out.

West Indian parents were such a plethora of contradictions. Her mother would conveniently treat her like she was still a child when it suited her needs but, of course, reminded her at every turn that she wasn't getting any younger and shouldn't wait too long to get a man. As if she had any control over that.

Although...

Her mind ran on Keiran, and she immediately dropped her fork, the loud clang echoing around the empty restaurant. Definitely not the man her mother would have in mind for her, but her mother didn't know him like she'd gotten to. He'd shown her something else of himself other than what the rumors said and what she'd assumed. Especially that day in the studio.

"Everything okay?" Her father's hand was gentle on her arms. He was the softie between her parents, and most times, she and Ava would run to him for soothing when her mother had chided them for some perceived slight.

She was definitely a daddy's girl.

"Yes." She mustered a smile. "I'm fine. I think...I might be having an epiphany about something, is all."

"About Jerome?" Her mother looked hopeful, and Cherisse almost busted out laughing. *Wrong guy, mother.*

But then she thought, why not? Why not just stop keeping things inside and say what was on her mind? It could've just been the sugar coursing through her veins, giving her a false sense of "don't care," but it was her birthday, dammit. She could do this.

"Not Jerome. Someone else."

Her mother's perfectly filled-in brow winged up. "Someone else?" she repeated slowly as if the idea of Cherisse succeeding in this on her own was ludicrous.

"I like him, and maybe you'll meet him at the party I'm not supposed to know about but obviously do. So, I'm gonna need you to abort your matchmaking mission. Please."

Her mother's eyes narrowed, and Cherisse refused to look away. The wheels were obviously turning in her mother's head, trying to figure out who the hell Cherisse was talking about. But her birthday wasn't the time for argument, and one would definitely erupt if she so much as mentioned Keiran's name.

"Looking forward to meeting him," her father said, offering up his usual smile as her mother continued to stare her down. "Seems like a great time for presents!"

Ever the peacemaker, her father's jovial attitude was catching, and by the time she was scheduled to meet Remi at the Hyatt, she was in less of a panic mode—by a smidge. The apprehension was still there, of course, because *what was she doing?* But step one was complete. She'd told her mother to back off on her matchmaking. She was still a mess of emotions and possibly falling headlong into something, but it was a start.

Even so, it was their birthday, and she shouldn't allow herself to check out because of *feelings*. The next step was checking into the Hyatt, then out with the girls tonight. Anything else could wait. Easier said than done, but she owed it to her girls to be present. Keiran was on her mind too much. The fact that it wasn't *just* naughty fantasies with him in a starring role was distressing, but maybe not as terrible as whatever her nervousness was doing to her gut. *Relax, girl. You got this. Keiran King is but a man.*

"Reba's apparently smuggling in some stuff." Remi tapped her phone screen as they waited in the lobby for Reba to show up.

"Stuff?" With Reba, that could mean anything from booze to sexy entertainment.

"Drinks to pregame. Something sweet? Who knows? She's being all cagey about it. So expect birthday surprises."

"Surprises? Father God, don't let this be a repeat of last year."

Remi busted out laughing, entire body shaking. "Listen, I didn't think she'd actually come through with that."

"You put it on the list!"

Last year, Reba had told them to make a list of things they'd want at a party. They'd gotten the surprise of their lives when a sexy dancer had shown up at the joint birthday party. Luckily, it had been just friends, no parents. The dancer had come complete with an old-school boombox and a costume that ripped easily away.

"It was a joke, a challenge. Reba's always talking about her connections, but I didn't think she'd actually hire that woman. Who even owns a boombox anymore?" Remi waggled her brows. "I don't know 'bout you, but I had a good time."

She sure had. Her bestie had enjoyed her lapdance lots. Cherisse had just watched on, amused. There was no official party this time—at least, not being thrown by them. She could be certain her mother's party would be tame, but who knew what shenanigans Reba would get up to? They'd forgone the list after that, but it didn't mean Reba wouldn't shake things up.

"I miss the list. We could've kept it."

"No damn way."

Remi pouted. "But I was so looking forward to sexy break-dancing firefighters this year."

"Maybe next year. Thirty should ring in with a bang, right?" She winked.

She had no doubt Reba would somehow come through with Remi's very specific request. It was one of the reasons Cherisse had hired her. She was connected. Her resume hadn't hurt either. Reba didn't talk about the details surrounding why she'd left her last job, but Cherisse suspected it hadn't been an amicable split. She was grateful for her, and they'd meshed well, becoming friends along the way. Sometimes, the lines blurred between work and friendship, but Reba never pandered to her, which Cherisse appreciated.

Reba told her if an idea was shit or if something just wasn't going to work. Plus, she got stuff done. She was an asset because Cherisse would have fallen behind on updating any social media related to Sweethand. Not to mention, Reba's pastry skills were a gift.

Reba arrived at the Hyatt with her bags casually slung over her shoulder and a small suitcase. Cherisse eyed her bags. "Do I even wanna know?" she asked as they went through the check-in process.

Reba grinned. "All shall be revealed when we get to the rooms. We got separate rooms for you and Remi since I don't know what after-party plans you birthday girls may get up to. Don't wanna cramp any potential sexy times. Ava and I'll share."

Remi didn't say a word but tossed Cherisse a look heavy with questions. Cherisse rolled her eyes. She hadn't specifically planned on any birthday sex, and it was probably for the best that she not reach out to her current supplier. Her plan tonight was to party with her girls and deal with Keiran later. "My after plans will probably be sleeping off a hangover," she said.

Reba wagged a finger at her as they followed the guy helping them with their bags. "Never say never, and I noticed Remi isn't saying a damn thing."

Remi looked up from her phone. "I'm deep in birthday wishes. Look, I got the Twitter balloons and everything! We'll see what goes down tonight, but good looking out, Reebs."

Reba pretended to dust off her shoulder. "It's just what I do. Okay, let's get settled in our rooms, then meet up by the pool in twenty minutes."

The room was a standard with one big bed and the classic Hyatt shower in the middle of the room. She'd always found the shower placement odd but figured it could be a good time with the right person. Refusing to dwell on that too much, she changed into a bright pink floral monokini and tossed a flowy cover-up over it before checking her messages. She had a couple across her platforms, mostly thanks to Reba sending out a blast on the Sweethand accounts that it was her birthday. She had a bunch on her personal account too.

She rarely did selfies—it frustrated her how many photos she had to take before being satisfied with one—but figured it was her special day. She looked and felt cute, so why the heck not? She took one of her lounging on the bed and played around with captions and tags before uploading to Instagram and sharing on her linked accounts.

Happy birthday to me!!! I think I make almost 30 look good, no? #birthdaygirl #29andfeelingfine #thefunnowstart

Remi, always on point with her posts and selfies, had already updated her Instagram with an adorable photo over breakfast with her parents and brother, Akash, and a tour of her hotel room on her story.

"So lovelies, me and the birthday twin bestie are about to go get our drink on by the pool. Then later, who knows what trouble we'll get up to?" She winked and signed off with a peace sign, all while wearing a lopsided "birthday girl" crown. It seemed Reba had already given out one part of her surprise.

By the time they grabbed drinks and Cherisse had been presented with her own crown, they'd taken a multitude of photos—mostly shots posing with their drinks, the infinity pool in the background—and Cherisse had been inundated with more messages, likes, and comments on her pics. She noted that **keirank** had liked all of them. She'd gotten a happy birthday text too, had shot back with a quick "thanks!" and nothing else. Today was her and Remi's day. No time to dwell on sexy men who made her moan and got her heart racing for non-sex-related reasons. Nope. No time at all.

WHEN AVA GOT TO THE Hyatt, Reba was sober-ish enough to meet her downstairs so she could organize a separate room key for her and get Cherisse a new one because her tipsy ass had already forgotten not to put her phone near her keycard. She'd only realized the thing had demagnetized when she'd tried to duck back into her room to grab the forgotten sunscreen.

At that point, Cherisse had said fuck it and not bothered, returning to the pool area, which was on their floor anyway. She wasn't exactly steady enough to traipse downstairs for another card, and none of the others wanted to either.

Ava met them in the water with cocktail in hand, bright yellow bikini nearly blinding them as the sun glinted off her.

"Happy birthdaaaaaay!" She kissed Remi and Cherisse on their cheeks, and they toasted with their drinks.

Cherisse couldn't recall what number cocktail she was on, only that it was delicious, and she was all buzzy, which was the perfect mix for bad decisions. She'd been itching to check her phone to see if a certain somebody had sent any more messages. Thankfully, her phone was on the lounge chair all the way over there, and they were in the water.

"We're gonna need a nap before we go out tonight." Remi yawned.

"I'm about that nap life," Reba agreed. "Don't listen to anyone who says naps are for babies and senior citizens. How do they think I keep going all night long?"

Cherisse raised a brow. "We still talking about dancing?"

"Yes, boss lady. Get your mind out the gutter! Although I *do* got that stamina."

Everyone cackled at that. Remi swished her hand through the water as she slurped her drink. Cherisse had no idea what Remi's drink was at this point, only that the glass was tall, the drink blue, and the garnish was a mix of pineapples and cherries.

"Oh, hey! I totally forgot!" Reba giggled. "I brought food and margarita cupcakes and rum punch! Surprise!" She clapped her hand over her mouth, looking around before whispering, "I hope no staff heard that."

The bartender had been steadily supplying their drinks since Reba excitedly informed him about the double birthdays, but either he was too busy to have heard her loud outburst, or he really didn't care. He didn't even look up from the bar. By five o'clock, they all agreed it was time to at least sober up a bit then nap to reenergize for tonight. They were toasty and tipsy. The four of them weaved their way back to Reba and Ava's room. Ava was the most sober, having opted to leave her drinking for tonight.

While Reba dished out what looked like an entire meal her mother would cook on a Sunday—Spanish rice, baked chicken, and pigeon peas with some fresh salad on the side—Cherisse caught up on her notifications, snapping some of the spread to post. She sent one to Keiran before she could stop herself.

Keiran: damn! On my way!

Cherisse: no boys allowed

Keiran: sigh. So cruel

This was safe. She could do this. Banter—without a side of talking about things better left said later, after she'd sobered up. Everything was way too sparkly anyhow. She was in no condition for serious conversations. Who knew what else she'd let slip? She didn't get to respond because her phone was pulled out of her hand. "Hey!"

Remi held Cherisse's phone over her head. Cherisse didn't even try for it. Remi was too tall, even in flip-flops. "It's time to eat, then nap, then ass shaking. All people with the last name King are banned today."

"Seriously? When did we make that rule?"

"Just this second because you're in no condition to be talking to Keiran."

Reba looked between both of them. "What did I miss?"

Remi lowered her hand, grip tight on the phone as Cherisse reached for it. "There's a lot of liquor sloshing around our insides right now. Trust me. We're both guilty of texting while tipsy. So I gave Ava my phone so I wouldn't drunk-text anyone."

"I was just replying to birthday messages," Cherisse lied, which was pointless because Remi was already on to her. She rolled her eyes and wiggled her hand. Remi released her phone, finger wagging.

"Don't you do it!"

"Ugh, fine." She stomped over to Ava and handed her sister the phone with no explanation. "Hold this for me 'til later?"

Ava took it, brow wrinkled. "Um?"

"Same deal as Remi. Save me from myself." She clapped her hands together, tummy rumbling as her eyes dropped to the plates. "Okay, let's eat!"

Chapter 30

Keiran

THE TWINKLING LIGHTS of the city below were a contrasting background to the smoky smells of BBQ wafting over from the tents that covered the food stalls. The lookout was lined with other cars. Some families were chowing down on food, and a few couples were all snuggled up against each other, taking in the view. Others snapped selfies, trying to get the perfect angle to capture all those lights down below.

"Well, this is romantic, isn't it?" Eric plopped down next to Keiran on the hood of his car, box of BBQ balanced on his lap. "I mean, I love you guys and all, but I wish Ava were here. No cuddle buddy to gaze at the stars."

"Ha! I'll have you know I give the best cuddles," Scott announced.

"That's debatable," Keiran said.

It *was* romantic, with the city lights glistening down below and the stars dotting the sky above. The lookout was well-known as a place for couples. Some food vendors had seized the opportunity and set up food stalls. There were more people coming just to get food and check out the view rather than only couples these days.

"Wonder how the ladies are doing?" Eric opened his box and took a whiff of his food. It overflowed with BBQ chicken, rice, and fries. The fresh salad was somewhere under all that goodness if the bit of green leaf that Keiran assumed was lettuce was anything to go by.

"Pretty damn good, I'd say." Scott waved his phone. "The 'gram don't lie."

Keiran had checked Remi and Cherisse's posts all afternoon. His conversation with Cherisse earlier that afternoon had stopped abruptly after she'd sent the photo of their lunch spread, and he'd joked about coming down there.

There'd been a pre-nap selfie of Remi hovering over Cherisse, who had clearly succumbed to the itis—lying on her stomach, hair spilled around her. She was either asleep or on her way there.

remi_d: nap time before party time :P @cherrygoody #somuchfood #birthdaytwin

He always got a kick out of Cherisse's Instagram name. She used the same name on all her social media and had mentioned how people kept thinking her accounts were porn sites when really, she only showcased food porn. The photo explained the aborted conversation.

He had to stop obsessively checking every update, but he was weak. He'd casually walked away from Eric and Scott as he scrolled, giving the illusion that he was taking scenery shots with his phone. Cherisse had posted a photo all dolled up, hair fluffed up in some kind of up-do, neck encased in a lacy black choker. He was so used to seeing her with her hair down that whenever she put her hair up, he zoomed right in on her neck. Knowing now that it was one of her zones didn't help. The way she squirmed when he nibbled at her throat right there...

"Daaamn, face beat to perfection on this one," Scott said, peering down at Keiran's phone. Jesus, he'd been so engrossed in the photo he hadn't even realized Scott had come up behind him to mind his business. Not that Cherisse *was* his business. But she could be. If she wanted that. But he didn't know what Cherisse wanted. She'd admitted she didn't know herself, and she'd all but ignored his request to talk. He shouldn't have pushed.

He closed out of the app and frowned. "Personal space, man. It's a thing."

Scott deployed his epic eye-roll. "You just salty you got caught. Whatever, be less obvious then." The words irked, but Scott was right. He hadn't tried hard enough to be covert. He should work on that. He still hadn't told Eric about the kiss or anything else.

"They just posting thirst traps for your ass, and you don't even know. Sad," Scott informed, cheeky grin plastered on his face.

"Oh, come on. There's no thirst trap setting."

"Maybe not intentionally by Cherisse, but when you have Remi "The Mastermind" Daniels as your bestie, I'd say trap's being set." Scott held up his finger. "One, I'll bet my comic book collection that Remi knows all the dirty deets about you and Cherry. Two," Scott carried on, a second finger joining the first one. "You've never been her favorite person because of that rivalry with Maxi back in the day, so I'm certain she's out there having Cherisse dialing up the sexiness to maximum just to have you panting. You, my friend, are sadly obvious. And, I know you're about two seconds away from driving to the Avenue to act like you just happened to casually be there to run into them."

He wanted to deny it, but the thought had crossed his mind. He'd vetoed it, but the night was still young. It was barely ten now.

"I'm not going down there," he insisted.

Scott looked skeptical, lips pursed, brow raised, arms folded in front of his favorite t-shirt. Grey and well-worn, the material of the t-shirt was so thin it molded easily to Scott's build. He'd been leaner back when he'd been modeling more, but he'd packed on some muscle since then. The words on the front were starting to get a little patchy from where the print was scraping away, bit by bit. Keiran grinned as he read it: *Part-time model. Full-time nerd.* Scott had had this t-shirt forever.

In the past, the sight of his friend in it, short sleeves flaunting the muscles shifting beneath his toned deep-brown skin, would have Keiran feeling some kind of way. The flutters had long since dissipated, leaving affection and warmth whenever his best friend shook his head at him, the way he did now.

"Don't get me wrong, I'm rooting for you. I just worry that you'll let her walk all over you just so you can be close to her. Not that I'm saying she'd do that," Scott added hastily. "You know she's my girl. Just be realistic about what your expectations are."

"I know." Of course, he knew all that. But Scott didn't know about Cherisse's confession. And Keiran didn't feel right about revealing it when Cherisse was obviously torn up about it. He'd gone into this claiming he was fine with whatever when that hadn't been the truth from that first kiss. He'd told her the power was in her hands. She could end this whenever she wanted. He'd been bracing since then for when she'd do just that. Could he take front and end it before he got any more caught up than he was?

"Why so serious?" Eric joined them, patting his belly, a satisfied, happy sigh escaping his lips. Clearly, the food had been tasty. "What're we discussing?"

Keiran felt Scott's stare on the side of his face. He could spill everything, let Eric into the loop. Eric was his boy, but he'd joined the crew later on after the Scott/Keiran duo had already been solidified. Back in school, when one was seen without the other, people would look at them funny, like something wasn't quite right. That bestie bond was strong. Eric made them the Three Musketeers, but there were just some things Keiran had never told Eric about. Especially the whole "I tried to kiss my bestie and got rejected hard, and then I wanted to fade away into nothingness because it was so awkward" incident.

"Tell you later," Keiran replied. "What'd you all think about a drive down to the boardwalk?"

THE CHAGUARAMAS BOARDWALK was the place to be on the weekend, it seemed. Well, for those who preferred to hang out away from the club vibes of the city. People walked about with families and friends as lights glinted off the dark sheet of the water. Some walked along the shore; others were set up on the beachfront walkway deck.

It was a chill atmosphere, one he hoped he'd get to walk with Cherisse sometime. He rubbed at his chest as if to keep the feelings bubbling up at bay.

"They've really fixed up this place," Eric observed.

They were set up near the railing, arms draping over it as they looked out at the water. This area had seen some major development over the years. It was evolving into a full-on hotspot for locals and tourists.

"Nice spot." Scott was on his phone again, and Keiran had a few guesses as to whose timeline he was checking.

"Anything interesting going on?" he asked casually.

Scott continued scrolling. "If by interesting, you mean all this thirst trap posting going on. Damn." He stared down at his phone. "Who's even allowed to have a face like that? Also, quit fishing." He looked up at Keiran. "If you want to see what she's up to, no one's stopping you."

Keiran rolled his eyes. He didn't reach for his phone. Instead, he caught up with his boys—even though Scott's eyes were still glued to his phone—and they talked about the wedding, work, anything that wasn't related to the birthday girls' current celebration.

The conversation was a good distraction from Cherisse and other things that were cropping up on the horizon, workwise. He'd finally spoken with his father because the track was officially done and ready to be teased to the public, except his father was being mum on exactly when they'd drop the teaser online.

They hung around the boardwalk until one in the morning when yawns started to break out, and tiredness crept into Eric's face. His friend was having a rough time at work with difficult clients and older employees who still felt he had to prove himself capable of running his father's company one day. Keiran didn't envy Eric in that regard at all.

They'd decided to call it a night after more yawns were deployed and were on their way to their respective cars when Keiran's phone chimed. He nearly dropped it when he checked his chats.

"Jesus, fuck." He skidded to a stop.

Eric and Scott stopped walking too. Damn, he'd said that out loud.

"Everything good?" Eric asked, concern clouding his face.

"Oh, yeah, just fine. Great."

"You sure?" Scott prodded.

"Yes, was just caught off guard by a...thing. But it's all good." Caught off guard was really selling it short. He'd damn near bitten his tongue off at the photo Cherisse had sent him. They'd clearly returned to the hotel. She was on the bed, lying on her side, fluffy white robe on, the front of it gaping open to reveal her lacy bra, a hint of stomach, then a slice of her matching lace panties. The message read: **make my birthday wish *come* true? Room 411**

It was a booty call, plain and simple. He told himself to ignore it. Go home. They had so much to talk about, and this was clearly not an invitation to talk.

"Keiran?"

He looked up. Eric and Scott were still waiting. He'd forgotten about them. That damn photo.

"Sorry. I'll catch up with you later. Message when you get home. I have to go meet someone to get...uh...something real quick, then home."

"At this hour?" Eric asked, brow wrinkled.

Scott's concern had vanished. He knew what was up. His arms were folded, eyes narrowed. Keiran stared back, challenged Scott to call him out, say something. Scott shook his head.

"Just be safe," he said, tossing a wave over his shoulder as he headed for his car.

Eric still looked confused, but he waved and followed Scott to where they'd parked. Keiran waited for the guys to disappear before heading to his car and replying to Cherisse's sexy photo.

Keiran: on my way!!!!

Cherisse: fined. For excessive use of ! but yes please hurry. I'm waiting

The emojis were followed by another sexy photo. This time, the robe was flipped back to reveal a bit of rounded ass cheek. Jesus, help him.

It took him fifteen minutes to get to the Hyatt, heart pounding, body buzzing. After he strolled into the hotel and ran up the stairs to the elevators, he realized he needed someone with a keycard to access the elevators. He'd completely forgotten that in his horny state. Luck seemed to be with him tonight as some people strolled over just as he was about to text Cherisse and used their card to call the elevator. He pressed the button for four and hoped he wouldn't run into Remi, Reba, or Ava.

He assumed Cherisse wouldn't have sent that invitation if she shared a room. Didn't stop him from moving briskly down the fourth floor to find the right room. It took a bit for her to answer the door after his **I'm here** text, but when she did, *holy Jesus*. Her hair was a rumpled shiny wave around her shoulders, the makeup around her eyes slightly smudged, but she looked decadently sexy in that loosely tied robe. Her saucy smile had him hard in no time.

She yanked him inside, closed the door, then dove into kissing him as she led him backwards to the bed. The tie of the robe gave up trying to stay in a knot and swung open. Keiran's hands swept up her sides, thumbs caressing the lacy front of her bra as they got to the bed. And he tried to be the voice of reason. He really did.

"We should talk, Cherisse."

"Talk after. Make me come *now*." Cherisse stumbled and almost careened to the side. "Whoops," she giggled loudly, righting herself, giving him a good look at her underwear through the gaping front of the robe.

Keiran pulled back, eyes searching hers. Her eyes were heavy-lidded, slightly glassy. "Cherisse, are you drunk right now?"

"Pssh. Maybe a little tipsy? It's all good. I know what I'm about. I've been drinking water like a good girl. See?" She waved at the bottle of water on the bed. She reached for him again, and he gently stopped her with a hand on her wrist.

"We're not doing this if you're not sober. If I'd known that was a drunken sext..." He hadn't even considered it, which was thoughtless of him. He'd stopped checking their social media updates, but they had started the drinking fairly early. His horny ass hadn't thought of anything else but getting under or on top of Cherisse.

"Fine." She pouted and crawled into the bed. "Stay until I sober up? Then we can have fun?" She patted the spot beside her. "I'll behave." Her smile said that was a lie, but Keiran kicked off his shoes and crawled next to her, back braced against the headboard.

She tossed the robe off the rest of the way, then rolled onto her side.

"This is you behaving?"

She grinned. "Not even a little."

He could handle a little teasing, no big. This full-on seduction routine presented more of a challenge. He nudged the forgotten bottle of water until it rolled against her bare side. "Drink." She drew the bottle to her mouth, red lips covering the entire head of the bottle then dragging it out slowly, eyes fixed on him. "Cherisse, c'mon," he pleaded.

"Okay, I'll be good." Her giggle said otherwise, but she let up on the water bottle fellatio. "Let's play a game."

He eyed her suspiciously. He should just go. Not because he wasn't getting the sex he'd come for, but this was starting to feel a little too cozy, and his willpower was frayed. "Does it involve stripping?"

"No, since you won't let me have any fun. And don't look at me like that, I know, okay? I shouldn't have drunk-sexted you and put you in an awkward position."

Well, they agreed on that. "So, what's the game?"

"Confessions."

That sounded like the worst idea. Yet, he wasn't heading for the door, too intrigued. She was pulling out all the weapons at her disposal right now, and he was a sucker. Brown eyes, all big and shiny, looked up at him as she sprawled there in just her underwear, bare skin tempting him to touch. Oh, she was devious. Whoever underestimated Cherisse was in for a rude awakening.

"Alright," he conceded.

She gestured to the side table. "Liquid courage if you need it. The hotel sent each of us a birthday bottle of champagne. Didn't finish it all. Room's chilly enough. It's probably still cool enough to drink."

He took a swig straight from the bottle and gestured for her to start.

"Hmm. I told my mother no more matchmaking."

Keiran blinked at her. "Why'd you tell her that?"

"Because." She sipped her water, small smile on her face as she watched him.

"Because?"

"Because I like you."

"Well, I already know that." It didn't hurt to hear it again, though.

"Shut up. Your turn."

He grinned, took another sip of the champagne. Fine, he'd play along. "Pizza Hut is overrated."

Cherisse gasped. "You take that back. I won't stand for this slander!"

"My mom's homemade pizza is way better."

"Hmm, never had it, so you better rectify that soon." She glared, and he thought she was ridiculously charming in this moment.

They went back and forth, confessing things that bordered on silly, steering clear of her earlier confession even as Keiran wanted to circle back to it. Why had she told her mother no more matchmaking? He needed to hear her reason. He couldn't make any assumptions. His poor heart couldn't take it if he was wrong about what it meant. All the while, Keiran knew he should slow down on the champagne. The whole point of the game was to pass the time while Cherisse sobered up, and here he was, downing the bubbly.

"I used to have a crush on Scott," he blurted. Shit. Fuck his loosened lips.

Cherisse blinked at him, hands flying to her face. "Oh my God, what? Are you serious right now, Keiran?" she shrieked. There went the cozy bubble they'd been encased in for the last—he stole a quick glance at his phone—thirty minutes. He waited.

"I can't believe this." The bed was shaking, and he swung his head her way. Was she crying? Laughter bubbled up from behind her hands, and Cherisse spread her fingers to peek through them at him.

"You're laughing." He stated the obvious. Was she cracking up like this because she thought he was joking about Scott? He considered pretending just that. It would be easier than what the alternative could be. Her entire body still shook from her laughter.

"Yes!" She removed her hands. "This is too funny! I had a crush on Scott too."

Say what now? He hadn't expected that. "What?"

"From Form 1 to about halfway through Form 2, which is when I just gave up since I knew I had no chance. I mean, can you blame me? Scott has always just been all good-looking, and he's never had an awkward phase in his life. Puberty was kind to him. This is so hilarious. We both had crushes on Scott!"

"Yeah, I just...wow. I thought your shock meant something else," he trailed off.

She stared at him, a frown forming a crease between her brows. "Wait, did you think I was upset?"

"It's cool," he rushed out.

"Keiran, shit. You thought I was upset because of that? Oh my God, I'm sorry I laughed. I didn't mean for you to think that. But yeah, fuck, I see how my reaction wasn't the best. I'm a fucking fool."

"Hey, it's fine. I just misread."

She grabbed his hand. "I don't care if you're—uh, I don't want to use the wrong word."

"Bi." It tumbled out before he could filter himself, brush it off. Make light of it. But dammit, he didn't want to. He wanted Cherisse to know him. "It's what I've been IDing as for a while now. I'm not out or anything. Well, just to Maxi, and Scott, who knows obviously because we kissed back then, and..."

"The fuck? You and Scott kissed?" Her mouth hung open.

His face heated. He was embarrassed to talk about it because it hadn't been his smoothest moment. He wanted to crawl out of his skin now. He'd kept this stuff to just his sister and Scott for so long.

"I kissed him. Even Eric doesn't know that."

"I won't say a thing. You can trust me on that," she assured him. "I gotta say, teenage me is jealous as hell. I bet he was a good kisser."

"Well, I sort of sprang it on him. He didn't really kiss me back. It wasn't a mutual thing. He let me down easily, but..." Was it possible for his face to go up in flames? Keiran rubbed his thumb over her hand. "It's funny how things work out because later on, I had a crush on you."

"You didn't," she whispered. She didn't pull away, just let him keep up his caresses.

"I did. I seem to keep having crushes that'll never work out. Well, I mean, teen me did."

She stared down at their joined hands. "Who says it won't work out now?"

His caresses stopped. "Are we actually talking about it now?" He held his breath.

"Uhh." She chewed her lip. "Sucky timing, I know. I told mummy no more matchmaking because there was someone I liked. I didn't tell her who because, well..."

"I'm not her favorite person."

"I don't care."

The knot in his chest loosened a little. "Really?"

She nodded. "Wanna come to my party tomorrow? My mom's throwing it. I guess she'll figure it out then. I want to try."

He lay down, so they were at eye level. "Try?"

She sighed like she was tired of his questions or just plain tired. "This. With you." She yawned, eyes fluttering closed. "So, you coming to my party?" she asked, eyes still closed.

He smiled, brushing her hair away from her face. She leaned into his touch. Did she even know she was doing that? Her eyes were still closed, her breathing shifted. Sleep wasn't too far off.

"Sure. Could be fun. So, to be clear. You're saying you're not going on any more dates? And we're gonna try this thing that we're not putting a name to?"

"No public hand-holding or anything, but yes." Her eyes closed again, and she'd definitely dozed off this time. Guess the confession game was over.

He should get his ass gone from this room, but drowsiness had descended. The champagne hadn't helped. Maybe he could take a quick power nap to make sure he was good for the drive home then leave. His eyes mapped every bit of her face.

She wanted to try being with him. It was everything he wanted, but he still hadn't told her about Sean. Tomorrow, he'd do it, when they were both sober and clear-headed, his father's edict about keeping mum until the release be damned. He prayed he wouldn't ruin everything before it even began.

Chapter 31
Cherisse

WAKING UP NEXT TO KEIRAN was weird but nice. A trivial word for the fluttering in her stomach and the thudding in her chest, but it was all she could muster at the moment. Cherisse allowed herself to just look and drink in every bit of his face, so serene in sleep. That mouth that had infuriated her countless times but was oh so inviting. She'd wanted to slap the grin off his face so many times, but then she'd allowed him to kiss her, and that mouth became a tantalizing thing.

That delicious, mind-whirling kiss.

How did she get here?

She should be hustling him out of the room before the others came knocking or teasing him awake for a morning quickie to make up for last night's aborted booty call. Yet, she kept mapping every bit of his face, a foolish grin on her lips.

"Now who's watching who sleep?"

He stirred and opened his eyes, and Cherisse froze. They stared at each other for several seconds—Cherisse becoming increasingly aware that she'd never washed off her makeup last night, and it probably looked a smeared mess. The slow sweep he did of her body also reminded her that she was still in her underwear.

He carefully propped himself up and yawned. "Hi."

"Hi."

"Do you remember what we talked about last night?"

Of course, she did. But she understood his careful question. She'd been tipsy and had felt brave enough to speak her mind, even though she'd couched it all in the confessions game. For him, last night may have seemed like a drunken confession that didn't hold any weight in the light of the day.

"I remember you owe me an invite to your mother's pizza," she said because how could she not tease when he looked so adorably sleep-rumpled? There was a line on his cheek from the pillow, and Cherisse thought it was the cutest thing.

She hadn't felt this in a long while, this feeling of falling, of finding the littlest things about *that* person so cute, she almost couldn't stand it.

"I remember it all, Keiran," she assured him after a moment of silence. "And I meant what I said about you and me. I also remember what you trusted me with, and I won't betray that." She placed her hand over her heart. "Scout's honor."

His eyes dipped to her chest, where her lacy bra wasn't hiding much, and his gaze heated.

"We don't have time." She didn't have a clue of the time—where was her phone?—but it was best they didn't try anything. No telling when the others would come a-knocking for breakfast before checking out.

"I know. I should go anyways."

"Yeah."

Neither of them made a move.

"I need to wash my face. My skin is crying for help after not washing this off last night and doing my routine," she said the same time he said, "There's something I need to tell you,"

The seriousness of the words and his sudden intensity scared her a bit because she couldn't fathom what he had to say. But her mind *could* conjure up all sorts of things. All sorts of impossible, it's-too-early-for-this things.

She slipped off the bed, getting to her feet, and Keiran did the same. "I gotta go, and *you* gotta go before the others come. I'm not hiding you or this thing. I just want to tell them my way."

Keiran raised the brow that she was sure could still infuriate her. "You know, there's a word for this thing. It's called dating."

"Anyways, I need to wash my face, and I'll see you later at the party?"

He sighed. "Fine." Tugged on her robe to pull her closer. She came easily. "I *will* see you later, and we'll work on you saying, "Keiran and I are dating," okay?" The forehead kiss startled her, and Keiran laughed softly. "Your face right now."

"Get out of here."

"Or you'll what? Spank me?" He sounded so eager and hopeful.

"You don't want to start this because you will lose." She struck a pose, and like a moth to a flame, his eyes traced the curve of her hip.

So damn easy, she thought. It was going to be fun winning.

Keiran exhaled deeply, eyes going soft. "God, I..." He froze, and her eyes grew wide, but he stepped back, looking around for his shoes. "Yeah, I really gotta go," he muttered.

Cherisse stared at the door after he'd left. He'd definitely been about to say something too serious and too soon for the moment. She needed to wash her face, dammit. Cleanse. Tone. Moisturize. Sunscreen. Focus on that.

She completely chickened out at breakfast because she knew her girls well. Reba would've shrieked, and all eyes would have turned their way. Cherisse didn't need an audience for this, and she didn't want Remi's judgment while she ate.

Once they'd gotten back to her apartment, she started pulling ingredients to craft a mini mock-up of the cake she envisioned for Ava's wedding. Baking soothed and drove her into this zone where nothing else mattered. Focusing on slicing the finished cake into layers, then plopping the prepared buttercream in the middle of each layer and slowly spreading it out before topping it with the next cake layer eased the anxiousness that had plagued her the whole ride back.

"Is she stress-baking *again?*"

"I don't know. She was mixing that batter a lil' intensely."

"You should go see what's up."

"Me? Nah, I'm good, thanks."

"She's your bestie!"

Remi and Reba's voices carried easily into the kitchen, and Cherisse smiled.

"Okay, fine. I'll go," she heard Remi announce, which was then followed by shuffling feet heading for the kitchen. Out of the corner of her eye, she saw Remi poke her head in. "Heyyy, buddy. Everything good in here? You know we have that surprise party in a few hours, right? So, uh, what do we have here, hmm?"

"Yes, I know. I'm trying to figure out how to tell you something. Plus, I just needed a visual for this. I'm doing a quick semi-naked mini cake prep." She didn't look away from the cake. She'd added all the layers and gone around smoothing the buttercream that peeked out between each one.

"Like that one you did for that birthday party last year?" Remi peered at the cake as Cherisse reached for the bowl of icing, spinning the cake stand, so the entire cake got coated in a light layer of frosting.

"Yup." She was one of the few local pastry chefs who had adopted the naked cake style. Her feature in the Island Bites magazine had drawn a good bit of people asking for them.

Cherisse reached for the spackle next, doing another go-round of the cake, removing some of the frosting, so the cake showed through. She hadn't quite decided if she'd go full-on naked with Ava's actual cake or semi, so she planned to make variations to show Ava and get some feedback.

"Figured out how to tell me whatever yet? My gut tells me this is Keiran-related so if he did something, I'm gonna eff him up."

She stared down at the cake, picturing how she'd place the flowers she had in mind as decoration. Remi swiped a finger through the frosting, prompting Cherisse to swat her hand away. Didn't do any good—Remi just came at the cake from another angle. "Remi, c'mon!"

Remi stuck out her tongue. "Party's in a couple hours. Finish the cake. Let me sample the cake. Practice your surprised face, and tell me what's up with you."

Cherisse rolled her eyes and looked up. "I told Keiran how I felt, and I invited him to the party, and we're sort of dating?"

"*Yes,* bitch, you lock down that fine ass man!" Reba shouted as she rushed over to the kitchen.

"Well, you've certainly been busy," Remi said, less enthused. "You could do worse, I guess. Have done worse."

"Wow, thanks for being so reassuring," she said sarcastically. Cherisse took no real offense because Remi would always tell her like it is.

"You don't need my reassurances. You know what you're about."

Is that what Remi actually thought? "I don't know what I'm doing. I just know what I feel. I want to try."

"Plus, she's getting that good sex," Reba pointed out, defusing the potential tension with her blunt words.

"Look, I just want you to be cautious as you always are and not jump into something because you're lonely."

"I love that you care. Keiran's not Sean. I feel that in my gut, and more importantly, he's shown that."

"Okay. Can I eat the damn cake now since you forced me to listen to all this feelings stuff?"

Cherisse pushed the cake at Remi. Getting between her and her treats was a mistake. She could work on another before they left for the party.

"So." Reba placed her elbows on the counter as she squeezed in between Cherisse and Remi. "I don't need to know girth or anything, but ballpark, what's he working with? Just tell me when to stop."

Cherisse watched as Reba placed her two index fingers in the air and kept widening the gap between them. Reba's mouth dropped open as Cherisse didn't tell her to stop.

"Damn, girl, is your vagina okay?"

Remi choked on the cake, and the entire situation was too funny. Especially because Reba still had her fingers apart, *way too far apart*, eyes open wide.

"I'll let Keiran know how much you overestimated. But enough dicking around, help me pick a cute outfit that'll make him weak in the knees."

AS SOON AS SHE ARRIVED at her mother's house, Cherisse was swarmed by family members and friends, wishing her a happy birthday. Most people hung outside under the covered garage or tents her parents had rented for the occasion. Some were inside, drinks in hand, catching up with family they hadn't seen in years. Her mother had basically turned her birthday into a small family reunion too.

Aunties she hadn't seen since she was a teen descended, critical eyes taking in her off-the-shoulder floral crop top and high-waisted shorts. She'd decided to show some leg today just to tantalize Keiran but hadn't considered it would be fodder for the aunties who loved to criticize about everything.

"Buh aye aye, where all that bumper come from? Too much good food, eh?" Auntie Veronica, from her dad's side of the family, sized her up.

Cherisse braced for a cheek pinch. It had been years since she'd seen this aunt. She was the oldest and loudest. Didn't have a filter, ever. Veronica always had some comment to make on her hair, or weight, or anything for that matter.

"Hi, auntie." She made the hug brief, hoping to escape before Auntie Veronica launched into the inquisition.

"Or too much happy times with the man?" Auntie Veronica leaned in, dropping a wink, tone heavy with insinuation.

Cherisse laughed—her default response to anything her older relatives had to say. This auntie would get the scoop soon enough. She wasn't inclined to tell her about Keiran because then everyone at the party would know. She didn't want Keiran strolling in with all eyes on him. He was already going to have to face her mother. Poor man had no idea what he was walking into. Perhaps she should have warned him first. Her family loved to pry, and Cherisse hadn't brought any potential guy around her family since Sean.

There went the butterflies battering away at her stomach again.

"Yuh not saying anything, so is true, eh?" Auntie Veronica persisted. "And I hope whoever it is, you not *just* hanging out. That cousin of yours always just hanging out with some girl. I swear is a different one every month, can't keep track." Her aunt sniffed. "What it is with you all and being scared of relationships? I tell you, I don't understand this generation at all at all."

She suffered through Aunt Veronica's speech about the failings of the youth today until her dad swooped in to the rescue.

"Hey, sis, I need the birthday girl a minute here." Her father linked their arms and strolled away from his sister.

"Thanks, daddy."

A smile broke out on his round face. "I know how she gets. She started in on me the second she got here." He patted his tummy.

Her father had only recently gotten the Gooding paunch that all his brothers seemed to grow as they got older. He hadn't gotten the hair loss yet. His short fro was going strong, if not a little greyer. Brown hands drummed idly against his belly as he walked them over to where some finger foods were laid out.

"So, your friend still coming?" he asked as he steered them over to the food table.

Cherisse's face prickled as she flushed. "Yeah."

"What you want to eat?" he continued, not pursuing the topic any further. She could always count on her father to not pry too much. It helped with her tumbling tummy, especially since she was braced for her mother's reaction.

Her mother's scolding didn't get any less harsh with age, but Cherisse would stick up for herself and Keiran if needed. But some food for fortification couldn't hurt.

There were Styrofoam cups of geera chicken and pork, fried wings with honey mustard dipping sauce, and pholourie with tamarind sauce. This wasn't even half of the food her mother would've cooked or organized with others to bring. These were just cutters, the appetizers to soothe any grumbling bellies. The main course wouldn't be served until later in the evening.

Cherisse reached for a cup of geera chicken. "This looks so good."

Her father looked around before reaching for the geera pork. He maneuvered her, so she stood directly in front of him, shielding his view from her mother's laser eyes.

"Seriously?"

Her father dug into the cup. "Listen, I not able to hear no talk from your mother about how I not supposed to be eating this. Just let me have this one cup."

The laughter burst out of her, loud and rambunctious, which was usually a siren call for her mother, who detested Cherisse's laugh and always found it unbecoming of a lady. She didn't care. It amused her that her father, who towered over her 5'2" mother, hid to eat some pork for fear of his wife's wrath. But when her mother got going, she wouldn't let a little thing like her height stop her. Her mother didn't raise her voice—because ladies didn't ever do such a thing—but she was so adept at cutting someone down with her words that you felt that tongue lashing for days after.

"Alright, but you better eat fast." She looked around. "Don't think because it's my birthday, she won't buff me too, for encouraging this."

As the afternoon wore on, Cherisse kept checking her phone. Still no messages from Keiran. She'd sent a casual photo of the food, not wanting to send any **Where are you?** texts just yet, which gave her pause. Why was she so hesitant to send that text? She definitely hadn't cared about sending a message like that before. Just because they were going to do the thing—she'd get around to being comfortable saying 'dating', it had just been so long—didn't mean she had to act different, be different. That was nonsense.

She sent the text, and still nothing. He hadn't even read it. Which didn't mean anything. He could have just gotten held back for some reason. She wouldn't think the worst. She'd done that enough with him before.

"Please tell me we're not related to him."

She followed her cousin's gaze, and *finally*. Keiran stood at the gate, hesitation visible in the tense set of his shoulders. Dressed in jeans and a short-sleeved grey Henley, he personified casual sexiness. Cherisse let her eyes wander over his shoulders, down his arms. The damn fabric clung. The Henley's material was so thin his nipples were saying a hearty hello.

"Nope," Cherisse said, cringing when her cousin Michelle shouted, "Hallelujah!" but she couldn't really fault her now, could she?

"Well, don't just eye-fuck him. Go get your man," Remi said, voice lowered but eyes on her like a hawk.

Cherisse broke away from their little group, aware her mother's eyes had already swung Keiran's way, but Keiran looked good enough to eat, and she'd deal with her mother later.

He stuck his hands in his pockets. "Hey. My phone died. Sorry, I'm late."

"It's okay."

"You're just the breath of fresh air I need right now." Keiran sighed like he had the entire weight of the world on his shoulders. What the hell happened after they'd parted those few hours ago? But before she could ask, he smiled. "It's weird, isn't it? We just saw each other a little while ago, but damn, Cherisse, my heart's working overtime."

Her face was certainly red right now. How could he say these things so bravely? "Is everything okay?"

He shrugged. "I don't know. I ignored several calls from my dad before my phone died. It's the worst time to do that, but I just wanted to get to you. I don't want anything to mess up your day."

She understood that his relationship with his father was tenuous, but this felt like more. Like something else was causing the furrow between his brows. "What can I do to help?"

"Nothing. It's your party. Anything else can wait. Show me off to everyone?"

That she could do. She didn't go so far as to hold his hand or anything, but her cousins were no fools. They were already playfully nudging each other as Keiran walked beside her.

"Hey, everyone, this is Keiran. My, um..." She cleared her throat. Why was this so hard?

"Yes, yes, he's your boo, we got it." Michelle extended her hand. "Enchanté."

"Girl, you not French," her other cousin, Venetia, commented.

Michelle sucked her teeth, whipping her hair over her shoulder. "We got French Creole in this family, don't try to police my heritage."

Keiran took Michelle's hand, then Venetia's. "Nice to meet you both."

Venetia held Keiran's hand a tad too long for Cherisse's liking, and what the fuck, was she jealous? "Damn, that's a good grip. Strong. Firm. Big hands. You know what they say about big..."

"Okay, we get it," Cherisse interjected, yanking her cousin's hand away. Keiran chuckled, not looking the least offended.

By the time the main course was shared, Michelle had apparently won the honor of locking Keiran down for conversation. The other cousins who'd been trying drifted away, defeated. Her cousin had even managed to snag a seat next to him at the table they'd commandeered. Cherisse was on Keiran's right, eating her curry, watching on amused as Michelle tried to find out how they came to be boyfriend and girlfriend—Michelle's words. When Michelle drifted off to get a drink, Keiran turned to her.

"Sorry about that. I didn't know if I should correct her about the labels."

"I haven't been anyone's girlfriend in a while, so it'll take some getting used to," she admitted. Sean had soured the entire experience for her, and while a tiny voice at the back of her mind cautioned her to not rush into anything, she didn't mind trying it on.

"I haven't been anyone's boyfriend for some time, either." He reached over for her hand and brought it to his lips to brush over her knuckles.

"So, it's true?" Her mother's voice cut into the moment. Keiran withdrew his hand, and Cherisse faced her mother. The entire table had gone quiet.

"Okay, then. Like up yuhself. You're an adult," her mother said before walking away.

"That went better than expected."

"The calm before the storm," Cherisse declared, returning to her food. She ripped a piece of paratha to scoop up some curry duck, pumpkin, channa, and aloo to stuff in her mouth. Perfuckingfection. Her mother's passive-aggressive shit wasn't going to get to her. Cherisse licked her curry-stained fingers, noticing the way Keiran's eyes briefly dipped to the fingers in her mouth before refocusing elsewhere. So damn easy.

Later, they could escape to have some private time. She wondered if it would be as frenzied as ever or tempered by emotions and feelings and shit. She was eager to find out.

"Let's go dance off this food," Remi suggested.

It was a great plan, sweat out some of this food. Otherwise, she'd be too sluggish for what she'd planned later. She was going to get her some birthday sex, and no curry was going to get in the way of that. Some guests were already up and dancing. She smiled at her parents, who were showing off their fancy footwork for everyone. Her mother made her want to scream many times with her overbearing ways, but they were so in sync up there.

"My parents are making us look bad, with their nauseatingly being all in love and stuff." Remi's parents were also out there on the floor. The song shifted to a slow tune. "Oh geez, here we go," Remi grumbled good-naturedly. Sure enough, her parents were being all lovey-dovey. Remi's father, with his giant self, smiled at her equally tall mother. The look in his eyes was the equivalent of the heart eyes emoji.

The Daniels made an adorable picture. With that bald head, dark brown skin, and bulky build, Roy Daniels was a good-looking dude, and Remi's mother, Shalini, looked gorgeous with her sleek black bob swinging about her round face and the short kurta she wore with jeans. They also made Cherisse seek out Keiran, who looked troubled again, but eventually his gaze swung to her, and his eyes cleared.

"Shall we, my lady?" He held out his hand, and Cherisse was teleported back to the only other time they'd ever danced. The moment that changed everything.

His hands on her waist burned. The tiny space between the end of her top and the waistband of her shorts left her skin bare to his touch. Not totally different from that other time, except now she didn't have to be covert about enjoying his touch, about reveling in the way his thumb stroked her exposed skin.

"I am so gonna wreck you tonight," she whispered just to see his reaction, and he didn't disappoint.

The sound that escaped his mouth was a cross between a cough and a wheeze. "Jesus, Cherisse." He looked around, but no one was truly paying them any mind. Of course, family members looked their way occasionally, and she still felt the weight of her mother's stare, but their private little bubble was intact.

She would allow nothing to ruin this moment.

Chapter 32

Keiran

DANCING WITH CHERISSE in front of her family was the balm he needed for his soul. Ignoring his father's calls would bite him in the ass. His churning gut said so, but all Keiran had wanted was to get to her, to have a moment where he didn't have to worry about anything else. Just for a little while. He chose to interpret his phone dying before he could return the calls as a sign. The phone was currently charging, and Cherisse was busy being pumped for information by a small group of relatives.

They occasionally glanced his way, and obviously, he was the topic of discussion. He threw them a small wave because why not? Cherisse's eye-roll was visible from here, but so was her smile. How had he gotten so lucky?

Tell her.

The chant had followed him all the way over here, and he'd pulled out every excuse to delay the moment he'd have to let her know about Sean and the plans for the video.

You're not supposed to tell anyone. Cherisse wasn't just anyone.

It's her birthday. You don't want to ruin it. You're making it worse by stringing this out.

You don't want her to return to looking at you like you're the accidental piece of shit she trod on.

No matter what excuse he told himself, that one was really the issue. This thing between them was new and fragile. He didn't want to shatter it before they'd really had a chance. But that was selfish.

N.G. PELTIER

He inhaled deeply, then released his breath slowly. Now. It had to be now. But first, he needed to check his phone. He'd left it charging near the DJ. Her cousin, who was managing that spot, pointed to his phone as soon as he approached.

"Someone's really trying to get you. Thing's been making noise non-stop." Roan? Roger? He couldn't recall the name—Cherisse had too many cousins—but he unplugged the phone.

"Thanks."

Numerous calls from his father, but it was the message sent a few minutes ago that felt like a kick to the throat.

Dad: Promo has gone live.

Shit! No, no, no.

He dialed his father's number. Why the fuck had he ignored him?

"What the hell? I thought we were getting an advanced heads up about going live?" he shouted as soon as the call connected.

"Good of you to finally return my call. We couldn't wait for you to decide to grace us with your time, so an executive decision was made." His father sounded bored, but underneath that casual tone, he was pissed. "We're already getting quite a bit of traction on social."

"Fuck." He couldn't blame his father for any of this. Ignoring the man always had consequences, and God, he needed to talk to Cherisse *now.*

"Is there a problem?"

"Yeah. Nothing you'd care about." He hung up and immediately noticed missed calls from Dale too, and a string of messages.

Dale: your dad called. we're going live apparently! Did you know it was today?

Dale: guess it's a surprise to everyone. I'm posting to our accounts.

Keiran needed to move, go talk to Cherisse, but he hadn't seen the finished teaser. He needed to know how bad this would be.

All they'd needed from him was the completed track. KKE was responsible for everything else. So, of course, the first thing he was hit with when he opened their DK Productions Instagram was a cut of his fight video with Sean as a sample of the track played over it. The caption talked about the collaboration between Sean and Sheila and DK Productions' role in it all, with a link to the full track and story behind the song. There was even the option to swipe for a more behind-the-scenes look.

Keiran slowly made his way back to Cherisse. Maybe she hadn't seen it yet. They followed each others' personal accounts, and he followed her Sweethand account, but he didn't know if she followed DK's. And the chances of her following her father's company on there was hopefully nil.

But the moment he saw her, the sinking feeling in his stomach escalated. She was with Remi, head bent over her phone.

Please, God.

"Cherisse."

Her head popped up, and Keiran wanted to smooth away the frown, but touching her right now wouldn't help anything.

"I was tagged in a post. I guess because people remember I was involved in the original video. So, mind explaining what the fuck is this shit?" She thrust her phone at him, but he didn't look at the screen. "You don't even have to look at it, do you? Because you already know what it is."

"Yes, but it's not what you think."

"Yeah? So, you two didn't set up this whole fight as some publicity stunt for your track? While clueless me acts a fool worried about your ass? Because that's what I think. *God,* did you play me so I'd have sex with you that night?"

"Cherisse, *no.* I swear to you, I would never. Sean and his publicist literally ambushed me the day after the fight and told me this is how it was gonna be. How we'd spin it. I was against it totally, but I had to consider the artiste, Sheila. She didn't deserve to get caught up in Sean and I's mess, so I went with it. I've been trying to tell you, but..." What excuse could her really give?

Cherisse folded her arms, a hand squeezing at her bicep. "How long have you and Sean been working together?"

"Don't say it like that. There wasn't some nefarious plan like you're making it sound. I didn't..."

"How long?"

"I got called into the meeting and given the edict the same day we were to meet up for our first planning session. It's why I ran late," he admitted.

Cherisse's jaw clenched, and the hand squeezed tighter. If she wanted to slap him, punch him, he'd accept it all. "That was weeks ago."

"I know. It's just we didn't exactly care for each other then, so I figured—"

"That Cherisse was smart," she cut him off. "I wonder where she went." Her laugh was bitter as hell, and Remi, who'd remained silent next to her the entire time, placed her hand on Cherisse's shoulder but continued to say nothing because she trusted Cherisse to handle her shit. While he hadn't, he realized. He'd used all those damn excuses, telling himself he was protecting her when he'd been trying to stop this very moment. Trying to not have Cherisse look at him like this. Like she didn't know who the hell he truly was.

"I'm sorry," he said. "I didn't tell you because I didn't want you to be upset."

"Well, I'm fucking upset!" She unfolded her arms and drew closer, lowered her voice. "How fucking dare you try to manage my emotions for me? That's not how this is supposed to work. You tell me and allow me to feel whatever, not try to protect me from it because of some misguided notion. *I* get to decide how I react to shit. Not you."

"You're right. I screwed up. Again."

"Actions, Keiran. Speak so much louder. How many times are you going to say sorry before the word means nothing? You should go. I need to think."

He nodded. "Okay."

The masochistic part of him clung to her last words. If she needed to think, that meant there was hope she'd forgive him, right?

"And Keiran? Consider this a 'don't call us, we'll call you' situation."

Well, then. That message was received loud and clear.

CHERISSE

"Fuck!"

Aunt Lucia, who stood nearby, looked scandalized as Cherisse grabbed a bunch of napkins to clean up the mess of her spilled drink. It was either cry or curse. The cursing seemed like the better option because she refused to cry. It was her birthday, and she could cry if she wanted to, but dammit, she would not.

"Okay, let's go inside," Remi suggested. There'd been no "I told you so" after Keiran's exit, and Cherisse was grateful for that. She couldn't handle that being thrown in her face right now.

"What's going on?" Ava appeared, concern etched on her face. She'd been the most pleased to learn about her and Keiran.

Cherisse shook her head, feeling the burn rising in her throat as she tried to swallow back the tears. She didn't want to say. Didn't want to admit how foolish she'd been allowing herself to take a chance on Keiran.

God dammit, they couldn't even last a few hours. Why did she ever think this was a good idea?

Ava grabbed her arm, steering her away from the noisy chatter, music, and her mother's hawk-like gaze, into her bedroom. "Sit," she commanded.

"But..."

Ava pointed to the bed. Remi, who'd followed behind, also sat. "What the hell happened? I don't know what's going on with you, but listen, if the stress is becoming too much, tell me. I'll find someone else to do the desserts. Might be cutting it close, but I'm sure I can figure something out."

"What?" Cherisse gaped up at her sister. "You don't want me to do the cake and desserts anymore?" Her stomach churned. She couldn't take Ava firing her from that major task, on top of everything else.

"No, *no*," Ava said, firmly. "It's not that I don't want you to do it, but if you're doing this only because you think that's what I want and not what you want to do, then you don't have to. I don't want you to feel forced into this just because we're sisters."

"No, I want to. I swear."

Ava eased down next to her. "So, what's going on? Talk to me."

Cherisse plucked at the sheets. Her sister's old room hadn't changed much from when they were growing up. Photos of her life unfolding scattered across the corkboard she had tacked to the wall. There were ones of them as children. Ones with their parents. Ava with her friends. With her fellow teachers and students. Ava and Eric. She figured out of everything Ava would take when she moved in with Eric, it would be that.

"It's Keiran."

"Oh?"

She spilled everything. The video, how it all just made her feel so shitty.

"Wait, wait, *wait!*" Ava interjected. "Keiran and Sean purposefully planned that fight?"

"No, he says it wasn't planned, but he could've told me all about it the minute he found out they were gonna spin it like it *was* planned. I thought he was different, is all. I thought I could do this with him, but maybe he's not really the guy I thought."

"Do you truly believe he kept all that from you for his benefit? Or maybe he did because he didn't want to hurt you."

"That's the problem! He did it for himself, not me. Not really. He didn't want me to get angry and end it." She grasped Ava's hand. "What's your secret? You and Eric make this whole thing look easy. What should I do?"

Ava busted out laughing. "Easy? Oh, no, honey. I'm glad we've given off this illusion of perfection or whatever, but not even close. Let me tell you a secret. Eric and I broke up two years into our relationship. For like a week, but the worst week of my life, I swear."

"What?" She hadn't gotten a whiff of anything like that in the four years of them being together.

"Oh, yeah. He, out of the blue, proposed, and I said no. Which, of course, became this whole big thing of him thinking I didn't want to be with him when I *did*. Just...we'd never even discussed marriage at that point. We'd both just been going with the flow. I wasn't ready, and I freaked out. *I* started thinking he'd just say to hell with this, with us, with me because I'd said no. Thank God he hadn't done some big splashy proposal." She smiled faintly. "Turns out, he felt pressured by his parents to propose. They'd given him this whole 'if you can't see yourself marrying her now, then why are you even together' speech, and that sparked off a whole other thing where I was all, 'I want you to *want* to marry me. Not because other people think that's where we should be right now.' It was a giant mess."

"Holy shit. Wait. Was this that week you demanded we have that pizza and wine weekend?" She distinctly recalled Ava being insistent about the pizza and drinks. "You told me that was work stress-related."

Ava shrugged. "I lied, obviously. That week was hard. But he realized how the proposal was just a big no when we hadn't even talked about marriage or children, and he'd just assumed, let his parents get into his head. I mean, I wanted those things, just not right then. And here we are." She squeezed Cherisse's hand. "My point is, I can't tell you what to do. What to want. You might think you don't know, but I'm saying you do. Don't let other people dictate your relationship. Any relationship, for that matter. And realize people are going to mess up because they're scared. I'm not saying you have to forgive Keiran. That's your call. But think hard on whether you're letting your past with Sean color things with anyone you could potentially have something with."

"I'm pissed off at him, yeah," Cherisse admitted. "I just need to decide how I feel."

Ava patted her hand. "Well, then. Sort it out. Just don't make a scene at my wedding."

"I promise I won't. You know I'm not about the drama," Cherisse assured Ava. She had some things to ponder on. "And I'm sorry I've been the worst maid of honor ever. I'll do better."

"Just make sure I don't pull a runaway bride, and we're good." Ava kissed her cheek and pulled Cherisse to her feet. "For what it's worth, Eric's been taking bets on you and Keiran forever. So, if it doesn't work out in the end, I get to keep my money. I thought for sure he'd won when Keiran showed up, but it's all still in the air now, isn't it? It's not like Eric needs any more dollars."

Remi snorted.

"Wait." Cherisse looked at Ava aghast. "You bet against us?"

Ava smirked. "I figured you two disliked each other too much. Should've known that would be grounds for some good old hate sex, at least."

Cherisse rolled her eyes. She had to get this whirl of emotions under control. Focus on the wedding. Maybe she could sort out the Keiran mess along the way.

Chapter 33

Keiran

CHERISSE'S VOICE ECHOED around the studio, and Keiran realized he'd hit an all-new low, sitting here, listening to Cherisse's vocals on that track when he could be doing anything else. The new track with Sheila and Sean had been well received, and even though his personal life was currently in shambles, his professional one was moving along smoothly. He hadn't reached out to her since her birthday party, as per her wishes, but he'd almost sent tons of messages that bordered on begging. That for sure wouldn't have solved anything and would just further aggravate Cherisse.

He had to give her space, and if she decided she wanted nothing to do with him, it was her call. What he needed to do was build some sort of fortification around himself before the rehearsal dinner because otherwise, he was likely to throw himself at her feet, a sobbing mess. He'd held back tears enough for one day. But it was all his damn fault, so he deserved the burning eyes and pounding headache. Trying to stem tears took a lot out of a person.

He stared hard at his phone as the vocals died away. What if he just sent a quick message making sure she was okay? Because that would go over so well when he was the reason she wasn't okay in the first place.

He rubbed at his throbbing head. *Just let it be.*

He had a best man speech to finalize. He should focus on that. His gift for the bride and groom had been sorted, and Keiran allowed himself a small grin. He'd more than nailed it. The urge to text Cherisse, tease her with that knowledge, made his fingers twitch towards the phone, but he forced his hand into a fist.

No. Just stop. You are pathetic.

Not so easy. Not with the wedding looming in the coming week. But he had to try.

"So, this is where the magic happens?"

Keiran nearly tipped backwards, so lost in thought he hadn't heard anyone come into the studio, and he certainly didn't expect to see Remi here. He righted himself and turned the chair to face her, heart racing. Had Cherisse sent Remi to end it? Was she that disgusted with him? No. Cherisse wasn't a coward like him. She would have come herself.

Remi peered down at him. "Relax, I'm not here to assassinate you or anything." She tilted her head as she leaned in to look at his face, her mass of curls nearly brushing his thigh. "Have you been crying?" she asked.

"What? You think it makes me less of a man?"

Remi sucked her teeth and walked over to the couch to sit. She crossed her legs, eyes fixed on him. "Don't even try that shit with me. I don't care if you were crying. In fact, you *should* be bawling your eyes out."

"So, you're here to witness my misery? Great. Take a pic, it'll last longer."

"I'm here because you two need to get your shit together. Don't get me wrong, I love reaping the benefits of Cherisse's emotional bakefest, but—" She held up her index finger. "There's only so much cake even I can eat. You need to fix this."

"What? I'm respecting her need for space."

Remi sighed like she was completely exasperated with him. He was confused, had expected a cuss out for hurting Cherisse, but Remi's reaction wasn't aligning with what he knew about her.

Fiercely protective of her friends, Keiran had been hearing Cherisse and Remi refer to each other as platonic soulmates forever.

So why was Remi going easy on him? Did he look so pathetic that even Remi was taking pity on him?

"She cares about you, and you're obviously in love with her. Even though you keep fucking up. God damn, get it together. I swear you are the one person that sabotages his own happiness so damn much."

"I don't understand what's happening right now. You're rooting *for* us?"

Remi rubbed the bridge of her nose and muttered, "Save me from clueless men, Lord Jesus," before getting to her feet. "Cherisse hasn't allowed herself to see anything with anyone in a long time. She's been cautious, and obviously, you wouldn't have been her first choice for that."

"Geez, thanks."

The look Remi shot him nearly murdered him on the spot.

"But," she continued. "Stuff doesn't always go as planned, and it's so obvious to me you didn't plan some malicious plot with that asshole, and look, Cherisse in her heart knows that. You don't even like him. They tried to spin those behind-the-scenes vids in a certain way, but I could tell you were getting frustrated with Sean. But you tried to manage her, which was a big no-no. Might not have been your intention, but you need to show her you're serious about her. Serious about admitting you fucked up and want to do better. Actions. Not just some pathetic apology saying I'm sorry. I'm sure you've said it so many times since you two were forced to work together, so *show* her you're genuinely willing to fix this. Apologies aren't always comfortable, so figure it out."

He opened his mouth to ask how the hell he was supposed to do that, and Remi held up a hand. "Don't even ask me. I've helped you enough. Bye."

Keiran leaned back in his chair, pondering. Remi had given him a lot to think about. It was easy to say sorry, but doing something to prove that? Not so much. But Cherisse deserved more than that.

When he finally allowed himself to pick up the phone and dial, his heart was thudding again. Was he really going to do this?

"'Sup, man?"

He took a breath and said, "I need a huge favor."

Chapter 34

JUNE

Cherisse

CHERISSE HAD NEVER felt more conspicuous in her life. It could be her imagination—after all, there was a lot going on. But she felt eyes on her and refused to look directly at anyone for fear of seeing their pity. Word would have filtered down to the rest of the wedding party, at least about her and Keiran supposedly being an item. Not everyone would be privy to what transpired after that, but who knew?

The wedding rehearsal and dinner that followed was lovely but awkward for her. First, she didn't know how to react, seeing Keiran again after a week of radio silence. Then she felt like she had to act like nothing was weighing on her, that she was fine because her sister didn't deserve a Maid of Honor who was too busy dealing with her own problems to give her all.

Everyone else was buzzing with excitement about the walkthrough at the Green Meadows venue. She was just trying her best not to look at Keiran while maintaining a casual air of being unfazed by his presence.

That didn't last because she could avoid him for only so long. The main con of their roles in this wedding.

Suck it up.

And so, she did, even as she felt his eyes on her the entire rehearsal as they did their walk up the runner that was laid out on the grass, leading right to the arch where the ceremony would take place. Most of the major setup was already complete. Tomorrow, her main duties were going over the dessert stations and the cakes setup with Reba and attending to Ava. Both she and Scott would be working double duty, him with the makeup and her with the desserts. Her plan for tonight was to get Ava and all the bridesmaids to have an early night after dinner. No one was showing up hungover on wedding day. She would see to that.

The last week had been her channeling her energies into ensuring everything within her purview was set for the wedding. Keeping Ava calm was key. Her sister appeared to be doing just fine. It was Cherisse who had a whirlwind inside her.

It was becoming more unstable as they were forced to do the walk several times because Cherisse kept trying to hustle through it so she wouldn't have to keep locking arms with Keiran to walk up the aisle, which was counterproductive because it made them have to do it over and over while her stomach was a jumble of nerves. She expended way too much energy, trying to act like everything was normal. Like she didn't care about him right now.

The pressure to keep up a certain appearance and simultaneously ignore her mother's questioning stare only added to her fractured emotional state. But she would not allow any of it to spill over to any aspect of Ava's wedding.

As they ran through the steps again, Keiran's body next to hers was too distracting. She didn't know if she could keep it together much longer, certain every emotion was plain for all to see, but that could just be her paranoia. She was holding on by a thread here, a slowly fraying thread because she didn't know what to do.

Ava swooped in as soon as that walkthrough was over, dragging her off to the side. "Everything good?"

"Yes, great, fine. Let's do this so we can get to dinner then rest. We all need some sleep. Big day tomorrow," she said as cheerfully as she could muster. Not well enough, it seemed. While Ava let her be, Reba and Remi shot worried glances her way. Did she look as pathetic as she felt?

She spied Scott talking with Keiran, but his sidelong glances irritated her. She was obviously the topic of discussion. When she excused herself to use the bathroom and found Maxine at the sinks after she exited the stall, she lost it, figuring she was here on behalf of her twin.

"Don't," she warned.

"I'm just here to use the bathroom. Same as you. Promise." Maxine held up her hands.

"Sorry," she rasped out, throat tight, tears threatening to burn their way out. She yanked the paper towels out until an entire set rolled down. "Fuck!" She ripped off what she wanted and wiped furiously at her hands.

Maxine's eyes widened. "Wait, hey, just let me help you."

"Forget it." She didn't want sympathy from Maxine or anyone. She just wanted her brain to sort everything out. She swept out of the bathroom and ran into Remi, who she waved off with a slash of her hand.

She called it a night by nine, coaxed Ava and the rest of the bridesmaids to do the same. She didn't look at Keiran when they left. Not once. Go her.

WEDDING DAY BROUGHT perfect weather. Cherisse gave a silent salute to the weather gods and begged them to keep the sky blue and the day cool. No oppressing heat or rain, please and thank you. Ava and the other bridesmaids were busy getting their hair and makeup done.

Cherisse expected to be called in for her session soon, but she needed a last-minute meeting with Reba. Reba was good about the actual setup. Cherisse had no worries about it. She'd gone through the process while Reba had assisted her with the baking of all the goodies for today except the main cake. But she wanted to make sure her frazzled brain hadn't forgotten anything, and that's where Reba came in.

"Cherisse!" Her mother was swiftly heading her way, face made up and hair done, wearing a silky blue robe that was securely cinched at the waist. "You have to get ready."

"I know." She still wore her setup wear of old shorts, a t-shirt, and slippers.

"Now! You're the maid of honor. You can't be out here still with this."

She rolled her eyes, backing away while still repeating details to Reba.

"Might want to watch where you're going, boss lady," Reba advised, and Cherisse whirled around, running right into Keiran. He wasn't dressed yet, either, still in baggy shorts and a t-shirt. The groom and his party were on the other end of the venue, ensuring Ava and Eric wouldn't see each other before the ceremony began.

"Sorry."

"It's all good," Keiran drawled.

She felt compelled to say something, anything to melt this wall of ice between them. But she wasn't at fault here. "Ball's in your court," she reminded him.

He nodded. "I know."

"Cherisse Amelia Gooding!" Her mother's voice rang out across the venue.

"You better go." Keiran turned away before she did, heading back to the groom's room.

The photographer was getting his official shots in when Cherisse entered the suite. Ava's makeup and hair were done. She was still clad in her robe, the wedding dress hanging nearby. Remi played secondary photographer with both her camera and her phone.

"Hustle your ass." Scott pointed to the chair. "I gotta get beautified, too, you know."

When Scott finished up her face, she helped Ava finally put her dress on. Her sister twirled once she was ready, hands on her hips. "Well?"

Cherisse blinked over and over. Her sister looked stunning. Scott tapped her nose. "I swear to God if you cry this off."

Her mother lost the battle first, sniffling. Then Julia, who looked ready to bawl all her makeup off. Only Remi remained dry-eyed, capturing all the emotions. Scott rushed to ensure no one had smudged, handing out tissues before hustling out to get dressed.

Against everything telling her to leave him alone right now, she texted Keiran, using their maid of honor/best man connection as an excuse.

Cherisse: we're at crying our makeup off stage. She looks amazing. Tell Eric if he runs, he'll miss this. And she'll hunt him down and kill him for screwing this up.

Keiran: No worries. If he pulls a runner, I'll tackle him

Cherisse: thanks

She left it at that. Let that be her one moment of weakness.

Assembly time came quickly. Remi nearly tripped over her feet when she spotted Maxine in her grey suit and a coral bow tie. Her usually flat-ironed hair fell in gentle waves, her flower crown resting over her bangs.

"Who thought this was a good idea? Women in suits are my kryptonite. I'll trip down the aisle, ruin everything," Remi hissed. "God, she looks like she smells good. She's wearing suspenders! I can't do this."

Cherisse nudged Remi with a finger to her side. "You'll live. Take your place. Go on. Don't fall." Not the best advice, but it would have to do.

Remi's place was next to Maxine. In spite of the chaos in her own love life, Cherisse smiled as Remi fidgeted next to Maxine. Her cool-as-a-cucumber bestie was losing her shit. Cherisse could relate.

Cherisse's dress had an intricate pattern on the top and a flowing coral skirt below, while the others had plain coral fabric on top. Ava had insisted she wanted Cherisse to stand out a bit as her MOH. Worked for her —she loved the end result.

The wedding party looked on point.

Scott, in his suit, looked gorgeous as usual, standing next to the equally stunning Julia. No matter how tight her throat felt, it was a beautiful day, and it wasn't about her. She moved to stand next to Keiran, hating how her heart pounded. Being angry at someone didn't mean you just didn't care anymore. But Cherisse had been clear. It was up to Keiran to show he was serious.

"Crown's a little crooked," he said. "May I?" She nodded, and he adjusted her flower crown. The guests were totally into their crowns. They damn well better be, after all the fighting up with them Cherisse had endured.

"Ready?" Keiran's breath washed against her ear, and goosebumps broke out on her skin.

Cherisse nodded again, taking deep breaths. She had to focus, watch her steps. No falling. Just get to the end of this runner. Don't ruin her sister's big day.

The wedding planner cued the band, A Roti and a Red Solo, whose front man was Remi's brother, Akash, and the procession began. Everyone took their places as they got to the front. From his side of the arch, Eric looked nervous. He shifted from foot to foot. Keiran inched closer to Eric. She had no doubt he'd take Eric down if he had to.

When Ava appeared with their father, Cherisse focused on getting shots of her sister. These pockets really came in handy for storing her phone and some tissues. Eric's eyes shone with love and awe as Ava glided up the aisle, and their father handed her off. Cherisse bit her lip, blinking rapidly.

The ceremony went by faster than expected. Eric cried. Julia kept sniffling loudly, then finally just gave up and let the tears out, dabbing at her eyes with the tissue Cherisse handed her. The guests clapped and whooped as Mr. and Mrs. Jones were announced, then they were swept away for the official photos and some silly pics they took with their own devices. Cherisse even ended up in a group selfie with Keiran. The photo was adorable—they were standing next to each other, and his smile...Jesus, help her—and had her all up in her feels when he posted to his account and tagged everyone, including her. Especially when the likes and comments started rolling in.

bishopX: bro who's dat?? She look lil familiar.

Merryberry69: aww so cuuute. Y'all make a cute couple for reals

jacobmorrow: but wha chubble is this? hoss link meh with the deets nah.

Beam_me_up_scotty: the cuteness! It buuuurns

Cherisse rolled her eyes at the last comment. Scott was ridiculous and a giant nerd. She was glad to get through the speeches portion. She'd labored over hers for weeks, nerves battering her insides when it was her turn.

"When Ava told me she'd said yes to Eric, my first thought was, 'hell, yeah, sis, get that money.'" Laughter echoed around the venue, and Cherisse smiled sheepishly at Eric's parents, ignoring her mother's scandalized stare. "Joking. We're not gold diggers, I swear! But seriously, I was so happy for them both. Yeah, money's all well and good, but finding someone who just gets you? Loves you with all your flaws—and lemme tell you, Ava and punctuality just don't mix, so good luck with that, Eric."

Eric shrugged. "I put our leave time as two hours ahead of the time we actually have to be there, so I'm good."

"Legit," Ava said, not even a little sorry.

Cherisse chuckled. "But you two make me believe I can find that too someday." She refused to look at Keiran, throat thick with emotion. She reached for her wine glass instead. "I couldn't ask for a better bro-in-law, but know if you screw up, I'll come for your romance novel collection." Eric gasped, and the crowd lost it. Cherisse beamed as laughter erupted again. "I love you and wish you all the happiness."

"I'll drink to that!" Ava replied.

She considered caving and pulling Keiran aside after the speeches to talk, but common sense prevailed.

Tears flowed when Keiran revealed his gift to the bride and groom, a surprise performance from their favorite local jazz singer, Douglas Charles. Douglas was extremely sought after and not easy to pin down with his packed schedule. Backed by Akash's band, Douglas had everyone grooving. Cherisse's gift was a fun video she'd put together for them, with close friends and family of the couple chiming in with hilarious anecdotes about Eric and Ava.

The bouquet and garter toss came around, and Keiran still hadn't approached her. A small part of her wondered if he'd given up so easily. She didn't want him to, even as she held on to her hurt.

She stole glances at him as everyone got in place. Who could blame her? In that suit, Keiran was scorching. She ogled the way the suspenders hugged his chest, the fit of his pants. He'd discarded his jacket as soon as official photos were over, and he was wearing the hell out of that shirt. This was pathetic.

"Come on, ladies!" Ava waved her bouquet enticingly.

The unmarried women were herded to the middle of the room. Some rushed for a prime spot. Cherisse lagged behind. She hated this part. People took this way too seriously.

"Mummy, you for real right now?" Keiran's voice echoed over the noisy chatter, and Cherisse snickered as she turned and found Ms. King next to her.

"They said, 'unmarried ladies.' You see any ring on this finger?" She waggled her hand, and everyone cracked up harder.

"Let the woman have her fun," Maxine called from the other side of the gathered women.

Keiran rolled his eyes. Cherisse's mother eyed her from off the side. She found herself in the middle of the gathering women, having been pushed there by her aunts. They weren't even being subtle. Ava counted down, bouquet clutched in her hand, then let it go. It soared over all the heads and landed right at Cherisse's feet. She stepped back. There was a scramble of limbs and some tugging as two women latched onto the bouquet, engaged in a tug of war, everyone else cheering on, rooting for their person. Michelle emerged victorious, waving the mangled bouquet in her hands. She grinned and whooped, eyes locked on Keiran, who watched the entire thing, amused. She blew him a kiss, and Cherisse tamped down the urge to bat the bouquet from her hand.

You will not fistfight your cousin at your sister's wedding.

The garter toss was next. Eric full-on dove under Ava's skirt.

"Like he searchin' for gold up there or what?" a guy Cherisse didn't recognize commented as Eric finally emerged from beneath Ava's skirts with the frilly band.

Eric tossed the garter, and for a minute, she thought it would land right on one of Eric's cousins, except a hand reached up, swiping it from the air. Keiran's grin was triumphant as he waved the garter around. His smile was too infectious. She couldn't help her goofy grin, even knowing her emotions were all up in the air now.

"Alright, people, we have a special guest performance. Calling Keiran King to the stage."

What the fuck? Cherisse's smile faltered as she watched Keiran heading for the stage.

"What's that boy doing now?" her mother asked.

Cherisse wanted to know the same thing. Keiran had the mic in his hand and was speaking to the band. He'd told her he didn't sing in public ever. Was that a lie too? He turned back to the now-curious crowd, and no, he hadn't lied about that. She was certain. His hand gripped the mic for dear life, and he looked ready to throw up. Oh no.

"This one is for someone special. I'm really sorry for subjecting everyone to this, but it's gotta be done." Keiran queued the band and launched into the worst rendition of "Hard to Say I'm Sorry" by Chicago that Cherisse had ever heard.

"Dear Lord." Remi slipped next to Cherisse. "Please make it stop."

It was a train wreck. Keiran couldn't carry a note to save his life.

"Seriously, Cherisse. Make him stop." Remi pushed her towards the stage, and she winced as Keiran croaked out a line. Okay, she needed to end this for all their ears.

"Stop. Please," she begged. "Get down here. Now." She tugged on his shirt as he handed the mic back to Akash.

"This band is no way connected with *that*. Just an FYI," Akash declared, and everyone laughed.

"What the hell was that?" Cherisse demanded. "If you were trying to guilt me into forgiving you, you should've just lip-synced. Jesus, my poor ears."

"I wasn't trying to guilt you. I just..." He shuddered. "God, I think I'm gonna puke. How do people just sing in front of others with no fear? How?"

He truly looked a shaky mess. "I'm sure they're still scared when they do, but they do it anyways. C'mon." She grabbed his arm, leading him away from the curious onlookers up to the deck space that would be utilized for dancing later.

The decorator had strung up fairy lights that added a romantic flair. She leaned against the railing, arms folded.

"I didn't know how else to show you I'm serious. I never wanted to hurt you, and I was wrong to keep the plan for the video from you, and I should have eventually told you about Sean."

"I know you didn't tell me because of how I'd react. I *know* that. But it just felt like that move was more about you than me. Do you understand?"

He nodded. "Yeah. I didn't want you to end it. I didn't give you the chance to decide for yourself. I assumed for you."

"Yes. If we're going to do this, you can't keep shit from me because you're afraid I'll get angry and end it." She took his hand. "That's no way to build anything. I can't be with someone like that. The terrible singing isn't a dealbreaker, but that is."

"I sang in front of people. Feels like I can do anything now." His thumb caressed her hand. "I can't promise that I won't mess up, but I won't disrespect you like that again."

"Good. See that you don't. I will be calling you on your shit. And I expect the same. I don't want to bury shit just because we decide to date. It wasn't easy for me to admit that I could feel anything more than frustration for you. I mean, sexual chemistry is one thing, but this other thing..." She bit her lip. It didn't get easier to admit. "That's way more terrifying. Knowing that I think about you with your clothes on too, all the damn time."

Keiran laughed. "I feel you. Not gonna lie, though. I think about you *without* your clothes on a lot too. Those dimples are pretty distracting." He dodged the elbow she tried to poke him with. "You still *like* like me," he repeated, almost a whisper as if he couldn't quite believe it. "That's not something I hold lightly. So, about labels?"

She narrowed her eyes. "Don't push it."

"How about I just refer to you as the woman I l—"

She clamped her hand over his mouth, heart racing. "Shh!" She felt his grin spread behind her hand. Mischief twinkled in his eyes, or maybe it was just the lights strung overhead reflecting in their depths. The wet flick of his tongue against her palm had her pulling her hand away. "Eww."

"I've licked more things than your hand. You'll be fine." He reached for her hand to rub at her palm. "There, all dry now." He inhaled deeply. "Okay, so no major declarations yet. Got it."

"Definitely too soon." Sweet God, she wasn't ready for that yet.

"Someday," he proclaimed, sounding so sure.

She rolled her eyes but didn't pull away, basking in the feel of his fingers tracing lazy circles on her palm. "I'm having second thoughts." She really wasn't. Just standing here with him touching her had her insides a jumbled mess.

"You think I'm gorgeous. You want to kiss me—" he sang.

"No, Keiran, I swear—"

"—you want to huuug me. You want to lo—"

She nudged him in the stomach with her elbow. "On second thought, the singing may actually be a dealbreaker. Please, no more! How are you so bad at this?"

"Not everyone can have your vocals. I'll just leave the singing to you then." He looked so hopeful as if she'd ever get in that studio to record anything again. The one-time deal was enough.

"I'd really like for us to kiss and make up now if that's okay with you?" He wet his lips, the damn tease.

"I should make you suffer more."

"Haven't I suffered enough? Didn't you see me almost pee my pants up there?"

Cherisse grabbed onto one side of his suspenders. "I think we suffered the most. For the record, please never try to serenade me for any reason. Ever. And if you have to work with Sean again, please tell me. I'd rather not walk into your studio unawares."

He placed his hand over his heart. "I promise."

"Good. Then go for it."

He leaned in to brush his lips against hers. It was brief, chaste. He leaned back before she could even reciprocate or really get in there, grinning as she narrowed her eyes because surely, he could do better than that.

She wrapped her hand tighter around that damn suspender, tugged him close, and licked her way into his mouth, relishing the taste.

"Think they got any supply closets around here?" he asked.

"That isn't going to become a thing."

A commotion headed their way had them drawing apart. The bride and groom were leading the charge.

"What's happening?"

"Ha! They're really doing it. Those nerds."

Cherisse was confused until she really paid attention to the song the DJ was playing. "Oh my God."

People were lining up on either side of the deck as Heavy D & The Boyz's "Now That We Found Love" pounded through the speakers. Leave it to her sister and her new hubby to recreate a *Hitch* scene. Rom com-loving nerds. She giggled as Ava and Eric made their way down the center as all around them, the guests clapped and cheered them on. Cherisse spied her mother, scowling her way, but she also got thumbs up from Remi, Reba, and Scott, who were waiting their turn to go down the line.

"Well?" Keiran was looking at her expectantly. "It's our duty as best man and maid of honor to get jiggy with it." He took her hand and brought it to his lips. There went that damn blushing again, and a chorus of awwws from the side.

"Alright, let's do this." She meant so much more than the silly dancing.

It was scary, thinking of this, of them together as something more. She squeezed his hand, and Keiran smiled down at her. Or maybe, it was the start of something sweet. And she liked sweet things, a lot.

Acknowledgements

THERE ARE SO MANY PEOPLE to thank. Where do I even begin?

To the romance community for embracing me. A girl from an island in the Caribbean who has had this dream of publishing a book for some time now. You all have pushed me to work harder and dig deeper with my writing. I'm just trying to be half as good as the amazing authors out here.

To my agent Lauren who pushed for this book from the beginning! Our plan took an interesting path but I'm always grateful for your guidance and having my back. Lucky to have you in my corner.

To my first set of readers: Leah, Jen, Carla, Keyanna and Avril for taking the time to read and offer great insight and feedback.

To Jen especially (yes I'm singling you out shh shh) for being my ULTIMATE cheerleader. Who just gets all the trini things I put in this book, and who gushed with me over my gawjus cover when it was just a rough sketch.

To Katrina Jackson and Mina Waheed for giving me such great advice when I was like "I want to do a thing help!!" Thank you so much. You continue to be amazing and an inspiration to me.

To my amazing cover artist Leni Kauffman. The moment I saw your work I said I needed you to do my cover. I couldn't have anyone else. Your work is exquisite! The final cover speaks for itself.

Finally, this book was written when I was not in the best frame of mind. Back in January 2017 I had been sent home from my job. The anxiety levels were off the charts and these characters came to me and said *wriiite me*. They were the balm I needed at the time.

Sweethand, while having gone through changes from what it first started off as, remains an ode to my island and the ways in which people can fight down a whole situation, but you know they're gonna get that Happily Ever After! ;)

I hope you enjoy this little slice of Caribbeanness I'm offering ♥

N.